RINGMAIN

'A circuit of high-speed explosive fuse
for the simultaneous detonation of
separate explosive charges . . .'

*School of Special Operations
Sungei Buloh, Malaya*

George Brown

RINGMAIN

BARRIE & JENKINS
LONDON

First published in 1991 by Barrie & Jenkins Ltd,
Random Century House, 20 Vauxhall Bridge Road,
London SW1V 2SA

This book is a work of fiction.
Any resemblance between the characters portrayed
and real persons, living or dead, is
purely coincidental.

BRITISH LIBRARY CATALOGUING IN PUBLICATION DATA

Brown, George
Ringmain
I. Title
823.914 [F]

ISBN 0-7126-3933-0

Phototypeset in Linotronic Ehrhardt by
SX Composing Ltd, Rayleigh, Essex
Printed and bound in Great Britain by
Mackays of Chatham PLC, Chatham, Kent

FOR PAULA – WHO REFUSED TO GIVE UP

PROLOGUE

The man in the darkened room raised the sashed window inch by inch until he'd made a gap of just over four inches. He waited a few moments, then, without disturbing the heavy curtain, rested a powerful night telescope on the ledge and surveyed the empty tree-lined road several storeys below him. After a careful study of the entrances to the grand apartments on the opposite side of the road he concentrated his attention on a building some three hundred yards to his right.

The telescope peered into the entrance bringing out a darker shadow, a man, motionless. The watcher removed his eye from the lens and blinked moisture into it then moved the telescope fractionally to the left. A second man stood in another doorway. The faint gleam from an adjacent street lamp reflected off a worn patch on the stubby Heckler and Koch machine pistol cradled in the crook of his arm.

He ignored the first floor of the building. It was in darkness.

The second floor showed only one lighted window.

The third had light leaking from every window.

He started from the corner of the building and through the lens checked each of these windows in turn. The curtains were effective; he could see nothing inside the apartment. But it wasn't the inside of the building that interested him. Half-way along the third floor and running almost the length of the building jutted a narrow balcony in front of four french windows. A man stood against the wall at either end of the balcony. They were both armed with machine pistols.

A third man with his back against the windows stared back at him through powerful binoculars, but saw nothing and moved on in his routine quartering of the surrounding area.

The man with the telescope glanced down at the luminous dial on his watch. Nine forty-five. Still on his knees he edged away from the window and stood up.

A tiny pinprick of light from a pencil torch guided him to the rifle already set on its sturdy tripod. Easing the bolt open he loaded a single round into the breech. Returning to the window he squatted at the far corner and, again without any sudden disturbance of the curtain, rested the tip of the rifle barrel on the ledge and adjusted the height of the tripod. There was just enough gap in the open window for him to see the entrance to the apartment through the powerful Schmidt and Bender power scope. The shadow in the doorway clicked into daylight-like shape. He fine-focused. The swarthy man's face was clear – he had a tiny nick in the corner of his upper lip where he'd cut himself shaving. His eyes never stopped moving. The man at the window touched the butt of the rifle with his finger, it was little more than a stroke, and tightened, gently, the lever on the ball and socket head of the tripod. The cross-hairs of the sight were centred at head height on the iron and glass door.

He glanced down at his watch again. Five past ten. He stroked the safety catch forward and placed his eye once more to the power scope. No change.

And then, in the silent, dark room, the small radio receiver on the floor beside him hissed into life.

'They're on their way down.'

He made no acknowledgement. His eye stared unblinking through the scope.

'They're coming out now,' said the voice from the receiver, urgently. 'Ghadaffi's man is in the light-grey suit. He's coming first – four close bodyguards, Libyans. They've got two more outside. The Minister's right behind him – black suit, white shirt.'

Two cars pulled up and waited, engines running, their exhausts spewing white steam into the cooling night air, and then the door opened and the two outside protectors closed in on the man in the light-grey suit; then the French Minister and his entourage spilled out into the entrance. The Libyan bodyguards' eyes were everywhere, their heads, like puppets, moving in all directions as they shepherded their charge across the pavement.

The man at the window loosened the lever on the tripod head and tightened his thumb round the ribbed stock of the rifle, bringing it tight into his shoulder. It took only a second. The cross-hairs moved from the head of the man in the grey suit and zeroed in on the temple of the man still standing at the door. No hesitation; the finger squeezed.

Phhht!

He didn't wait to admire his handiwork.

The explosive bullet thudded into the French Minister's head and shattered it like glass. The men behind him, his protectors, hit the ground while the people escorting the Libyan crowded round him, pressing his head down, protecting him with their bodies as they swept him off his feet and rushed him into the car. It took off at high speed.

The French bodyguards recovered quickly and fanned out into the quiet, tree-lined avenue searching for movement in the windows and on the roofs above them. But they did it without conviction. This had the hallmark of a professional killing.

The radio crackled again: 'Jesus, Siegfried – you've shot the wrong bloody man! You've killed the bloody Minister!'

He continued dismantling the rifle and tripod and for the first time answered into the machine. 'Close down,' he said coldly. 'Don't acknowledge.'

He went down the back stairs and slipped into the closed garage. A dark grey Citroën was the only car there. He leaned into the back, pulled up the armrest and the back section fell forward. The specially constructed brackets accepted the rifle and clicked back into place. The tripod went into the boot and fitted into the slots reserved for the jack. He lit a cigarette and opened the garage door. He waited a few seconds until the converging sirens wailed to a halt, then drove out and headed towards the, now, crowded street with its traffic jam of ambulances and flashing police vehicles. It was swarming with serious-looking men in dark suits. Four policemen clutching sub-machine-guns surrounded his stopped car and two of the dark-suited men appeared on either side of him. He kept his hands on the wheel. Between his fingers was a small leather card-holder. 'Slowly,' said the man on his side of the car.

He handed him the wallet. The other man leaned in through the offside window and watched. In his left hand he held a 9mm Browning automatic. It was pointed ostentatiously at the driver's head while the first man studied the card in the wallet.

'Merci, monsieur,' he said respectfully and handed it back. 'You'll have a job parking – can I get someone to do it for you?'

'No thanks.' He eased his foot off the brake and the Citroën moved slowly along the street, until it was lost in the chaos of parked ambulances and patrol cars.

'Who was that?' asked the other dark-suited agent.

'Maurice's man. Gerrard.'

'Who's Maurice?'

'Head of the Special Security and Intelligence Bureau at the Elysée.'

CHAPTER 1

December 1985: Dublin

The American was the last to arrive.

He took his raincoat off and threw it over the back of a chair. He nodded to the man by the fireplace, nothing friendly, a casual acknowledgement that they'd already met, then ignored him to concentrate on the six men standing nearby.

'My name's Meier,' he said to no one in particular, glancing round the huge, dimly lit Georgian room. 'Eugen Meier. Which of you gentlemen is IRA?' He paused for a second as if trying to recall the structure of that organisation. 'The Provisional IRA?'

A pair of heads offered the suggestion of a nod.

Meier acknowledged them curtly and allowed his gaze to fall on the two men furthest away from the group. They were both big men, well built and wearing identical navy-blue suits. They appeared unimpressed, even bored, by their surroundings and stood casually by the heavily curtained window smoking long filter kings. They stared flatly at Meier and waited for the question.

He didn't ask it, instead raised his eyebrows and tilted his chin interrogatively.

'IRA,' said one. 'Official.'

Meier nodded absently to himself then turned back to the man standing nearest to him – a thick-set man with thin lips and a coarse peasant Irish face, at the moment shrouded by a lungful of expelled cigarette smoke. The Irishman stared back into Meier's eyes.

'So I can take it that you and your friend are INLA,' Meier said to him. It was a statement not a question and was acknowledged by the thin-lipped man with a fractional depression of his eyebrows. He held Meier's eyes for a second longer than necessary then looked away and brought the cigarette up again to his mouth.

Meier reckoned he'd spent enough time on introductions. He walked towards the head of the long pedestal dining-table, pulled the heavy carver out from under the leaf and sat down, staring for a moment at the silent, blank faces of the Irishmen – the heads of the three main Irish Republican terrorist organisations.

One of them sat down, uninvited, and the rest followed suit. Meier didn't object. He peered through the haze of cigarette smoke and set his sights somewhere in the middle of the group.

'I've been sent here to clear the British out of Northern Ireland for you,' he said crisply.

The silence that greeted his announcement lasted almost ten seconds.

'Oh, fuckin' hell!' A fist slammed on to the table-top and a chair was pushed back angrily as one of the Provisionals stood up. 'You've brought us here to tell us that?' The Provo pointed his finger menacingly at Meier. 'That's the big deal that brought us down here? That you've been sent to clear the British out of Northern Ireland! Jesus Christ! What the fuckin' hell d'you think we've been doing up there for the past twenty bloody years?'

Meier stared dispassionately at the interrupter.

'I know what you've been doing for the past twenty years,' he answered calmly. 'But you haven't shifted them. They're still there. And they'll still be there in twenty years' time, because you haven't brought enough pressure to bear on them – and you won't the way you're going.'

'Balls!'

Meier ignored the expletive. 'I *know* how to pressure them. And I know what'll shift them. I said I'm going to clear the British out of Northern Ireland and that's exactly what I'm going to do.' Meier frowned at the far end of the table. 'All you've got to do is listen.'

'Sit down and let him say what he's come to say,' interrupted a gruff voice, 'and then let's get the bloody hell out of this place.'

The Provisional sat down reluctantly. 'OK, Yank. Go on then, tell us how to pull nails out of concrete. But before you do, I know why *I* want the bastards out of the North – what's your interest?'

'Interest?' Meier stared at the speaker. 'My interest . . .' He stopped himself and started again. 'Our interest is the same as yours: a profound desire to see a free and united Ireland.' His cold eyes embraced the other five Irishmen. 'Nothing political, nothing material – pure sentiment.' Meier closed his eyes for a brief second. It must be jet lag.

Sentiment? These evil bastards wouldn't know what the word meant . . . And as Solomon Boelke had said yesterday in New York: 'If you can talk those thick

Irish potatoes into accepting that, Meier, they ought to make you the first German/Yiddischer king of Dublin! What do you think, can you take them along with you?'

'Will the IRA help?'

'They'll all help.'

'Money?'

'Help yourself.'

Eugen Meier opened his eyes and looked at his audience. Nothing had changed.

'That's all our interest is.' And he repeated: 'Pure sentiment. We just happen to love Ireland – nothing more than that.'

'OK,' said the Provisional's spokesman, caustically, 'so you love Ireland. Great! We can all sleep with our eyes shut tonight! Now that you've got that bit of bullshit out of the way, how about telling us how you're going to disinfect the North of Ireland.'

Meier ignored the sarcasm. 'We think it's time to stop terrorising the British and bring political pressure to bear from the international community. Until now, Britain's been allowed to have its own Gaza Strip and get on with it. That's got to stop. Only if my Government turns the political screw on the British and demands their withdrawal from Ireland is there any likelihood that they'll go.'

The two branches of the IRA looked at each other with scepticism. Meier ignored the looks. One of the older IRA men raised his eyes to the ceiling; he looked like a man reading the graffiti on the wall while he emptied his bladder in a Falls Road pub bog – there was not a lot of conviction in his expression.

Meier looked about him. 'We have to take out a public figure who is so important that it will create shock waves around the world. Not another Mountbatten or Airey Neave or the Thatcher near-miss at Brighton but bigger than anyone ever hit before.'

One of the INLA men, Belstead, had the answer. 'Let's kill their queen.' His suggestion was met by unanimous and enthusiastic nods.

Meier jerked them back to reality. 'Killing British royalty doesn't solve anything. It stiffens people's resolve – it's non-productive.'

'But it's good headline stuff!'

'Wrong. It's bad headline stuff. The world's waiting for you to humiliate the British and they'll applaud you when you do it . . . But they're not waiting for you to kill an old woman; you won't make any friends in that direction.' Meier paused for a second and peered through the smoke at the animated faces of men who smelt blood and wanted to taste it.

They hadn't got the message.

'How about the Duke of Edinburgh? We got a lift out of Mountbatten – we could always make it the pair.'

Meier gave it the pretence of consideration then slowly shook his head.

But Belstead insisted. 'We've gotta have a splash. You said so yourself. We have to get the big one.'

Meier nodded his agreement. 'It's been taken care of,' he said carefully.

'Who?'

'That comes later, with the dots and pins of the detailed briefing, but accept my word, he's big – you'll get your splash. Bigger than you expected.' *But whether it's going to please your friends is another question.* Meier's eyes hooded briefly as he stared at the INLA chief. *There's only one man going to get a dividend out of this rolling head . . .*

September 1985: Washington

'Don Rourke's only got another year to bumble around the stage as President, Eugen, then he'll be able to loosen the clips that are holding his face together and go back to riding the range on Tonto – or whatever he calls it . . . What d'you think of Vincent Beaune's presidential chances in Eighty-eight?'

'Hundred per cent, Solly. Vice-Presidents always do well. This one'll ride home on Rourke's popularity.'

'I think you're right. And then comes Kennedy next time round – Kennedy's got charisma.'

'I disagree, Solly. Kennedy's got fuck-all except a name and a couple of flashy brothers in Arlington. They had charisma. Vincent Beaune'll swamp him too – it'll be embarrassing.'

'Right again, Eugen, Vincent's going to embarrass a lot of people.'

'What people?'

'Never mind what people, Eugen, take it as read. Vinnie'll have to go now, before he gets started.'

'He's not the only Republican runner, Solly. There are others.'

'Let's start with Vinnie. We'll deal with the others as it happens.'

'I thought you got me up here to talk about Ireland?'

'This is about Ireland, Eugen. It's all to do with the other thing we talked about . . . How're you getting on with that? Have you got the British worried yet?'

'It's coming together, Solly. I've got a network in England making all the right contacts for me. Give me three months, and I can go and talk Irish. It's being arranged. The three top crews fighting the war in the North are being negotiated into a position where they'll talk to each other – and then listen to me! But this thing about Vincent Beaune? I don't want to go off on a tangent, Solly – not at this stage.'

'I was thinking aloud, Eugen. Vincent Beaune and Ireland are interlocking – they're both part of a ringmain.'

'How's killing Vincent Beaune going to help Ireland?'

'I didn't say anything about helping Ireland, Eugen. I don't give a fuck about Ireland. I'm splashing paint over a much wider canvas than a third-rate bit of swamp land in the Atlantic. This goes deep, Eugen.'

'I've lost you, Solly.'

'Don't let it worry you. You get on with what you're doing, and the rest'll slot into place. You don't need to know anything else for the time being.'

'How does Kennedy fit into your plans?'

'They want to put the big hat on his oversized bonce. If Vincent Beaune gets in next year he'll be there for the next eight years. They can't wait that long – Teddy's losing his youth and charm. He'll be up the road with the other two if he misses out in Eighty-eight.'

'I can't see the connection between booting the British out of Northern Ireland and putting Kennedy on the throne . . . Maybe it's better I don't know, Solly?'

'Maybe you're right . . . But don't worry, I'll tell you all about it, Eugen – all in good time. Let's get back to Vincent Beaune.'

'Let's.'

'As we anticipated, Vinnie Beaune will be making a European tour next year. Vinnie and his entourage will be in England in the middle of next summer . . . The British have arranged for him to carry out a little dedication ceremony down in London Docks. They're about to demolish some old warehouse or shed where Eisenhower had his last crap or something before D-Day – the British want to put a mark on the water where it all happened.'

'How d'you know all this, Solly?'

'I've got someone who helps draw up his programme.'

'So we can get the IRA to do the business for us?'

'Exactly.'

Belstead continued staring at Meier. 'I've got another question,' he said.

Meier raised his eyebrows.

Belstead leaned forward on the table and jerked his thumb over his shoulder. 'Who's that guy sitting in the corner back there?'

Meier said, 'That's Lieutenant-Colonel Frederick Lambdon.'

The Irishmen stiffened noticeably, and heads lifted round the room. 'That sounds English to me.'

'He is. But let Mr Malseed tell you about him.'

'He sounds English too.'

'He is. Mr Malseed co-ordinates on the British mainland. He is my representative over there and is in supreme control of this entire operation – under my direction, of course. He will also take care of the political aspect and the post-withdrawal negotiations with the British Government.'

Six pairs of suspicious eyes studied Malseed, who returned the scrutiny blandly.

The American studied the Irishmen's disquiet and added firmly, 'Mr Malseed has the complete trust of the executive behind this operation.' He didn't get any further.

The shoulder blades of one of the Official IRA men were twitching.

'Let's go back to this lieutenant-colonel, whatever you said his name is, before things get too complicated for a simple Irish country boy like me . . .'

Like humour, sarcasm was wasted on Meier. 'Very well.' He raised his voice slightly. 'Will you join us, please, Colonel Lambdon?'

The assembled heads turned with curiosity to the dark corner where, beyond the edge, and out of the lambency of the central chandelier, the shadowy figure of a man rose from a deep armchair. He'd sat there throughout the meeting, silent and unmoving, listening to the hum of conversation. He'd made no movement to draw attention to himself until his cue arrived, then, with all eyes on him, he strolled unselfconsciously across the room and into the full glare of the stage. He posted himself, casually at ease, beside the American's chair and stood like an applicant for a job, waiting for the interview to commence.

Meier didn't keep him waiting.

'Please sit down, Colonel. Mr Malseed? Perhaps you'll introduce the Colonel to our colleagues . . .'

Malseed was in his element. He was a politician. There was no doubt about it; it was the way his mouth shaped itself for a long rambling discourse. But before anything came out, Meier said politely, 'Briefly, if you don't mind.'

Malseed's disappointment showed. He let his breath out slowly and said, 'Colonel Lambdon is an ex-member of British Security Service – MI5 . . .'

'I don't think I'm going to like this,' one of the Provisionals said loudly and tensed the muscles in his thighs ready to get up and leave.

'I think you will,' Malseed assured him.

'Is he the man from Whitehall?' a voice interjected.

'What man is that?' Malseed raised his eyebrows, but kept his eyes on the speaker.

'I heard we'd got a man sitting with the British spy brass in London. I'm asking if this is him.'

'Where did you hear that?' Meier took over from Malseed.

'It's done the rounds. What I heard was that a guy named Lynch was spouting about it in a pub in Poolbeg Street . . . some time ago. Months ago.'

'Who was this Lynch?'

'A Dublin lip. Started blowing his mouth off about the IRA playing high flyers in British Intelligence. A couple of their people were in the pub too.' The speaker nodded at one of the men in navy blue. 'They put a bag over Lynch's head and carried him down to the rubbish tip . . .'

'What'd they do with him there?' asked a voice, unnecessarily.

Nobody answered. They all knew what happened on rubbish tips.

Meier took charge of the interrogation again. 'What was the name?'

'I just told you – Lynch.'

'Not that one, the name of the person in Whitehall.'

'I don't know. I don't think a name was mentioned.'

Meier looked at each of them in turn. The globular eyes behind the rimless glasses were as cold as two wet shillings and the flat tone of his voice warned them to accept his word or get ready to go and join hands with Mr Lynch.

'There's no such person,' he said, 'not in Whitehall, not anywhere else. Is that clear?'

Nobody answered. It was clear enough.

The Official IRA man broke the silence that had descended on the room. 'You were going to tell us what makes our soldier here so special . . .'

Malseed was glad to change the subject. 'Do you remember a raid on the Felton Army Depot near Catterick a few weeks ago?'

The man nodded and inclined his head towards the earlier speaker. 'Sure I do. It was his people, Provo. Useless. Wasted effort. Put everybody on their bloody toes, and all they walked away with was a couple of old Brens and half a dozen SLs. What about it?'

'You didn't mention casualties.'

'Two Brit squaddies killed, one wounded. No PIRA casualties. So what?'

'Colonel Lambdon organised that raid and led it. He killed the two Brits himself.'

'It could have been set up . . .'

'No it couldn't.' The younger of the Provisionals spoke up. 'I was there with him.'

The Official scowled at Lambdon and said to the room in general, 'OK, so now we've got a British colonel wearing the green hackle!' His eyes came back to Meier. 'But you still haven't said what he's doing here tonight.'

Meier took over again. 'I've got a particular task for him that won't wait . . . It'll interest you, Belstead.' Meier blinked through the smoke at the INLA man, then swivelled his eyes back to Lambdon. The other Irishmen looked on curiously.

'Your knowledge of the European mad dog scene I would imagine is fairly extensive?' he said to Lambdon.

Lambdon said nothing.

Meier took his silence as agreement and went on, 'You'd have firsthand knowledge of men who kill for a living – jackals . . . Europe's full of them, wouldn't you say?'

Lambdon's eyes hadn't left Meier's face. He'd heard Meier's earlier conversation with Belstead and had a good idea what was coming next.

'No, Mr Meier, I wouldn't say that at all.' Lambdon's voice was classless, very English, with none of the high-pitched drawl that Irishmen associate with British colonels. They almost liked the sound of him. 'Europe's *not* full of top-class professional killers. What Europe's full of is half-trained, soft-boiled terrorists who take a chance, and the money, on the quick kill. No skill – just straightforward gun merchants hyped up for a quick in-and-out.'

Meier's expression remained attentive. 'Point taken. Go on.'

'But if you're looking for the real thing, the man with the killer factor, the professional, he's there somewhere – hard to find, but he's there – about half a dozen of them – no more than that.'

'Could you recommend three?'

'Depends on the target.'

Meier's eyes searched Lambdon's face, but whatever it was he was looking for he couldn't find. He blinked behind his glasses and nodded decisively. 'OK. Give me a list of these three individuals – as soon as you like.'

'They don't work in teams,' said Lambdon.

'I know that,' said Meier tartly. 'A team isn't my intention. I've got work for only one smart technician but it's a strange quirk of my nature, Colonel Lambdon, I like to have a choice. Is that all right with you?'

Lambdon ignored the sarcasm. 'Of course. But if you told me the target it might help me make my recommendations. It becomes a question of specialities.'

Meier's face remained bland, but the eyes showed Lambdon that this line of enquiry had reached a dead end. Meier shook his head.

'The target comes with the final briefing.' He placed a mental tick beside that subject and moved on. 'An estimate of the cost, please, Colonel?'

Lambdon tried from a different angle. 'Again, it would depend on the subject.'

'Naturally. But think high, very high, say, er . . . head of state, king, queen . . . erm . . . prime minister . . . Go along those lines.'

Lambdon didn't hesitate. 'Half to three-quarters of a million pounds.'

Meier didn't blink. 'Very well, take the upper level for the very best. Your budget is three-quarters of a million pounds. I want those names within two weeks. Can you produce?'

Lambdon nodded thoughtfully.

'There's something on your mind, Colonel?'

Lambdon stared at the American for a second, then said, slowly, 'There are some very, very good technicians in the States, top-class professionals . . . I know of a couple who'd make the Europeans look like fairground workers . . .' Lambdon left the statement in the air. Meier knew what he was getting at.

'I have my reasons, Colonel. He's got to be European. That means no Americans, and . . . ' he paused for a second and caught Belstead's eye, 'no Englishmen.'

After Lambdon left the room the meeting began to disperse.

The Irishmen stood up and stretched their legs and began talking seriously to each other in deep hushed voices. Belstead detached himself from the Irish group and approached Meier, now shrugging into his damp raincoat. Something was troubling him. Something would always trouble Belstead.

'How long's that Englishman been on our side?' he asked.

'Which one?' said Meier.

'The soldier.'

Malseed answered for Meier. 'He's been with us just over two and a half months. He's been screened and double-screened. The word from London is that he's as clean as I am.'

The comparison didn't seem to impress Belstead. He turned his back on Malseed and addressed himself again to Meier. 'Is he in on the final briefing? Is he going to know the target, the timing, the location?'

'I haven't decided yet.' He turned back to Malseed.

But Belstead wasn't finished. 'Is the plan finalised?'

'Yes.' Meier showed his impatience. 'It was put to bed three months ago. Every detail . . . It's all been carefully researched. Nothing's going to go wrong.'

'How many copies of the plan are there?' persisted Belstead.

'One.'

'How many people have seen it in its final form?'

'Two. And one of them's standing in front of you.'

'And the other one?'

'A man called Felix Schoernberger. His was the tactical brain – he re-searched and planned it. Apart from myself he's the only man who's seen where the pin goes in the map.'

'Great,' said Belstead caustically. 'And how secure is he?'

'They don't come any securer than Felix Schoernberger.'

'Is that supposed to impress me?'

'It should – he's been dead three months.'

October 1985: Washington

The two young men, one in a mid-blue blazer and the other in a light-grey suit, detached themselves from the crowd and came up on either side of Felix Schoernberger as he left the restaurant, and, without a word, steered him into the waiting car.

'Evening, Felix,' said the man in the blazer. He smiled at Felix as he made himself comfortable on the back seat. 'Steak well done and to your liking, was it?'

Felix wasn't disturbed. He recognised the haircuts and the after-shave – he knew CIA when he smelt it.

'Whatever your problem is, boys, let's get it over quickly, I've got an after-dinner date that won't keep.'

'This won't take much of your time, Felix. It's about your friend Solly Boelke.'

'What about him?'

'He's been seen stretching his podgy little fingers towards the east . . .'

'What's that supposed to mean?'

'Somebody saw him standing on the sea-shore shading his eyes with his hand and gazing towards England.'

'Very Homeric, gentlemen, but I'm still not with you.'

'Felix had a classical education,' the man in the blazer told his companion. 'What do you make of this then, Felix? Standing beside your friend Solly was your friend Eugen Meier with a rolled-up map of Great Britain under his arm. What are they up to, Felix?'

'I don't know what you're talking about . . . Who's your boss?'

It was the turn of the man in the grey suit to smile. 'We're self-employed, Felix – no boss.'

'You're CIA?'

'Sort of.'

'I don't think I like the sound of that . . . Take me to your leader!'

'Well done, Felix! They said you had a great sense of humour.' The smile vanished. 'What're Solly and Meier up to, Felix?'

'I've no idea . . . But I'll tell you two clowns what I *have* got.'

'What have you got, Felix?' asked the man in the grey suit.

'I've got some very powerful friends in very powerful places.'

'You sure about that, Felix?' said the other man.

'What, about my powerful friends?'

'No, I know all about them. I'm asking if you're sure about the other thing – about old Solly and Meier.'

Felix shook his head. 'Quite sure.'

The man in the blazer stared at him for a second then shrugged his shoulders. 'OK, Dick.' He turned to his companion. 'Let's take Felix to the massage parlour.'

The massage parlour was four concrete walls of a large underground garage. There was one chair in the middle of the garage. Nothing else.

'We got the idea from an old gangster movie,' the man in the grey suit told Felix. 'It's soundproof too.'

Felix wasn't worried. He sat in the chair and said, 'OK then, let's play gangsters . . .'

'D'you want to change your mind?'

'No thanks.'

'Dick, I'm going to break Felix's ankle.'

'Which one?'

'Which ankle do you walk on, Felix?'

'What movie did you two comedians get that bit of dialogue from?'

'It's not funny, Felix, I'm going to cripple you if you won't chat with me . . . You're quite sure you don't want to change your mind and tell me about Solly's thinking?'

'I've just told you . . . I don't know what Solly thinks about.'

'You'll have to wear an iron boot, Felix. It's going to be bloody uncomfortable clomping about in an iron boot. You won't be able to foxtrot any more.'

Felix shrugged his shoulders. He knew they were bluffing.

The man in the blazer nodded slowly. 'OK, Dick, go and get the stuff.' He smiled at the unconcerned Felix. 'And don't forget the aspirins. I don't want to have to hang around all night trying to make sense out of Felix's screams . . . You're still quite sure about this, Felix?'

Felix didn't reply. But suddenly he wasn't quite sure. The juices in his stomach confirmed it and started an upward journey when the man in the grey suit returned with a long-handled fifteen-pound sledgehammer. The joke had gone beyond a joke – his throat dried up.

His change of mind came a few seconds too late.

The two men worked like a cabaret act.

Felix's mind boggled.

One of them stuck a handful of fingers hard into his midriff. When he opened his mouth to shout his pain the other one forced a tennis ball between his teeth and rammed it into his mouth as far as it would go. His eyes popped out. But it didn't make any difference, they were well into their act. They strapped him into the chair and pulled his legs apart over the seat as if he were in the saddle and out riding in the park.

'Which ankle – the right one or the left?' Dick asked his friend.

'I don't think it matters. Does it matter, Felix, which side you hobble on?' The man in the blazer smiled down at Felix, but nothing came past Felix's tennis ball. The message that he'd changed his mind and now had things to say remained stuck firmly behind it.

'We'll do the left one first . . . We're going to do the left one first, Felix!' The man in the blazer raised his voice as if the tennis ball was also inhibiting Felix's hearing. 'Hopefully we won't need to do the other ankle . . . I can't imagine the racket you'd make, Felix, stomping in and out of the club with two iron boots! Dick, give Felix a little jab now, it might deaden a bit of the pain, and then give him another good dose when he comes round.'

Felix tried to tell the man in the blazer what Solly Boelke and Eugen Meier were planning, but the man had dropped out of sight; he was down on his hands and knees and, with the help of his friend Dick, was rolling up Felix's left trouser leg.

'You can leave his shoe and sock on, Dick.'

Felix tried to faint when he felt fingers exploring his ankle, and then he felt a sharp prick in his calf – there was no question of fainting now.

The man in the blazer said, 'I reckon about there . . .' His fingers gently massaged Felix's ankle bone through his sock. 'This little bit that sticks out, Dick . . . What do they call it?'

'Buggered if I know! Ankle bone, I think.'

Felix thought they sounded like a couple of first-year medical students playing with their new plastic skeleton. But his thoughts were short-lived. The man in the grey suit stood up, gently touched Felix's ankle bone twice with the cold hammer head, raised it level with his shoulders, and swung . . .

When he woke up, and had stopped screaming, Felix told the two men what Solomon Boelke had planned for Ireland.

There was no mention of Vincent Beaune.

'Is it workable?'

The man in the blazer smiled bleakly at his superior. 'Certainly, Director, there's nothing wrong with Meier's thinking. The only holes I can punch in the thing are the guys he's going to have to use. The IRA are like red-tipped matches – rub 'em against anything and they're liable to go off.'

'Where's Felix now?'

'He had a nasty motor-car accident, Director. It rolled over and over and caught fire – he'd just filled it up with gas. Poor old Felix was burned to a frazzle. They could only just tell what he was, let alone who he was.'

'Has Solly been informed?'

'The Police Department did all that. Apparently Felix had dined and wined too well – particularly wined . . . The restaurant confirmed that, they said he was quite the worse for drink when he left.'

'They said that . . . ?'

'No, they said he was loaded to the gills.'

'I hope they weren't put up to making statements like that.'

'Never let it be said, Director.'

'Poor Felix . . . Solly'll be quite upset.'

'Poor Solly!'

'OK, so you've got it all on tape and film?'

'And in my head.'

'What about Dick?'

'What about him?'

'Is he safe with something like this?'

'Sure he is. He wouldn't want to join Felix.'

'You're a hard bastard.'

'So they say.'

'OK. Go diplomat. I'll inform Grosvenor Square. When you get to London the man you want to see is General Sir Richard Sanderson. I'll inform him you're on the way. He'll leave a message at the Embassy telling you where you can meet. You two should get on quite well – he's like you, a hard bastard.'

'It takes all sorts.'

'Give him everything, be open and frank – he likes fine detail.'

'Is this from CIA?'

'No, from me . . . Personal favour . . . Erm, one other thing before you go.'

'What's that, Director?'

'Tell Sir Richard to look under his bed.'

'He'll know what he's looking for . . . ?'

'Tell him, if you don't mind a metaphoric cocktail, that there are indications that the Micks have got a friend swinging from the chandelier in the boardroom.'

'Red?'

'Could be . . . Come and see me when you get back.'

CHAPTER 2

Lieutenant-Colonel Fred Lambdon moved briskly up the steps of Green Park Underground. He stood at the entrance and stared into the sunshine of Piccadilly for a few seconds then, with a shake of his head and a frown, retraced his steps and slipped into one of the empty phone booths in the ticket hall.

His follower went to the news-stand and bought a copy of the *Sun*. He moved out of Lambdon's line of vision, propped himself against the wall and, with one eye on the phone booth, opened his paper and studied the inside back sports page.

Lambdon turned his back on the crowd, dialled his number, and said into the mouthpiece, 'Let me speak to the General, please.'

'Who wan – '

'Don't ask questions, Coney, go and get him.'

'Sorry, Colonel, I didn't recognise your voice.'

'Sanderson,' a new voice said.

Without preliminaries, Lambdon said, 'You were right, Richard, there's a hairy creature with a wobbly mouth using your executive loo . . .'

'What does that mean in English, Fred?'

'There's a mole in the shop.'

'Just what we need. What about the other thing?'

'You were right. The Irish have got a big bang planned, and the Yanks have taken over. They've sent over a hard bastard named Meier to organise the party.'

'I know all that – *I* told you, remember? I'm more concerned about the other bloody thing at the moment . . . Didn't they drop a hint as to who this mole might be?'

'Not a word. Just that there was somebody collecting the carbon papers in Whitehall; somebody senior, who wasn't to be mentioned under threat of joining the last bloke who was indiscreet . . .'

'And where's that?'

'Gasping for air at the bottom of the Liffey.'

'Try and keep it serious, Fred. What's your position with them at the moment?'

'You did too good a job on me, I'm almost an honorary Irishman.'

The voice didn't smile. 'Don't let it go to your head, it was either you or the tea lady. You had the broader shoulders.'

'A fitting testimonial! Which brings me to the raid on Felton . . .'

'Forget it. It was very realistic.'

'Too bloody realistic. Sorry about the two lads who bought it.'

'Three. The other soldier died in hospital. But don't burst into tears. If you hadn't done it one of your new playmates would have obliged. Don't give it another thought, we've got plenty more soldiers. Have you got anything else for me?'

'You're becoming quite a hard bastard yourself in your old age, Richard. Look, isn't it enough that somebody's down for the chop?'

'Have you got a name?'

'No. But it's big, very big – Mountbatten proportions. Meier's asked me to sign up a top European gun. He wants a list of three so that he can make a selection – he's talking in terms of half to three-quarters of a million pounds.'

'And when is this due to take place?'

Lambdon dived into his memory, but didn't stay there very long. 'It wasn't mentioned, but I doubt that it could be sooner than three to four months. There's a lot of ground work to be done yet.'

'And no hint of the target?'

'None. But your mate in the boardroom's going to be there for the briefing.'

'Hmm . . . which three have you got in mind?'

'He specified no Brit – and for some reason, no Yank.'

'Interesting. So what are you left with?'

'Not a lot. I can think of only three men in Europe who could command that sort of fee.'

'I wouldn't have put it that high myself.'

'I won't argue with you. It's two plus one. The one is unobtainable, and like everything else unobtainable he's the best of the bunch – I'd rate him the best in the world. Unfortunately he's gainfully employed – he's French, he kills for the DGSE and he's definitely not on the open market.'

'OK, Fred, make up your list of two. When you've done that let me know and I'll supply you with the name of the winner of the competition. When do they want the list by?'

'Two weeks.'

'Plenty of time. What's his name?'

'What's whose name?'

'The DGSE man. The one who's unobtainable.'

Lambdon hesitated for a second then said, 'Siegfried.'

'Siegfried?'

'That's right.'

'Sounds more like brother Hun than a Frenchman. I wonder why they didn't call him Maginot?'

Lambdon said nothing.

Sanderson didn't seem to care. 'Siegfried?' he said again. 'Siegfried what? What else does it say on his gun licence, Fred? What did his mother call him when he was a lad?'

Lambdon grunted. 'He's a bastard, Richard; I don't think he ever was a lad – and I doubt he ever had a mother.'

'You know him?'

Lambdon grinned to himself. 'He joined me in the SAS in the mid-Sixties and we wandered hand in hand around the Far East, then the Middle East, for about three years. I managed to teach the bastard the difference between his arse and his elbow. His name's Gerrard. Michel Gerrard.'

'And you don't think he'd like to come and play with our bat and ball?'

'Like I said, Richard, he's got his own room in a French whorehouse . . . His masters are not generally known for going around touting work for him.'

'Ladies have been known to forsake the security of the whorehouse for the excitement of the street.'

'You'd be wasting your time. There's an Italian who might play it our way, though . . . I'll sound him out.'

'Don't do that, Fred. Do nothing until we talk again. Ring me in ten days, earlier if you feel your ears are burning.'

'Goodbye, Richard.'

Ten days later Lambdon went to Baker Street Underground and dialled the same number. His watcher bought himself the *Daily Mirror* and this time stood a little closer; it was wishful thinking – he knew there was absolutely no chance that he was going to hear anything Lambdon said. Lambdon knew he'd got a watcher.

He'd been there, just behind him, for three weeks; he'd become part of Lambdon's scenery. He was nothing special. A stocky, dark-haired man in his early thirties wearing a clean shirt and a tie and a well-cut navy-blue blazer with six shiny brass buttons on it. A bright splash of colour stood out from his breast pocket – a crest, regimental or rugger – he looked the rugger type – player, not spectator. He opened the paper at page three and after a quick interested glance at the tits of the day concentrated on trying to read Fred Lambdon's lips.

Lambdon turned his head in the opposite direction and listened to the pips beeping in his ear.

General Sanderson answered the telephone himself.

'Richard?' Lambdon said, again without preliminaries. 'Does the name Brocklebank mean anything to you?'

'Brocklebank?' repeated Sanderson.

'That's right. Spelt the way it sounds.'

Lambdon was left momentarily with just an electrical hum for company. It was only a brief pause. A pause for reflection and a quick look round while General Sanderson dredged his memory. He stared without recognition at his watcher before turning back. The man didn't look up from his paper. Sanderson's voice came back down the line.

'Doesn't mean a thing to me, Fred. What's it supposed to do?'

'I'm not altogether sure. The other day I was sitting in the corner minding my own business when this name Brocklebank was mentioned. I wouldn't have given it another thought except the minute it was out one of those unaccountable silences came over the company. Actually it was more of a freeze. Nobody said a word for about half a minute and they all sat looking at each other.'

'In what connection was it mentioned?'

'Hit-men ... One of the clowns said, how d'you get hotshot trigger-men into a country like England where they jump up and down and foam at the mouth if a pussy cat comes through the wrong channel. One of the others told him, "Brocklebank takes care of things like that." As I said, I wouldn't have given it a second thought, other than Paddy's bought himself an immigration inlet, except for one thing. As soon as bullet-head mentioned the name he swallowed it as if it were a bad oyster, and Malseed cut the man off with a glare and a very pointed look in my direction.'

'Brocklebank.' Sanderson had his bone again. He pronounced the name slowly and let it roll off his tongue like the taste of a good claret. 'I can't say it means anything at the moment, Fred, but I suppose we could consider it as slightly better than nothing. Could be code, of course. I'll have it run through the system and see if anything changes colour . . . I'll talk to you about it next time round.' He paused. 'You mentioned a name – Malseed. Who's he?'

'He's my contact. Meier thinks highly of him. He's going to negotiate the peace terms on behalf of the gutter people.'

'Hmm. D'you know anything about him?'

'There's something vaguely familiar about him. It's a Paddy name but he sounds English. Probably a paper name. I've seen his face before, but he's not my type; it must be a box face – could be politician. He's also a trapeze artist, but that's neither here nor there.'

'What's a trapeze artist, Fred?'

'You're leading too sheltered a life, Richard. He's a man's man.'

'I'm still not with you.'

'He's queer.'

Sanderson coughed quietly and changed the subject.

'Have you sorted out those two names for your list?'

'Yes. D'you want them?'

'No. Add this one to it: Michel Gerrard, French; operates under the codename Siegfried . . .' Sanderson paused again, then added, unnecessarily, 'Siegfried as in *Nibelungenlied*.'

'How did you do it?'

Sanderson wasn't letting on. 'He's in the freelance business now. You didn't know?'

'No.'

'You ought to keep your ear down on the railway line, Fred. I'm surprised you hadn't heard he'd moved out on to the pavement and set up his own stall.' Sanderson seemed to be enjoying himself. 'He's a private dealer now and he's offering himself as a candidate for that highly paid bit of temporary employment you mentioned. All you have to do is make sure he gets it.'

'Is there anything else I need to know?' asked Lambdon sceptically. 'Is there anything funny about this sudden movement on to the streets of the star whore?'

'Not that I know of. A word of caution, Fred – I don't want you to discuss your dual nationality with Gerrard when he appears on the scene, and he's not to be told of your connection with me.'

'There's a good reason for that, Richard?'

'Yes.' Sanderson didn't elaborate. 'Convince him that your role in this affair is merely one of intermediary and nothing more. I don't want him to know anything about your undercover role – that's of no interest to him and has no relevance to his contract. Play it like that, Fred, and we won't be tossing and turning in our beds all night. I hope I'm making myself clear.'

Lambdon grinned lop-sidedly. 'You are, Richard, but what if Meier falls in love with one of the other candidates?'

'Don't be negative, Fred. I thought I'd just made it perfectly clear – Siegfried's got to have the job. If your people don't fancy him as favourite he'll have to attend to the others, one by one, until his is the only name left – just get him the job. Understood?'

'Absolutely.'

'Anything else?'

'Just one thing.'

'What's that?'

Lambdon moved his body slightly so that he could look round the edge of the partition. The man in the blazer was still gazing into the inside pages of his *Daily Mirror*.

'Have you given me back-up, Richard?'

'No. Why?'

'I've got a Harry Darkers. If he's a Company face get him off, and quickly or he'll blow the whole bloody game wide open. If he's rumbled as a back marker my run'll end with a red-hot poker up my arse in a plastic bag in somebody's back garden. And that'll be the least of my problems.'

Sanderson paused for a second. 'But it shows somebody cares!'

'Goodbye, Richard.'

CHAPTER 3

The taxi-driver turned his head a full ninety degrees and studied his passenger through the gap in the glass partition.

'This is it, guv,' he said after a pause. 'Trafalgar Square. What you asked for . . . Anywhere round here do?'

The passenger stared back at him and watched the traffic lights at St Martin's-in-the-Fields change from red to orange to green. 'Carry on round,' he said pleasantly, 'I'll tell you where to stop.' He cut off the beginning of the driver's protest with a raised hand and said, 'The lights are green.' He finished his directions to the back of the driver's head as it swung away rapidly to face the front. 'Make as if you're going all the way round to St James's, and be ready to pull in the minute I tell you.'

He glanced out of the darkened rear window, just a quick glance, then leaned forward, resting one knee on the tip-up bucket seat and spoke into the driver's ear. 'Pull up over there, by the entrance to the Tube.'

He fell back into his place, still with the same untroubled expression, and watched the driver's lips tighten as he half turned in his seat and swung the wheel hard over. The taxi swished across the startled rush of early morning traffic and pulled up, with the faintest suggestion of a rubbery squeal, just beyond the Admiralty Arch entrance to Charing Cross Station.

'This suit you, sir?' The driver turned his head again and looked into his passenger's face.

If he'd expected to see shock from the violent manoeuvres he was disappointed. He received a gentle smile. 'Perfectly, thank you. What do I owe you?' A pair of cool brown eyes regarded him with mild amusement. 'Without foreign visitor excess.' The accent was barely noticeable, his English impeccable and idiomatic, but not nearly enough for the driver.

'Two pounds twenty-five . . . You must be from France, sir.' There was a trace of reproach in the Cockney voice.

'Must I?'

The smile had vanished by the time the Frenchman stepped out of the cab and stood looking over the roof of the taxi at the traffic hurtling round the square. He shrugged his shoulders – the mad bastards looked as though they were driving over-powered dodgems. He looked to his right and watched another taxi disgorge its occupants and then heard the Cockney give an impatient cough. He ignored it and watched the traffic move up towards the Arch and then, as if satisfied that London was still everything it always had been, bent down and addressed the driver.

'How much did you say it was?'

'Still two pounds twenty-five, guv'nor. *Service non compris!*' The driver smiled into the Frenchman's eyes.

The Frenchman didn't smile back. He placed a five-pound note in the outstretched hand and without waiting for his change turned and vanished into the thin morning crowd.

He walked briskly past the old Malaya House, his well-polished Church's brogues making no sound on the warm, dustless pavement. He wore a light-grey, single-breasted summer suit and a narrow-red-striped shirt with a plain maroon Dior tie. In his left hand he carried, casually bunched, a light fawn-coloured raincoat and in the other hand a rolled-up daily newspaper; he presented an elegant and inconspicuous appearance; nothing out of place, nothing to draw attention to himself. His movements were unhurried. A man without a definite purpose – he looked like any other well-dressed Englishman in a crowd, killing time with a sunny morning stroll along the Mall.

He continued along the right-hand pavement under Admiralty Arch where he slowed almost to a standstill to gaze upwards at the stone span. He allowed his glance to follow the curve across the road to the point where it entered the main Admiralty building. He studied this building casually, like an architectural student reminding himself for the tenth time how it should be done, then, after a cursory glance at the pavement on the other side of the road, moved on.

He passed into the Mall, turned to the kerb, waited for a gap in the down-coming traffic, then chose his moment and sprinted to the middle of the Mall where he stood patiently, but intent, looking to the right and then slightly longer to the left. He waited for another gap between the traffic heading towards the Palace and squeezed between two black taxis, then sprinted to safety on the Citadel side of the Mall. Without a backward glance he walked briskly under the trees by the great Citadel wall and turned sharply into Horse Guards Road.

Forty yards behind him a heavily built man in a dark-grey suit moved purposefully in his wake. As soon as the Frenchman was out of sight he quickened his pace and turned abruptly by the Citadel. He caught the Frenchman up before he reached the beginning of the Parade and touched him lightly on the back.

'Don't stop, Gerrard,' he told him quietly. 'Keep walking across the square.'

The Frenchman didn't turn his head. 'Hallo, Fred. Nice to see you again.'

'You're supposed to sound surprised,' said Fred Lambdon. 'I've been watching you do the Iban tracker act since you left your hotel.'

'I know. Navy-blue taxi . . . Can we stop playing games?' Gerrard turned his head and studied Lambdon's profile. 'How did you know I'd left the Company, Fred?'

Lambdon looked innocently into the Frenchman's eyes. The mock sincerity came quite easily; it was second nature after a lifetime of practice. Sometimes it was harder to tell the truth. He changed his innocent expression to one of knowing.

'Word gets about in our trade, Michel, particularly when somebody like you changes his striped pants for a labourer's overall. It's bound to be noticed. But it's not important.' Lambdon blinked and stared up at the sky. 'Don't read anything sinister into it.'

'You're not saying then?'

Lambdon lost interest in the sky. He looked down and shook his head.

'OK, Fred.' A lot of the camaraderie left the Frenchman's eyes. 'Then tell me what MI5 wants with an ageing French ex-civil servant . . . And try to remember who you're telling it to.'

Lambdon shot a quick sideways glance at the tall man walking beside him. He took in the receding hairline above a long lean face, with deep-set brown eyes that gazed steadily ahead over an aristocratic French nose; it was a face that smiled easily and frequently, but had no laughter lines round the mouth. It was a face liked by women – a long way from being handsome, it had hardened into a good-looking, well-worn ugliness. It was the face of Michel Gerrard, spycatcher and licensed killer for Department Maurice – the powerful but unpublicised Presidential section of the DGSE. And if he would have him believe it, now out running with the common herd. Lambdon decided to keep his reservations to himself and looked straight ahead.

Before Lambdon could reply the air echoed with the shouted commands and stamping feet of dismounted troopers as the guard changed under the archway at the exit to the square. It brought the two men to a halt and they turned instinctively to watch the toy soldiers perform their ritual. Neither man spoke for a few minutes, then Gerrard, frowning at the noise of clattering boots that echoed under the cobbled archway, brought his companion back to the question.

'. . . keep it fairly simple, Fred.'

'Keep what fairly simple?' Lambdon was enjoying the spectacle; he continued watching the changing of the guard.

'Fred, you didn't bring me here to watch soldiers playing games.'

Lambdon dragged his eyes away from the Household Cavalry and back to Gerrard. 'It's not MI5 that's calling you in.'

'Who then?'

Lambdon shook his head and side-stepped the question. 'It's a kill job. Somebody's had a cross drawn on his forehead. A big, unmentionable, political somebody that's going to take one of the best in the world to send him away . . . Are you interested?'

'You haven't told me anything yet.'

'I was hoping not to have to go into too much detail until you showed some sort of enthusiasm. What if I mentioned the amount of money involved?'

'Start again, Fred.'

'I can only give you more words. You're supposed to be one of the best in the world, if not *the* best. You're now running outside, operating a private firm, and the people I represent are offering you a job. It's nothing more than what you've got on the brass plate outside your door. I told you what it is. The offer's three-quarters of a million pounds. All you have to do is nod your head. If you don't fancy it, shake your head and I'll go for the next one on the list.' Lambdon was chancing his luck and he knew it. He looked back to the soldiers but they'd finished stamping their feet and gone for a cup of tea. The two men did another ten yards in slow time, and in silence.

Then Gerrard said, 'When do you want a decision?'

'Then you're interested?'

'I didn't say that. You and I both know that a reward of three-quarters of a million pounds reflects the near-impossibility of fulfilling the contract. To put it bluntly, Fred, you're not offering that sort of money to dispose of one of those horse soldiers over there – '

'It's a feasible contract,' interrupted Lambdon.

'It's not its feasibility that makes me hesitate,' said Gerrard, 'it's you. It's your unusual vagueness that's putting me off.'

'What's that supposed to mean?'

'It means you're doing it all wrong, Fred. You're standing there hopping from one foot to the other like a tart with her first customer. You've got me worried.'

'It's your Gallic imagination.' Lambdon gave a rare grin. 'Ask me something else then.'

Gerrard wasn't affected by the Lambdon grin. He merely nodded an acknowledgement. 'All right, tell me who these people are who admire my style and want to pay me all this money?'

Lambdon shook his head.

Gerrard hadn't expected anything more. 'And who's worth three-quarters of a million pounds to them dead?'

Another shake of the head.

'And when we've got that out of the way we can get down to the serious stuff . . .' They had reached as far as they could go across the square and turned back the way they'd come. 'But first I want to know who you're working for.'

'What's that got to do with it?'

'We both know that the British Government doesn't employ foreigners to do its killing, and I know that there isn't a department in M.I. that could afford to pay my laundry bill, let alone the sort of money you're suggesting. And then I want the target. That'll do for now.'

'I don't know who it is.'

"Do you think I'm a child? How do you expect to sell something if you don't know what it is?'

'You've missed the point, chum. I'm not selling jobs, I'm gauging interest and setting up interviews. If they think you're interested – and you're the man they've chosen – they'll sell it to you. My part is to see if you want to earn that much money, I'm the contact man, I've got the boy's job because I'm the only dummy on the team who knows Michel Gerrard by sight.'

'What's so important about that?'

'My people are worried that the English might stick in a ringer. Does that stop your balls twitching?'

'I don't know about that, but it's making me very curious.' Gerrard grinned crookedly into Lambdon's unsmiling face. 'OK, tell me who's been robbing the bank and drawing crosses on people's foreheads.'

Lambdon heaved a silent sigh of relief. 'The Irish. Actually it's an Irish stroke American deal, but it's American money paying the fiddler.'

'So what's your status? Are you working for the Irish or the Americans? Surprise me.'

'I'm the man you're dealing with today. That's all you need to know. When you've satisfied me you go on to the next rung, and that's where you'll be shown the dirty postcards and all those noughts on a Swiss cheque. All I want from you is a yes or no and I'll pass you on.' Lambdon rasped a trace of impatience into his voice. 'I wish I knew what the bloody hell you're fart-arseing about at. It's only a job of work, and you go home with seven hundred and fifty thousand pounds' worth of francs – that's an awful lot of bloody francs in anybody's back pocket.'

'I've already got an awful lot of bloody francs in my back pocket, Fred, and I'm fart-arseing about because there's something wrong with all this. I'm trying hard, but I somehow can't fit you in with the Irish. The mixture's not on. Are you sure you're being straight with me?'

'Did you ever know me not to be?'

Gerrard slowly shook his head. 'I still don't like it.' He looked Lambdon squarely in the face. 'The last time you and I got drunk together you were popular in high places . . . That wasn't a long time ago. A year? Not even . . . and here you are now, a full-blown Irish messenger boy – a bagman. What's it all about, Fred?'

'It's none of your business, but take it that I'm earning myself a better pension. Anyway,' said Lambdon harshly, 'we're not here to discuss me, we're here to discuss a job of work. I think we've done prying, is it yes or no? Are you in or not?'

Gerrard decided it had gone on long enough. He stopped to light a cigarette, cupping his hand round the flame and inhaling deeply before flicking the match with his thumb into the wind. He looked up at Lambdon with narrowed eyes. 'You puzzle me, Fred. There's something doesn't smell right about you and your change of colours – something stinks!' Gerrard didn't smile.

Neither did Lambdon.

Gerrard shook his head. 'Reluctantly I'm going to buy your new status, but only for the time being . . . and I warn you, Fred, I'm going to put my ear to the ground and if I find you're taking me for a fool . . .' He left the threat unfinished and held his packet of cigarettes out. 'Here, d'you want one of these?'

Lambdon heaved another inaudible sigh of relief and presented a blank face to Gerrard. 'No thanks, not at the moment.' He paused and looked intently at the Frenchman. 'What about this job then?'

Gerrard nodded. 'I'd like to hear more about it.'

'Then I can tell them you're interested?'

'Sure, but that's all it is, Fred, just interest. No commitment either way until I'm told a bit more than you've been able, or prepared, to tell me. You'll fix something up?'

'Aye. Leave everything to me. I'll push off now and start the snowball on its way down the hill. I'll be in touch as soon as they can get some brass over from Dublin to talk to you.' Lambdon looked up and down Horse Guards Road. 'Looks like a shower,' he said, and got ready for the dash. 'I'm off . . . But one last thing.' He checked himself. 'They might contact you direct, but more likely I'll have to come and pick you up and tell you what hands you've got to shake . . . Expect to hear from me later today or some time this evening. If you want me for anything in the meantime you can get me at this number.' He rummaged in the side pocket of his jacket and brought out a crumpled brown envelope. He turned it over, frowned at what was written on the reverse then carefully tore it in half, putting one segment back in his pocket and scribbling on the other with a gold Parker. He passed the scrap to Gerrard and held out his hand.

'Let's have a drink tomorrow, after they've stamped your cards,' he said unsmiling. 'See you!'

''Bye, Fred.' It was a firm handshake and distracted Lambdon sufficiently for Gerrard to lift the other half of the torn envelope deftly from his pocket.

He stood on the kerbside and watched Lambdon disappear into the crowd. As he shrugged into his raincoat the man on the other side of the road left it just that little bit too long. Stocky, dark-haired, in a navy-blue blazer with a Royal Artillery crest emblazoned on the breast pocket, he looked like a tourist. But a tourist without the trappings; no camera, no umbrella, no raincoat – and nowhere to go and nothing to look at. His eyes lingered a fraction too long as Gerrard held his glance.

Gerrard looked away and headed towards Birdcage Walk. As he passed the Guards Memorial he stopped and lit a cigarette. Then, openly, and without attempting to conceal his actions, he held the two halves of envelope together and studied the typewritten address. It read: Lt-Col. F. Lambdon MC, c/o Barclays Bank Plc, Circular Road, Hastings. The address had been lined through with a pencil and another written neatly by its side; 4 Clarence Garden Mews, London W2.

He turned it over.

The piece that had made Lambdon frown had written on it in shaky biro the one word BROCKLEBANK. Underneath this was a series of numbers, *8597514*.

Casually he screwed the two halves of envelope into a ball and put his hand into the metal waste bin hanging on the railings beside the great Memorial. He withdrew his hand, with the scraps of paper neatly palmed in his half-opened fist, and strolled on in the company of a bunch of Japanese sightseers. He didn't look round. He knew exactly where the blue blazer was, and exactly what it would be doing.

He crossed the road and headed towards the square again. As soon as he was on the other side he covered his movements by placing a parked DOE service van between himself and the man in the blazer. He waited a second, then cut back under cover of the van and stood by its front door window. He had a perfect view. He knew what to expect. He wasn't disappointed.

The man with the Artillery badge was hunched over the rubbish bin. Both his hands were deep in its interior as he rummaged through the collection of grubby and sticky balls of paper like a hungry tramp scenting a half-eaten steak and kidney pie. His anxiety showed in the back of his thick neck; it showed as his head bobbed up and down every time a likely ball of paper turned out to be a discarded chocolate or ice-cream wrapper, and it showed with the increasing frequency with which his head turned towards the distant, partly obscured, exit to Whitehall and gauged the latitude he'd allowed his quarry.

The unpleasantness of his task helped settle his priorities. Abruptly he abandoned the rubbish bin and took off at a fast walk in the direction he'd seen Gerrard heading. He was half-way across the parade ground before he realised the fox had left him without a smell – he'd been done by a rubbish bin. He looked over his shoulder and stared blankly at the DOE van, then continued on his way towards the arch.

He was still swearing fluently to himself as he walked past the dismounted troopers and out into the tropical downpour that thundered angrily down an almost deserted Whitehall.

Gerrard sat and watched the same rain through a window in the Pond restaurant. He drank his coffee and, after copying what Lambdon had written on the back of the envelope, tore the two halves into tiny pieces and set fire to them in the ashtray. As he gazed out of the window at the teeming rain he crushed the ashes, absently, into powder in the glass bowl and wondered why he'd taken the trouble to remove the envelope from Lambdon's pocket. He thought Lambdon had handled the morning show with all the skill and verve of an amateur cardsharp. Something was wrong. Lambdon hadn't got his act properly together – he was being shunted – and he was getting old. Gerrard finished his coffee but didn't get up. There was nothing but rain outside; even the Japanese had gone home. He lit another cigarette, and pulled himself up short – he was treating Fred Lambdon like the other side, but he'd known Fred Lambdon most of his adult life. It left a nasty taste in his mouth.

The stocky man in the navy-blue blazer darted through a sudden flush of traffic and headed towards the telephone kiosk on the opposite side of Whitehall.

It was empty and unvandalised.

He held the door open with his foot while he dialled. It answered immediately.

'Murray here,' he said. He didn't wait for an acknowledgement. 'Get hold of Smithy right away and tell him to meet me at the pub on the corner of Scotland Yard. He knows the one, it's opposite where the horse soldiers play. Have you got that?'

'Hang on.'

He lit a cigarette while he waited and watched the eddy of blue smoke snake its way out of the crack in the door where it dispersed in the wet driving onslaught that slanted down Whitehall. When he was bored with watching smoke he raised his eyes and gazed blankly at a tall figure waiting outside.

'Are you going to be much longer in there?' It was a voice that came through a mouthful of plum stones.

Murray raised an eyebrow and removed his foot from the gap in the door, allowing it to slam shut. The wet figure jumped backwards and glowered. Murray puffed contentedly on his cigarette and stared back, unconcerned, through the thick glass pane – but the confrontation was over before Murray had time to settle down and enjoy it. The umbrella descended on the face and the wet feet moved on.

Murray looked at his watch, then drew on his cigarette, inspecting carefully the length of ash at the end, before flicking it into the rubbish collected in the corner of the box. He opened the door again and whistled tunelessly through his teeth as he watched the rain bouncing off the pavement; Murray seemed to be gifted with an inordinate amount of patience – he seemed almost to be enjoying the wait.

'You still there, Murray?'

Murray brought the receiver back to his ear, and grunted.

'He's on his way,' the voice went on, 'give him about half an hour. What do you want him for?'

'I want him to watch Lambdon,' said Murray laconically, 'all on his own.'

'Bully for Smudger. But hang about, I thought Lambdon was your personal bag of bones – you going on holiday or something?'

'Don't be funny! Put your teeth back in and listen carefully; Lambdon's gone dry – he's doing exactly what he's expected to do. But I don't trust the bastard; he spends far too much time on the bloody phone for my liking, and when he's not doing that he's doing fuck-all to make my life interesting. I'm moving to pastures greener.'

'There'll be bloody hell to pay if Lambdon turns out to be a face card and Smithy buggers it up.'

'He won't. Listen, and jot this down somewhere on your shirt cuff . . . Lambdon met a stranger to the game at Horse Guards this morning. A tough-looking bastard, fairly prosperous by the way he was dressed, fit and mean, somewhere in his forties. I don't like the look of him so I'm going to make him my business. I'm going to attach myself to him for the duration – that's if I can find the bastard again!'

'In London? – you're joking!'

Murray wasn't. 'I'm going to have a chat with F. Lambdon Esquire tonight. He's going to tell me all about this new bloke, isn't he – he's going to tell where he comes from, where he's going, and what the bloody hell he means by chatting up my pet poodle on the bloody Horse Guards.'

'You expecting me to make a note of all this, Murray?'

'You're the bloke with the pencil!' Murray opened the door a fraction and took a deep breath of rain-laden air. It made him cough. He let the door slam and put the phone back to his ear. 'You still there?'

'I've nowhere else to go.'

'Good, make a note of this then; the last time we spoke I told you Lambdon spends a lot of time on the phone, didn't I? I've decided he does that because he's made me and doesn't want to show me who his friends are. He thought he'd lost me this morning.'

'And did he?'

'That'll be the day!'

'If he's running a solo through the phone box why are you sticking with him?'

'I've just told you, I'm not – Smithy is, and if you were interested, or

34

could understand the finer points of dirty bastardry, you'd realise that sneaking around the way we do does Lambdon's ulcers no end of good. It's also beneficial for him to know he's not been allowed to drift through his new life unnoticed and unaccompanied. When old Lambdon's made my acquaintance and we've had our little chat he'll be inclined to drop his guard a bit because he'll know I've shown him my cards – which means, as far as he's concerned, that I'm back in the pavilion. He might well feel free then to let Smithy into some of the more evil aspects of his life style. He might move more of his conversations out of the phone box and on to the parade ground, but one thing's for sure, he won't be expecting a lad like Smithy to be doing a man's work – not after he's had the real thing on the job, now will he?'

There was a longish pause while the information was digested at the other end; then, 'Are you taking Smithy with you tonight?'

'No, this'll require a different sort of finesse – the sort you get at the arse-end of a Suffolk Punch. I've got just the bloke.'

'You mix with some very peculiar people! Anything else?'

'No. I'll be in touch.'

Murray dropped the receiver on to its rest with a clatter and let himself out of the box and into Whitehall. The rain was still coming down in torrents. He turned up the collar of his blazer and ran for the sanctuary of the King's Head.

CHAPTER 4

Fred Lambdon was tired. He'd been in the shadow game too long – he was slowing down; he knew he was slowing down because the taste of the whisky was not as important as the effect. After over thirty years in the grey zone Fred Lambdon suddenly realised he'd had enough – it was time to go home and cut the grass. He gulped from the large glass of whisky he'd been nursing, while, with his free hand, he loosened his tie and opened his shirt collar. He pulled a face at himself and his eyes met their reflection in the mirror above the mantelpiece. He grimaced at the reflection, glanced down at his wrist-watch and walked across the room to the telephone. He dialled the code for Dublin and followed it with the number written in his address book under the heading, Central Electricity Board.

The response was immediate.

'Lambdon here,' he said and, without a further preamble, 'The answer's maybe. He wants more detail and he wants it direct from one of you.'

The silence lasted several seconds; then, 'Maybe's not good enough, Lambdon – what we want is a yes or a no. I don't want to come over there just to sit in the park and talk French. You're supposed to know him, make a guess – will he or won't he?'

The voice in Lambdon's ear was distinctly English. He knew who it was. He waited for a moment before answering, then weighed his response carefully. 'I'd say he was interested. I wouldn't go as far as saying keen and enthusiastic, but definitely interested.'

'You've got an opinion on how far his interest extends?'

'Sure. I think he'll do the job if you show him the rules and play the game in the open. If you try bullshit you won't see his arse for dust . . . And as for sitting in the park with your dictionary – forget it, he speaks English like you and me.'

There was no reaction, just a curt, 'Where is he now?'

36

'At the Crinton. He's waiting for me to contact him again. He'll stay there until I call him.' Lambdon drank from his glass and listened to the crackle and splutter in his ear – it sounded as if a bucketful of Irish Sea was working its way into the line. When it cleared the voice came back loud and crisp.

'Tell him somebody will collect him tomorrow morning and bring him to a rendezvous. The courier will call on you first; take him to Gerrard and make the introduction, then remove yourself from the scene. Go away for a few days. Good night, Lambdon.' The line went dead.

Lambdon put his fingers on the cradle and dialled the Crinton Hotel.

'Michel?' he said. 'It's Fred. I'll be bringing someone round to see you tomorrow morning. Wait in for me, will you? They haven't given a time. The bloke I'm coming with will take you outside somewhere to meet one of the big spuds – he can talk contracts and sign. Is that all right?'

'Fine, I'll be waiting.' Gerrard's voice softened slightly. 'Fred, I forgot to ask this morning; how's Marjory?'

Lambdon was less than forthcoming. He sounded in a hurry. 'She's all right, Michel, thanks. Don't see enough of her nowadays, but yes, she's fine. I'll tell her you asked.'

'Do that, Fred. Give her my love. And how's your baby daughter?'

'She's fine too. Grown up a lot – you wouldn't recognise her. So I'll see you in the morning?'

It was like talking to an answering machine. Gerrard gave up.

'Goodbye, Fred.'

The phone went dead in Lambdon's ear. He replaced the receiver with a thump and stood looking at it, as if daring it to answer back. It remained silent. He studied his watch again then emptied his glass with a gulp and poured another generous measure from a litre bottle of Grouse; this time he doubled it up with lukewarm water from the tap. He carried the drink back to the telephone but before he reached it the door-bell rang. He opened the door without thinking. He realised his error too late.

Two men blocked the entrance and, even as the warning bell clanged in his brain, a large fist powered into his stomach. He heard his lungs empty with the whooshing sound of a blown tyre. The pain was just behind.

As his legs disintegrated he doubled forward – the only way he could get any breath past his throat – and didn't feel the hand on his shoulder that steadied him and prevented him from pitching out into the cobbled yard. But he did see, through his streaming eyes, a smiling face. The face was saying something to him but Lambdon could only hear the roaring in his ears.

'Hallo, Freddie, old chum,' the face bellowed cheerfully, loud enough for anybody outside to hear. 'Yes, of course we've got time for a drink.' Murray knew how to do it – he'd done it all before. He lowered his voice and said quietly to his companion, 'Give him another one – same place.'

The second pile-driver thumped just below Lambdon's rib cage and Murray, with his hand on the door frame for balance, placed his right foot gently on Lambdon's heaving shoulder and sent him hurtling backwards into the room

Lambdon died. But the relief was only momentary.

The roaring in his ears was replaced by a high-pitched scream. He knew where it was coming from, but he did nothing about it – he wasn't ashamed – there was no other way of getting air into his collapsed lungs.

Murray closed the door quietly behind him and, after a studied professional glance at Lambdon, curled foetal-like among the splintered wreckage of a broken table, nodded to his companion and waved his hand around the compact mews flat.

The other man nodded back and vanished.

Murray straightened up from the door and strolled across the room. He stood looking down at Lambdon for a second or two, then placed his foot on Lambdon's face and pressed it into the carpet. Lambdon kept his eyes open, but only one of them had vision. There was no point saying anything; the rules were that the man winning was the man who did the talking. He continued staring across the carpet – a one-eyed worm's view – and could now see, vaguely, the second man moving about the room. But there was no time to get excited. Suddenly everything went black. His eyelid had dropped and he was left in the dark. It was an automatic reaction to the cold cylindrical tube pressed firmly into the corner of his eye socket.

'Good evening, Freddie.' The voice seemed to come from a long way off. 'This is a .45 Browning I'm holding to your eye.'

Lambdon didn't need the confirmation.

'Get up slowly,' the voice continued, '. . . very slowly. Turn that armchair back on its feet and sit in it.' As he spoke, Murray took his foot off Lambdon's face and straightened up; the pistol was raised but continued to point at Lambdon's eye.

Lambdon did exactly as he was told.

'Well, Fred . . . ?' Murray began, and stopped. The buzzing telephone interrupted whatever he was going to say. It set Lambdon's nerves screaming.

Nobody moved.

'Shall I answer it, Dave?' The other member of the team, a tall, heavily built second-row forward, poked his head round the bedroom door.

Murray narrowed his eyes, but kept them, unwaveringly, on Lambdon's face. 'Who is it, Fred? You expecting any calls?'

Lambdon shook his head. The effort almost made his eyes pop out of their sockets.

Murray said quietly over his shoulder, 'Pick it up, Bernie. Find out who it is and get their number. Say Fred'll ring back later.'

The tall man picked the phone up and after a short exchange of mumbled words replaced the receiver and said, 'Bird named Melanie.' It was a strangely gentle voice coming from a face that had seen more than its fair share of rough treatment; a voice with its origins well to the east of Aldgate pump. 'She wouldn't give me a number.' He looked blankly at Lambdon but got no reaction. 'Said 'e'd know who it was and what number to ring.'

'Who is she, Fred?' Murray asked.

'Just a friend. I met her a couple of days ago.'

'You sure about that, Fred?'

'I'm sure.'

Murray winked at the large man and looked back quickly at Lambdon. 'That's funny! Don't you think that's funny, Bernie? And you too, Fred,' Murray brought everybody into the joke. 'I think you'll find it funny as well when I tell you, Fred, that in the several weeks I've been doing a blanket job on you the only woman named Melanie that's flitted across your screen was Melanie your daughter!' Murray's face creased in a broad grin. 'Sorry, Fred! I can see you don't feel too much like laughing. Maybe you'll feel differently in a minute.'

Lambdon stared blankly into Murray's face.

Murray wasn't finished yet. 'So, goodbye Melanie! Now what about Marjory?'

Lambdon's throat had gone dry. It was nothing to do with the thumping he'd received from Murray's mate.

'Who's Marjory?' he rasped.

'He asked who Marjory is, Bernie. Will you tell him or shall I?'

The Cockney shook his head. 'You tell him, Dave. You tell 'em better than me.'

Murray beamed. 'Marjory's your wife, Fred. She lives down a nice little backwater opposite the churchyard in a place called Chennington-something-or-other in Sussex. Isn't that right?'

'I don't know what the bloody hell you're talking about.'

Murray stopped smiling. 'You're a fucking liar, Lambdon!'

Lambdon shrugged his shoulders – a lump of ice had replaced his stomach. Murray watched closely, he knew his business – he knew what was happening to Lambdon's stomach. He gave it another little stir. 'But let's forget your wife and daughter for the moment. We can always come back and chat some more about them if our little conversation runs out of steam. OK?'

Lambdon found his tongue. 'You'll be wasting your time. I don't take work home with me.'

Murray's humour was restored. He smiled into Lambdon's eyes and tapped him on the knee with the automatic.

'We'll see, Freddie, we'll see.' The smile, which had never really caught on, vanished. 'OK, that's the social part of the occasion over with – let's get on with making the pudding. We all know what the form is . . . My name is Bastard and you are Fred Lambdon former member of Her Majesty's cloak and dagger brigade currently running the three-legged race with a Dublin set.'

'And you are?' grunted Lambdon.

'I told you, I'm Bastard. You and I are wearing different strips, Fred – we're on different sides, we don't like each other – we're enemies . . . And that's enough about me. His name . . .' He nodded in the direction of the big Cockney who'd moved over to the small sideboard and was busy pouring whisky into two cut-glass tumblers. 'Well, it doesn't really matter to you what his name is, but for interest's sake it's Gallagher – Bernard F. for "Fuck me, I've killed the poor bugger and I only tapped him across the nose!" Bernie's one of your original Iron Age men – tough as a concrete block – they dug him up out of the Dagenham Marshes . . . Isn't that right, Bernie?'

Gallagher nodded without looking up from the bottle and glasses. One thing at a time was Bernie's mental capacity – pouring drinks and making conversation were two.

Murray stared at the back of his head for a few seconds, shook his head and pulled a face at Lambdon, 'So for Christ's sake, Fred, try not to upset him.' He frowned back again at the big Cockney. 'Bernie, don't forget to pour one of those for Colonel Lambdon . . . Make it a big one.' He smiled kindly at Lambdon. 'You look as though you could do with one of those, Fred.'

40

Lambdon made no reply. He accepted the glass Bernie handed him and, hiding his gratitude, took an enormous swig. It made him cough violently when it hit the back of his throat.

'There you go, Fred! I said you needed that, didn't I?'

Murray pulled up a dining-chair, turned it round and straddled it with both arms resting across the top. He held the pistol, a very large and well-worn Browning .45 automatic, limply in his right hand and rested his chin comfortably on his forearm.

'OK, Freddie,' he said amiably. 'Let's start with these three fellows you keep bumping into in Dublin. Ready? Good. First of all, who are they and what are their names? Second, who do they represent? Third, what's the address of your next meeting place? And, finally, for the time being that is, who was the chap you spent the morning marching across Horse Guards Parade with?'

Lambdon stared at him, expressionless. Instead of answering he took a slow drink from his glass, swirled the whisky round his mouth and swallowed. Then he started again.

Murray wasn't offended. 'I'm not too keen for Bernie to have to drive all the way down to your seaside home at this time of the night to confirm any dodgy answers with Marjory.' He waited a second. 'And then come all the way back for *tête-ah-têtes* with Melanie. Got it, Fred?' He nodded encouragingly. 'So, let's get it right first time, OK? Good. Off you go then. Start thinking and talking at the same time.'

'I've never seen all three together at . . .' Lambdon stopped dead when the pistol barrel bounced on his knee.

'Just a minute, Freddie boy,' Murray snapped. 'Just hold your horses.' The chumminess disappeared with his smile. 'I didn't ask anything about whether you'd seen them in a gang or on their bloody tod, did I? Now think over those questions again, and as I said, answer them the way I put them; think, consider, then answer . . . And get ready to duck if I don't like it.'

Lambdon started again. 'The names are probably all paper ones, but the one who usually hears my confession calls himself Jack Keighly. He's IRA . . . Official . . .'

He saw Murray's eyes swing upwards to a point just above his head, and caught movement in the corner of his eye. He started to duck, but was too late. An open hand, the size of a dinner plate, exploded on the side of his face. He nearly passed out with the agony. It felt as though his cheekbone had been driven through to the other side of his nose.

He wasn't given time to recover.

Beyond the galaxy of stars and a mist of pain he saw Murray's lips moving. The sound came back to his right ear in time for him to catch the end of the sentence.

'. . . and the next time, Fred, I'll tell him to hurt you.'

Lambdon opened his mouth and moved his jaw from side to side. 'All right,' he tried to say, but it was difficult to articulate with one side of his face numb and frozen – it was like talking to the dentist with his fingers wrapped round the last back tooth in a dead mouth – 'The name you want is John Malseed. He's the cut-out man. I tell him, he tells them, and then the procedure's reversed. I sit in the ante-room and count my fingers . . . He does the eyeball bit. You should be talking to him, not me – I'm only the boy who makes the tea.' He stopped talking and delicately touched the side of his face with the tips of his fingers.

'Put your hand down,' Murray said absently. 'What did you say that name was again?'

'Malseed.'

'I see. And who does he play for? What's his position?' Murray lit a cigarette and looked over the match at Lambdon while he waited for his answer.

'IR – '

Lambdon saw it coming this time and dropped his chin, allowing the blow to fall on the back of his head. The huge fist bounced like a black-smith's hammer off the anvil. It didn't break any bones but Gallagher swore in agony and waved his hand around like a Chinese fan.

'You all right, Bernie?' Murray looked at the big man without concern. 'You took your eye off the ball then, didn't you, you silly bugger? You want to watch what you're doing with those hammers – I don't want the poor old sod snuffed – not yet anyway.'

'Christ Almighty, Dave! 'e's got an 'ead like a bleedin' cannon-ball!'

'All right, Bernie, leave it out now, and for Christ's sake watch where you're waving those bloody things.' Murray turned his attention back to Lambdon. 'How about you, Fred – can you hear me?'

Lambdon felt as if his head had been split in two. He opened his eyes and winced at Murray. 'Look,' he hissed through clenched teeth, 'if this bloody ape touches my head again I'll have nothing left to think with, let alone talk. Tell him to lay off, will you?' He put his hand to his head, but dropped it quickly when Murray shook his head. 'OK, tell me what's disturbing you. What don't you like, the name or the IRA?'

Murray's eyes were frank and open. 'Fred, you keep saying IRA, when I know these three are not. They're not Provo; they're not Official; and they're not INLA. I know everybody who's anybody in the Dublin Kremlin and there's nothing on my tablets that mentions any of your playmates. They're from outside somewhere, all three of 'em. They're talking big and they're playing some sort of game – I want to know what that game is, Fred, and you're going to tell. At least you're going to tell me the bit you know about it or, in about ten seconds flat, you're going to have a bowl of blancmange on your shoulders instead of a head.'

Lambdon opened his one good eye and focused it on the speaker. 'Can I have another whisky?' he asked.

'Of course you can. Get him a large one, Bernie, and a small one for me. Put a drop of water in mine. Fred'll take his neat.' Murray turned his dark eyes back to Lambdon. 'You've told me fuck-all so far, Fred. But then you know that, don't you? I've wasted half an hour on you and we haven't even got going yet. I find it very hard to believe that anyone could know so little about what he's supposed to be doing.' Murray shook his head admonishingly. 'Personally I think you're coming the daft ha'porth with me, my old *Sturmbannführer*, so, knock that drop of whisky back quickly and get ready to try and dissuade me from turning Bernie loose on you. You've got about five and a half seconds to think about it.'

Lambdon was indeed thinking. He was thinking about Murray and wondering which corner of the Irish problem he'd wriggled out of. Or was he something else? There was supposed to be room for everybody in this corner of the shit-house – a well-known fact behind every locked door in MI5's Gordon Street emporium. Irishmen, theirs and ours, were all grabbing a bit of the space – they were all crawling around in the undergrowth with their eyes closed and their mouths clamped tight like a virgin's knees, and half of them didn't know who the other half was. Undercover was a lovely word for the comic papers, thought Lambdon in his five-and-a-half second communion, but it meant bugger-all when you didn't know who was yours and who was the one with the shamrock printed all over his 'Y' fronts. He looked at Murray through his one good eye.

MI5? You don't look as if you'd know where bloody Gordon Street is, let alone what letter of the alphabet they're playing under. Irish accent – why not RUC's EA4? Why not? – you're not going to bloody say. And what about our lot? Army? 14INT? Could be. And by the same bit of uneducated guesswork you could be a UVF leg breaker, but you're not going to chat about that either so who the bloody hell does sign your pay cheque every Friday afternoon? If I could find a bloody fool to take it I'd bet a pound to a bent pin the bastard smells of Jameson's and whistles 'Danny Boy' between swigs. It's got to be. We don't breed runners like this evil bastard – or employ them. Or do we? You're not going to find out by sitting here and letting this refugee from the Stonehenge show pound your head into a jelly. So why don't you tell him what game you're playing and hope he's on our side? And if he's not? Fuck it! And what about Gerrard? What about him? Because, you stupid bastard, you pointed for them and the bloody bog brigade's had time to paint his picture – that's what about! Have you forgotten? This bastard said he'd made Gerrard on Horse Guards this morning. Maybe it was passing curiosity, nothing more than that – showing off that he's got eyes and can watch like the best of them. Maybe he's forgotten about it . . . ?

He hadn't.

Murray brought Lambdon's mind back into the warm.

'Let's leave the Dublin song and dance act for the moment, Freddie, we'll come down that road on our way back.' Murray studied Lambdon's face critically as he spoke. 'So now tell me, without bullshitting and shilly-shalling around, who the fellow was you trooped the colour with on Horse Guards this morning, and what his business is. You seemed to have quite a lot to say to each other, but you'll be telling me all about that, won't you?'

Lambdon frowned hard at Murray for a few seconds, then allowed a gleam of comprehension to flash into his eyes; he tried to laugh for added sincerity, but couldn't make it with only half a mouth functioning – it came out as a gurgled grimace. 'Horse Guards? This morning? Funny, I didn't see you hanging around there . . . You must be thinking about old Harry.'

'Must I?'

'He's the only person I met this morning.'

'Then that's the one we're talking about,' said Murray patiently. 'What about old Harry?'

Lambdon continued grimacing his set smile. 'Harry's an old friend from the bullring – we did the blood and sand bit in Aden together. He's looking for a job and thought I could help him out. Nothing sinister. Just a bloke looking for a job.'

Murray blew smoke in Lambdon's face and raised his eyebrows. 'Go on,' he said.

'Go on what? That's it – an old friend looking for a job.'

'How did he know where to find you?' The fly moved gently across the stream towards the basking trout.

'The O & M Club gave him my phone number. He rang me last night.'

'What's old Harry's full name?'

'Biskitt. Er . . . Harry Biskitt.'

'Biscuit?'

'That's right.'

'As in custard cream?'

Lambdon said nothing.

Murray grinned. 'Where does Harry Biscuit live?'

'He's staying at the O & M Club while he looks for somewhere to rent. He'll give me his new address as soon as he finds a place.' Lambdon was pleased with the little extra touch, it sounded convincing.

Not to Murray it didn't.

There was no change in his expression, not a blink, nothing. It came without telegraph or warning. His hand shot out like a snake's head and the barrel of the automatic cracked noisily across the back of Lambdon's hand. Two knuckles and the forefinger broke with the sound of crunching bone. There was a thin silence which lasted a fraction of a second. Then Lambdon screamed.

The pain shot up his arm straight into his brain. He threw his glass of whisky away in horror and grasped his hand in an attempt to dull the shrieking agony. When he looked down he nearly passed out at the sight of bone, gristle and the bloody gore that had been his right hand. He screwed his eyes up and bowed his head while the ruined hand jerked uncontrollably, shaking off large thick droplets of blood which splattered heavily on to the pale-grey Wilton.

Murray was on his feet. He was in control of himself but his eyes blazed and he glared at the top of Lambdon's bowed head.

'What a load of bloody rubbish,' he snarled, 'I've never heard so much bloody shit in all my life. What sort of Chinese idiot d'you think you're dealing with, Lambdon? Give me a bit of credit, for Christ's sake. Even that bloody moron behind you wouldn't be taken in by a load of crap like that. Right – I reckon that's your bloody lot. You obviously don't fancy the gentle ways, do you? You want to be a tough guy? You want butcher's shop? OK, that's what you're going to get then – fuckin' butcher's shop.' Murray winked at Gallagher over Lambdon's head. 'You heard that, Bernie? You can stop fucking around now. Next time hit the bastard.'

Gallagher winked back, glad to be part of the game, and on the winning side. He leaned over Lambdon's shoulder and looked down with clinical interest at his mutilated hand.

'I don't think you're going to be able to use that 'and again, mate,' he said knowledgeably. 'You're in trouble . . . You know that, doncha? If you want my advice I sugges' you stop taking the piss and start wondering how you're going to open your fly button wiv'out fingers. You continue fuckin' Mr Mu – Dave abaht and he'll do the same to the other 'and – or worse.'

Lambdon came out of shock with a bump. He was angry and hurt – and very afraid. 'Get bloody stuffed, you big stupid bastard!' he hissed over his shoulder. 'And the same goes for you.' He blinked in pain at Murray and, ignoring the gun pointed at his midriff, half rose out of the armchair. It was as far as he got. He felt a stunning blow on the back of his head and a searing flash in his neck. He heard a brittle crack which was followed by a series of flashing lights and in a deathly silence he dropped painlessly into a numb, dark oblivion.

Fred Lambdon's neck had snapped like a dry twig.

Murray sat unmoving and stared, as if hypnotised, at Gallagher's huge hand folded into a fist and frozen like a heraldic device over Lambdon's collapsed figure. He shook his head in disbelief. Then he looked up, and very quietly through clenched teeth, hissed, 'You bloody great stupid bastard! You've bloody well killed him!'

Gallagher stared at his clenched fist, shaped like a ten-pound hammer, and shook his head.

'You stupid, bloody, homicidal, moronic bastard.' Murray felt like squeezing the trigger on the big man standing in front of him. 'Now just who the bloody hell am I going to sit down and talk to now? God, please help me!' He closed his eyes in supplication. 'You clumsy great bastard! What the bloody hell have you got in that fuckin' thing on your shoulders besides nuts and bolts?' Murray shook his head as he stared at the big Cockney. 'You stupid bastard!'

Gallagher opened his mouth to say something, but got no further.

'Just shut up, will you! Shut up for a soddin' minute and let me think.'

Murray grasped Lambdon's hair and lifted his head. Somewhere behind the ear a bone grated, bringing a look of distaste to Murray's face. He wrinkled his nose and looked into the dead man's glazed eyes as if willing him back to life, and in exasperation shook the head backwards and forwards like a rag doll's before letting it fall loosely on to the back of the armchair. Murray turned his tight-lipped attention back to the big man and stared at him.

'I only tapped 'im,' Gallagher got his side in quickly in the hope of forestalling another stream of insults, 'and you did say 'it the bastard next time. Besides, how the fuckin' 'ell was I to know the stupid old bugger 'ad a bleedin' weak neck?'

Murray controlled his anger with difficulty. He was no stranger to vio-

46

lent death but this one was not only unnecessary, it was bloody inconvenient. He stared at Gallagher and bit back the words that came easily to his tongue – he'd already used most of them once and swearing at Gallagher was like swearing at a concrete lamp-post. And all the swearing in the world wasn't going to make Lambdon's tongue waggle again, and it certainly wasn't going to put him alongside his marching companion from the Horse Guards Parade. So, that's that – fuck it! he growled under his breath. We marked Old Freddie down as expendable – and so he would have been after he'd sicked up the name of his playmate – but he didn't, did he? He said bugger-all and here we are back at the bloody beginning with nowhere to go except home.

He gazed blankly at the dead body slumped in the armchair in front of him, its head lolling to one side, and unconsciously allowed his thoughts to become words.

'So what am I going to do about all this, Fred?' he murmured to the dead man's face. 'How am I going to find that hard-faced bastard you were talking with this morning?'

'What about his old woman?' Bernie thought he'd been forgiven. 'He could have told her about this Mr Biscuit.'

'Don't be bloody – !' Murray's head shot up and he stared at the Cockney's innocent expression. 'Say that again.'

'What – Mr Biscuit?' Gallagher's face creased into a smile.

'No, you stupid bastard! Never mind – it doesn't matter. Forget it, I think you've just given me the answer . . . Lambdon's bloody wife! And why not?'

'What?'

'Marjory'll know who Mr-bloody-Biscuit is.' Murray ignored the big Cockney's puzzled expression. 'Why am I telling you? Forget it. Do something useful – go and put that on the bed and cover it up.' Murray jerked his chin at Lambdon's sagging body but remained deep in thought. He issued instructions to Bernie automatically as he worked out in his mind his next move. 'And when you've done that come and clean up some of this mess, and while you're doing it see if you can find his address book, not that there'll be anything in it that we don't already know. But get a move on, I want to get out of here – I've had enough for one bloody day.'

Murray was right about the address book. Lambdon had left nothing for him to make a story out of; it was an empty-handed Murray who pulled the front door shut behind him. Murray was philosophical about the way the ball bounced – some you win, some you lose; it didn't worry him all that much even though the day that had started with such promise had ended in near disaster. But it was only near disaster – Mrs Lambdon might yet save the day. 'Cheerio, Fred,' he called over his shoulder. 'Thanks for the drinks.'

CHAPTER 5

Michel Gerrard stared out of his bedroom window at the dawn of a typical English midsummer day.

The rain teemed down like lengths of silver stair-rod and struck the window with a din that mocked the soundproof powers of the expensive double glazing. He winced when a brilliant fork of lightning cut through the brown morning light, and steeled himself against the clap of thunder that exploded almost in unison with the flash. He lit a cigarette and swallowed another mouthful of lukewarm coffee, and swore loudly at the echoing roll of thunder as it rumbled across the wet rooftops.

'What a country! No wonder everybody looks so miserable.' He grimaced when his next words were drowned out by the beginning of another salvo.

'I'm not miserable, Michel! But I will be if you don't come here quickly.' The voice, muffled and plaintive, came from the depths of the royal-size bed that dominated the luxury apartment. In the storm-inspired gloom the bed looked shapeless and mysterious but, somewhere in its centre, a gentle mounded sheet offered a suggestion of occupation.

Gerrard turned away from the window and stared at the bed.

A long, sensuous arm languidly uncurled from its depths like a waking cobra rising for its breakfast. It uncoiled slowly, shedding the protective sheet until it revealed a delicate silken armpit and the gentle curve of a firmly rounded breast. A long elegant finger crooked in his direction, and again the voice slithered across the semi-darkened room.

'Come back to bed, Michel.' It was a warm, sleep-laden voice, husky with sex. 'Come and hold me, thunder terrifies me ... And I'm ready ...' she paused and gave a soft laugh, ' ... to be told goodbye! Quick!'

Gerrard stubbed his cigarette out in the saucer of the coffee cup and walked across the room to the bedside.

The tousled blonde head was buried deep in the large soft pillow, but her eyes were open and she peered innocently as he stood beside the bed looking down; then she smiled through sleepy eyes and pouted her lips. 'Please?' she whispered appealingly.

Gerrard didn't move.

She said it again: 'Michel, please? Don't be cruel.' It was an insistent childlike demand to have her toy returned.

'You're being greedy,' Gerrard told her. 'You'll wear it out . . . You'll go blind.'

'Come here.'

'Sorry, there's no time. I've got to get dressed . . .' There was little conviction in his voice. 'People are coming to see me. Do you want them to sit drinking their coffee on the end of the bed waiting for you and me to untangle?' He broke off when the shadowy hand descended and, searchingly, found its way through the gap in his dressing-gown.

'They can wait,' she said hoarsely. 'I can't.' And after a second's pause, and with a giggle, 'And neither can you!'

Gerrard's will-power was never at its best first thing in the morning. He shrugged his shoulders out of the blue towelling robe and, still guided by her soft, but determined hand, slid under the covering sheet and into her warm liquid body.

'Don't move,' she implored him, then moaned with her open mouth pressed against his shoulder, 'for God's sake don't move . . .' Her body was now still and she lay passively under the hard weight of the Frenchman's expended force. Her appeal was unnecessary. They were both powerless to move and lay joined and trapped in each other.

She was the first to recover.

'How?' she whimpered into his ear, and began to shiver. 'Why you?' Her voice trembled as she quivered under him and she gripped the back of his hair and dug her fingers into his neck. 'I didn't think . . .'

'Don't . . .'

'It'll never be the same again.'

'Flatterer. I bet you say that to all your friends.'

'Don't be unkind, Michel.' Her body at last quietened and she took her mouth away from his shoulder and searched for his. 'I never knew that could happen . . . Nobody ever took me down that road before.' She wriggled underneath him to show which road she meant. 'Why have you come along to ruin what I've always thought was a perfectly good thing?' She searched the inside of his mouth with her tongue, then whimpered, 'What am I going to do, Michel?'

Gerrard raised his head and looked into the lovely features beneath him. Her eyes were closed but her mouth remained open, searching; he touched her lips gently with his, then placed his hand lightly across her mouth. 'You can stop talking for a minute,' he told her, 'and remember what they tell little girls about their dinner.'

'What do they tell little girls about their dinner, Michel?'

'That they should always leave a little piece on the side of the plate for the angels . . .' He breathed heavily into her ear and she began to wriggle again. 'Apply that rule to this, and when you've built up all those little portions I'll come back and take them off you again.'

'What a sweet little story. When?'

'Ah!' Gerrard kissed her open mouth and tried to raise himself off her, but she opened her eyes, smiled mischievously, and kept her hands locked behind his neck.

'Just a minute,' she whispered, 'I think . . .'

'Forget it! It's out of the question.'

'Not even that tiny little angel's bit . . . ?'

'Not even . . . It's a physical impossibility.'

'Not for me it isn't.'

'It is this time.' Gerrard pulled himself away from her and stood up. 'And it's time to go,' he said brusquely. He looked at his watch. 'In case you've lost touch with time it's eight o'clock; time you were in bed – your own bed! Planes have been known to be on time. They've even been known to be early . . . I don't think your husband would be over the moon to stroll in and find you handing out angel's portions to strange Frenchmen.'

'Planes . . . ?' She stared, perplexed. 'Husband . . . ?'

'Wake up, Audrey! You're meeting your husband. Remember him? He's arriving in London in an aeroplane this morning . . . That's what you told me last night.' He looked askance at her. 'And I suppose now you're going to tell me you've forgotten you have a husband?'

She didn't wilt. 'No. I'm going to say, look at the effect you've had on me!'

'Come on, get up,' he said harshly. 'It was very nice, but it's another day. Playtime's finished. Out!' He ripped the bedsheet off her, but she didn't move; she remained still, proudly naked, and gazed up at him unashamedly.

'Michel,' she said, and put her hands behind her head. 'When shall I see you again?'

'You won't,' said Gerrard cruelly. 'Go and meet your husband. Take

51

him home and be nice to him, and don't place any lasting value on an amusing night. And Audrey . . .'

She lay very still and stared up at him.

' . . . don't make a habit of getting yourself picked up and taken to bed by strangers in hotels – you're not that sort of person – and you know it . . . Come on.' He reached down and took one of her hands from behind her head. 'I've got work to do and I don't want an irate husband, boiled up after eighteen months in the sun, bashing on my door looking for his wife.'

She made a face as he pulled her upright. The top of her head reached his shoulder and as she continued looking up into his face he relented, and broke into a grin.

'Go and eat some oysters,' he said, and kissed the tip of her nose. 'Because when your man starts unwinding, God knows when you'll see the light of day again!'

She stared at him open-mouthed, then shook her head slowly. 'You really are a cruel bastard . . . I thought you were only putting it on.' She opened the top of his dressing-gown and kissed his chest. 'But you're a nice cruel bastard . . . I think I could take this up as a hobby – in fact I would if I was sure I was going to meet you every time.' She didn't give him time to reply; he watched her pert bottom disappear into the shower.

Gerrard remained where he was, staring at the bathroom door as he lit a cigarette. The beginning of a frown creased his forehead, but he shook it away and flopped wearily into a large armchair.

But it wouldn't go away completely. It had been too easy; far too pat.

A beautiful woman, young, attractive, alone in a hotel bar, and at the twitch of a stranger's eyebrow she was between the sheets, quicker than a Marseilles whore on a time bonus. It didn't seem right. Nobody was that lucky nowadays.

He pulled thoughtfully on the cigarette and listened to the water patting musically against the shower screen in the bathroom. *The trouble with you, Gerrard,* he told himself, *is that you've never been able to accept presents from Father Christmas. Why don't you take a day off for a change? Nobody's running beautiful spies around the system this year – it's out of fashion. She's what she said she is; a lovely little nymphomaniac in town for the night to collect a returning husband . . . And if she's into the honey trap game then there's a couple of very weary people going to be wandering around London today. And one of them's got nothing to show for her hard night's work except sore lips . . .*

*

She kissed him lightly before leaving. 'Did you mean what you said about not doing this again one day . . . or night?'

'Yes,' he said gruffly.

'Ships that pass in the night, and all that sort of thing?' she said wistfully.

'Something like that,' he replied unemotionally. 'Goodbye, Mrs Scott.'

'Goodbye, Monsieur Gerrard.'

Gerrard turned the cold tap in the shower full on and winced when the needle-sharp jets pounded into his shoulders. He moved out of range and soaped himself from head to foot. His stomach muscles ached and his head began to throb in gentle sympathy; but he still managed to raise a smile at the thought of a lost night.

His smile broadened as he poured shampoo over his thinning hair. Mrs Scott was a lovely girl – a beautiful body; energetic in the right places, perfect for the man who thought he had the exclusive rights – even better for the ship that passed in the night . . . Gerrard's smile changed to a grin and his headache vanished almost as abruptly as it had come. He moved back into the water flagellation of the needle jets and forgot all about the beautiful Mrs Scott.

But the beautiful Mrs Scott hadn't forgotten Michel Gerrard.

She sat on the newly disarranged bed in her room at the Crinton with her back resting against the padded headboard and she puffed contentedly on a long filter cigarette. She wore only a large bath towel, draped sarong fashion around her damp body, and her bare shoulders still glistened with the undried water from her second shower since leaving Gerrard's bed. She held a cream-coloured telephone loosely near her right ear and listened to the ringing tone. When it stopped, a male voice answered.

'Can I talk?' she asked.

'Yes. Did you have any difficulty picking him up?' The voice was brusque and businesslike.

She laughed. 'I didn't have to try. We locked eyes over the bar and the next minute he was rolling back the counterpane.'

'Did he say very much?'

'You mean during . . . ?'

'You know what I mean.'

She stopped smiling. 'His name you already know; real or bogus it's

Gerrard . . . And he didn't call himself anything else in his dreams! I presume you know what he does for a living?'

'I do.'

'Well?'

'Well what?'

'Geoffrey – I've just spent the night with him! Stop being so bloody mysterious. What does this Frenchman do in the daytime? And what makes him so interesting to you?'

The voice was matter of fact. 'He kills people for money. He goes under the code name of Siegfried. He's Europe's number one assassin.'

'Good God Almighty!'

'Satisfied?'

'You could have told me before.'

'Why? Would it have made any difference?'

'Not really.' Audrey shrugged her shoulders, and watched a droplet of water trickle between her breasts. 'Was I supposed to be finding out what he's doing here in London?'

'No, I know what he's come for. You were supposed to confirm that he's legitimate – that he's not drawing wages from more than one source.'

'How do you mean?'

'I want to be sure that his mind is completely on the business he's come to England for and that he's not doing a tap-dance routine to somebody else's music. I rather hoped that with your persuasive powers of making a man forget whether he's standing on his head or the other thing he'd scream out all his inner problems into your busy little ear . . . Sounds as though it didn't quite work out that way.'

''fraid not, Geoffrey.' Audrey tried to keep her voice even, but it didn't work. It betrayed, like the two red spots that suddenly appeared below her eyes. *It was the other way round, wasn't it, Geoffrey? It was him doing the persuasive power bit and me doing the screaming . . . He knew what he was standing on all right – so did I. It wasn't his head . . .* She bit her lip to ward off memories that had been made only half an hour ago.

The voice was speaking again – it had picked up the vibrations and was cold and critical. It served as a bucket of cold water over her wandering thoughts.

'Pity.' The voice contained no remorse. 'But at least you've made contact, so it's not all down the plug hole. There's a lot more I want to know about this bloody Frenchman. I've got a feeling about him, I think there's more to him than meets the eye, so, I think you'd better devote a bit of time to him. Go and get yourself a French dictionary and do the thing properly.' The voice broke into a brief chuckle. 'Now that you've become good friends he might loosen up, particularly next time, by when his mind should have moved away from the fire and up towards the mantelpiece.'

'Don't be crude, Geoffrey. Is there anything else? I want to get dressed and go home. I've had enough of the Crinton – I've got an old-fashioned yearning for my own bed.'

'Hold on a minute, Audrey, don't rush off just yet. When are you seeing him again? Tonight?'

'No. He doesn't want to. I tried, but he warned me off. Told me not to make anything out of a brief encounter so I didn't push it – you don't push people like this one, you wait for them to do the pushing . . . Sorry about that.'

'Never mind. You sure he doesn't use both barrels?'

'What do you mean?'

'That bit about not wanting his afters. You sure he's all right . . . ?'

'Geoffrey, Gerrard likes girls, not boys. There's nothing wrong with him . . . He's being careful about trailers. He'll have somebody else testing his stamina tonight; no ties, she'll get the same treatment as me in the morning.' She managed to keep the regret out of her voice. 'By the way . . .'

'Be quick.'

'He's expecting to meet some people this morning. He suddenly decided he was in a great hurry. That was when he threw me out of his room . . . said these people were coming to the hotel and then he was going out, presumably with them.'

'Thank you, Audrey.' The voice was flat and non-committal. 'I know all about that. I know who he's meeting – and I know what the meeting's about . . . Pity! Seems like a wasted night.'

Audrey heard the click in her ear as the receiver was put down at the other end. She shivered and pulled the bath towel tighter around her.

CHAPTER 6

In the ground-floor flat of a tall Victorian house a couple of miles to the north of the Crinton Hotel, Clive Reason poured boiling water over the tea-bag in his Gemini mug and swirled it around until the water changed colour. He poured in milk, stirred it, then deftly hooked out the soggy bag with the end of a spoon and flicked it into the sinkful of dirty crockery. He carried the mug across the room and sat down heavily at the table by the open kitchen window and looked at his tree through the rain. It was the only tree in sight. The only tree in urban development gone mad. It gave him a sense of being over-endowed in a concrete world.

The rain was heavy, but it came skimming with the wind over the top of the tall house and funnelled down the narrow garden to shake the tree's branches like a wet shaggy dog. Somewhere out of sight the sun succeeded in breaking through the thick black rain-laden clouds and produced a faint rainbow-streaked halo of fine displaced raindrops around the quivering tree. It was much more entertaining than morning television.

Reason continued staring, for want of something better to do, until it became his ordinary common or garden vanishing species of a London tree again, then he sighed and reached delicately for his tea. His movements were slow and deliberate, pandering to the fierce hammering behind his eyes that threatened to split the inside of his head into two useless, pain-racked lumps. He blew across the rim of the steaming mug and took a tentative sip of its contents. He grimaced at the taste, then winced in discomfort when the telephone rang.

He lifted the receiver and listened in silence to the payphone pips. When they faded into a series of hollow clicks he pushed the mug away, slopping weak brown liquid over the pale-blue Formica, and closed his eyes. There was no relief; the throbbing in his temples went on unabated.

'Clive?'

He recognised the voice and pushed his headache into the background.

'Yes, General.'

'You alone?'

'Yes, sir.'

'Good. Two things.' Sanderson's voice was crisp and authoritative; he sounded like a man in a hurry. 'There's a person staying at the Crinton Hotel named Michel Gerrard. I want a couple of your scruffy friends to go there with a camera and a high-powered telephoto and follow him. I want pictures of anybody he meets. D'you know anybody at the hotel who can point your people towards this man?'

'Yes, sir.'

'Both Gerrard and the man, or men, he's meeting will be expecting uninvited company. Warn your people to be ready for evasive tactics, but don't, under any circumstances, get caught out ... Hold on a minute, don't go away ... What's the matter with this bloody thing?'

'It needs more money, sir.'

Reason's eyes remained closed; his expression blank. He reached blindly for his mug of tea but remembering its taste changed his mind. General Sanderson's voice rattled against his headache again.

'... better to abort the thing than let Gerrard and his friends know we're interested.'

'What was the other thing, sir?'

'I've lost touch with somebody and I want you to go and look for him. It could be serious, possibly terminal. Go and look at his place. If he's around just look at him, but don't let him see you. Don't try to make contact. All I want to know is whether he's still in an upright position. When you've done that let me know immediately – and make sure it's only me you tell. And, Clive ...'

'Sir?'

'There are others interested in the game so watch your step. Their play is inclined to be a bit terracy – a bit on the rough side.'

Reason gave up nursing his headache. 'What's this guy's name – the one you want me to wink at?'

'Lambdon.'

'Fred Lambdon?'

'That's right.' Sanderson didn't elaborate.

Reason did it for him. 'Ex-Company man – last seen playing hurley in Dublin with a Northern team?'

'That's the sort of thing that got the cat into trouble,' said Sanderson.

Reason's smile vanished. 'What is, sir?'

'Curiosity, Clive. When I want you to go down to the river bank and join in the gossip with the village washerwomen I'll let you know. In the meantime, go and have a discreet look at that address. If it looks from the outside like a funeral parlour get yourself inside and have a look around. And I'll want to know something about the other affair as well, as soon as it happens. Goodbye, Clive.' The phone went dead in Reason's ear.

Reason placed a large finger on the bar of the telephone, waggled it up and down once or twice, listened to the tone, then dialled a local Camden number.

Shortly after Reason made his call, the solitary figure of a man splashed its way down Kempton Street, W1.

His head was bowed low into his chest and his thin shoulders brushed wetly against the side of the Crinton Hotel as he sought its protection from the driving rain. He was draped in a pale-grey plastic mackintosh held together by a belt made of knotted segments of parcel string. A transparent plastic hood totally covered his head, leaving only his face exposed to the rain. This face was as wet as if he'd just walked out of the sea. The rest of him looked like a large, raw, king prawn.

He was black, and his dark, wet features stared fixedly at the pavement as he walked. His expression was set at miserable. He looked as if, with every step he took, he was cursing his mother and father for bringing him to this horror climate when he could have been happily strolling along a warm and dusty Barbadian shoreline.

He stopped before a large iron-shuttered entrance, ran his wet sleeve across the lower part of his face and poked his head round the corner of the half-open wicket gate.

'Wha'cha want, son?'

An elderly uniformed security guard stood with his back to the wall behind the door. Two medal ribbons flashed prominently against the drab material of his uniform tunic and he wore a white-topped peak cap, the shiny visor of which had been shortened and flattened, guardsman fashion, so that it completely covered his eyes. A thin stream of smoke drifted gently upwards and over his shoulder from the cupped hand which skilfully hid the burning cigarette, and explained his partially concealed position. He raised his chin and looked over the flattened bridge of a broken nose at the soaking black youth.

'. . . I said what d'yer want, boy?' he repeated.

The youth stared back into the shaded eyes. 'Wanna see me dad,' he said and shivered uncontrollably.

'Who's your dad? What's 'is name?'

'Bliss.'

'Bliss what?'

'Mr Bliss. He's doing the eight to four shift.'

'All right, sonny, don't cummit wiv me . . . I've kicked manners into bigger arses than yours. What d'yer want 'im for?'

'If it's any of your business, General, I've got a message for him.'

The guard frowned and took a quick drag from his cigarette, then nodded his head. 'OK, come in 'ere aht the bloody rain, you look like a bleedin' fish standin' aht there.' He waited until the boy was inside then stared into his face and said, ''Ang abaht, I'll call 'im.'

'Cheers.' The black youth showed his teeth in a grimace. He sniffed, shivered, and then ran a forefinger under his nose to dislodge a large dewdrop of rain that had collected on its tip. 'He's handy then, is he?' he asked.

The guard managed a smile. 'I bleedin' well 'ope so! Don't go away.'

The shiny hobnailed boots echoed loudly in the confined area as the ex-guardsman clomped across the concrete floor. His voice took up the racket with a bellowed shout to the unseen Bliss: 'Hey, H.T.! Yer've got a visitor.'

'I'm busy. Who is it?' The voice seemed to come from a long way off.

'It's your baby boy. Says he's got a message, a note from the ol' lady.' The stentorian voice bounced off the curved wall and vanished down the corridor. The old soldier waited for a second then followed the words up with a parade-ground laugh. 'She wants to know why you didn't go 'ome last night. And if you don't get a move on she's coming rahnd 'ere 'erself!' He turned and winked at the youth and got a sickly smile in return, but before he could produce the next line of barrack repartee a tall coloured man, also in uniform, turned the corner and patted the elder man on the shoulder.

'Thanks, Dusty,' he said. He wasn't smiling.

Dusty was disappointed. He went back to his position by the door and pulled another eighth of an inch from his cigarette. He watched his big partner confront his son.

Bliss didn't move. His expression remained blank, but his dark intelligent eyes were very wary as he looked the young man up and down.

He waited for the youth to say something.

There was no greeting. 'It's private, Dad,' the boy said, and looked pointedly across the room at the other security guard.

The old soldier got the message. 'I'll go an' finish me fag in the rest-room. Gimme a shaht when you've finished.' He vanished quickly, his boots clattering away into the distance.

The tall black man's eyes remained wary. 'OK,' he said to the youth, 'who are you and what do you want?'

The boy tried a half-hearted smile. 'It doesn't matter who I am,' he said softly. He kept his ears cocked in the direction the other man had taken, listening for the heavy clump of shiny boots coming – or going. 'We both do as we're told by the same people.'

'Who's that?'

'Reason. And if you don't like my face you know his number.'

'You're right about that,' interrupted Bliss.

'Right about what?'

'I don't like your face.'

The young man's smile vanished. 'OK, go and give him a ring. I'll wait. But listen, sunshine, do it quickly and don't waste my time – I've got a lot to do and not much time to do it in. What I haven't got is time to fart-arse around with old soldiers and spy games.' The young man's voice had changed. In place of the West Indian lilt was a sharper, educated tone. It carried authority and changed the atmosphere in the hollow surroundings.

He held the uniformed man's wordless scrutiny without blinking until, with a shrug, and a glimmer of amusement, Bliss thrust out a large hand, palm upwards, and said, 'OK, what's your game then, Mr Bond?'

The young man was not amused. He touched the outstretched hand lightly, and said, 'There's a man staying in this hotel named Michel Gerrard. I want him pointed out. That's all, just a finger – we'll do the rest.'

Bliss looked thoughtfully at the young man's mackintosh then raised his eyes to the plastic hood. 'What've you got under that?' he asked.

The young man smiled. 'Rastafarian,' he said.

'You mean dreadlocks, beads . . . the lot?'

'S'rite.'

'It's a joke?' said Bliss.

'No joke. Can you think of a better cover?'

Bliss stared incredulously at the youth for a moment – he didn't know whether to laugh or cry.

'Cover ... ?' he managed at last. 'Don't make me bloody laugh, sonny. That bloody stuff's about as good a cover as my bare arse on a Sunday morning! Tell me, boy, can you see yourself in your black curly rings and ribbons sitting quietly, unnoticed, in the main foyer of the Crinton Hotel?' Bliss waited for a second for a response, but got none. 'Well, can you?'

The young man listened politely without taking his eyes from the older man's face. He offered no comment and made no move except to twitch his nose to remove another droplet of rain that had made its way down from his wet forehead. He waited patiently for Bliss to finish talking.

'Of course you bloody can't.' Bliss flicked the grey plastic with a long black finger and scowled into the young man's face. 'OK, now tell me something that I can laugh about when I'm drinking my pint of bitter tonight; tell me what your other half's made up as ...' He held his hand up and grinned. 'No, I'll tell you what, let me guess; he's a friggin' circus clown.'

The young man suppressed a desire to laugh. 'Not quite. But close! He's a sort of scruffy skinhead type. You'd probably call him a punk. He's the one who takes the pictures.'

H.T. Bliss raised his eyes to the ceiling. 'Christ All-bloody-mighty!' He spoke through clenched teeth. 'I suppose I've gotta believe all this. Where's this character now?'

'Sitting in the car.' The youth pointed over his shoulder. 'Just up the road there. Any chance of getting him nearer to the front of the hotel?'

'No. Leave the car where it is for the time being. It'll be all right there, the worst you can get is a ticket. Go and collect this skinhead of yours and make your way round to the front entrance. When you get there, hang around outside. Try and look normal – Christ knows how, but try. I'll nip upstairs and point you out to the under-porter; he'll be at the door, the one not wearing the top hat. He's the man you've got to watch, so keep your eye on him all the time. He'll make the mark for you when your man leaves the hotel. After that it'll be up to you and your buddy, OK?'

Bliss didn't wait for a reply. He wrinkled his face in a mirthless grin and added, 'And next time you get yourself a posh hotel job, sunshine, take a tip from me; put on a ginger wig and stick half a table-tennis ball on the end of your beak. It'll be a bloody sight less conspicuous than the gear you're got up in now.'

The young man shrugged his shoulders without smiling. 'Thanks,' he said. 'And perhaps we might meet you some time, dressed up like that on Broadwater Farm! But don't worry about us, uncle, we'll get by. And it's been nice chatting with you . . . See you around.' He held his hand out and the big man slapped it.

By the time Bliss had removed the grin from his face the youth had ducked out through the wicket gate and disappeared into the rain.

CHAPTER 7

Gerrard inspected the razor nick on his chin before slapping a handful of Monsieur Balmain's after-shave over the damage. He moved away from the mirror, gingerly picked up the soggy cigarette still smouldering on the glass shelf and pulled a damp mouthful of smoke into his lungs. He studied the butt end with distaste, coughed throatily, then dropped it into the lavatory and flushed it out of sight.

He was fully dressed and showing signs of impatience.

He looked at his watch, stared hard at the pink telephone, and absently lit another cigarette, his seventh of the day. He picked up the unopened morning paper and sat on the edge of the bed. He looked at his watch again – the hands hadn't moved. He leaned back against the headboard, put his feet up on the bed, and waited.

It was half-past nine.

At twenty-eight minutes to ten the red light on the telephone blinked a warning and an apologetic buzzing filled the room. Gerrard dropped the newspaper to the floor and lifted the receiver.

'Gentleman at reception for you, Mr Gerrard.' The silken whisper brushed against the nerve ends in his ear.

Gerrard smiled to himself: where did they find them?

'Thanks,' he said.

'Shall I have him shown up to your room?' Liquid sex in an English accent – the Yanks must love it.

'No thank you. Hold him there. I'm on my way down.'

The girl with the golden voice caught his eye as he approached the desk and parted her lips to show him her excellent bridgework. It came close to a smile, automatic, but uninviting; like plastic flowers it was only for show. She tapped her teeth with the end of a black Bic as she gazed frowningly across the foyer, then pointed the pen like a dart at a corner to the far side of the hall. 'There you are, Mr Gerrard,' she said. 'There's your visitor, the gentleman sitting just to the right of that pillar. Do you see him?'

'Man in a dark suit, white shirt?'

'That's him.'

'Did he give a name?' He didn't even look like Fred Lambdon. Gerrard turned his head and studied the girl's innocent expression.

'No, but he said you were expecting him. There's nothing wrong, is there?' The perfect lips parted slightly and the small white teeth opened to accept the tip of the black pen; she waggled it up and down as she stared into Gerrard's face. Gerrard smiled into her unconcerned eyes and murmured, 'No, there's nothing wrong.' He nodded his thanks and made his way across the lobby.

The man in the corner watched him come, but made no move to meet him.

Gerrard stopped in front of him. 'I'm Gerrard,' he said. 'You wanted to see me?'

The man inclined his head, but didn't get up. He was an anonymous individual, featureless and deliberately inconspicuous; he was a permanent member of the crowd; he blended into the scenery like a guardsman in a colour trooping ceremony, and he was at ease – very comfortably at ease.

'That's right,' he said casually. 'You have an appointment this morning with a Mr Malseed. I've come to take you to him.' The accent blew his anonymity straight back across the Irish Sea. 'Now. If you're ready?' he added.

Gerrard stared down at the man, then glanced back over his shoulder at the reception desk; the girl was busy gazing into the eyes of an American; she was still tapping her teeth with the Bic. When he looked back to the Irishman he forced a twinkle of amusement into his expression. It was a difficult exercise – there was nothing funny, or amusing, about a flat-faced Irishman with Lambdon's baton tucked under his arm while Lambdon was supposed to be still running around the track.

'It sounds exciting,' said Gerrard, 'but are you sure you haven't made a mistake? I don't think I know any Mr Malseed, and I know I don't know you – I've never seen you before in my life.'

The opening moves were completed.

The two men continued to stare at each other. The Irishman wasn't put off by Gerrard's rebuff. He went on, quite unruffled. 'The meeting was arranged yesterday by Fred Lambdon. He was supposed to be here with me to make the introduction. You're going to tell me now you don't know Fred Lambdon?'

'What did you say your name was?'

'I didn't.'

'OK. So where is Lambdon?'

'I was hoping you'd be able to tell me that. It was all arranged last night – late. Like I said, it was down to Lambdon to make the introduction, but there was no reply from the address they gave me.'

'How did you find your way here?'

'I was told this was where you were staying. I had to take the chance and try picking you up without Lambdon holding my hand. It's an urgent business this, Gerrard. Too bloody urgent to be sitting here playing games.' The unruffled Irishman was beginning to ruffle under the pressure of time; his deadline was staring at him like a huge eye from the large clock over the canopied reception desk. He confirmed its accuracy with a quick glance at his left wrist before looking back up at Gerrard. 'Mr Malseed's come over specially to see you.' His voice suddenly took on a hoarse tone, as if he'd suddenly remembered what he was – and where he was. 'And I don't think you should disappoint him.' He started to push himself out of the chair. 'Can we go now?'

The Irishman's urgency failed to impress itself upon Gerrard. He put both hands in his trouser pockets and leaned against the imitation marble pillar. The clock wasn't worrying him.

'What was the address you said you went to – the one where Lambdon was supposed to be waiting for you?'

The Irishman wasn't deceived. He allowed himself to drop back into the chair with another quick glance at the foyer clock. A tiny nerve under his right eye twitched momentarily – it was as close as he could get to an understanding smile. 'You're still not happy then?' He didn't wait for an answer, he could see it in Gerrard's face. 'OK. Lambdon's staying at number 4 Clarence Garden Mews. That's on the other side of the park there, round the back of Marble Arch.' He studied Gerrard's uncompromising expression for a moment and added, 'It's got a dark-blue front door. But like I said, he's not at home. If he is he's not answering the door today. Does that satisfy you?'

Gerrard nodded and waited until the Irishman stood up. He wasn't very tall.

'I asked you for a name,' demanded Gerrard.

The Irishman was busy struggling into a navy-blue raincoat. He didn't stop for the question. 'My name's of no consequence,' he said. 'We won't be meeting again. I'm only the escort, I hand you over and then I'm finished. You ready to go now? Have you got a raincoat? It's pissing down out there.'

'I'll order a taxi.'

'That won't be necessary. It's not far, we can walk.'

The Irishman's assessment of the intensity of the rain was exaggerated. The thunderstorm had passed over the centre of London and headed east, leaving just enough of its fringe to moisten the air with a light, delicate drizzle. Gerrard stared up at it sceptically then shrugged into his raincoat on the steps of the main entrance before joining the Irishman on the pavement overlooking Park Lane.

'We'll cross over to the park and head towards the Serpentine,' said the Irishman. 'Don't worry about looking behind, I'll attend to that part of it.'

It was not the sort of morning for a walk in the park and the few people using the pathways were not doing so for pleasure; there was no loitering or aimless wandering hand in hand – this was a businessman's promenade, everybody was going somewhere. *Nothing to make your arse itch here, Paddy!* Gerrard looked sideways at his escort and smiled to himself as he pulled the collar of his raincoat up round his neck. There was nothing more to talk about. He put his hands in his pockets and walked in silence, hardly aware of the equally taciturn Irishman splashing stolidly beside him.

The walk was longer than Gerrard had expected.

The Irishman stopped abruptly and put his hand on Gerrard's arm. 'Here we are,' he said.

The bandstand looked lonely in its island of empty wet seats.

'This isn't the Serpentine.' Gerrard stared blankly into the other man's wet face.

'It doesn't matter. Go and find yourself a seat. Mr Malseed'll join you in a couple of minutes.' He took a long hard look at Gerrard and turned back the way they'd come.

'Just a minute,' Gerrard called. It stopped the Irishman dead in his tracks. Gerrard reached out and withdrew the sodden newspaper from under his arm. 'You won't need this,' he said, 'and I think you'd better go and get your Mr Malseed one as well, it's not going to do his piles much good sitting on these wet seats.' He bared his teeth in an artificial smile and made his way down one of the aisles. He sat down uncomfortably on a wet seat and stared, without interest, at the empty bandstand.

The damp had barely worked its way through the Irishman's *Daily*

Mirror when Gerrard's ears picked up the approaching footsteps. He didn't look round.

The footsteps halted beside him. 'How do you do, Mr Gerrard. My name is Malseed.'

Gerrard looked up at him. He was a tall man and wore a dark impermeable – a tailored raincoat, with a black velvet collar that glistened with rain droplets that had found a way under the protective umbrella.

'Please don't get up,' he said, and placed a restraining hand on Gerrard's shoulder as he eased past his knees to take the seat on Gerrard's left. He tilted the chair fussily and cleared it of rainwater before carefully covering the seat with a neatly folded pink newspaper. After a quick, experienced glance at the sky he collapsed his large black umbrella and waved the drops from it into the row in front. He sat down and gripped the umbrella between his knees and crossed his hands primly on the ridged bamboo handle. He looked comfortable and at ease. The only thing missing was the band.

'It's kind of you to meet me like this,' he said and half turned towards Gerrard. He studied the Frenchman's profile openly as he spoke. 'Sorry about the discomfort.' He smiled apologetically into Gerrard's unresponsive face. 'But I think you'll find it a rewarding discomfort.'

'Can you get to the point, Mr Malseed?' Gerrard cut him off without apology.

'Of course.' Malseed's lips tightened and the bonhomie was replaced by a sharper, more brusque approach. 'I spoke to Fred Lambdon last night. He told me you might be interested in our proposition but that you need confirmation and evidence of our good faith. I'm here to offer that to you.'

Gerrard glanced sideways at Malseed and studied him as he removed the cellophane from a new packet of Gitanes.

He was a tall man. Gerrard had noticed that when Malseed had arrived, but he was still tall, even sitting down. He was hatless and his well-groomed silver hair gleamed with a combination of rain and old-fashioned brilliantine. He had a narrow moustache, the same colour as his hair, and this added an element of military distinction to his long thin face. His accent was upper-class English, and Gerrard, for some strange reason of his own making, was surprised – he'd expected a voice dripping with Guinness and peat smoke and found instead vintage port and the aroma of fine *Habanas*. He grinned inwardly; the scuffle over the water was becoming increasingly complicated.

'Cigarette?'

Malseed studied the packet of French cigarettes briefly, then shook his head and smiled. A little of the bonhomie crept back into the atmosphere. 'No thanks.' He brought a black leather case from the inside pocket of his coat and selected a long filter cigarette. 'As I was saying,' he began, then turned his head sharply with a look of exasperation. His eye had caught movement in their private auditorium.

The look changed very rapidly to one of annoyance when the tranquillity of the deserted bandstand was shattered by the clatter of heavy boots on metal. In a matter of seconds the movement and the noise joined together on the far side of the bandstand in the shape of a shaven-headed youth in a full set of skin-tight leathers complete with chains, safety pins, the lot. He balanced himself shakily on the slippery chairs, like a drunken clown on a frozen pond, before skidding and stomping his noisy way to the centre of the bandstand.

Malseed glared across the rows of empty chairs and drew furiously on his filter king without glancing at the smiling Frenchman.

'That's one of our problems in this country,' he said, 'English youth. What we need is another bloody good war. That'd get rid of half of them and the other half'd come back like normal people – to heel!' He smiled to show it was only a pipe dream. 'Can we get down to business now?'

'I'm listening,' said Gerrard. He injected a note of impatience in his voice. It wasn't lost on Malseed.

'All right, I'll give it to you briefly; on the twenty-fourth of this month, exactly ten days from now, the Vice-President of the United States will be attending a dedication ceremony at Western Dock.' He forestalled Gerrard's query. 'Western Dock's in Wapping, just off the Thames near Tower Bridge. We want to kill him on that day. You've been told the price. Let me repeat it; seven hundred and fifty thousand pounds – three-quarters of a million.'

He turned fully in his chair to face Gerrard.

Gerrard allowed a few minutes to pass before he answered. He could feel the tension building up in the man beside him but ignored it and concentrated his attention on the antics of the punk, now on the far side of the bandstand. He had been joined by a rastafarian youth with dreadlocks. Gerrard watched them, weighing up the chances that he and Malseed were under surveillance, until the voice came again in his ear.

'I'd like your decision, please.' Malseed's patience had run out.

'I accept. Subject to certain conditions.'

'Good! We also have conditions. Let's compare them.' Malseed's breathing was easier and his tone more relaxed. 'You go first,' he suggested.

Gerrard dropped his half-smoked cigarette in a shallow puddle and looked straight at Malseed.

'To start with,' he said, 'I shall want half the money right away – in cash. Secondly, when I've convinced myself, and proved to you, that the project is feasible and has more than an even chance of success, I shall want the balance. That's before I touch the trigger. I want no interference, and my plan of action is to be known only to my paymaster.' Gerrard drew on his cigarette without taking his eyes from Malseed's face. Malseed was riveted, he'd even forgotten about the next war and its future soldiers. Gerrard continued, 'In addition to the contract fee I want expenses of up to fifty thousand pounds. This, of course, will be accountable. Lastly, and above all, I want no contact with your people after the job is done. Those are my conditions.' Gerrard turned away, lit another cigarette and crossed his arms. He didn't look at Malseed.

Malseed didn't hesitate. 'I agree to half the money now, but with the proviso that if, for reasons not of our making, the job is called off, or you find it, to use your term, "unfeasible", the amount, *in toto*, is to be refunded.'

Gerrard gave it a few seconds' consideration. 'Less ten per cent administration charges – plus normal expenses.'

'Agreed,' said Malseed. He looked briefly contented, then reassumed his sombre expression. 'But I can't, I'm afraid, agree to your next point – the copyright question. For three-quarters of a million pounds I'm afraid your audience is going to have to be bigger than one. I probably haven't made myself as clear as I should have – let me put that right now.'

Gerrard sensed a long speech coming. He turned to watch the two youths again, now at play on the bandstand itself, and decided they were probably genuine. He let Malseed's voice ramble on in his ear.

'I have people to answer to.' Malseed hadn't paused for breath. 'People who make up committees. One in particular is the planning committee and the members will want a complete briefing of your proposals well before the date of the operation. The planning people won't sanction the final payment of your fee until you've convinced them in person that your plan is going to work – which, I think you'll agree, is quite understandable considering the size of the cheque they're willing to sign.' He looked askance at Gerrard. A trace of anxiety had again crept into his voice. 'And don't ask me the names of these people. They're serious men – I can fully guarantee their discretion.'

Gerrard shrugged his shoulders. 'The names wouldn't mean a thing to me, but if you're making this an essential condition I shall want to know at least what they are. Not who, Mr Malseed, but definitely what.'

'I don't follow you.'

'Then I'll explain.' Gerrard lit a new cigarette and sat back in his chair. 'In any assassination portfolio there are only two men at risk – the target, and the assassin. The people financing the operation, the men with most interest in the outcome, risk only the loss of somebody's provident fund. When it's all over they can stroll up to the *guichet* and collect their winnings. I'm not complaining. What I want to assess is the strength of my security; I want to know who's going to be shooting his mouth off in the pub about the big score. I want to know beforehand the rank of the person whose big mouth can put me away.' Gerrard turned and looked at Malseed to make sure he was getting the point. 'If you want me to work for an audience, Mr Malseed, you're going to have to tell me what that audience is. It's either that, or the job's off right now.'

The two youths had worked off their frustration by kicking the slatted chairs around in the bandstand and left by climbing over the back balustrade. The silence around the two men in the auditorium was broken only by the twittering of sparrows surprised at the sudden reappearance of the sun and the tink, tink, tink of raindrops bouncing off the metal seats from the wet, overhanging branches of the surrounding trees. Gerrard's buttocks ached from sitting on his own hard, unyielding park seat, but he sat still after delivering his ultimatum and wondered whether his demand had been too fierce for Malseed's stomach.

Malseed coughed after a long pause. He spoke slowly, as if he had tried out every word in his mind before saying it aloud.

'This is quite exceptional to my mandate,' he began pompously, 'and I break our own security only as an added sign of our, or rather my, good faith in your professionalism. But I ask one thing of you,' he allowed himself a troubled sideways glance at Gerrard, 'that under no circumstances do you divulge to my colleagues, when you eventually come face to face with them, that I have revealed their designation.' Gerrard nodded his acceptance and Malseed continued: 'Apart from myself, the people you will be briefing are two of the architects of the operation – both Irishmen from America – plus the chiefs of staff of both branches of the IRA and the top executive of the INLA. Also present will be the newly appointed head of combined Irish operations in England, and the resident IRA Military and Intelligence Co-ordinator. These, Mr Gerrard, have no tongues for the fears you expressed. Oh, and I nearly forgot,' Malseed's enthusiasm carried him over the threshold and he broke Meier's commandment, 'also present will be the man who's going to supply you with detailed plans of British security arrangements and their intelligence assessment of its effectiveness in this instance. We are well served.' He allowed the trace of a smile to touch the edge of his mouth and looked at Gerrard from the corner of his eye. 'An impressive audience, wouldn't you say?'

'They're just people to me,' Gerrard murmured, 'so many mouths. Which one of them is in charge?'

'What do you mean?'

'Which of them sits at the head of the table? Which one presses the button?'

'Ah, you mean Mei – ' Malseed stopped himself. 'It doesn't matter. The head of this organisation won't be attending.' He gave a shy deprecating smile. 'An American, he doesn't like Europe – or Europeans. Dublin's as near as he'll come to the crucible. He's the modern American gangster – Harvard and a degree in social science. On the Israeli borders he'd be called an adviser in terrorism. In Dublin he's a co-ordinator of military tactics. Let's hope he finds it all worthwhile.' Malseed shook his head slowly. It was light relief now, he'd cleared the main hurdle – it was all systems go. 'Anything else?' he asked finally. The cigarette bobbed up and down jauntily between his lips as he spoke.

'By the sound of it the commander in chief doesn't seem to have earned your unqualified admiration.' Gerrard turned his head slowly towards Malseed as he drew on his cigarette. 'Something lacking in that quarter, is there?'

Malseed smiled, but didn't answer the question. 'Politics, my friend,' he said easily, 'it's all a question of politics. I don't give a bugger whose spoon I use to eat my rice with provided that while I'm doing it he's out there fighting the battle for me. That's what's happening here, Gerrard. I'll still be eating rice when it's all over – they'll get what they want and move on, but I'll be here to pick up the pieces.' Malseed raised his eyebrows at his new confidant. 'And why not me? I don't have to love the people who stoke the boiler for me – do I?'

Gerrard exhaled noisily. It was time to bring Malseed down from the clouds and back into the boiler room.

'I'm not interested in the politics of your business,' he said caustically. 'As long as the money ends up in one of my accounts the job'll be done.' He looked at Malseed without smiling. 'You say the Irishmen will be here in London for a briefing? How soon will that be? I don't want to

71

have to rush through the preliminaries to meet an unexpected deadline.'
He left the sentence unfinished for Malseed to take up.

'You'll be told when. And in good time. A lot of your preliminaries will
have been taken care of.' He glanced slyly out of the corner of his eyes to
study the effect. It was a disappointing effect.

'Fair enough,' said Gerrard. 'How soon can you let me have everything you've got? I want all the information you have on the target's visit
and his timetable leading up to the site you mentioned.' He hesitated
deliberately. 'You say this thing happens in ten days' time?'

'That's right, the twenty-fourth.'

'So the details of the contract are fairly well known among your
people?'

Malseed looked indignant. 'I wouldn't call my committee public – but
yes, certainly they know whose head's going up on the billiard-room
wall; they ought to – it was their decision.'

'OK, then; this material you have that you call the preliminaries, is
that also well known?'

Malseed smiled enigmatically and shook his head.

Gerrard persisted. 'You mentioned something about security
arrangements laid on by the British. You also said you had access to
some of the intelligence aspects of the occasion.'

'Correct.'

Gerrard stared at Malseed for a few moments, then said, 'Good, I can
use some of this information, unless it's some drunken Irishman making
wild guesses from Dublin.'

Malseed picked up the ball with hardly a break in his stride. 'I was
hoping you weren't going to take me up on that – not just at the moment.
But I suppose you have to know some time.'

Gerrard didn't push him. He sat and waited and smoked. His attitude
of unconcern persuaded Malseed to break the seal on the file.

'The wild guesses, as you call them, are not from Dublin, and neither
are they wild. They're blue chip – they come from the man who helped
draft the plans for the protective screen.'

Gerrard continued to look sceptical. It worked. Malseed was un-
stoppable.

'We have a man among the top people in British Intelligence circles.
It's all there for the asking. Tell me what you want and I'll pass it on.'

Gerrard thought for a moment, then said, casually, 'Better he and I
talk direct. Can you arrange a meeting with this person?'

Malseed shook his head, but before he could voice a flat refusal,

Gerrard added quickly, 'He and I will speak the same language, and as some of the things I want to ask are highly technical I wouldn't want to take the chance of answers becoming distorted on their way through an intermediary. Make it as soon as you can, if you don't mind.'

Malseed's eyebrows pinched together and he turned once again in his seat to face Gerrard. There was no hesitation in his manner. It looked as though he realised he'd already gone too far into the swamp.

'I don't, at this juncture, consider it prudent for you to meet him or know anything more about him,' he said crisply. 'You'll have that pleasure at your briefing when you demonstrate to us how you're going to fulfil your contract. In the meantime, draw up a list of the data you require and I'll see that it reaches the right hands. I think we've gone far enough now, don't you?' He looked down at the gold wafer on his wrist. 'So if there's anything else?'

Gerrard shrugged his shoulders. 'I'll let you know what I want in due course.'

Malseed bristled. 'I can assure you . . .'

'I believe you.' Gerrard changed the subject abruptly. 'What about my expenses?'

'That, and the first part of your fee, will be delivered to your hotel after lunch.'

'One more thing,' said Gerrard. 'How do I contact you? Do you want me to come through Lambdon or can you give me a direct line?'

Malseed reached between his legs and tore off a section of the *Financial Times* he was using as a cushion. He wrote a number in the margin alongside the mining news.

'Twenty-five past eight any evening you'll find me at this number. If you want to see me personally I'll arrange for someone to collect and deliver you, so keep me informed of your movements. And don't forget, you've only got ten days.' He rose stiffly to his feet and looked down at Gerrard. 'May I say how much I've enjoyed our little chat?' He didn't offer to shake hands – there were no farewells, no pleasantries; Malseed left as he'd arrived, silently and without warning.

CHAPTER 8

Clive Reason studied the front door of 4 Clarence Garden Mews as he pushed the tiny glowing ember behind the plastic button of the electric doorbell.

He could hear the muffled ringing inside the small house. It rang in concert with the overloud bell of a telephone from behind one of the other doors in the mews – it was a happy sound, but nobody was getting any joy out of it.

Reason removed his finger from the button and looked over his shoulder. The deserted mews looked as if it had been plucked from an old Ealing film set; brightly painted, different-coloured doors, over-stuffed window boxes and Victorian street lamps. They'd left the cobbles in place as a legacy of what it used to be like when everybody had a horse – and nobody had a telephone.

Reason scowled at the continual buzzing of the anonymous telephone and jabbed his finger back on to his own problem. *Maybe they didn't answer bells in this mews.* Losing patience, he rapped his bare knuckles against the woodwork. It sounded thick and solid, and didn't give an inch. It didn't open either. He glanced over it again quickly. It had no door-knob and no letter-box. *Playing safe, Lambdon? Don't you fancy being blasted from the hole in the door? Or doesn't anybody write to you?* Reason kept his mind busy with charitable thoughts as he continued surreptitiously inspecting the door. *A Yale at shoulder height, that's how you get in. And a security Chubb lower down – that's how you make sure nobody else gets in.* Reason nudged the door with his knee. He didn't expect it to swing open. It didn't. The door was firmly shut.

He looked over his shoulder again and smiled his good intentions to anybody with nothing better to do than watch a man break into their neighbour's house and, shielded by his long black raincoat, extracted a short length of paper-thin steel from an inside pocket. He moved his body in line with the Yale and, with a quick short prayer to anybody who was interested, slid the blade into the door jamb. He eased it down in little testing jerks until it met the tongue of the lock. A little more pressure, and as metal rasped on metal he leaned his knee against the door. *And if that bloody Chubb's been turned you can do the same thing, Reason – you can turn round and go home.* He managed to keep the grin out of sight behind his closed lips when the blade loosened. He felt the luck bubbling through his fingertips. There was no Chubb. The door was open.

The strange phone bell continued to ring behind him but, as if on cue, it died as he slid through the open door; it died with an uncomfortable gurgle in the middle of its throat, as if someone had strangled it.

Reason stood in the semi-darkened room with his back firmly against the door. With a gentle pressure from his shoulder blades it closed with a solid, reassuring, and well-oiled click. His eyes moved rapidly round the small room. The curtains were still drawn, but the sun ignored them and illuminated the room with the power of a strong electric light bulb. Reason relaxed – the room was empty of people.

Without moving his feet he leaned forward and peered into the doorless kitchen. The curtains on the small window which overlooked the mews yard were also drawn. The room was empty and had the sterile smell of disuse. He straightened up and slipped the catch on the Yale behind him, but remained with his back still against the door. His attention was riveted to the closed door on the other side of the room. It looked solid and firmly closed, and without thinking about it too long, Reason knew that on the other side of that door it would be dark. A dark, closed room. The bedroom – it worried him.

Reason kept still. He was unarmed, and regretted it.

A small tic started to flicker under his left eye and threatened to go out of control. He squeezed it shut and blinked nervously several times in an attempt to clear it, but it refused to disappear. He bared his teeth in as near a grin as he could manage and moved towards the door. There wasn't a single unemployed nerve in his body – and they all shrieked caution. He heeded the advice and tiptoed across the room.

As he moved he caught out of the corner of his eye the reflection of broken glass; tiny diamond like fragments picked out by the sun's slanted rays and diffused into coloured lights. With the same glance he noticed the broken side table propped tidily against the armchair. *Don't say it – you clever bastard . . . !* He moved stealthily towards the bedroom door.

Reason squared his broad back against the wall and slid his hand slowly down the door panel until it found the large round knob. He began to turn it towards him. When the door moved he released the knob and pushed it slowly open with one long finger. The whites of his eyes reflected brightly as he watched the gap widen and the tic stopped dancing when he pressed his temple against the door jamb and inspected the room.

It was exactly as he'd expected – quiet and dark. As he breathed in silently he caught the stuffy sweetness of a used bedroom and, he sniffed delicately, a faint cloying overtone usually found on the inside of an occupied coffin. Reason wrinkled his nose and slid his large frame through the gap and pressed himself against the inside wall.

The dark room lightened as his eyes adjusted to the gloom and his nerve ends settled – it was just another empty room, no one had been waiting for him behind the closed door. He let his breath out in a whoosh, and, almost in the same moment, he noticed the mound on the bed.

It was a small room and two long strides took him to the bedside. He hesitated for the briefest second, then carefully lifted the corner of the duvet and gazed into the dead face of Fred Lambdon. It wasn't a pretty face. Reason folded the duvet back, switched on the bedside lamp, and went down on one knee. Lambdon's protruding eyes stared back at him; opaque, flat eyes, with a blue death film masking them; they looked like the eyes of a newly killed salmon nestling in its bed of ice on a fishmonger's slab.

Reason gazed curiously at the slack, sagging jaw and then, with a puzzled frown, put his head closer to examine the coagulated liquid blocking the dead man's pinched nostrils.

'That's very interesting, Mr Lambdon,' he whispered into Lambdon's uncaring face, 'the last time I saw something like that crawling out of a bloke's honker was from a guy who'd got himself a busted neck. I wonder if that's what caused you to take to your bed?' He lifted Lambdon's head gently and immediately regretted his flippancy. The whole side of Lambdon's face was one massive purple bruise. It hung on the underside of his jaw, spread up the ridge of his nose, and puffed out half his mouth like a grinning clown's mask. It glowed like a gigantic port-wine birthmark.

Reason winced and shook his head. 'Jesus wept!' he hissed between his teeth. 'What a bloody awful last fifteen minutes you must have had . . . You poor old sod, you should have stayed on our side.' He continued staring, transfixed by the ugliness of Lambdon's death, and when he stood up he was still shaking his head and whispering to Lambdon, 'I wonder . . . ?'

What d'you wonder, Reason?

'I don't suppose it could've been one of our weightlifters who caught up with you and won the argument? Could it?'

Reason asked himself the question again, silently, and wasn't altogether convinced that his shaking head was the correct response.

He gave it up and turned Lambdon's body on to its back and carefully searched it from head to toe. He removed all trace of Lambdon's identity, turned him back on to his face, and covered him with the duvet again. When he straightened up he had another good look around the room. It hadn't changed, he saw nothing that he hadn't seen on his earlier inspection; it was still an uninteresting, featureless bedroom; a place to sleep in, or, in Lambdon's case, a place in which to get your face smashed in. He turned away and, without another glance at the heap on the bed, slipped out of the room pulling the door shut behind him.

He walked straight through the small drawing-room – it was much easier going out than it had been coming in. He even had time for another glance into the kitchen on his way. That hadn't changed either. But when he reached the front door he stopped, with his hand grasping the latch of the Yale, and frowned. He remained still, unmoving, for several seconds, his eyes focused not on the door in front of him but somewhere inside his mind. The frown disappeared and he turned abruptly and walked back into the tiny kitchen. He stopped in front of the draining board and stared hard at the half-empty bottle of whisky standing in almost solitary splendour. Almost. But not quite. It brought a smile to Reason's otherwise expressionless face. It was not the bottle, or its contents; it was the cheap stubby glass tumbler that stood beside it, the sort of heavy imitation-crystal tumbler that came as a give-away with half a pound of inedible, vinegary mustard. But there was no mustard in it now. Reason was staring at quarter of an inch of neat whisky – just enough to wet the bottom of the glass.

He picked the tumbler up carefully by its base and emptied its contents down the drain, then wrapped it in a plastic bread bag and slipped it into one of the pockets of his raincoat.

Reason whistled gently to himself as he left the kitchen. This time he managed to get the front door open without finding something else to drag him back. He stopped for a moment on the front doorstep and as he closed the door called out in a loud voice, 'Cheerio, Fred!' It wasn't loud enough to wake Fred Lambdon, but there was enough sincerity in it to dissuade any nervous finger in the background from dialling emergency.

Reason shrugged his shoulders as he crossed the cobbled yard and headed out towards the real world. The thought that had just crossed his mind didn't bring a change of expression to his sombre features – in different circumstances it might have generated at least a weak smile, but not today – it was the thought that for the number of people he'd encountered among the mews dwellers, and the amount of activity going on, they could all be humped up under their duvets just like old Fred Lambdon.

Somewhere in the mews a door slammed, as if to contradict his thoughts, and behind one of the coloured doors a plaintive telephone started crying for attention again. But Reason had lost interest in Clarence Garden Mews, and he kept walking. He didn't look round.

Reason darted into the first empty telephone booth he came to in Bayswater Road. He spent two minutes with the dead receiver glued to his ear, watching the corner of Stanhope Place. Nobody turned the corner; nobody hesitated, nobody stopped to light a cigarette near the box. Nobody was interested in Reason. He took his finger off the phone rest and dialled a number. When it answered he turned his back on the road and spoke into the mouthpiece.

'That friend of yours, sir . . . the one you asked me to go and look at.'

'Yes?' General Sanderson's voice was flat, almost incurious.

'He's dead.'

The line went silent for a respectful second.

'I see. And . . . ?'

'He looked as if he'd gone fifteen rounds with King Kong before they pulled the chain on him. He was in a bit of a mess. Not a pretty sight.'

Sanderson's voice remained unaffected. 'Get on to Tommy when you've finished talking to me and tell him to go and tidy it up. I want Lambdon's place done over completely and then closed down. We won't be using it again. Tell him it's to be a no-action job – make it suicide, or an Irish accident, whichever he can carry through.' He paused, long enough for Reason to gaze up and down the Bayswater Road again. 'How did they finish him, Clive?'

'They broke his neck, sir.'

The line hummed with silence. Reason waited patiently.

'Hmmm. Different,' said Sanderson eventually. 'Any idea who did it?'

'I might have. I'm having it checked out.'

'Keep me in touch. What about that other thing?'

78

'Bit early yet, sir. I've had two people on the job but I don't know yet whether your man was fished out by his contact or not. If he was, my two'll be there with him.'

'Good.' It was an unconvinced grunt that came down the line. 'It's a bit too soon after breakfast for more bad news. Now, about this Frenchman – Gerrard. I want to see him today . . . this morning . . . so get yourself to the Crinton and pick him up and bring him over to Chelsea. Make sure he's had his meeting, though, I don't want that interrupted.'

Reason wasn't happy about it. 'I hope you're not trying to tell me we've got Frenchmen horning into our game. Whose side's he whoring for?'

'I'm not sure I like your choice of words. But keep the fact that he's French to yourself. I'll tell you all about him when you bring him to Chelsea . . . Better still, I'll give you a copy of the script – I've got a vacancy for a new actor.'

Reason caught sight of himself in the phone-box mirror and winked at his serious reflection. 'About this vacancy . . . ?'

'What about it?' said Sanderson guardedly.

'I don't suppose the opening's coincidental with Lambdon being dropped through the hole in the ice?'

The answer came back quickly. 'As I've said before, Clive, don't ask me any questions and I won't have to tell you any lies.' There was no laughter in Sanderson's voice. He ended the conversation abruptly. 'Don't let me keep you any longer. Go and find your Frenchman.'

Gerrard threw his damp trousers into the corner of the room and swung round from the foot of the bed to answer the telephone.

'There's a gentleman asking for you at reception, Mr Gerrard.' The voice sounded breathless and excited at the news.

Gerrard grunted and reached for his cigarettes but didn't take one out of its packet. 'That'll be Lambdon,' he said to himself, 'and about time.' He spoke under his breath, but the vibrations travelled.

She was very receptive to vibrations. 'I beg your pardon, Mr Gerrard?'

'Sorry, I was talking to myself . . . Just a minute, did he say his name was Lambdon?'

'He didn't give a name.'

'Well, would you ask him if he's got one, please?' Gerrard's patience with an attractive female voice was infinite.

'He's gone,' she whispered, 'but he said not to hurry. He's going to have coffee in the Raffles Room. Will that be all, Mr Gerrard?'

'Thank you.'

Gerrard finished changing his wet clothes and walked the three flights down to the Raffles Room. He ran his eye cursorily around the room and shook his head. Fred Lambdon would have to be mad to be sitting in amongst this lot – noisy, unattractive, and raucous – it was like the parrot house in Regent's Park Zoo. He frowned. No Lambdon – unless he was lying under a table with his fingers jammed in his ears.

Gerrard stared again across the noise and saw only one man sitting among the elderly chickens. It wasn't Lambdon, unless he'd been under his sun lamp all night. The big black man returned his glance and studied him over the rim of his coffee cup. It was an impassive, almost incurious scrutiny, like one Englishman of another in the ante-room of a cheap Kuala Lumpur knocking shop.

Gerrard made his way directly to the corner table where the black man sat.

Reason lowered his coffee cup slightly and watched Gerrard's determined approach.

'My name's Gerrard. You asked for me at the desk.' Gerrard's voice was cold and unfriendly, but Reason ignored the tone and continued to sip his coffee as he gazed squarely at the standing Frenchman.

'I thought it was probably you.' He smiled disarmingly. 'Want a cup of coffee?'

Gerrard ignored the invitation. He pulled one of the bamboo chairs out from under the table and sat down. 'What did you want to see me about?' he asked.

The black man's smile remained in place. He was quite unaffected by the lack of cordiality. 'Have some coffee,' he insisted. 'I ordered for two.'

Gerrard looked steadily across the table. After a second, he nodded. 'Yes. No cream.' He placed a cigarette between his lips and offered the packet across the table. Reason's large hand came away from the coffee pot and hovered in mid-air. After a moment's hesitation he said, 'I've given up,' and plucked a cigarette out of the blue packet. He placed the cigarette between his teeth and grinned as he went back to pouring Gerrard's coffee. He refilled his own cup before leaning across the table to accept a light from Gerrard's Dupont.

He drew smoke contentedly down his throat and allowed it to trickle gently through his nostrils. He looked like a man who'd been deprived of smoke for a long time. 'Thanks,' he said. 'My name's Reason, Clive Reason. General Sir Richard Sanderson sent me to . . .' He stopped in mid-sentence and pulled a face at Gerrard's raised eyebrows. 'The telephone's outside that door.' He pointed his finger and jerked his clean-shaven chin towards the entrance to the Raffles Room. 'Turn right and it's in the far corner.' He scribbled a number on a scrap of paper and handed it across the table. 'Go and have a word with him. He wants to see you. You can either come with me or he'll arrange an ambulance for you – I'm easy either way.'

Gerrard studied the unsmiling face for several seconds then abruptly pushed back his chair and walked off in the direction of Reason's pointed finger. He was back within minutes. His expression was unchanged, but his manner was decidedly easier when he sat down.

'OK,' he said. 'Tell me what you were going to say about General Sanderson.'

Reason took another long pull on his cigarette and gave a little choking cough when the taste brought back memories of his hangover. 'The General would like to chat with you about your meeting this morning . . . He asked me to come and fetch you – that's all. You ready to go and see him now?'

Gerrard kept his misgivings to himself. He nodded and pushed his coffee cup away. 'I'm ready when you are.'

Reason said, 'Good, then this is how we'll do it. You'll stroll out of here on your own and make your way to the front of the hotel. Get the guy at the door with the top hat to call you a taxi. Make sure it's the first one in the queue, and act like a man without a tongue until it pulls away. As soon as the wheels start turning tell the driver you want the hotel staff entrance. I'll be waiting at a big shuttered door marked "Staff Only", and when your taxi pulls up there we'll be able to see how good your tail's performing, won't we?' He grinned cheerfully and waved at the waitress.

The taxi turned off the crowded King's Road into Oakley Street.

Reason was satisfied that anybody waiting outside the Crinton to log Gerrard's movements had been left floundering around in Mayfair's one-way traffic system. But it didn't stop him staring automatically through the rear window of the cab before tapping loudly on the glass panel between him and the driver.

'Stop on the corner of Phene Street,' he told him. He ignored the bad-tempered grunt and dropped three brass coins into the man's hand. 'Don't bother with the change.'

'There ain't none.'

'Too bad.' Reason turned his back on the cabby and joined Gerrard on the corner of Oakley Street and Phene Street. He stood a few minutes and gazed up the tree-lined avenue towards the King's Road before nudging Gerrard into Phene Street. They walked the few yards in silence before Reason steered left into Oakley Gardens and stopped in front of a large, imposing Georgian townhouse. He jabbed a long black finger on the brass bell-push and listened to the peal of bells that clanged urgently just behind the solid oak door. He seemed quite happy that the door wasn't thrown open immediately and continued staring stolidly in front of him.

After a minute he rang the bell again. He held his finger on the button for much longer this time and as it clanged again behind the door he muttered, 'And about bloody time too.'

A heavy bolt was drawn just as he removed his finger from the button and after a short pause the door swung smoothly open.

The man standing in the doorway was sixty. His short back and sides, more grey than black, was pasted flat to his head with a glossy, scented brilliantine and was separated from his bushy eyebrows by an inch and a half of frowning forehead. The tip of his nose drooped and overhung an ugly harelip. It was a lip that still carried the hallmarks of an early, crude attempt at remedial surgery, and its failure probably accounted for the abrasive manner with which he regarded the unafflicted. He wore a spotless white shirt, a striped tie in the colours of a famous regiment of foot, and a pressed, but badly fitting, navy-blue suit. The gloss on his black shoes matched the shine of his hair. He was an ex-regular soldier; there was nothing else on earth he could have been.

''Mornin', Mr Rason.' The man's voice rasped like sandpaper. His eyes, unblinking under their hairy canopies, remained fixed steadily on Gerrard.

'Reason,' said Reason. 'The General's expecting us.'

Two hard, fit young men stood watching on the far side of the hall. There were no friendly smiles on their faces. They both clutched the inevitable folding machine-pistol with the easy comfortable manner of men who knew how to handle it, and studied the two newcomers with undisguised interest.

'Come in, Mr Rason,' said the harelip superfluously, 'and if you'll close the door behind you I'd like to see what Mr Jerrud has brought with him.'

Reason wasn't smiling. He ignored the harelip and looked Gerrard in the eye. 'You carrying a gun?' he asked.

Gerrard shook his head.

'Nevertheless . . .' The old man flicked a finger for Reason to move to one side and curled his lips at Gerrard. 'If you don't mind?' he rasped.

He ran his hands expertly over Gerrard's body, then stepped back two paces with Gerrard's thin gold Parker pen, his heavy silver Dupont lighter, and a packet of Gitanes. He tossed the cigarettes back after a quick glance inside the packet, but studied the other two items like a jeweller assessing a newly cut stone. He was only half happy when he shook his head and reluctantly handed them to Reason.

'If you're ready, gentlemen, I'll take you to the General. He's expecting you.'

The two men followed him across the bare hall to the large staircase which curved in a half-circle against the wall and rose smoothly to a banistered landing.

Half-way up the stairs Reason turned to Gerrard and jerked his chin at the ramrod-stiff back of their guide. 'His name's Coney,' he said. He spoke in a normal conversational tone and made no attempt to lower his voice. It was as if the old soldier was on a different parade ground, miles away and out of earshot. 'Sergeant Coney,' he added. 'I'm not sure which bloody army he was a sergeant in, but the sooner he moves up the road and joins those other old buggers the happier I'll be.'

The short back and sides continued up the stairs without losing step. Reason could have been talking in Swahili for all the interest the back of Sergeant Coney's head displayed. Coney's day was being made; he'd got at the black man – Reason's irritation was showing.

'But,' Reason growled on, 'if he calls me Rason once more I'm going to pick the scrawny bugger up by those bushes over his eyes and swing him around like a bloody bolo until his balls fly off into the blue!' Reason winked at Gerrard and set his face in a scowl.

The ramrod stopped on the last step before the landing and the craggy, mirthless face turned and looked Reason in the eye.

'What's a bolo, Mr Rason?'

'I like him really,' Reason told Gerrard.

General Sir Richard Sanderson, KCB, DSO, MC, stood by one of the three large windows which dominated the room.

It was a room in direct contrast to the sparse hall below with its beleaguered bunker effect; this was an elegant room, a man's room furnished in good taste with an emphasis on comfort; it looked as though General Sanderson spent a lot of time in it.

'Go and sit down,' he told Gerrard, 'I'll be with you in a second.'

Sanderson was on the slippery side of sixty-five but carried himself with discreet athleticism. Tall, and slim with it, he looked fitter than most men who'd been born ten years after him. Dressed in a formal dark-grey suit with waistcoat he made no concession to the heat of mid-summer and ignored the overpowering warmth of the sun-baked room. Air-conditioning had been considered and rejected.

Gerrard wandered across the room towards the large Adam fireplace, dominated by a long, comfortable-looking settee and flanked by deep armchairs and gleaming pie-crust Georgian side tables. The hearth was shielded by an elaborately embroidered fireguard and over the mantel-piece hung an enormous painting of an elderly, bewhiskered officer wearing the scarlet tunic of a much earlier British army; the years had done nothing to soften the choleric bulge of his eyes, which glowered with stern rebuke across the room at the gentlemen who were sharing his trip into eternity: gentlemen in sombre black, the dullness of their coats relieved only by white or faded yellow stocks tied neatly round long-dead throats, their expressions set in contemplation of a timeless boredom.

Gerrard lowered his eyes to room level and heard Sanderson say, 'All right, Coney, carry on. I shan't be needing you for the time being. We're not to be disturbed.'

Coney nodded, and closed the door quietly behind him leaving Reason on the inside.

'I'll call back then, sir,' Reason began, 'I've got – '

'Cancel it, whatever it is,' said Sanderson tersely. 'It's nothing import-ant, is it?' The polite query was a formality, like a sergeant-major's solicitude, but its meaning was clear. Reason kept his face blank as he joined Gerrard by the fireplace.

General Sanderson moved in the opposite direction. 'Sit down,' he commanded, 'both of you, and let me get you a drink. Gerrard . . .?'

'Whisky.'

'Water or soda?'

'Water. Half-way up the glass, please.'

'Clive?'

'Gin, please. With tonic.'

Silence descended on the room while Sanderson busied himself among the decanters and bottles on the mahogany sideboard. It was an intense silence, emphasised by the gentle clink of ice cubes dropping into fine crystal, and lasted until Sanderson placed a small tray with three tinkling glasses gently on the glass-topped coffee table.

'Smoke if you want,' he said and sipped delicately from his glass before lowering himself on to the settee. 'Cheers,' he offered as an afterthought, and looked hard across the table at Gerrard. 'What did you talk to the IRA about this morning? Did they nibble?'

It took only a few minutes for Gerrard to convey the gist of what had passed between himself and Malseed in Hyde Park that morning but it was enough to bring a gleam of satisfaction to General Sanderson's pale-blue eyes and a fractional raised eyebrow from Clive Reason.

'And he's going to do it all on his own?' asked Reason.

'No. You're going to help him.'

Reason allowed himself a slight, cynical smile. 'Then may I ask a question, sir?'

'Certainly,' replied Sanderson.

Reason drew on his cigarette and directed a lazy stream of smoke towards the ceiling; he removed a tiny speck of tobacco that had stuck to his tongue, inspected it, and flicked it away before nodding his head towards the quiet but watchful Frenchman.

'How is it a Frenchman's been allowed to gatecrash our domestic squabble with the tribe O'Grady?'

'Good question.'

'And then I'd like to know who, and what, this Frenchman is.'

Sanderson frowned at Reason, then looked hard at Gerrard. 'He works for French Intelligence – loosely speaking. Department DGSE . . . But it goes a bit deeper than that. He's a technician – a specialist. He operates under the codename Siegfried.'

'Specialist at what?'

Sanderson smiled coldly at Reason. 'He's considered to be one of the three top specialist killers in the world today – if not *the* top.'

Reason sat up in his armchair and studied Gerrard with renewed interest. He bit off the comment he was about to make; instead, without taking his eyes off the Frenchman, he said to Sanderson, 'So what's he doing at our party?'

Sanderson sipped his gin again and tapped his lips delicately with the back of his forefinger. 'He's come to do a spot of killing for us.'

The black man's eyebrows shot upwards. 'The American Vice-President?'

Sanderson waved a limp hand at him and almost smiled. 'No, Clive – forget about Mr Beaune, we're not killing friends this month. The man Gerrard's come to kill wears a different set of responsibilities – which I shall explain in a minute. But let me bring you up to date. It'll make Gerrard's presence in the paddling pool so much easier to understand if you join the conspiracy.' He showed his teeth to Reason. 'Membership's very restricted at the moment, but I think you'll understand why there's room for another if I tell you that the key figure is Fred Lambdon.' Out of the corner of his eye Sanderson noticed the Frenchman's head swing round sharply, but ignored it – he was more interested in Reason's reaction. He wasn't disappointed.

'I might have expected Lambdon to be involved somewhere along the line,' said Reason bitterly. 'I seem to have spent the whole day with his name, one way or another, drumming in my ears. I almost felt sorry for him when . . .'

Sanderson stopped him with a frown, and shook his head, an almost imperceptible movement that wasn't lost on Reason. He subsided back into the depths of his armchair and raised his glass to his lips. Sanderson let him off lightly. 'You jumped the wrong way there, Clive. Fred Lambdon hadn't changed colour – he went under the wire for me. We set it up between us. I carefully blotted his copybook and threw him out into the weather hoping the Irish would offer him a poncho. They did. And he's been out there tightroping ever since. Fred Lambdon was planted on the Irish.'

Gerrard merely raised his eyebrows but Reason knew what was expected of him. 'Why was Mr Lambdon planted on the Irish, General?' he asked obediently.

'To look for a man who's been doing a Burgess and Maclean for the IRA.'

'Dangerous,' muttered Reason.

'Of course it's bloody dangerous, which is why Fred Lambdon was floundering around without friends. I dared not tell anybody. This bastard with the long nose is worth his weight in lorry-loads of Armalites to the IRA and he sits high over here, that's the bloody nub. He's almost unflushable.'

'How high?' asked Reason.

'I don't know. Our Cousins' term "high" means unacceptable. That's enough for me. That's who Freddie Lambdon went over to look for.'

Reason pulled a face. 'Did he come back with anything?'

Sanderson shook his head slowly. 'Nothing significant. No name . . . well, not a real name; a paper cover that ends where it started – somewhere in the blue. Brocklebank. That's all Fred managed to put together. I've tried it out. It's code. It goes nowhere.'

Gerrard's face remained blank. He wondered if General Sanderson would have downgraded the 'nothing significant' to 'nothing at all' if he

86

knew that his star turn had been wandering around London with the 'paper name' carelessly scrawled on the back of a used envelope in his jacket pocket.

Reason had the right idea. He must have read his mind. 'I think I'd call that nothing and leave it at that.' He tilted his glass and negotiated another mouthful round the piece of lemon. 'If you're sure that's all he came home with.'

Sanderson almost smiled. 'Not quite. He also brought with him an invitation for somebody who knew what shoot means to sit round the table with the mysterious Mr Brocklebank and discuss the assassination of the American Vice-President. And, as it was put to Fred, a top-level discussion in London by interested parties to fire the starting cannon.'

Reason refused to meet Gerrard's eyes. 'Sounds a promising invitation, but it still doesn't explain to me this Frenchman's presence.' He nodded briefly in Gerrard's direction. 'When there's at least half a dozen men who know the difference between a gun and a cock sitting outside there in the bushes who could quite easily reach across a table and stick a gun up your colleague's nostril and squeeze the trigger . . . And my arms are no shorter than anybody else's.'

General Sanderson nearly balked at Reason's use of the term colleague, but decided to let it pass. He smiled sadly and stared at Gerrard. Gerrard loooked away and bent his head to light another cigarette. He remained in that position, studying the glowing ember, when Sanderson answered Reason. Gerrard had no intention of speaking yet.

'It's not that easy, Clive. I used the word invitation rather airily. It's a bit more complicated than that – as I'll explain in a minute. But I want to go back for a minute to this Brocklebank person.'

'Is he an Irishman – as a matter of interest?' Reason relaxed back into his chair again.

'I thought he might have been at first but then I sat down and thought about it and decided he's not a Johnny-come-lately Irish wonder boy, far from it . . . I think he's much deeper than that, deeper than an Irish plant – in fact, I think his involvement with the Irish is what I said earlier – a little bit on the side. I came to the conclusion that he's Moscow-inspired, a bit of Soviet opportunism which we're becoming used to, or if we're not, we ought to be. I think this man's been around for a long time. I think he's a Soviet missionary, a long-term sleeper, and it's taken the Irish to point him out to us – plus of course a bit of luck by Fred Lambdon. That's my opinion.'

Reason grinned and threw back the remains of his gin and tonic. 'It's your educated guess, is it, sir – about him being Red I mean, or have you noticed another of your colleagues with his hand on his hip mincing pigeon-toed along the corridor to the executive loo?'

Sanderson stared at Reason for several seconds, as if doubting his sense of humour, then gave him the benefit of the doubt and answered his question seriously. 'Of course it's bloody guesswork. But if you'd been messing around with these people for as long as I have you'd find it not very difficult to visualise this chap's slippers warming in front of the log fire in the Caucasus – or wherever it is these fellows retire to, to write their memoirs. I can't see him doing that in a peat shed in Killarney.'

'Or on Bondi Beach?' Reason kept a straight face.

Sanderson wasn't amused. He didn't smile. He stared at Reason for a second or two, as if he hadn't noticed the interruption, then continued, 'Of course the bloody man's Moscow-inspired, that's where his leaning is. Even Cambridge would've been hard pressed to spew up, thirty years ago, an English twit with an ideological bent towards Irish political aspirations ... It wouldn't have been fashionable, anyway.' Sanderson stopped talking to stub out his cigarette in the ashtray. There was the glimmer of a smile in his eyes as he looked at Reason and waited for the big man's expected question.

Again, Reason obliged. 'Why thirty years ago?'

'Because, brilliant or otherwise, it'd take a chap that long to move in any direction in our system.' Sanderson was emphatic. 'There's absolutely no doubt about it in my mind, the man's got snow on his boots. They've lent him to the Irish for the duration, and that's their big mistake. The silly buggers have shifted his foundation. He could have gone on for ever if we hadn't got a whiff of him from the other direction – from Dublin.' Sanderson took another sip of pink gin from his glass and touched both sides of his moustache with a long, thin forefinger. He smiled thinly at Gerrard. 'Gerrard, if the details you were given this morning are correct you're going to find yourself in conclave with not only my Russian missionary but all the brains of the Irish stroke American big bang committee. They asked for a decent assassin. That's what they've got – we're going to give the whole damn bunch a bloody good send-off. Poor old Freddie laughed all the way across the Irish Sea.'

'Poor old Freddie?' queried Gerrard.

Nobody answered him.

Reason said, 'How did Lambdon come up with the name and address of our French friend here? Couldn't he find an Englishman with the right qualifications?'

Reason's mocking tone was lost on Sanderson. 'They specified no Englishman. Something to do with trust and loyalty.' He almost smiled, but changed his mind and shook his head instead. 'You wouldn't credit the way the Irish mind functions, would you? Can you imagine any dedicated killer being accused of either trust or loyalty when he's looking down a telescopic gunsight at seven hundred and fifty thousand pounds? Most of them'd shoot their only daughter for half that amount.' He frowned at Gerrard. 'Present company excepted.' Gerrard didn't smile either.

Sanderson turned back to Reason. 'Lambdon and Gerrard were in the SAS together. That's how he came up with Gerrard's name. They'd kept in touch. He knew what Gerrard's business was in France. He mentioned it to them – they bought it. Then he mentioned it to me – and I arranged it. Simple as that!'

Reason wasn't happy. 'His cover's been over-elaborated. The SAS connection won't work. The Irishmen's man in London would have been through to Exeter and had the records checked the minute his name was mentioned. Paddy may be thick, but he's not that thick; he knows you don't get Fro – Frenchmen, in the SAS. They would have been on to him right away; Lambdon's dropped a bollock by trying to be too clever.' Reason looked at Gerrard again and shrugged his shoulders – it was almost a gesture of farewell. 'I'd send Gerrard back to France if I were you and start all over again. He might have stood a chance without the SAS embroidery, but for my money his next meeting with the bog brigade won't be in Hyde Park – it'll be on his back somewhere, with a bright light burning holes in his eyeballs. Take my word for it.'

'Your lack of faith surprises me sometimes, Clive,' said Sanderson genially. 'I hope these people have checked Records – I want them to get on to Exeter, and I'll tell you what they'll find there. They'll find that Capitaine Michel Gerrard was seconded on special arrangement from the Third Parachute Battalion, *Légion étrangère* – Foreign Legion to you – to the 22nd SAS Regiment. It will show that he served for just over three years and saw action in Borneo and Aden. He left with the rank of major and returned to his parent regiment. It's all there in the records. That's what they'll find under the cobwebs, Clive. Now can I get on?'

Reason tightened his lips and looked again at Gerrard. He made no attempt to hide the cynicism in his eyes.

Gerrard decided his moment had come. 'Why didn't you tell me about Lambdon, General?' he said quietly to Sanderson.

'If I had told you, would it have made any difference to the outcome?'

'None at all. It seems an unnecessary precaution. Why are you telling me now?'

Sanderson shot a brief glance at Reason before answering. 'Fred Lambdon and I were the only two who knew what the game was about. As I've already explained, we were at great pains to establish Freddie's credentials both to those on our side of the chalk line and to the IRA's recruiting office. So, where do you stop when you start sharing your ideas with your fellow shopkeepers? We couldn't afford a whisper, not even the suggestion that things were not as they appeared to be, and least of all when there was a possibility that the man you've set the hounds on to could be sitting at the same table . . . Good God, man! He could have been asking me to pass the sugar, and stirring his tea with my spoon! We took no chances. Fred and I kept it as a twosome – and look at the bene-fits it's reaped.'

'Then why are you spreading the risk now?' persisted Gerrard. He kept his voice deliberately toneless. He had a good idea what the answer was going to be.

'Fred Lambdon was killed last night,' said Sanderson bluntly.

Gerrard didn't burst into tears. 'IRA?'

'No idea – Clive?'

'Definitely Irish.' Reason had worked it all out. 'Lambdon had a Watcher. The Watcher was in on the old soldiers' big reunion and went to Lambdon's home to ask who his new pal was. Lambdon said, It's my Frog friend from the SAS who's come to do a spot of killing. Who for, Fred? For General Sanderson.' Reason took a long drag on his cigarette and stared into Gerrard's face. 'You're blown.'

Sanderson shook his head. 'Try again, Clive. Neither Lambdon nor Gerrard knew what the other was up to. I made a deliberate point of keeping them both in the shadow – for that reason. If I hadn't, and one had fallen, they both would have gone into the dustbin. Gerrard's still clean. They must have wanted something else from Fred.'

'How about one of our own people showing a bit of mild interest in Lambdon's new circle of friends and tapping his nut too hard?'

'We don't do that sort of thing,' said Sanderson curtly. He sounded as if he'd lost interest in who killed Fred Lambdon. 'But when you do come across the fellow who did it perhaps you'll let me know what the conver-sation was all about. What is it now, Clive?'

Reason had also lost interest in Lambdon – for the time being. He changed the subject. 'You said our friend here works for the DGSE . . .

Works for, you said, not worked, so I presume you've got him on loan – a degree of co-operation with our co-Marketeers that surprises me, and that's putting it mildly.' He raised his eyebrows at Sanderson and nodded towards Gerrard. 'What sort of inducement did you use to persuade his ringmasters to kick him out of the tent and on to the pavement with us?' He smiled mock shyly at Sanderson. 'You know how nervous I am with strangers. If I'm going to share somebody's bed I like to know who their friends are and why they're standing on the street corner selling it.' Reason helped himself to another of Gerrard's cigarettes, lit it, and sat back comfortably in the armchair.

Sanderson smiled benignly at Reason. 'It was coincidence.'

Reason blew a long stream of smoke towards the ceiling. It was the only way he dare show scepticism. It didn't offend General Sanderson.

'I told you, when Fred Lambdon was searching his soul for names of applicants for this job,' he said, 'he mentioned Gerrard's name. He also mentioned the DGSE. Now it just so happens that I know the man who heads the DGSE section responsible for special activities. His name's Maurice. He and I did a bit of Resistance together in France during the war.'

'That's a coincidence?'

'Maurice has always insisted he owed me a few favours. Gerrard became one of those favours.' Sanderson didn't elaborate.

Reason leaned forward. 'You said earlier that only you and Lambdon knew about this undercover business of his. How many people know about it now?'

'You, Gerrard, and me.'

'And about Gerrard's game?'

'The same, plus Maurice in Paris. Anything else?'

Any further questions Reason might have had were interrupted by a discreet knock on the door. It was followed by Coney's head appearing round the gap. He addressed Sanderson.

'There's a, er . . . erm . . . person called to see Mr Rason, General. Won't say what 'e wants.' The bushy eyebrows twitched fractionally in Reason's direction, then back to Sanderson. ''e said it was personal between 'im and 'im. They're 'olding 'im dahnstairs.'

He nimbly side-stepped Reason's charge through the door, nodded politely to Sanderson, and managed to close the door noiselessly before rushing off in the black man's wake.

Reason was back within seconds. He clutched a large manila envelope, heavily bound with wide strips of transparent sticky tape, which he laid carefully on his corner of the coffee table. He began dismantling it.

Sanderson watched him for a moment without comment, then, with a puzzled expression on his face, said, 'What did Coney mean by an "er . . . erm . . . person", Clive?'

Reason gave him a lop-sided grin. 'He was referring to one of my Brownie pack who has this strange way of dressing. Coney wouldn't understand his haircut either. The boy reckons it helps him to blend into English society. He was on the job this morning wandering through the park with our friend here, hopefully as noticeable as a tree in full leaf. He's one of my star turns. Coney's suggesting that he doesn't look like an officer of the Household Cavalry in mufti.'

Gerrard looked over the flame of his lighter as he lit another cigarette and said, 'Which one was he? The black boy with the dreadlocks or the white one with a shaved head?'

Reason looked up sharply and said, 'Shit! Did anybody else make them? Did this man Malseed notice anything going on?'

'Nobody made them,' Gerrard reassured him. 'Malseed noticed the white boy. He said you British needed a war to solve your social problems. Are those the pictures they took?'

Reason nodded hopefully. He ripped the top off the packet and carefully separated two ten-by-eight photographs from the envelope's debris and held them out with a finger and thumb for Sanderson's inspection.

They were crinkled and mottled from overheated quick drying and immediately rolled up like a maverick venetian blind. Sanderson reached over and flattened them out with his hand. He barely glanced at the top picture and allowed it to roll up again.

It fell with a hollow bounce on the table and Gerrard picked it up. He unwound it and gazed at himself and the untalkative Irish courier walking through a rain-soaked Hyde Park; he rolled it up again and stood it on its end and joined the other two men poring over the second photograph.

Sanderson was staring hard at the print. He tilted it towards the sunlit window and studied it obliquely as if trying to force another dimension into the flat image. He glanced at Reason, then back to the picture.

'You know who that is, don't you?'

It was Gerrard who answered. 'Malseed,' he said. It was a crisp, clear picture of himself, and a somewhat less clear, slightly fuzzy-edged image of his companion; the two of them sitting near the deserted bandstand – they looked like two English optimists waiting for play to start at a rain-soaked test match in an empty Lord's.

Sanderson allowed the picture to roll itself into a tube and handed it back to Reason. He shook his head slowly. 'No it isn't . . . It's Adam Follington.'

Reason spoke first. 'Who's Adam Follington?'

Sanderson frowned into the puzzled expressions on the two men's faces. 'I'd have thought you'd know all about him, Clive.' He looked as if he'd got a bad oyster somewhere near the back of his throat and didn't know whether to spit it out or swallow it. 'Follington's got one of those foreign, anti-British north London seats . . . Parliament,' he added for the Frenchman's benefit. 'Keeps out of the limelight. Has the same passionate love of the IRA as most of his Irish constituents, but keeps his mouth shut about it in public. Lets his more vocal neighbours take the flak. But don't have any doubts, he's just as dangerous a bastard – probably more so because he has a modicum of intelligence.' Sanderson stopped for a second to wash his mouth out with a good swallow of pink gin. 'Funny this, though,' he said thoughtfully, and tapped the outspread picture with his finger, 'he must have a lot of bloody confidence in this venture to poke his head out into the rain!'

'He said he was expecting to find some pieces to pick up,' said Gerrard.

'We'll see about that!' snorted Sanderson. 'He didn't say what these pieces were, did he?'

Gerrard smiled and shook his head.

'I don't suppose his middle name would be Brocklebank by any chance?' asked Reason. He'd stuck the rolled-up photograph on his forefinger and waggled it backwards and forwards like a man with a bandaged finger; the expression on his dark features was as wishful as his thinking – he knew it wasn't going to be that easy.

'Not a hope,' said Sanderson. 'All right, Clive, is there anything else on the subject?'

'Nope.'

'Gerrard?'

The Frenchman shook his head.

'Good.' Sanderson gave a nod of approval. 'Then the two of you go and put your heads together while I deal with the Cousins. They're going to want to be in on this at every stage.'

'How many of our side have you got running with you, General?' Reason looked dubious.

'Relax, Clive.' Sanderson's smile became genuine. 'Nobody's run-

93

ning with me except picked elements of the SAS. You're handling the people at the top table, and we're taking out a few cells of Irishmen who thought nobody knew they were here. At this stage only the SAS commanding officer is on nodding terms with the general layout of both parts of the operation.'

'Harris?' persisted Reason.

'My number two,' explained Sanderson to Gerrard's raised eyebrows. 'No, Clive, not even Harris. But that's enough.' He turned to face Gerrard. 'Go ahead with this thing that Follington has proposed. Put something together for them, something with teeth in it, mind you. It's got to sound convincing, otherwise they'll smell it and scatter all over the bloody place before you can pull the plug out. We might as well make martyrs out of this lot, along with disposing of Brocklebank while we have the opportunity. It'll save me having to cook 'em one by one.' He paused, and frowned at Gerrard's lack of enthusiasm. 'You can manage that, can you?'

'Everything's possible, General,' said Gerrard, slowly. 'Given the opportunity.' He watched the frown lift from Sanderson's forehead, and smiled. 'And this looks as good an opportunity as any. Multiple targets don't often present themselves in a tidy group, not unless their confidence borders on stupidity, so it looks as though we dispose of this lot in matchboxes . . . An explosion; a bang with imagination will suffice. But I shall want some time to think more about it.' He searched Sanderson's expression for a sign. It was as flat as Reason's – and his own. 'You don't want details now, do you?'

Sanderson held up his hand, as if warding off the devil. 'Good God, no! I don't want any details at all. All I want is to hear a bloody great bang and see a pall of our colour smoke rise somewhere over London.' He paused and looked doubtfully at Gerrard – his curiosity had got the better of his intentions – 'How are you going to get enough stuff into this meeting to make an explosion?'

'The exact thought that was running through my mind.' Reason came out of his trance with a look of genuine curiosity on his face. 'But I didn't want to spoil the atmosphere.'

Gerrard looked from one to the other. 'That is the problem,' he said. 'I don't think they're going to let me walk in on them with a box of waxed gelignite under my arm, and I can't prepare anything beforehand because they're going to keep very quiet about where the meeting will take place . . . let alone when. What I need is to spend half an hour with a good tricks man who still has a few fingers left.'

'I know the very man,' responded Sanderson. 'Clive, introduce Gerrard to Archie Williams, see if he can't come up with some little toy that'll help him out.' He beamed at Gerrard, and washed his hands of the problem. 'Archie'll sort you out, Gerrard; be open with him, paint him a general picture – nothing specific, mind you – he'll understand.' Sanderson uncurled himself from the settee and stood up.

'Just two things before you go.' He stopped Reason and Gerrard at the door. 'I think we ought to know as much as we can about the people who punched Freddie Lambdon's card for him. I'd like to be sure that they are Provisional or INLA, and not some new bunch of yobbos nosing around and getting in everybody's way.' He didn't give Reason a chance to interrupt. 'You said you had some idea who killed him?'

Reason shook his head in surprise. 'No, sir, I don't think I said that. I said I've got something that may point us in the direction. Nothing substantial or definite, just a fingertip or two on a glass of booze left in Lambdon's kitchen.' Reason curled his lip. 'Which will probably lead us about as far as the end of Lambdon's arm. But I'll see it through, just for the hell of it.'

'Of course you will. Now, Gerrard.' Sanderson turned his serious expression to the Frenchman. 'I think I'd better make it perfectly clear that, apart from Clive here, you are entirely on your own.' He pointed his chin at the tall black man. 'You have no friends in this country except him – don't forget it.' He stopped again and frowned. 'But,' it came out almost as an afterthought, 'and it's a "but" you want to take a lot of thought in exercising, if you find yourself enmeshed in this country's other national emblem – red tape – and need some sort of official muscle, the man who can give you that muscle is Commander Roberts of SB's C19.'

Gerrard nodded. He knew all about Special Branch's C sections, particularly C19. But Sanderson was making no assumptions. 'C19 is anti-terrorist. Runs along with, and supplies legal backing for, MI5's F Branch. Roberts controls C19. He's trustworthy – he ought to be, he's one of my people. But as I said – use him only in emergency. You can get him through Audrey Gilling, his liaison officer.'

Sanderson frowned into the Frenchman's face. 'Don't use your own name, not even with him. Identify yourself as Michael – Mr Michael. And,' he tapped Gerrard's arm with his finger, 'don't get into trouble before you pull the pin out on Follington's party – I don't want even Roberts to know of your presence before that happens.'

Sanderson didn't offer to shake hands when they left but patted

Reason's shoulder as he passed in front of him. 'Clive,' he said softly, 'if you go to David Street at any time don't mention Gerrard's name in front of Harris.'

Gerrard caught the look of surprise on Reason's face but said nothing until they were both standing on the pavement outside the house.

'What happens at David Street?' he asked, and without waiting for Reason's reply, added, 'And Harris, I presume, is the one he . . .?'

'Yup. You heard him say it.' Reason had been expecting the question. 'He's the Old Man's number two. Trusting old sod, isn't he?'

Reason pointed Gerrard towards the King's Road and fell in beside him. 'D'you want to join me for a bite or are you going back to the hotel? They do a very good hamburger over the road – lots of chips.'

Gerrard shuddered, but smiled. 'No thank you. I'm going back to the Crinton. You didn't say anything about David Street.'

'Ah . . . David Street. That's where our shop hides itself. It's our front office, shows up in the KGB's guide book as a travel agency. They tell me it actually makes money selling theatre tickets and things. Funny old game, isn't it?'

The two men arrived at the King's Road and Reason pointed to the slow-moving line of traffic. 'You can get a taxi if you wait here long enough. I've got a bit of business to attend to. I'll call in at your place later this afternoon. OK?'

Gerrard nodded.

Reason hesitated. 'One thing before I go,' he said. 'There's nobody from our shop watching your rear so if you find you've got company it'll be some other firm. Just lose 'em, but for God's sake don't kill 'em! Not at this stage.' He grinned broadly again and pointed at a garishly decorated shop further down the road. 'You quite sure you don't want a hamburger lunch?'

Gerrard shook his head firmly. '*Au revoir*, Reason,' he said.

Gerrard ate a solitary lunch at the Crinton. It was a grander affair than Reason's offered hamburger and he said goodbye to the rest of the afternoon with the best part of a bottle of Beychevelle and a large Delamain. It had the right effect. He had to struggle to keep his eyes open as he made his way gingerly up the stairs to the third floor and his bedroom.

He lay flat on his back on the bed and slid thankfully into a sweaty, temporary death.

But it was very temporary – a three-minute death.

The telephone hummed gently against his right ear and he began the trip back, wallowing sluggishly upwards like a diver reaching for the rippling brightness of the water level until his head broke the surface. He kept his eyes closed as he reached for the receiver.

The silence when it touched his ear almost sent him sliding back into the warm dark sludge, until one of the sensual voices from the morning reception show breathed life into his ear and asked him if he'd like to see a Mr Reason.

He opened his eyes, and closed them again quickly against the fierce glare of unobstructed sunlight.

'Let me have a word with him,' he grunted.

Reason sounded surprised. 'You got company?' he asked.

'No. I like the sound of your voice. Before you come ask them to send up a very large pot of coffee and some hot milk – and two cups if you want some.'

Gerrard flipped the receiver back on its bracket without waiting for a response and wandered into the bathroom. He filled the washbasin with cold water and dunked his head. It did the trick. He combed the water from his hair, slipped on a pair of trousers and a clean shirt and, in bare feet, padded through to the small lobby and slipped the catch on the door.

Back in the bedroom he pushed one of the armchairs to within leg distance of the end of the bed and sat down with his feet propped on the mattress. He lit a Gitane, inhaled luxuriously, and waited for his new partner to arrive.

Reason threw his jacket across the back of a chair and flopped heavily on to the bed. He looked hot but not bothered.

'I ordered a sandwich with the coffee,' he said and made himself comfortable on the bed. 'No lunch – too busy.' He looked as though he would like to curl up and go to sleep.

Gerrard studied him for a second. 'Tell me about Fred Lambdon,' he said.

'Good friends, were you?' There was no sympathy in Reason's expression, only mild interest. Reason wasn't yet old enough to have developed a twenty-year-old friendship.

Gerrard nodded. 'Pretty good . . . How did they kill him?'

Reason told him, then went on to describe what he'd found at Lambdon's place. Gerrard lit another cigarette and listened in silence, looking not at the big man on the bed but at the ceiling, flat, white and unreflective with the only movement up there the scurry of smoke disturbed by the brush of conditioned air and the only sound the deep resonant bass of Reason's voice.

'Not a very dignified end,' Gerrard murmured when Reason had finished, and pulled reflectively on his cigarette. But Reason wasn't listening. He wasn't interested in ends – dignified or otherwise.

Gerrard flicked his eyes back into focus and cleared the frown from his forehead. 'When did they kill him, last night or this morning?'

'By the way he was hardening up when I saw him this morning I'd say he waved goodbye some time last night.' Reason swallowed the last of his sandwich and his tongue explored the side of his mouth for roast beef, but it didn't stop him talking. 'But what you're particularly interested in is how soon after he was talking with you did they round him up and start squeezing his balls. Right?'

Gerrard said nothing.

'And,' continued Reason, 'you've been lying in this dustbin ever since you finished your fish and chips wondering whether you can accept that it was you who caused them to start squeezing?'

Gerrard still said nothing.

Reason swallowed a mouthful of coffee. 'It was,' he pronounced.

Gerrard shrugged his shoulders. 'How do you know?'

'Simple. It doesn't take a genius to figure that until you strolled on to the stage it was the comfortable game; the gentle version, the one according to Lambdon's rules; our people believed he'd gone Irish and kept a casual eye on him. The Irish thought he had but didn't trust him entirely. Both of us logged his contacts: the Irish to make sure the crooked act was genuine; our people to study his footwork and to see if there were any new faces on the battlefield. And then, when everything has settled into a routine, he spoils everybody's game by trooping his colour across Horse Guards with just that – a strange face. So, some-body – them or us – said, Righto! If that's the way old Lambers wants to play we'll go and have a little chat with him and see what it's all about – find out what's with this new bloke.' Reason stopped to let it sink in, then, 'Did you notice anybody out of sequence when you were talking with Lambdon, anybody who shouldn't have been around when two old chums meet up?'

Gerrard brought his eyes down from the ceiling. 'Somebody popped his head up as we were leaving Horse Guards. Definitely "trade" but nothing special; he could have been anybody's; Irish, British, Special Branch, anybody at all.' Gerrard paused for a moment and smoked, then added, 'But there was something distinctly British about his uniform.'

When he described how the watcher had been dressed Reason frowned for a moment then blew out a long stream of smoke. 'The cheeky bastard! But it doesn't sound like your average Irishman, does it?'

'Doesn't it?'

Reason pulled a face. 'I don't know – I suppose I ought to know better by now. Paddy seems to look like everybody else nowadays so I really shouldn't be surprised to hear that one of them's strutting around London dressed like the Prince of Wales! Did you have any trouble losing him?'

'None at all. If he was Fred Lambdon's man he would have been torn between the two of us. It's always difficult when you've got options – you usually end up with nothing – as he did.'

'Except he knew where to find your friend Freddie.' Reason stretched his arms over his head and yawned. But he wasn't finished. 'The big question is who this guy was representing and how much Lambdon told him about the state of play before he closed the book on him. There's always the possibility that he was persuaded to throw mud at the neat set of credentials that have been repesented to the Irish on your behalf.'

'Sanderson said Lambdon was in the dark as far as I was concerned,' said Gerrard.

'Was Lambdon a fool?'

'Far from it.'

'Then give the fellow his due, Gerrard, he'd know more than you or Sanderson gave him credit for. Think the worse and come back to my original question – what did he tell them about you?'

Gerrard shrugged.

Reason stared at him for a moment, then said, 'Whatever it was it means that before you start shoving dynamite down your socks and presenting yourself to the firing squad I'm going to have to have a chat with this careless bastard.'

'Careless?'

Reason grinned broadly. 'He has to be. To start with, he lost his new face in the morning, which is bad enough, but then bugger me if he doesn't go and blow out the candle of his one definite marker. Stupid bastard! There he was, waiting for Lambdon to come up with your name, rank and number, and instead all he got was the old man's head bouncing into his lap. That means information-wise he finished up with fuck-all – hopefully! I call that bloody careless. But all is not lost.'

Gerrard didn't respond.

Reason poured the last of the coffee, now cold and insipid, into two cups and passed one over to Gerrard. He grimaced when he tasted his own and hurriedly replaced the cup on the tray. 'So, we've got an Irish ex-artilleryman lumbering around in the china shop. You're quite sure he's ex-Royal Artillery?'

'That was the badge he had on his jacket pocket.'

'You'd recognise that?'

'Of course. Everybody I know in England is an ex-gunner. Aren't you?'

'Nope, Two Para.'

'An exception. You were saying all is not lost.'

'Right! When I was leaving Lambdon's house this morning I happened to spot a little glass standing all on its own on the draining board. It had half an inch of whisky in it. I reckoned it was left over from the party so I emptied it and shoved it in my pocket.'

Gerrard didn't look excited. 'Lambdon could have left it there before the troops arrived.'

Reason shrugged his shoulders. 'I reckon it's just the sort of daft thing an Irish gunner would do – pull some poor bugger's head off his shoulders, drink all his whisky and stack the dirty glasses neatly on the draining board for the maid to wash up in the morning! I've sent the glass off to be looked at by people who know about these things. I want to see smudges. And they won't be Lambdon's – any bets?'

Gerrard stifled a yawn as he shook his head. 'When are we going to meet Sanderson's bombsmith?'

Reason wasn't put out by the sudden change of subject. 'Archie?' he said. 'I've arranged a little session for Sunday morning. Is that OK?'

'Sure. It'll give me time to go and see Marjory Lambdon. Somebody's going to have to tell her about Fred.'

'Does she know you're in town?'

'Fred might have told her,' said Gerrard, reluctantly.

Reason's expression was deceptively innocent. 'Fairly open with her, was he? Kept her up to date on everything that was going on?'

The innocence wasn't deceptive enough for Gerrard. 'Calm down, Reason,' he said. 'Lambdon might have told her I was in London – but that's all he would have told her. And forget it – he wouldn't have discussed his, or my, affairs with her. For anything else she's safe. Discretion is part of Marjory Lambdon's way of life, always has been – she's had a lot of practice at it.'

Reason kept his face blank. 'She'll be on their list. If Lambdon didn't help them sort out the identification problem then they'll move in on her.

I'm not doubting your friend Marjory's discretion, but it becomes one hell of a bloody luxury when some nasty big bastard's screwing your nipples off with a set of Petersons. She can identify you; she can place you; she can blow you right out into the open. Get her out of the game, Gerrard – they'll have her if you don't.'

Gerrard shrugged his shoulders but said nothing.

Reason persisted. 'Is she in London?'

'Sussex.'

'Go and get her out of there,' repeated Reason. 'We'll hide her up here – I'll give you a safe house. What about children?'

'A daughter from Fred's first marriage.' Gerrard smiled half-heartedly as he lit a new cigarette. 'You're running a bit wild, Reason. Why don't you leave it up to me?'

Reason shrugged his broad shoulders. He didn't look the least bit wild. Still relaxed, his hands still clasped behind his head, his expression remained unchanged.

'Where's the girl – with her mother?' he demanded.

'Her mother's dead. She was only a little kid when I last saw her. About five years old.'

'How long ago was that?' Reason didn't wait for Gerrard's reply. He pulled himself off the bed and disappeared into the bathroom. His voice carried over the sound of running water. 'And how old does it make her now?'

Gerrard stared at the bathroom door for several seconds, then looked at the ceiling for the answer. 'Twenty years ago – when Fred and I first met.'

The silence in the bathroom lasted long enough for Reason to add twenty to five and wrap a skirt round it. His head appeared round the corner of the door. His face was dripping water. 'It's a joke?' he asked.

Gerrard was still gazing at the ceiling. He said nothing.

Reason went back for a towel and stood drying his face. 'I make that about twenty-five.' He draped the towel round his neck and grinned at the unresponsive Frenchman, 'You might be better off going to see her and leaving Marjory for the next time round . . . You could be in for an interesting surprise or two!'

'Have you finished?'

Reason laughed throatily. He threw the towel on the bed and picked up a sheet of hotel notepaper from the side table. 'Get 'em both up to London,' he said, 'and then we can relax. I'm giving you a couple of numbers where you can get me at short notice.' He was serious now, the joke was finished. He leaned on the desk and scribbled, speaking as he did so. 'I move around quite a bit but either of these numbers'll get me – eventually.' He handed the sheet to Gerrard. 'Don't leave it lying around. One of those numbers has got a pair of legs like a silk stocking advert – I wouldn't want it to get into the wrong hands!'

He collected his coat and moved towards the door. He hesitated, then turned to face Gerrard.

'By the way,' he began. There was no amusement left in his face. 'Forget the empty place at the dinner table in Sussex. Your friend Marjory doesn't qualify for a peek at the latest casualty list. Sanderson's put his thumbprint on Lambdon, and it extends to his old lady.'

Gerrard stared at Reason.

Reason stared back and pulled a face. 'She's not privy to this one – not yet. Same for his daughter. Lambdon's trip's a non-event – the only people with tears in their eyes are you, me, General Sanderson and the dustman. The bloke who chopped Lambdon's head off has his own emotions – I doubt whether he's going to run around telling everybody what he did and how he did it. But I'm afraid your old friend Marge's widowhood is going to have to be postponed until after you've handed your trowel back to the stores.'

'You're a callous young bastard, Reason.' Gerrard spoke quietly, there was no venom in his voice.

Reason took it in his stride. 'Lambdon's gone abroad. It came up suddenly last night – a short-notice emergency somewhere where the sand is hot and the nights are cool! It's going to take a few days to handle – a couple of weeks at the most. Blanket stuff. He's got to stay cold. She'll understand. You said it yourself – she's had lots of practice.'

Gerrard inclined his head in acknowledgement of the big hand Reason held up.

'Cheerio,' said Reason and closed the door quietly behind him.

Gerrard looked down at the sheet of paper in his hand. He studied the numbers for a few seconds then went into the bathroom and flushed the screwed-up paper down the lavatory.

He lit a cigarette and looked at his watch; it was exactly a quarter-past three.

At that precise moment a man wearing a navy-blue blazer with a Royal Artillery badge on the breast pocket stepped on to the doorstep of Marjory Lambdon's house in Sussex and rang the bell.

CHAPTER 9

Gerrard woke the next morning to the screaming of the telephone from the table by his head. He picked up the handset and enjoyed the silence for a second before glancing quickly at his wrist; half-past seven . . . He groaned aloud, pushed the thin cotton sheet down to his stomach and reached for a cigarette.

'Hallo,' he coughed.

'Ring the desk and get them to send you up a *Daily Express*,' said Clive Reason. 'There's a small item you should read on the back page. It's in the stop-press column.'

Gerrard coughed again over another throatful of smoke. 'Read it to me and save me the bother,' he said brusquely – morning had never been his best time of day.

Reason was unrepentant. 'I'd rather not if you don't mind,' he said. 'I think you should read what it says, think about it, then call me back from somewhere other than where you are at the moment. Oh, and while you're thinking about it throw a few things into a bag and get yourself out of that place in a hurry. Don't ask questions, it'll probably become all too clear to you when you've read your newspaper. If it hasn't I'll tell you why when I see you. Use the number I gave you yesterday. OK?'

'OK.' Gerrard replaced the receiver and punched the service button.

It took them half an hour to put together a large pot of coffee, half a dozen croissants, butter, jam, and a *Daily Express*. The tray arrived outside his door at just past eight.

Gerrard studiously avoided the folded newspaper and drank a large cup of indifferent coffee to prepare his system for the good or bad news, then lit another cigarette. He put his hand on the croissants. They were stone cold, so it didn't matter, they could wait. He picked up the *Express* and turned to the back page. He found Reason's item exactly where Reason had said it would be; it was clear and to the point and very brief and showed what it was – something slipped in late, almost as an after-thought.

Marjory Lambdon's name jumped out of the printed box like a familiar face in a group photograph. He knew what it was going to be before he started reading. It said a woman had been found dead in her home in Chennington Magna, Sussex. The woman's bound and half-naked body had been discovered late last night by her stepdaughter. The police were making no comment. The victim's name was Marjory Lambdon, married, aged thirty-eight.

Gerrard read the short paragraph twice and threw the paper, un-opened, into the waste basket. Poor Marjory – what a terrible waste.

He closed his eyes and summoned up the memory of their last meeting; but it was a brief requiem, dispelled with the next mouthful of luke-warm coffee and erased with a long thoughtful pull on his cigarette. So, Reason was going to bare his big white teeth and say, 'I told you so!' No big deal. But he also had a point – a game of mental leap-frog took one from Fred Lambdon to Marjory Lambdon to Michel Gerrard, care of The Crinton Hotel, London.

Gerrard smiled grimly to himself as he lifted the lid of the coffee pot to inspect its contents. It was empty, which gave him a mild sense of relief. He buttered the last half of doughy croissant, ate it, and washed its taste away with the dregs from his cup. He pulled a face and shuddered, and stood up to look out of the window. He had a feeling about today; it had got off to a bad start. He stared out of the window at the morning sun – why wasn't it raining?'

He threw his cigarette end into the empty coffee cup and offered a loud and emphatic '*Merde!*' to the world in general, then lowered himself to the floor and began ten minutes' vigorous exercise. It helped – not very much, but, like absolution, it cleared his mind.

Gerrard left his one lightweight bag with the hall porter and strode down Park Lane to Hyde Park Corner where he found a vacant telephone kiosk. Reason answered almost before he'd finished dialling the final digit.

'I agree with you,' Gerrard told him.

'What about? I haven't said anything yet.'

'You're going to say that you were right.'

'I thought it might be a bit too early for that. I'm not sure about your sense of humour.'

'You think this is funny?'

Reason's voice became serious. 'I don't think the culling's complete yet. If whoever it is isn't on to you already I think they'll go for the last of the Lambdons – they won't know you haven't seen his daughter for twenty years. But I have a nasty feeling that Marjory will have blown your cover. We'll see. In the meantime, have you booked out of that hotel yet?'

'Yes, but I've got to go back for my bag.'

'Leave it. I'll collect it later.'

'Thank you. About Lambdon's daughter – Melanie. Any news other than that reference in the paper?'

'Nothing so far. But then I haven't been able to do anything yet. I've been too busy wasting my bloody time sitting here waiting for you to get your finger out and ring me back. I didn't want to block the line.'

Gerrard smiled. 'Your patience is an example to us all, Reason. Keep calm, they're going to have just as much trouble finding Melanie as we are. Or have you an address already?'

Reason laughed deeply. It made Gerrard's eardrum buzz but helped his mood move upwards another notch. Reason said, 'Give me a quarter of an hour to wake some people up, and put some others in a bad mood, and I might have something to talk about. How about breakfast? Have you eaten yet?'

Gerrard shuddered, he could still taste the heavy croissant and the awful coffee of his 'continental' breakfast. 'I've had all I want for this part of the day, thanks. But don't let me put you off, I'll come and blow smoke in your face and drink coffee. Where did you have in mind?'

'Get a taxi and go to the Grosvenor Hotel.'

Gerrard looked at the traffic. 'I'll walk.'

'OK, walk, but be a good fellow will you, and do me a favour?'

'What's that?'

'Look over your shoulder once or twice on the way there. I've got a nasty little feeling that somebody's made open season on you and I don't fancy having rusty nails whistling round my ears while I'm eating my breakfast! Just make sure you come alone. *Au revoir.*'

The telephone clicked and died. Gerrard repressed his irritation at Reason's patronising tone, and glanced about him as he replaced the receiver. Two girls with bare shoulders and tight impatient mouths who'd been staring at him earlier had got bored with waiting and left. Hyde Park Corner looked as normal as the early rush hour would permit, and every other man wore a blazer with brass buttons. Gerrard walked thoughtfully down Grosvenor Place towards Victoria Station, his casual manner disguising a needle-sharp awareness of the movements about him.

The Grosvenor Hotel restaurant was crowded, but Clive Reason made an easy target. He sat alone at a corner table by the window and stood out like a six-foot-three-inch, seventeen-stone, Savile-Row-suited black man. He looked up and nodded as Gerrard approached, but didn't stop eating.

Gerrard sat down and poured himself a large cup of black coffee. He swallowed a mouthful and pursed his lips in approval – it was much better than the Crinton's. He lit a cigarette to celebrate and tossed the blue packet on to the white linen tablecloth. He waited for Reason to demolish his breakfast kipper. That done, Reason wiped his lips with a large crisp napkin and reached across the table for the packet of cigarettes. He winked at Gerrard. 'Kippers,' he said. 'Beats frogs and toads any day!' He stuck a cigarette between his lips. 'Got a light?'

Gerrard held out his Dupont. 'We only eat the legs,' he said defensively.

'Very cruel! Not nice.' Reason inhaled luxuriously, grinned to show that it wasn't serious – yet – and sent a stream of smoke towards the high ceiling. When he lowered his head and looked across the table the grin had gone.

'OK,' he said, 'let's talk about the Lambdons.' He removed a piece of kipper from between his front teeth with his finger and inspected it as he spoke. 'Now we've got two of them to talk about.' He flicked the piece of fish away and looked back at Gerrard. 'Yesterday we had one, today we've got two – I've decided they were both knocked off by the same people, and for the same reason.'

'Me?'

'Correct.'

'Irish?'

'Or British.'

'You're joking?'

Reason didn't smile. 'Sanderson told you yesterday that nobody on the shop floor had been told about Lambdon's high-wire act.'

Gerrard stared at him.

'Stick your hand in the bag and pull out a number! The British can be just as curious as the Irish about a French face with a worn trigger finger. And who to go to for pointers? Old Fred Lambdon – last seen paddling in the same pond as the IRA; next, trooping the colour across Horse

Guards Parade with Al Capone!'

'But you don't know for certain?'

Reason shook his head. 'And I don't think I want to. I've lost interest in the dead Lambdons – it's the live one who's worrying me at the moment. I want to break this bugger's sequence – if Marjory was no use to him I don't want him getting to you through the girl. At least not until you've done what you came to do. Does she know you well enough to excite our man's lustful nature?'

'She doesn't know me at all. I told you yesterday, I haven't seen her since she was a child. Your Irishman's run up against a wall.'

'He could be a Brit.'

'You've already said that. Can we put the girl somewhere out of reach?'

'We're going to have to, and quickly. When they arrive at the Crinton and find you've bolted, and when they make up their minds that she's been shown the dirty pages in the book, they'll move in and start tweaking her little nipples for your new address. You can count on it.'

'She wouldn't know anything about it.'

'That's not important. They sound like people who enjoy their work. I think you're going to have to collect her. She may remember you; she's probably heard Fred and Marjory speak of you. She'll trust you. You can bring her up to London and I'll sort out a secure cupboard for her. Will you go this morning?'

Gerrard nodded. Reason passed the coffee pot across the table. 'Finish that up, I'll order some more in a minute. Work on it while I make a couple of phone calls. Shan't be long.'

Reason helped himself to another cigarette as he sat down, and said, 'Old Coney took a call yesterday afternoon at three-thirty from a lady who said she was Marjory Lambdon.'

Gerrard replaced his cup carefully in its saucer, lit a cigarette, then held the flame under Reason's. 'And?' he said.

'And nothing,' replied Reason, 'that was all she said. She cut off after saying her name. As it was a number used only for emergency calls it would appear that something must have been breathing down her neck. Whatever it was it didn't give her a chance to unburden herself. It had to be the guy who killed her.'

Gerrard smiled condescendingly. 'And I bet he had an old-fashioned cannon embroidered on the pocket of his navy-blue blazer.'

Reason pursed his lips and frowned, but he let the suggestion pass without comment and continued, 'The other little item concerns one Bernard Gallagher, of Dagenham in Essex.'

'Who's he?'

'Bernard Gallagher's the bloke who left his unfinished whisky on Fred Lambdon's draining board last night. He also left his fingerprints all over the glass. He put it there, like a well-brought-up tripehound, for the maid to wash in the morning after he'd tried to pull old Lambdon's head off his shoulders.'

Gerrard stared coldly at the black man. He didn't say anything. He let Reason continue.

'I mentioned that Lambdon's face looked as though a cultivator had been driven across it, didn't I – apart from the broken neck, that is? Well, here's a bloke who owns a pair of mitts which, I'm told, can punch holes through concrete blocks. Your friend's head would have been like an onion to him.'

'Is he in the Business?' Gerrard's show of interest was genuine. He sat forward and drew heavily on his cigarette.

Reason shook his head. 'A part-time potato lifter – a helper-out, which explains why he was present at Lambdon's farewell party. I'd better go and have a talk with him, just to make sure Lambdon didn't open the book for this guy's friend. Sanderson expects it too – he likes a couple of eyes and some teeth for an eye!' Reason stopped talking and drained the cold dregs from his cup. He didn't pull a face – he seemed to like the dregs. 'And it'll keep me occupied until Sunday.'

Gerrard nodded. 'Any news of Melanie?'

'She's staying at a pub called the White Hart in Chennington Magna, where your friend Lambdon's house is. I can understand the girl preferring the pub.'

'Have you got me a car?'

'Coney's arranging it. It'll be downstairs in the car park in about half an hour. But just in case, have you got Coney's number?'

Gerrard nodded.

'And mine?'

Instead of replying, Gerrard stubbed his cigarette out and lit another one.

Reason seemed oblivious to the snub. 'We've got time for another pot of coffee, and another thousand fags before I head for the rain forests of Dagenham. Do you mind giving me a lift, we're going in the same direction.'

'What about my bag at the Crinton?'

'I told you, I'll collect it later. Don't go anywhere near it.' Reason looked quizzically at the Frenchman. 'About this car . . . ?'

'What about it?'

'You done much driving in London?'

'No. I'll pick it up as I go along.'

Reason grinned. It was a little sickly. 'Perhaps I ought to go by Tube.'

CHAPTER 10

Gerrard turned the car into the slip road at Barking station and switched off the engine.

Reason tried not to heave a sigh of relief as he touched his damp top lip with a handkerchief. He said to Gerrard, 'I thought you were joking when you said you'd pick it up as you went along.'

Gerrard didn't smile. 'I'll take you for a drive round Paris one day.'

Reason unwound his large frame from the passenger seat and stepped on to the kerb. He stooped and looked at Gerrard through the open window. 'I'll see you when you get back,' he said. 'Give me a ring as soon as you hit smoke, you know where.' He stood on the kerbside for a couple of minutes after Gerrard had disappeared into the lunchtime Barking traffic, then moved off to look for Bernard Gallagher.

Bernie Gallagher was, to say the least, a little bit surprised to be approached by a 'bloody great big spade with a poofy accent' – the billiard-hall messenger's description – but his curiosity got the better of him. Five twenty-pound notes and Reason's offer of an interesting bit of axe-handle work compensated for the sitting pink. After a taxi ride, and a little ingenuity, he was persuaded into what Reason termed his dispensary – a semi-derelict building overlooking the Regent's Canal near the Cat and Mutton Bridge in Hackney.

Reason spent an hour with him.

To Gallagher it seemed more like twenty-four, most of the time lying in a corner with Reason's foot pressed into his face. He was most co-operative and answered all Reason's questions. Reason thanked him and gave him a cigarette before handing over to the two heavily built young men who called him 'sir' and who took turns in making the tea.

But their duties went beyond that.

After Reason had left they wound a wide strip of binding tape several times round Bernie's head to cover his mouth and stuck him back in the corner until the sun went down. When it was dark one of them looked out of the window, smiled at Bernie, and nodded to his companion.

They bounced Gallagher down the stairs, carried him across the road and squeezed him through the railings bordering the canal. They left him gazing at the reflected lights in the water, then shortly returned, staggering under the weight of a stripped cylinder block.

There was a lot Bernie wanted to say about all this but all he could get past his lips was a tiny insignificant squeak. If it was heard it was ignored.

A rope attached to the cylinder block was tied tightly around his waist.

One of the young men said, peering critically into Bernie's face, 'You don't think his head'll stick out above the water?'

The other man replied, 'It's a shade more than ten feet deep here. Even if he stands on the bottom and waves his bloody hands about he still won't break the surface. And how's he going to get his hands out of his pockets with this bloody great rope around his waist? Come on, let's get it over with, I'm dying for a beer.'

Bernie just had time to feel his heartbeat accelerate from fast to critical before they lowered him, and his cylinder block, silently into the water.

Reason jammed open the door of the public telephone box with his foot and stuck the greasy receiver to his ear.

'Is that you, Coney?' he asked when it answered.

'I'm recording, Mr Rason,' replied Coney. 'Go on.'

Reason opened the door a little wider and breathed in some fresh air.

'Memo for the General,' he said. 'Our former friend departed without blowing the game. The interest was the Frenchman. Nothing's been smudged so it looks as though everything's back to last week's square one. The man who waved our friend off has gone to join him, but there's a new face in the game called Murray. He was also at the farewell party. He's the guy who's directing the orchestra. He's Irish, from the North. I don't know who stamps his card but I'm hoping to have a word with him. That's all, Coney.'

'You've been busy, Mr Rason.'

'Goodbye, Coney.'

CHAPTER 11

Murray held the pint of bitter at arm's length and studied it critically before putting it to his lips and swallowing the top three inches. He put the glass back on the table, wiped his mouth with the back of his hand and winked at the man sitting opposite him.

'Bit on the cold side that, Smithy,' he said, 'but otherwise a reasonable pint. It won't touch Mulligan's draught Guinness, but it's drinkable.'

Murray's commentary on the state of the beer didn't placate his companion. He wasn't at ease. He fidgeted with his glass and looked up at the door every time somebody came through it. He'd stuck his long legs out deliberately blocking the narrow passage between himself and the adjacent table in case one of the new arrivals took it into his head to claim the empty place on the bench seat beside Murray. His long face wore a painful expression and he sipped his dry white wine without pleasure. When he spoke he kept the glass near his mouth so that his words were distorted. 'There must be better places to meet than this, Murray. For Christ's sake! – a bloody London pub!' He looked pointedly at the table on Murray's left where three young girls in skimpy T-shirts giggled into two spritzers and a half-pint of lager and lime. 'From a security point of view . . .' he began, but gave up.

'Sod the bloody security point of view,' said Murray, and reached for his glass again. 'Let me worry about the security point of view.' He spoke in a normal voice as if he didn't care whether the whole pub stopped to listen. 'But first, be a good chap and go and fill this up for me again.'

'Where did you get the name Michel Gerrard from?' asked Smithy when he returned with Murray's pint.

'A lady gave it to me,' said Murray.

'What lady?'

'Just a lady – why?'

'Michel Gerrard used to work for the DGSE.'

'Go on,' he said.

'Ever heard of a man called Siegfried?'

Murray lowered his glass fractionally. 'Kraut who made lines for British soldiers to hang their washing out on?'

Smithy pretended he hadn't heard. 'Siegfried,' he said, 'is the name given to the top DGSE executioner. Has his own office in the clouds somewhere above Paris. He's the official liquidator of people who get on the wrong side of French Intelligence. He's killed dozens of people. If you could name a handful of the top hit-men in the world he'd be right at the top of the list.'

'Does this eulogy have an end to it, Smithy?' Murray tilted his glass and drank.

'His other name is Michel Gerrard.'

Smithy waited for a reaction. There wasn't any.

Murray took a few more gentle swallows then raised his eyebrows. 'And . . . ?'

'And?' Smithy choked on his dry white wine. 'You're missing the point, Murray. This bloody Frog is a top-class assassin. He's dangerous, and the Lambdons' deaths have just provoked him. He's not going to be an easy man to take on.'

Murray went back to sipping his beer with little pouting movements of his lips. But his eyes had taken on a thoughtful, almost satisfied look; a look that seemed to stop half-way across the table and left Smithy feeling as if he'd been talking to a drawn curtain. He tried again, 'I said – '

'I know what you said,' Murray's eyes clicked back into focus and he lowered the glass from his mouth, 'but what you didn't say was who this hotcock's working for now.'

'What do you mean?'

'You said he *used* to work for the DGSE.'

Smithy nodded. 'He did – but he left them about six months ago to set up shop on his own. He hires out now for the big hit. He's very exclusive, takes on only impossible contracts, and by the sound of it it's got to be bloody nigh impossible to justify the fee he commands for the use of his finger. There's nothing nominal about him. The size of the fee restricts his targets literally to heads of state and his paymasters to oil sheikhs upwards.' Smithy stopped talking and tapped the base of his empty glass. It had no effect on Murray.

Murray wasn't even listening. He'd stopped listening when Smithy had told him Gerrard was running loose. He was now silently con-gratulating himself: *so that's what the bloody game's all about, is it? Old man*

Lambdon was busy setting up a million-pound shot for the Dublin Gathering and you, you clever bastard, Murray, you hung on the branch and knocked off the bloody apple! Lambdon was only the go-between. It's Mr bloody Siegfried hyphen Gerrard who's the potato; he's the boy who matters; he's the one we want to play liar dice with. Easy! All we've got to do is find the bastard! He brought his eyes back into focus and smiled at Smithy.

'So, what are you going to do about it now that you know you're on the way out?'

'What are you talking about, Smithy?'

'Murray, you're in a different bloody game now. If you've annoyed this chap, and he's caught a whiff of your after-shave, you might just as well say goodbye! You'd be well advised to leave him to the people who can handle him; people like the other kill-masters at the top of that list. That's what I'm talking about.'

Murray fixed Smithy with a hard stare. 'I want you to go back to the girl. Take up where you left off.'

'But what about her father?'

'Forget him. She's back in favour.'

'Fair enough. But I think you ought to know I haven't set eyes on Lambdon since you gave him to me. I've nothing to give you back.'

'You're not likely to now,' Murray said harshly. 'Lambdon doesn't matter any more. Forget him.'

'Oh?' Smithy raised an eyebrow and searched Murray's eyes.

'He's gone on his holidays, we won't be troubling him for some time. But that's not your concern; your concern is his daughter. I want you to stick so close to her that you run the risk of being canned for indecent behaviour. Get it, Smithy? She's my favourite girl this week, I don't want her getting up to anything without my being told about it.'

'Who am I looking for – in particular?'

'Can't you guess?'

'I'd rather you told me.'

'The bloody Frenchman for starters.'

'You're joking?'

'Like bloody hell I am! If you see a bloke with a beret and a string of onions hanging from the handles of his bike turn up on her doorstep you put your slippers on and start running in my direction! Where is she now, this Lambdon girl? Still in Highgate?'

The young man looked unhappy. 'I've no idea, but don't let it put you off your beer, I'll find her.'

Murray looked askance at him but said nothing.

'I don't know whether you know it, Murray, but the Lambdons have a place down on the south coast; she might have gone there for a few days.'

'She might well have done that,' said Murray woodenly. 'But concentrate on her Highgate pad, pick her up the minute she pokes her nose out of the door and stay with her until I tell you otherwise. OK?'

'OK. But satisfy my curiosity. What's a nice girl like that supposed to be doing with a top people's hit-man?'

Murray shook his head. 'You don't ask what's inside the sausage roll, Smudger, you just stick the bloody thing in your mouth and start chewing.' He frowned at Smithy's blank look. 'In other words, let me worry about her motives – all you've got to do is watch her.'

Murray stood up and squeezed between the two tables.

'Where are you going?'

'To get myself another pint of bitter and a wedge of their home-made veal and ham pie. Then I'm going to sit down quietly and eat it. D'you want a piece?'

'What about the Frenchman?'

Murray grinned again and reached down to pick up Harry Smythe's empty wineglass. 'Bugger the Frenchman! With all that money you say he gets he can afford to buy his own bloody pie!'

CHAPTER 12

Gerrard lowered himself into an overstuffed leather armchair in the lounge of the White Hart Hotel in Chennington Magna. He refused the offer of afternoon tea, instead lit a cigarette and wondered what twenty years had done to a sad little doe-eyed child with a page-boy haircut.

He looked up and studied the woman who stood at the entrance to the hotel lounge. Seven other pairs of male eyes did the same.

She was tall and slim with a halo of honey-coloured hair surrounding a soft, sun-tanned oval face. She was unbelievably beautiful.

She scanned the room with a sweep of her head. When her gaze fell on Gerrard she stared for a moment, gave a light, hesitant smile, and moved towards him. There was nothing for the other seven.

She kept her eyes glued to his; no smile, just a steady searching inspection as she walked towards him.

She was even lovelier close up.

This exquisite creature was the skinny little child who had hugged his neck and begged him to take her away? Jesus Christ! The smile was making his face ache. Where's the catch? He looked for the flaw – there wasn't one. But it can't be all perfection, it never is – she's got to be the type who hangs men's balls on the bidet handle as souvenirs. She'll have a voice like a Toulouse prop forward . . . But surely not with those eyes?

'You're the only man in this room who could possibly be Michel Gerrard.' She spoke just above a whisper in a voice that was soft and uncomplicated.

None out of ten for perception, Gerrard! He managed to remove the smile, but it left his mouth dry and unresponsive. He didn't reply. He felt like the village idiot.

She touched his arm lightly. 'Congratulations. You haven't changed. You're exactly as I remember you.' She raised herself on to the tips of her toes and brushed the side of her cheek against his. Gerrard had a brief sensation of the heady scent of exclusive perfume, and then it was gone. 'It's nice to see you again, Michel. You must have heard about Marjory. Is that why you've come to see me after all this time?'

Gerrard found his voice. 'I thought I'd wait until I outgrew my shyness – beautiful women have that effect on me.'

She knew the effect she'd had on him. She stared into his eyes for a second opinion. She'd already seen it when she'd crossed the room; the searching look, the scrutiny that went beyond the friendship for an old friend's child. As Gerrard had surmised, she knew what thoughts men had when they looked at her. She brushed a wisp of fair hair from her forehead with a tight, nervous gesture. She was on edge. It showed she hadn't been totally spoilt. Gerrard stared back approvingly.

She was dressed in a fawn linen skirt whose tailoring emphasised her flat stomach and the delicate, womanly curve of her hips, and a navy-blue shirt which hinted provocatively at full, firm breasts. At the open neck of the shirt Gerrard could see a tiny mole-like beauty spot on her collar bone. It was smaller than the other one that had nestled cosily in the smooth join of a little girl's thigh; oval, in the outline of a small brown mouse, it was the giggling party trick of an uninhibited five-year-old in-nocent; the tiny nude exhibitionist, pink and powdery, running from bath to bed: *Do you want to say good-night to little mouse, Uncle Michel?* There was nothing wrong with Gerrard's memory either.

When they sat down, Gerrard said reminiscently, 'The last time I saw you, you were a tiny little thing, skinny matchstick legs and big round eyes – but soft, and very cuddly. You spoke with a lisp and had crooked milk teeth.'

She crossed one long, exquisitely shaped leg over the other and modestly patted the edge of the skirt where it rose above rounded, well-tanned knees.

'I can see why you waited so long!' She smiled and clenched her teeth for his inspection. They were small and white and perfectly even. 'They're straight now – and I don't lisp any more! Got any other memories?'

'Oh, yes – lots.'

'Forget it. I don't think I trust your memory.' Her tone changed rapidly from banter to serious, as if there was a danger of letting the memories take over. 'Where's Daddy? Is he on his way?'

'I don't know.'

She looked at Gerrard sharply. 'What does that mean? That you don't know where he is, or you don't know whether he's on his way?'

'Both. I haven't seen him. I read about Marjory in this morning's paper and came down straight away to see if there was anything I could do.' Steady, Gerrard, he checked himself. Don't overdo it. Let her ask the questions.

A note of disbelief edged into her voice. 'Well, do you know how I can get hold of him? I've tried everywhere I know and all I get back is a great big hollow silence.'

Gerrard shrugged and managed to keep his eyes neutral. Nothing seemed to be the best thing to say to that.

His lack of response spurred her on. 'Surely he can read the newspaper like everybody else, and if you know about Marjory why in heaven's name doesn't he? Just a minute . . . !' She paused, and the frown grew into a suspicious narrowing of the eyes. 'If you haven't seen him how did he know you were staying in London?'

'Were you particularly close to Marjory?' Gerrard asked.

The question and the change of subject took her by surprise. She answered automatically, 'Not really . . . Not all that much. Well, no, not at all . . . We're different types and different ages. Come to think of it, the only thing we had in common was Daddy. Why do you ask?'

'You don't seem as upset as I imagined you would be. I wondered.'

'Would you prefer that I burst into tears?'

'I didn't mean that.' Time to change the subject again. He chose his words carefully, 'About your father . . .'

'Yes?'

'I saw him in Paris a couple of days ago. I told him I was coming to London, that's how he knew where I'd be. Don't ask me what he was doing in Paris because I don't know, he didn't tell me. All I know is that he was going on from there and didn't know how long he'd be away. You don't want me to explain any more than that, do you?'

She shook her head thoughtfully.

'Good. So, that's why you can't contact him and that's why he doesn't know about Marjory. Try not to worry about it. He'll be in touch with you as soon as he's back. Does that answer your question?'

'No.'

Gerrard swallowed the dryness in his mouth. 'Why not?'

'Because he rang me the night before last and asked me to tell Marjory he'd be coming home last night.' The frown had gone from her forehead but suspicion still lingered in the searching hazel eyes. 'When is he coming back to England?'

Gerrard squirmed inwardly. 'I don't know,' he replied, and then said, abruptly, 'I'd like you to come to London with me.'

She didn't seem surprised. 'When?'

'Now.'

She glanced at the small diamond watch on her wrist and shook her head.

'You've got an awful cheek, Michel Gerrard. You ignore me for twenty years, wander in here and tell me what an ugly child I was, then expect me to come trotting, without a whimper, up to London with you!' She smiled coyly. 'Do I look that simple?'

'There's a reason.' Gerrard didn't smile back.

'Tomorrow morning,' she said firmly. 'After you've bought me a conciliatory dinner and told me what you've been doing for all these years.'

Gerrard relaxed. 'Agreed. Can I get a room?'

'You can get anything if you know how to ask for it!'

'I have a feeling I've missed a very important phase of your life.'

'You have?' Melanie's eyebrows rose. 'What phase was that?'

'The one where you grew up and learned how to play naughty girls to helpless old men.'

'You could be in the middle of that phase right now!' Melanie stood up and took his hand. It was just like old times. Gerrard hoped she couldn't feel the rush of blood through his fingers. She said, 'Let's go and book that room for you and then we'll go for a walk on the beach and you can tell me all about it.'

'All about what?'

'Relax, Michel!'

He watched as she walked on the edge of the sand where it met the Channel; where the creeping, unstoppable water clawed its way out of the sea with a million little multi-shaped fingers; where it stopped for the breadth of a second before drawing frothily back leaving a dark fringe of smooth sand. She walked some distance in front of him, barefoot, leaving hardly a trace of her passage in the forgiving sand and, every so often, paid the price of daring and had to jump with a little animal-like squeal as a wave, more aggressive than the others, climbed higher up her legs and threatened to wet the skirt she held high above her knees.

Gerrard watched the child at play. But she wasn't a child any more – she was a woman, and she was happy splashing along the shore; happy, as any woman could be who didn't know her father was screwed up in a polythene bag and an Irish dimension was hovering over the middle ground. He tried to block his mind to it but Reason's voice boomed into his head; as persistent as the corpse-collector; as loud as the breakers waiting in line for their turn to come ashore; Reason's brutal words that had no pity on the imagination, and refused to go away.

'And when they make up their minds that she's been shown the dirty pages in the book, they'll move in and start tweaking her little nipples . . . You can count on it.'

Gerrard stopped thinking and walked towards the girl with the beautiful legs.

She met him half-way. 'I'm ready for that drink you promised me.' She put a hand on his shoulder and stood on one foot while she brushed wet sand from the other. It seemed nice and intimate, a most natural thing for her to do. 'Have you sorted things out yet?' She didn't look at Gerrard when she spoke. She changed position and worked on the other leg then smoothed her skirt over her hips and patted her thighs with open hands. 'Have you decided to tell me why Marjory died, and what sort of game you and Daddy are playing?'

Gerrard watched her hands tracing the outline of her hips and thighs before looking up into her face. She was a mind-reader. It was time to change thoughts.

'Let's go and see whether the news of champagne has reached Chennington Magna yet.' It had turned out to be a lot easier than he'd thought.

'You've done it again, haven't you?'

'Done what again?'

'Changed the subject. But it won't work, you know. I want to know why Marjory died.'

Gerrard regarded her for a few seconds. He relaxed his expression and smiled, then slowly shook his head.

'What?' she asked.

'Twenty years haven't changed you much.'

She stared back. 'In what way?'

'I speak as a man who's sprinkled talcum powder over your smooth little bottom!'

'Answer the question.'

'You're still a very lovable child.'

She smiled suggestively into his wary eyes. She didn't blush. But it lasted for only a second. 'If you think that's going to stop me asking about Marjory . . .'

CHAPTER 13

Malseed lay on his back and stared at the ceiling of his bedroom.

He was unable to sleep, but he wasn't worried about it, there was plenty of night left in which to catch up. But there was a lot to think about. A cigarette would have been a comfort – a glass of Glenmorangie a balm to his restless imagination, but he resisted both and lay silent, listening to the deep contented breathing coming from the silk-covered pillow by his head.

When the telephone rang he started with a guilty feeling of relief. He picked up the receiver and keeping his voice low murmured, 'Adam Follington.'

He had no fears about the security of his telephone – he'd had it checked by the best in the business, and then rechecked both officially and privately, and besides, they wouldn't dare, they knew the strength of his voice.

'Brocklebank,' said the voice in his ear, and without further preliminaries, 'First post in the morning you'll get a copy of our head salesman's itinerary. It'll show times, stops, and placement of every friend he's got; the undercover, overcover, and contingencies are all attached. I'd like you to pass it on to the onion man. Whatever you do don't let it out of your sight. He won't take notes, he's too professional for that. Let him have a good look at it and as soon as he's finished take it home, burn it and flush the ashes down your loo. Any questions?'

Malseed studied the face of his sleeping companion then reached out and ran his long fingers down the naked boy's stomach until he reached his groin. He spread his hand and rolled it gently from side to side; the boy's eyelids flickered but he otherwise made no movement. Malseed spoke into the telephone. 'Are you keeping an eye on the Frenchman?'

'Of course.'

'Where is he now?'

'South Coast. Place called Chennington Magna.'

'What's he doing there?'

'Fred Lambdon's daughter if he's got any sense!'

Malseed gazed down upon his young friend and curled his lip; he re-peated his question as if he hadn't understood the crudity. 'What's he doing at Chennington Magna?'

'He was last seen with an optimistic look on his face, eating candy floss and walking hand in hand along the beach with Melanie Lambdon.'

The silence seemed interminable, then Malseed coughed, cleared his throat and said, 'You seem to know a lot more about him than we've given you credit for. You'll continue to keep your eye on him?'

'Right up to Guy Fawkes day. He won't be doing much without my knowing about it. Anything else?'

'Is it still Tuesday? Is it definite?'

'Definite. The rest is up to you.'

Malseed pursed his lips. 'Then it's all arranged. Our friends will be coming over separately, and by different routes; the Frenchman's the only one who hasn't been told the date of the meeting so far. He'll be the last to know. You'll be there of course?'

'Yes. Let me know by the usual method if there's any last-minute change.'

'Naturally. Good-night.'

Malseed slid back into place alongside the young man. The need to lie alone with his thoughts was gone; he was aroused and excited, the ciga-rette and the drink could wait – this wouldn't.

There was more than a smile on his face when he took the sleeping youth in his arms and pressed his fingers hard into his buttocks. 'Wake up, darling,' he whispered, 'and be specially nice to me. This time next week your Adam'll be the most important man in England.'

CHAPTER 14

Gerrard drove slowly up Highgate High Street and turned into the narrow tree-lined backwater of Miller Street.

He'd jumped a red light and taken a deliberate wrong turning in Islington; this caused a series of small backstreet wriggles before he was able to filter back into Holloway Road.

The red light had taken care of the blue Granada that had picked them up outside Chennington and the backstreet shuffle lost the anonymous BMW who'd joined the party as they'd crossed Vauxhall Bridge. Gerrard frowned at the ease with which he'd lost them. But he didn't tell Melanie about the company.

A third of the way down Miller Street Melanie told him to stop. She pointed to a small, elegant Georgian cottage set about ten feet back from the road.

'Come and have some lunch.' She was half-way out of the car.

'I won't if you don't mind, I have a lot to do.'

'I do mind.' She wrinkled her nose at him and slipped back into the car, then leaned towards him and put her hand on his knee. 'Very much.'

He looked down at the hand on his knee and felt his good intentions melt towards his groin. He shook his head half-heartedly. She got the message.

'Right. That's sorted that one out! Come on.' She slipped out of the car in a flurry of legs and perfume and walked across the pavement to the bright yellow door and disappeared inside.

Gerrard sat in the car for a few minutes longer and studied the narrow street.

It looked safe and anonymous; a street of expensive miniature town houses, discreet behind the overhanging plane trees and secure behind the thick curtains and gaily coloured doors. Gerrard looked hard at Melanie's yellow door. Behind that, would she be safe – a shadow in a roomful of shadows – until he could get her somewhere secure? What if she refused to go? They would be looking for her at Chennington, not Highgate – there was no reason why anybody should point themselves in this direction. He narrowed his eyes into the rear mirror and counted the cars parked neatly behind him; they were that sort of car, they too looked as though they belonged.

But still he wasn't happy.

Four cars behind, and slotted nicely between the cars that belonged, Harry Smythe sat forward in his little BMW and watched Gerrard enter the house. He waited until the yellow door closed then left the car and strolled casually towards Highgate High Street. He knew where the telephone box was. He went straight to it and dialled Murray's number.

Melanie watched without expression as Gerrard cleared his plate of the last morsel of cheese. Her own omelette was hardly touched.

She sat sideways at the table with her legs crossed and an unaccustomed cigarette smouldering between the fingers of her right hand; she held the cigarette like a painter about to attack a blank canvas with a dripping brush, but there was none of the thrill of desecration in her eyes – the bubble of the car journey had burst somewhere between the iced melon and the *omelette fines herbes*.

They sat in the postage-stamp-sized garden, protected from the sun's rays by the branches of two huge chestnut trees growing in the large wood beyond the protective wall. It was a metropolitan oasis. Quiet and tranquil, its almost complete isolation broken only by the high-pitched whine of an overhead jet as it slipped into its flight path for descent into Heathrow. They were far too frequent.

Gerrard watched the latest arrival flit across a gap in the leaves as he munched slowly on the cheese. He watched the plane until it disappeared, then reached across the table and removed the smouldering cigarette from her fingers – she hadn't smoked it for some time and its long ash bent dangerously off the perpendicular. He crushed it into the grass. She didn't object.

'Does that mean you want coffee?'

'No. It means I want to talk about Marjory.'

She uncrossed her legs, turned round to face him and picked up her glass of Chablis. 'I think the coffee can wait.'

Gerrard lit his cigarette. 'The people who killed Marjory were looking for me.'

Melanie paled. But that was all. 'What had Marjory got to do with you?' There was a trace of suspicion in her voice – female suspicion.

It wasn't lost on Gerrard. He said brusquely, 'We think – '

'We?' she interrupted.

'Colleagues. We think they visited Marjory because your father and I are, er . . . co-operating, on a security project. I'm the person our . . . competitors want to talk to. They couldn't ask your father where I was so they asked Marjory.'

'Asked?' said Melanie, scathingly.

Gerrard stared at her for a second. 'She couldn't have told them very much,' he said bluntly, 'so they killed her.'

'I see.' Melanie was silent for quite a long time, during which she studied Gerrard's expression. He wasn't quite sure what she was looking for. 'That was the only reason you came down to Chennington Magna yesterday?' she asked.

Now he knew what she was looking for. 'I intended coming anyway,' he said lamely.

She wasn't impressed with his answer. She shrugged and said, 'Why did you ask me to come back to London with you?'

It was time to stop tiptoeing. 'Because I think the people who killed Marjory will want to talk to you. I couldn't take that chance.'

'You mean you were afraid I might tell all, even though I hadn't the foggiest idea what's going on?'

'Not quite. I didn't, and don't, want you hurt.'

'I have a feeling I ought to be wagging my tail and waiting for you to pat my head.'

'Don't wag it too hard.' He didn't smile. 'There's something I'm going to have to insist on.'

'Is there?'

He didn't like the way she said that, or the frostiness that had appeared in her, up to now, warm hazel eyes. 'I think you should drop out of circulation for a few days. We have houses where nobody – '

'You mean I should go into hiding?'

He sensed that she wasn't going to be easy to persuade. Before he could make a convincing case she held up a decisive hand and said, 'Absolutely not. I have my own life and I'm not going to be intimidated by a bunch of thugs. Anyway, Daddy will be back any day now – you said so.'

Gerrard shifted uneasily on his seat. 'Well, you're not to go back to Chennington until I tell you it's safe to do so – no matter how long it takes. And I want you to be very careful about who you see and who you go out with; stick with those you know and avoid any social contact with strangers.'

'This is because you don't want me hurt?' she interrupted. Her face had softened – she'd never been spoken to like this before – not by an adult male. It was an almost enjoyable experience.

'And because I'm very fond of you.' Then he spoiled it. 'And I promised your father I'd keep an eye on you.'

She stared at him coldly. 'Anything else?'

'Don't get yourself chatted up by smartly dressed, healthy young men.'

She couldn't help it. 'What if they've got grey hair and a bit of aged experience in their eyes?'

He relaxed his expression and smiled. 'Especially those. For different reasons.'

'Steady, Michel Gerrard!'

He stopped smiling. 'Be very suspicious of anybody who suddenly moves into your circle; anybody who says he's a friend of old so-and-so who told him to look you up whenever he was in town; and above all, be particularly wary of anybody, man or woman, who asks too many questions.'

'About what?'

'About anything. One last thing . . .'

'Thank God for that!'

'Do you want a cigarette?'

'No thank you. Was that it?'

Gerrard smiled. Her perplexity made her even more beautiful – it also made her look very vulnerable.

'No. When was your father last here?'

'He's never been here.'

'You're sure about that?'

'Quite. The nearest he's been is to stop outside in the road and peep his horn, and I can't remember the last time he did that, it's so long ago. Certainly more than a couple of months. Why?'

'Just curiosity. I'd like that cup of coffee now.'

It was as if she hadn't heard. 'Will you be staying in London?'

'I don't know.'

'Pardon?'

'I don't know where I'm staying.' Gerrard smiled to take the sting out of his words. 'May I call you in a few days?'

'Why don't you stay here until you finish whatever it is you're doing?'

'No thanks. I wouldn't be able to concentrate.'

'If that's your idea of flattery I can understand why you're a lonely man.'

Gerrard smiled in spite of himself. 'Can I use your phone?'

'Help yourself.' She didn't smile with him, not because she was afraid – she convinced herself she wasn't; apprehensive maybe, but not afraid; a little jiggle of ice nudging against the adrenal gland – but because she was suddenly very aware of the fluttering in her stomach and the accelerated beat of her heart. 'The phone's in there,' she pointed into the house, 'on the right.' She watched him move towards it and wondered about the unpredictable nature of desire.

Gerrard sat down in the cool darkness of the drawing-room and dialled one of the numbers Reason had given him.

'Yup?' The voice was heavy, black, and male. It wasn't Clive Reason.

Gerrard waited for a clue. The voice didn't help. Gerrard's patience ran out first. 'Is Clive Reason there?' he asked.

There was no reply and the line went dead – not hung up dead but the flat dead when a hand is placed over the mouthpiece. Gerrard lit a cigarette while he waited for the interpreter to arrive and pushed the spent match deep into the damp soil of Melanie's potted begonia. The voice came back with the same indolent lack of urgency.

'Say a name,' it said. The voice now had a West Indian lilt to it.

'Gerrard.'

'Hang on.'

Gerrard uncoiled from the chair, flicked the ash from his cigarette into the pot plant and picked up a silver frame that stood on the other side of the plant. A twenty-year-old Fred Lambdon smiled bashfully from under a beret with a Parachute Regiment badge gleaming on it. He leaned towards the camera at a slightly unnatural angle to show the shiny pip of a newly commissioned second lieutenant on each shoulder; a black and white picture, it would have been just before Arnhem. Gerrard replaced the frame and turned it away so that Fred Lambdon gazed out into the sun-soaked garden. As he straightened up, the telephone came to life again.

'Got a pencil?' asked the voice.

'Yes,' said Gerrard.

'Ring 201 0931.'

Gerrard said nothing. He replaced the receiver and started the process again. The new number produced a nicer voice. Female. But she got no further than 'Who wants – ?' when the phone was taken from her and Reason's deep baritone thumped down the line.

'Hallo, friend,' said Reason. 'Welcome back. How was your trip to the seaside?'

'Bracing. Anything happening?'

'Plenty. First a message from your paymaster. He wants you to get in touch as arranged. Looks as though you're about to start earning that winkle money.'

Gerrard frowned at the telephone. 'Malseed?'

'Himself. And there's more. Look, why don't we get together and rattle a bone or two over a drink? Where are you now?'

'I brought Melanie Lambdon up from the country with me. She gave me lunch at her place, that's where I'm ringing from.'

Reason gave a deep belly laugh that made the earpiece of Gerrard's phone vibrate. 'Still in pig-tails, navy bloomers and little white ankle socks?'

Gerrard peered through the shadows at the woman pouring coffee in the garden and smiled into the telephone. 'She's taller than I remember, and she's filled out a bit here and there. She can cook now. Stubborn, too. She insists on staying here and not taking cover. Where do you want to meet?'

'Whereabouts are you?'

'In Highgate.'

Reason gave a grunt of satisfaction. 'Couldn't be better. There's a decent pub near you that attracts some quite nice tit on a hot Saturday evening – it's called the Fusilier. We can sit outside, have a drink, and look at the girls. Can you meet me there at about seven?'

Gerrard looked at his watch and frowned. 'I'll be pushed,' he said, 'I've got to find myself a place to sleep tonight.'

'Didn't you make out with the girl then?'

'You've got a one-track mind, Reason.'

'I wouldn't have it any other way.'

'Where's that pub you were talking about?' Gerrard interrupted Reason's belly laugh and dampened down the atmosphere.

'OK,' Reason dropped the bantering tone and became crisp again, 'listen, forget about looking for somewhere to sleep tonight, leave it to me, I'll sort it out for you. Just get yourself down to the Fusilier – that's F.U.S – '

'I know how to spell fusilier.'

'Good. So about seven then? Oh, and Michel . . .'

'Yes?'

'How safe is that house?'

Gerrard frowned, then leaned forward to make sure Melanie wasn't within earshot. 'It's out of the way and can't be on anybody's list. Fred Lambdon hasn't been near for several months so he couldn't have brought any of the friends to look it over. If she stays out of sight until after the bang there's probably no way she can be marked. If they want her they'll look at Freddie's place in Sussex. It's second best, but I'm happy.'

'I'll remember you said that. See you at seven. Cheers.'

Gerrard replaced the receiver and stood up.

At that moment the front door-bell rang.

Melanie was still in the garden. She hadn't heard it. Gerrard walked across the room, waited for a second, then opened the door abruptly and looked up into the face of a six-foot four-inch beanpole. He had about twenty-five years on the clock and weighed as much as half a dozen newlaid eggs. Gerrard stared into his face, but, after a brief acknowledgement the young man's tired-looking eyes glanced over Gerrard's shoulder and his sombre face lit up with a smile. Gerrard knocked another three years off his age for the smile.

'You there, Melanie?' he called out. When Melanie appeared, his otherwise blank face beamed. 'Didn't know you were back in town . . . Didn't even know you'd gone away come to that! Like that fellow who used to pluck the Froggies off the bumbril – I sought you here, I sought you there . . . But no Melanie – you'd vanished!'

'Stop talking for a minute, Harry, and come in.' Melanie's head vanished but her voice continued from the kitchen, 'I'll get you a glass.'

But the thin young man didn't stop talking. He glanced briefly and apologetically at Gerrard as he slid past him into the room. 'Tried to raise you the other day but you were battened down for gale force. Where are you now?'

'Kitchen,' she called out.

'Can I come through? I thought you might like dinner later – if you're free that is?' He glanced over his shoulder at Gerrard and gave him a friendly nod before wandering into the kitchen. He came out again immediately with a glass in one hand and Melanie's waist in the other.

'Go into the garden, Harry,' she told him, 'and help yourself to a drink. We'll be with you in a minute.'

'What the hell is that?' whispered Gerrard.

'It's like this all the time,' she hissed back, 'I don't get a moment to myself!'

'Who is he?' Gerrard insisted.

'A friend.'

'How long have you known him?'

'It's immaterial how long. Take it that I know him very well.'

Gerrard raised his eyebrows. 'I see,' he said.

'No you don't!' she snapped. 'Why don't you come and have a drink with Harry?'

Gerrard shook his head. 'Sorry, I really am in a hurry now.'

'Where are you going?'

He touched her lips lightly with his finger and shook his head. 'Don't forget what I told you – don't make any new friends for the time being. Stick with those you know.' He stared again at the young man in the garden. 'And don't go back to Chennington until I've been in touch.' He continued staring into the garden. There was something troubling him. 'Goodbye, Melanie,' he said.

She stood on her tiptoes and gently brushed his mouth with soft moist lips. He tasted the fragrant perfume of her breath and saw that her eyes were open as she kissed him; it wasn't really a kiss, it was a meeting of mouths on her terms but it was enough to send the blood coursing through his veins. She stayed like that for several seconds, her lips touching his and her eyes searching, then she pulled away and said, 'I can almost remember the last time I did that! This time don't leave it so long. Another twenty years and it will definitely be too late!' She didn't say what for.

When she stepped back he had a clear view over her shoulder of the man in the garden. He was watching them across the rim of his glass.

'Why didn't he ask who I was?' said Gerrard.

She was taken by surprise. 'Why didn't who ask what?'

'Your friend in the garden there, why didn't he ask my name?'

'Because he's not like that. He's not nosy, and besides, it's no business of Harry's who I entertain to lunch – ours is not that sort of friendship.' She stared into his eyes, she wasn't smiling. 'It's like you and me – platonic!'

Gerrard grinned. 'That would worry me if I were as young and beautiful as you.'

'Your flattery comes too late! Ring me soon.'

'What did you say his name was?'

'Who, Harry? I didn't, but it's Harry Smythe. Depending on how friendly you are you can call him Smithers, Smithy, or Smudger, but I don't think that's going to concern you – I don't think you're going to get beyond Harry Smythe.'

Reason put two dripping glasses on the table and shook the spillage from his hand. He sat down, lit a cigarette, and allowed his head to rest on the wall behind him.

'I turned over the letter-box you'd arranged with Malseed. He'd left you a little billy-doo. He wants you to get in touch, as arranged, at half-past eleven tomorrow morning. Sunday.' He gripped the cigarette between his teeth and grinned. 'I hope that's not going to interfere with Holy Communion?'

'Was that all?' said Gerrard.

Reason shook his head. 'There was somebody watching it.'

Gerrard sipped his beer thoughtfully. 'Why would Malseed take the trouble to have the drop covered?'

'He wants someone to see you so they'll know they're picking up the right bloke on the day you're called in for the board meeting. The cover's the turnip who's going to take you to the *ceilidh*. It must be getting near shooting day – Malseed knows how shy you are about meeting strangers so he's doing it this way.'

'But he already has someone who knows me. You've seen his picture. The silent guy who picked me up in the hotel and took me round the park. Why would he want another?'

Reason studied his cigarette, took a final drag from it, and slid it under the heel of his shoe. As he ground it into the dust he said, 'He hasn't got that one any more. He's gone over the hill. He won't be coming back.'

'What caused that to happen?'

'He had an unlucky day – I recognised his picture. It was a face from the past that I owed a little pain to.'

'What had he done, trodden on your toe?'

'Billy Meehan,' said Reason, 'worked as a rat-catcher for the mob who called themselves the 3rd Ardoyne Battalion IRA, but you have to be as nutty as them to take any notice of the military suggestion.'

'Is that all you had against this character – that he called himself a soldier?'

Reason drank some beer and swilled it round his mouth like mouthwash. 'Meehan and a gang of scrags uncovered a friend of mine. He was doing a bit of undercover earwigging in a little old pub down in the pointed end when Meehan's lot crawled in from the gutter and rolled him up like an old second-hand carpet. When they'd finished with him Meehan hung a grenade with a long fuse round his neck and walked off into the blue. The poor bugger had to sit there for what must have seemed for ever, tied to an old kitchen chair with this bloody grenade ticking away just below his chin.'

Gerrard pursed his lips. 'Not nice,' he murmured. He could have been pronouncing on the taste of a bottle of corked Margaux. 'So you weren't too pleased with Mr Meehan? What did you do with him?'

'I hung a grenade between his legs and let him sweat.'

'For how long?'

'Half an hour.' Reason grinned. 'I took the detonator off the fuse. When I pulled the pin it made the right noise, but Billy wasn't to know there was nothing in there. I told him to have a nice trip and left him to it. I don't know how long he sat looking at the thing between his legs, or whether he bothered counting, but he'd fainted when I went back. Did me no end of good it did.'

'I don't think you're a very nice person to know, Reason. What did you do with him after that?'

'Couple of lads and I had quite a long chat with him. He was what you might call pliant when we got around to him, so we taught him the error of his ways and asked him to help us with our enquiries.'

'Where is he now?'

'In protective custody.'

'What does that mean?'

Reason stopped grinding the cigarette under his heel and looked up. 'It means he's in an old manure sack about eight feet under Epping Forest.'

'OK,' said Gerrard with a thin smile, 'thank you for telling me about Mr Meehan and your friend! Now tell me what Malseed's going to say when your lavatory man reports back with an empty envelope?'

'He won't be doing that. He's been flushed down the loo.'

'He's been what?'

Reason grinned again and reached for another cigarette. 'There was a little miscalculation and he and I came into contact. I didn't want him to go dashing off to Mr Malseed and tell him you'd got a sudden over-dose of the sun so I had a couple of fellows pull the chain on him. He's no longer interested in what's going on up here.'

Gerrard reached for his beer. 'You've been a very busy young man, Reason – do you get paid by the head?'

'No, I do it for the laughs.' But Reason didn't laugh. He pulled heavily on a new cigarette and paused long enough to indicate a change of subject. 'I spoke to the chap who killed your friend Lambdon.' The smoke left his pursed lips with a thin whoosh as he spoke. 'He was exactly what I expected: big, thick and ugly – a nothing person.'

'Was?'

Reason nodded. 'You could have spread this big bastard's brain on a pinhead and still left enough room for his guts. It must have been old Lambdon's unlucky day.'

Gerrard shrugged his shoulders, his expression remained blank. 'You going to ask for qualifications when your turn comes?'

Reason grinned broadly. 'He'll have to be a union man! The ape's name was Gallagher and the guy who employed him to help despatch Lambdon is an Irishman from Belfast, named David Murray. From the description Gallagher gave me I'd say he's the boy who played spot the Frog with you on Horse Guards the other day.'

'Is David Murray one of ours or one of theirs?' asked Gerrard.

'He sounds too tough to be one of us,' said Reason, with a hint of condescension. 'Apparently he had Lambdon in his sights for a couple of months before he decided to break his neck. My Bernie reckoned something must have caused him to pull the pin out of the plug up his arse because he suddenly took off after the good Colonel and started slapping him around the ear. But, according to Bernie, they'd only just started winding the clock up when he, Bernie that is, tapped Lambdon on the back of the head and broke his neck. He swore with his dying breath that it was an accident and said Murray nearly went into orbit when he realised the old man had snuffed it. Bernie reckoned he came very close to joining Lambdon in the sack himself, until Murray calmed himself down and said, "Fuck you, Gallagher, that bastard was the end of my bloody line!" Sounds quite volatile for an Irishman, this Murray, doesn't he?'

Gerrard looked hard at Reason, but made no comment.

Reason went on, 'And again, according to my friend Bernie, Murray was after something that he reckoned only Lambdon could help him with. Which makes our friend Murray's tizz perfectly under-standable, doesn't it?' Reason stared at Gerrard's blank face. 'Well, it does to me, anyway. I can just imagine the guy standing there listening to his last chance rattling his life away down a broken throat.'

Gerrard said, 'Did your friend say anything about Lambdon's wife,' he paused for a second, 'and family?'

'Yes, he did. He said Murray was going to chat her up. Murray had already told Lambdon that before he sent the poor old sod to byebyes.'

Gerrard stared at him. 'Did he know where to go?'

'Sure, Chennington. Not very clever, your friend Lambdon, was he?'

'Anything else?'

'Oh, yes! He told Lambdon if he didn't get any joy out of his wife he'd go and put his hand up his daughter's skirt and see what she had to offer. D'you want another beer?'

'No.'

'I forgot to mention the reason for Murray's sudden burst of activity.'

'You don't have to. It doesn't matter now. I'll be quite happy to talk to him any time, provided he doesn't mind walking around on his knees for the rest of his life.'

Reason grinned, but it was only a fleeting grin. 'What have you said to Miss Lambdon?'

'She's been warned about strangers and told to keep quiet for a few days. As she refused to accept protection there wasn't much else I could do. With luck nobody's going to come looking for her in this backwater.'

Reason picked up another of Gerrard's cigarettes and as he lit it he shook his head slowly. 'I wouldn't count on that. I wouldn't count on anywhere being a backwater, not nowadays.' He crossed his leg and carefully balanced the half-empty glass of bitter on his knee; he studied it for a moment, frowned, then looked at Gerrard. 'Are you well covered back home?' he asked.

'How do you mean?'

'If somebody didn't like your face and, with only your name for starters, wanted to put a few facts together to make an operational contract for an IRA or INLA execution squad, could it be done with money, or coercion – or by asking the right questions in the right place at the right time?'

Gerrard glanced sideways at Reason, but Reason was still intent on the balancing act of the glass on his knee. He didn't look up. But he was listening.

'It's been tried before,' Gerrard told him. 'And it's not recommended. Somebody would blow the whistle on them before they had time to ask their second question. They wouldn't make it.'

Reason gave up his balancing act and smiled as if some private thought had amused him. He raised the glass to his lips and spoke out of the corner of his mouth as he tipped the glass up. 'What odds will you give me against someone with an Irish accent raising your name in Paris within a week of your pulling the rug from under Malseed's feet?'

Gerrard shrugged his shoulders. 'I'll give his Irish accent twenty-four hours from asking the first question – twenty-four hours from mentioning my name and he'll be shivering, stark naked, in a cold little room at Vincennes. No windows, a thick soundproof door, a single bulb hanging from the ceiling. Got the picture?'

'I like it!'

'All that and a bloody great electrode clipped to the end of his *pin*.'

'The end of his what?'

'His cock. And there'll be a man with skin-tight rubber gloves tapping him across the ear with a copper bar every time he screams. By the time you and I get there he'll be ready to crawl up your leg, begging you to listen to what he's got to tell you about any subject you care to mention. Wouldn't you like to have a chat with an eager Irishman?'

Reason emptied his glass and placed it on the table. 'At the moment I'd rather eat.'

'Lead the way.'

Reason left the telephone box and climbed into the car.

'That was a friend,' he told Gerrard. 'She's got a nice face, a nice disposition, and a nice flat – and it's not too far from here. I've agreed to feed her tonight and in return she's giving you the run of the flat – much better than buggering around with hotels at this time of day, and you'll be out of the way.'

'Sounds cosy,' said Gerrard as they picked up speed. 'Is she on the game, this friend of yours?'

Reason looked hurt. 'She's a friendly. She's Colonel Harris's slipper girl – looks after his paper-clips and sits on his knee and shows him how to work the typewriter. You go through her to Roberts, remember. You'll be all right with Fanny Gilling, she's well brought up, a nice girl, she'll look after you and make sure you're not bothered by the unwashed.'

'Is it wise doing bed and breakfast with somebody in the trade?'

Reason grinned. 'Not unless you take it into your head to spend the early hours rolling around her pit discussing the wherefores and whys of what you're up to over here.'

'What did you tell her about me?'

'I said you were a Frenchman who looked like Yves Montand and had done me a favour in Rhodesia.'

'That sounds suitably convincing,' said Gerrard caustically.

Reason wasn't put out. 'Not at all. There were all sorts of people stumbling around in the undergrowth out there so the odd Frenchman hoofing it around wouldn't have been out of place. You could have been Rhodesian SAS or the Selous people – nothing wrong with them. Anyway, ⌐he said she likes Frenchmen, and she wasn't curious so why don't we ι. ⁄e it at that?'

'What were you doing in Rhodesia?'

'A bit of this and a bit of that. You might not have noticed but I've got the sort of face that didn't stand out like a Victoria plum among Mugabe's raggy-arsed militia so I could go in and out fairly freely. Just as well! I never did fancy tribal life – I'm a beer and tit man myself. Quick! Where that car's pulling out . . . Grab it before that bloody Roller gets his nose in . . . Jesus!'

The chocolate-coloured Rolls reared out of the way like a startled pony when Gerrard cut across its tracks and thumped the car into the empty space. Reason waggled his fingers amiably at the anonymous face behind the smoked glass but received nothing in exchange.

'He must have known you were French.' Reason wasn't smiling.

The restaurant was shaped like the letter 'L' with a balcony floor along the top end of the room and a small bar which filled the horizontal stroke of the 'L'. It was full and noisy and explained the happy expression on the proprietor's face.

Gerrard was about to finish his third whisky when she came through the door. He stopped drinking and stared, then, with the glass still at his lips, watched as she was directed to the corner of the bar where he and Reason sat.

'Is this your woman?' he murmured to Reason.

She was beautiful and poised and her eyes twinkled with the knowledge that most of the men sitting or standing at the bar had already worked their minds down to her flimsy white lace briefs; but she looked troubled, it affected the twinkle as she approached the two men.

'No,' said Reason out of the corner of his mouth. 'Yours. Mine's big, fat and black. She comes later.' He slid off the bar stool and put his arm round the woman's waist. 'Hallo, Audrey. This is the Frenchman who's looking for pint-size Bluebells. Michel Gerrard, Audrey Gilling.'

'He said your name was Fanny,' Gerrard told her.

She smiled fleetingly. 'He would, he's got a warped sense of humour, most of it centred in one area.' She parted her lips in a nervous smile and permitted a tiny tip of pink tongue to run drily over them as she stared into his face.

'I prefer Scott to Gilling,' Gerrard said to her.

'OK,' Reason broke in, 'is one of you going to let me in on the joke?' His smile embraced them both, but his eyes were like black diamonds; Reason didn't believe in coincidence.

Audrey did. 'No joke, Clive,' she said carefully, 'just a little coincidence ... I met Michel the other evening in the Crinton – he thought my name was Scott, God knows why!'

Gerrard held her eyes for a brief moment. 'Is Audrey your working name?' he asked, without smiling.

She frowned and made light of it. 'It depends on the circumstances, Michel. When I'm thirsty and sitting upright I prefer Audrey. Other times ... ?' She shrugged her shoulders. 'A large whisky please, Clive, lots of ice and water.'

Reason didn't move. He raised his eyebrows at Gerrard. Gerrard pushed his empty glass across the table. 'I'll have the same. No ice.'

Reason still didn't move. 'How did you two meet?' he asked Gerrard.

Gerrard let his eyelid flicker. Audrey wouldn't have noticed it. 'I'll tell you later,' he answered. 'It's nothing sinister, purely sexual.'

Audrey's eyes widened.

'But let's have that drink, the girl's tongue's hanging out and she's got some work to do with it.'

'Oh my God!' She blushed and laughed at the same time.

When Reason went to the bar Gerrard stood up and said, 'Come and sit over here and tell me all about this coincidence, Audrey.'

She slid past him and sat down and felt his thigh press hard against hers. It wasn't sexual. It frightened her. She tried to move away, but there was nowhere to go, so, with another little wriggle, she turned and looked directly at him. 'I'd rather not say too much in front of Clive,' she said huskily, 'can't we leave it to later?'

Gerrard smiled. It didn't reach his eyes. 'You mean you need a little more time to put your story together?'

'That's not fair,' she began, then whispered, 'Here he comes – I'll tell you later.'

'I think you've been stood up, Clive,' suggested Audrey after another two whiskies. 'She probably poked her head round the door while you weren't looking, saw what the bottom of the barrel looked like, and ran screaming home to Mummy!'

'There's a great big fat black girl just walked through the door.' Gerrard gazed unsmilingly over Reason's broad shoulder. 'She seems to be looking for somebody.'

Reason shot a startled glance at Gerrard before looking slowly over his shoulder.

She was a vision in anybody's language. An exquisite figure poured into a simple, tube-shaped cream dress, she stood waiting, tall, elegant and at ease; her light coffee-coloured skin glowed like a late sunset and her jet black, shoulder-length hair glistened in the subdued light of the restaurant.

Reason was on his feet in a flash and the ripple of interest that shuddered up and down the bar faded with his appearance.

Gerrard turned to Audrey. 'OK, Audrey – while Reason's getting the strength back in his knees. What are you doing here?'

'I thought we were going to leave it to later?'

'I've decided I can't wait. I won't enjoy my dinner. Surprises give me indigestion, and indigestion makes me bad-tempered and cruel. Say something quickly.'

'OK, but don't push me too hard.' She reached out, helped herself to one of Gerrard's cigarettes and tapped it nervously up and down on the table. She bit her bottom lip for a second then said, 'Clive and I belong to the same Brownie pack; same hive, different compartments. Hasn't he told you?'

Gerrard's head didn't move.

She shrugged her shoulders and shaped her mouth into a moue. 'What I'm doing here has nothing to do with work. It's Clive's fault, blame him. He rang me this evening and asked if I had room for an old friend of his.'

'I know about that – I was there. What were you doing at the Crinton?'

'My boss had a word popped in his ear by his Special Branch chum that a Frenchman, known in the business as Siegfried, had passed through Immigration. You weren't furtive enough for Special Branch so they passed you on to our people and I was sent to look you over for future reference.'

'Who's your boss?'

'I don't think I should say.'

'Was that all he wanted?'

She wet her lips with the tip of her tongue. 'No. He wanted to see if I could talk you into telling me what games you were proposing to play over here.'

Gerrard began to smile. When it reached his eyes she smiled with him.

'We're very good at things like that over here,' she said. 'Our masters are the spy world's great innovators; they're still working on the Mata Hari theory that a man will tell a woman anything provided the props are authentic and the sheets are crisp and clean – and she's the one underneath.'

'I understand now your yearning for romance.'

Audrey hesitated, and then smiled coyly. 'Look, why don't we leave the rest of this until tonight?'

'Is there more?'

She shook her head. 'Not really. But I do feel I owe you something. I can't quite put my finger on what, but tonight seems as good a time as any to try. That is, of course, if you still want to stay at my flat?'

Gerrard smiled again – it was becoming a habit. It gave her confidence.

'I know I shouldn't ask, but are you and Clive working together, or are your relations, if you'll pardon the expression, purely social?' She tilted her head and looked openly into his eyes.

Gerrard covered her hand with his. It was a friendly, intimate gesture but it didn't help. 'Clive's teaching me how to drive on the wrong side of the road,' he told her. 'He might call that work, but I don't!'

She got the message and wrinkled her nose. 'Have you known him long?'

'Long enough.' The smile remained on his lips. 'Why don't we leave it until tonight and I'll explain it in depth?'

'I feel like I'm going to blush again.'

Gerrard broke off abruptly and reached under the table and put his hand high on her thigh. He squeezed. 'Here he comes now. Watch what you say, and don't mention the name Siegfried in front of him. He's not on the list. OK?'

He tightened his grip, causing an intake of breath.

'You're hurting me!'

He let go. 'Not a word.'

'OK.'

Gerrard brought his hand back on to the table and reached for a cigarette and wondered whether he'd done enough to convince her that Reason was only there for laughs. He clicked the lighter flame out and replaced it on the packet of cigarettes. 'Sorry I hurt you,' he said.

Audrey recovered quickly. 'For Christ's sake, Michel, don't apologise! I'll look forward to some more of the same later on – provided I'm allowed to join in!' She stopped whispering, looked up at Reason and widened her eyes. 'What happened to the girl you were waiting for, Clive?'

'What girl was that?' the vision in cream asked.

'Somebody big, black and buxom,' Audrey told her.

The girl smiled. 'That's my mother. She'll be along to relieve me later!'

Reason wasn't amused.

Gerrard sat it out like a guest at the honeymoon.

The conversation was light and superficial, Audrey saw to that, but he wasn't happy. She'd marked the evening; she made it feel as if the whole idea had been hers. Maybe it was . . . He stared hard at the back of her head as he followed her across the restaurant towards their table. There was no clue there, nor was there in the confident way her slim hips swayed under his hand. Audrey Scott, or was it Audrey Gilling, was relaxed and happy . . . And what was her real name, Scott or Gilling? As if it made any difference.

Gerrard moved up alongside her and put his hand round her shoulder. He lowered his head and spoke quietly into her ear. 'What's your name, Audrey – Scott or Gilling?'

She could almost have been waiting for the question. She paused, turned her head and searched his eyes for a second, then smiled. 'Gilling,' she said, 'but I'm not hysterical about it. I'll answer to anything if the circumstances are right.'

'What circumstances are those?'

'If you don't know, darling, I don't know who does.'

'Naughty!' He dropped back and smiled. And looked into Melanie Lambdon's eyes.

Melanie and Harry Smythe were seated at a small table partly hidden in a shallow recess. Melanie wasn't laughing. If she'd heard the conversation it didn't show on her face.

'Hallo, Michel,' she said softly. 'I wondered why you galloped off so quickly after lunch.'

Nobody laughed.

Audrey didn't rush off. She whispered sexily, 'Don't be long, darling, your oysters'll lose their effect if they're kept on the ice too long!'

Harry Smythe winced and swirled his spoon nervously around his dish of oranges in brandy; he gave a stiff embarrassed smile to Gerrard, and a longer, more interested look at Audrey Gilling. She didn't return his inspection. He went back to his pudding and looked as though he'd rather be somewhere else.

Gerrard rested his arm against the wall of the alcove and looked down into a pair of misty, hazel eyes.

'Is this the only restaurant in London?'

Melanie knew what he was getting at. 'I've no idea,' she said coolly, 'but whatever it is you're thinking, we were here first.'

Gerrard stared into Melanie's unamused eyes for a second or two, then straightened up and turned to go. 'My friends are waiting,' he said.

'No they're not. They're tucking into a bottle of champagne. They obviously know the sort you like – or at least one of them does.' Melanie looked across the room at Audrey's table. 'And I think I can see your oysters coming, you'd better go.' She turned her attention from Audrey back to Gerrard and smiled innocently into his eyes. 'But before you go, do you want to tell me where you're staying tonight – just in case?' She emphasised the where, she had a fair idea with whom. 'I don't suppose you're going to still be at the Crinton?'

Gerrard glanced briefly at Harry Smythe before answering.

'No,' he said sharply, 'I shan't be at the Crinton, I've moved from there.'

Melanie's eyes went back to Audrey. 'I see,' she said softly. 'Where are you staying then?'

Harry Smythe spooned up the last of his burnt brandy and sat back in his chair. He smiled sympathetically at Melanie as he touched his lips with his napkin, but avoided looking at Gerrard. He couldn't believe it was going to be this easy.

It wasn't.

'I don't know where I shall be staying,' Gerrard told her. His tone signified the end of that line of enquiry and his expression warned her not to ask the next question that was itching spitefully in her throat. She swallowed and resisted the temptation to look across the room again. Gerrard rested his hand on her shoulder. 'I'll phone you.'

'I might not be there,' she said with a touch of childlike petulance.

'Yes you will. And don't forget what we talked about at lunch.'

'Have you got my telephone number?'

Gerrard smiled apologetically at Harry Smythe, then shook his head. 'Write it on this.' He tore the lid off the top of his cigarette packet and put it down beside her plate.

She wrote on it and gave it back with a tight little smile. 'I've put the address on as well in case there's no reply!'

'Make sure there is.'

Harry Smythe didn't laugh.

Gerrard slipped the piece of card into the small leather wallet and replaced it in his jacket pocket. 'Good-night, Melanie,' he said, and winked at Harry Smythe. 'I hope I haven't ruined your evening for you, but if her mood doesn't improve try sprinkling her with talcum powder.'

'Pardon?'

Melanie smiled sweetly. 'Good-night, Michel.'

CHAPTER 15

Harry Smythe eased the pillow up behind him so that it rested against his neck. He pulled his tie loose, undid the top button of his shirt and slipped his shoes off, pushing them lightly with his stockinged toes so that they slid untidily off the edge of the bed; then he lit another cigarette and removed the receiver from his ear.

The ringing tone continued, as it had done for the past two minutes, hollow and monotonous; he could hear it ringing when he held it at arm's length. He stared at it blankly, bored with the regularity of its music, and finally replaced it on its rest. He wiped the sweat from his ear with the corner of the pillow and gazed at the ceiling. He could still hear the ringing tone from memory. He finished his cigarette then dialled another number. It answered immediately.

'I can't raise Murray,' he said into the mouthpiece. 'I tried him twice this afternoon and again just now. Nothing at all. Dead.'

A voice laughed. 'Murray or the phone?'

'What?'

'Dead.'

'I don't find that funny.'

'Too bad . . . OK – he's gone to see his old granny: oh, two, three, two.'

'Belfast?'

'Bull's-eye.'

Harry Smythe replaced the receiver, lit another cigarette, then dialled the Belfast code.

The bell on the telephone beside the bed clicked before ringing. It was enough to wake Murray. His hand shot out from under the light cotton sheet and lifted the receiver before the clapper touched the bell. Murray slept like a chicken in a snake pit – he was awake and alert before the receiver touched his ear.

'Did I wake you, Murray?' asked Harry Smythe.

'No, Smithy, I was sitting on the edge of the bed on the off-chance you'd call. What d'you want? Just a minute – your end clean?'

'Yes. Listen, I met your Frenchman twice today – once at the girl's house and later at a watering hole in Hampstead. He's been down south with her. He brought her back this morning.'

'Has he moved in with her?'

'No.'

'Did you go with him to get his new address?'

'You told me to stick with the girl.'

'That was so we could get a lead on him, you silly bugger. Didn't you follow him home?'

'I took the girl back to Highgate. Perhaps I should have left her sitting on the kerb outside the restaurant while I rushed after your bogey man?'

'Slow down, Smithy,' warned Murray, 'I'm not in too good a mood either. Was the Frog eating alone?'

'No, he was with a big black chap the size of Battersea Power Station. He looked as though he knew what it was all about.'

'Was he a Brit black or one of theirs?'

'Theirs?'

'French, American, Eskimo.'

'He was a local boy.'

'Tradesman?'

'Hard to say. Could be.'

'OK, anybody else?'

'Two birds. One belonged to the black, she looked half and half; the other was a snake – lovely face, nicely put together, upmarket page three stuff.' Harry Smythe blew a smoke ring towards the ceiling. 'She seemed a bit more than friendly with Gerrard. I'd say this wasn't the first time they'd held hands under a restaurant table.'

'French?'

'No, English. He called her Audrey.'

'What'd she call him?'

'*Chéri.*'

'Is he screwing her?'

'How the bloody hell would I know? What's that got to do with it?'

'Everything. Get your snow-boots on again, Smithy, and go and find that little snake.'

'Why?'

'Because that's where our Frog'll be – warming one side of her bed until he starts polishing his bullets. He'll have moved in. They don't like crowds, these fancy trigger-men; but what they do like is a good regular poke, it's supposed to keep their eye in.'

'Very interesting! Good-night, Murray.'

'I haven't finished yet. You've increased our chances of picking up the Frog from just one girl, to one girl plus a black built like a brick shit-house with a coffee-coloured girl-friend, and a fancy Harrods rattler who's arching her back the French way. A gang like that shouldn't be too difficult for you to run down. Any one of them'll do, Smithy. Start casting around, I want something to chew on by the time I get back.'

'When are you coming back, Murray?'

'Tuesday, p.m. flight. Ring me. OK?'

'OK, Murray. Good-night.'

'Just a minute, Smudge.'

'Yes?'

'The Lambdon girl. Are you sure the Frog didn't tell her where he's staying?'

'Quite sure. She asked him in the restaurant. He wouldn't say. After watching him throw down a few oysters on the other side of the room she decided she wanted to go home, so I took her there and whistled back as soon as I could to the restaurant.'

'And the revellers had all skipped off to their respective pits by the time you got there?'

'That's right.'

'D'you think the Frenchman's been screwing the Lambdon girl?'

'You've got screwing on the brain, Murray.'

'Well, is he?'

'I don't know. I doubt it. I don't think she's the sort of girl who screws.'

'I knew there had to be one somewhere! What's the matter with her? She's not a tennis player, is she?'

'What does that mean?'

'Copies the boys – a dike . . . Lesbian.'

'I'm not prepared to discuss it.'

'OK, Smithy. But before you go dewy-eyed over this bit of crumpet take advice from your leader.'

'Good-night, Murray.'

CHAPTER 16

Audrey Gilling lay on her back and gazed at the ceiling.

The only light in the room, a pale moonlight, came through the large uncurtained Georgian window. It cast no shadows, but shimmered over her damp body like a ghostly hand, painting in the contours and highlighting the hard tips of her breasts before moving shyly across to outline the other person in the bed.

She turned her head and studied Gerrard's profile, etched like a chiaroscuro painting against the light wall. His eyes were closed tight, she could see that, and his chest rose and fell but she knew he wasn't sleeping. She gave a little shiver, but it didn't disturb the hand that rested lightly on her stomach, quiet and as still as a mamba, a sensor that told her she wasn't going anywhere without his knowing about it. But she wasn't complaining. She enjoyed the sensation. Perhaps it was time to talk . . .?

She raised herself on to her elbow and felt his hand slip downwards until it stopped, cushioned in the soft warmth between her legs. She squeezed her thighs together trapping his hand, and, with a shallow hiss of pleasure, felt his fingers slide into her. She gave a little moan to tell him she liked it and reached out and smoothed her hand on his chest with a gentle circular movement.

'How long are you staying in England, Michel?' she whispered.

Gerrard's eyelids moved fractionally. He could see the outline of her head silhouetted against the white ceiling but the details of her face were blanked out by the shadow of her hair. But details weren't necessary – he knew what sort of expression she'd be wearing – Audrey's probing technique had all the finesse of a jealous wife – give him the works, offer him more, and then slip it in between the groans! They all had it – that childlike over-estimation of the persuasive powers of their loins – poor Audrey no less than others; the gifted amateur, the girl in a man's world who liked this part of the job far too much ever to make a living at it.

'Go to sleep.'

But Audrey wasn't tired. 'Who was the girl in the restaurant?'

'Daughter of a friend of mine.' He was on the edge of sleep.

'Pretty girl, interesting face. She looked familiar. What's her name?'

'Melanie.'

'Melanie what?'

'Lambdon.'

Audrey stiffened. 'Anything to do with Fred Lambdon?'

It was said in little more than a whisper. But it was enough. Gerrard was wide awake. He didn't move. His eyes stayed closed and there was no change in his breathing; it remained that of a man almost asleep.

'You know Fred Lambdon?' he murmured.

Her voice was muffled by the position of her head and he had to strain to hear her reply.

'Yes – but I never knew him to take time off to make daughters.'

'Where do you know him from?'

'He was my mentor – he taught me how to walk on water and tell lies. The last I heard of him he was playing snakes and ladders with the IRA. But it's all out of character – Fred Lambdon wasn't like that.'

'Neither was Philby.'

'That's a point.'

'What does your boss think about it?'

'Not a lot. He'd have had him castrated before putting him out on the street. Reckons Freddie Lambdon's as bent as a paper clip, won't have a nice word said about him. Funny, Fred being a friend of yours. Where is he now? I haven't seen him for ages, have you?'

'No. Who are these people you said he's supposed to have made friends with?'

'Provisionals.'

'I thought you said someone else?'

'I didn't actually.' Audrey wasn't suspicious; after all, the sheets, if no longer crisp, were at least clean and Gerrard was the one underneath. She stared at his closed eyes. 'But there are others. I heard he was talking to Americans as well as the Irish. Irish from the South that is. Not run of the mill, something new and different – if you can accept that of the Irish. I have heard a whisper that they've got Russian help – which puts two pins in Freddie's effigy.' She lay still, listening and waiting for a reaction. Nothing happened.

'You asleep, Michel?' she breathed.

Gerrard grunted – the tired groan of a man already half-way to oblivion. Audrey wrapped herself tighter round his body and, gripping his thigh between her legs, she squeezed gently, and whispered, 'But what about her, Siegfried, what about the virginal-looking Melanie Lambdon – are you going to show her the facts of life too?'

Gerrard's groin twitched in spite of himself, but he lay still and awake until Audrey stopped talking to herself and loosened her grip and drifted into a deep sleep.

He timed his breathing with that of hers, but he knew sleep wasn't going to come that easy – he shouldn't have stopped to listen.

Audrey was only going through the motions; an exercise to show that if her heart wasn't in the right place her mind, at least, was making an effort. There hadn't been enough knife behind her probing to suggest a serious examination, but then it was like everything else she had done so far – she'd given more than she got! So, who are the curious ones – apart from Reason's Irish friend Murray? A good question . . .

Gerrard opened his eyes and stared up at the ceiling. *Murray wouldn't bother sending a girl like Audrey to do men's work, he'd want to do the asking himself – and, by the sound of it, with the help of the thick end of a silenced Browning.* He looked out of the corner of his eye at Audrey, naked, and curled up like a baby python. He didn't smile. *So who sent you to join the party, Audrey?*

He gave her another long look and went back to the ceiling. *It was Reason who brought her to the restaurant . . . Reason? Don't even think about it, Gerrard! Leave it at coincidence – there's enough of it about! What about Audrey's Colonel Harris?* Audrey's *Colonel Harris? General Sanderson's Colonel Harris! He's bobbing around in the act like a used French letter – and nobody wants him to know anything – so he has to do it for himself, poor lonely bugger! But lonely or not he'd want to know what French gunmen were doing in his garden, so, get your knickers on, Audrey and go to work. But the poor sod wasn't getting much value for his money out of his star turn – well done, Audrey!*

It was going to be a long time till dawn. Gerrard closed his eyes again, and, as if she'd been listening to his mind, Audrey stirred, and from the depths of her dream came a sensual whisper and an indecipherable demand. Gerrard listened and tried to make out who was taking her past the winning post this time, but she wasn't telling and her excitement subsided into a little choking snort. The jockey must have fallen off. Gerrard took pity on her.

She moaned softly as he turned her on to her back. When she

realised it wasn't a dream she opened her eyes and smiled sleepily. 'It's times like this,' she murmured jerkily under his weight, 'when I wonder why I don't consider taking it up as a full-time job.'

Audrey moved in the early hours before dawn.

She was almost clear when the disturbance half-awoke Gerrard. He opened his eyes, closed them again and moved like a crab to envelop her. She relaxed and accepted him sleepily, moving her body just sufficiently to show interest, then carefully slipped from under him when he went back to sleep. She lay beside him, listening to his regular breathing, and when she was satisfied it was genuine slipped off the edge of the bed and crept across the thick carpet to the bathroom. On the way she removed the small wallet from Gerrard's coat pocket.

She locked the bathroom door, switched on the small vanity light above the mirror and sat on the closed lid of the lavatory. She opened the wallet, removed the slip of card she had seen the girl hand to Gerrard in the restaurant and studied it briefly, without expression. She then copied what was written on it, replaced the slip exactly as she had found it and closed the wallet.

It didn't look the same.

She opened it again. Another scrap of paper had slipped from behind one of the credit cards and curled over. She removed it, held it to the light, and read: BROCKLEBANK *8597514*. She studied this for several seconds, turned it over, then abruptly replaced it in the wallet behind the credit card. She made no note of the inscription.

Gerrard was still sleeping soundly when she crawled back into bed and snuggled up against him. She lay silently and unmoving for several minutes, listening to the dawn, then reached down and modestly pulled the sheet up over their naked bodies. She went back to sleep almost immediately.

'I had no idea it was going to be him. I nearly peed myself when I walked into the restaurant and saw it was Gerrard!' Audrey Gilling crushed her cigarette into the saucer of the coffee cup and wrinkled her nose at her reflection in the dressing-table mirror.

The voice at the other end of the telephone jarred against her ear. 'Where is Gerrard now?'

'I don't know. He left a few minutes ago. I rang you as soon as it was safe.'

'Did he ring anybody before he left?'

'No, just upped and went. Said he'd see me later.'

'He didn't get in touch with Reason?'

'No.'

'OK. So Reason rang you last night and said he was looking for a pillow for a friend of his? Just that, nothing else?'

'He didn't put it quite as crudely as that. He said this friend was passing through London and didn't want to make a song and dance about it; he was looking for somewhere quiet and out of sight for a day or two. I was expecting somebody big and black – somebody a bit like Reason.'

'Didn't he say he was French?'

'I think he did. But I was rather expecting some black chum of Reason's. But what does it all mean? What's going on, Geoffrey? Do I start worrying now or wait until Gerrard's using me as a chest expander?'

The voice became matter of fact, unemotional. 'If Reason's tagging around with Gerrard there's a fair possibility they're in business together. If that's so there's a great deal of trouble about to break over my head. Reason spells shit, Audrey – if *he's* moved in there's a whole load of the stuff about to hit the fan.'

'Geoffrey . . . ?'

'Just a minute. You've seen them close up – did you get the impression they were working together?'

Audrey hesitated only long enough to light another cigarette. 'Quite the opposite. Without any prompting from me Gerrard said he didn't want Reason to know anything about his business or the fact that he goes around hiring himself out in the name of Siegfried. He said that part of him was pink file as far as Reason was concerned.'

'Why wasn't it pink file as far as you were concerned?'

'Because I told him I already knew all about him.'

'You did *what?*'

'I told him only what you told me, Geoffrey. And please don't shout at me, I've had a gruelling night and I'm feeling delicate. And I've got a headache.'

'That should come in useful tonight, then.'

'I don't think Gerrard subscribes to those rules! As I said, I only told him that I knew he was Siegfried and that he pulled triggers for a living. It made us buddies, and stopped him breaking my leg.'

'Did he say how he came to be skipping through the park with a hard nut like Reason?'

'No, but Reason told me they'd met in Rhodesia during the Mugabe quarrel and Clive owed him favours for something the Frenchman had done for him out there. He didn't say what it was. Neither did he give me the impression they were lifelong buddies; just that he was an acquaintance – somebody he owed a favour to.'

'It sounds almost convincing – like a rehearsed cover story.'

'How could it be, Geoffrey? Gerrard didn't know it was me until I sat on his lap, I'm quite convinced of that. You're going to have to accept it, Geoffrey, the situation's kosher.'

'I don't trust kosher situations, Audrey. I don't like friendships between top French trigger-men and people like Reason. If there's the slightest hint that that big black bastard's more than just friends with Gerrard then we close up shop and get out.'

Audrey whistled smoke through her lips and raised her eyebrows at herself in the mirror. 'Aren't you overestimating Reason? He's only a big black boy; he's just run of the mill, not some sort of super-bogey.'

'And that would be another mistake of yours.'

'What would?'

'Taking that bugger lightly. He's like a bloody iceberg is Reason – you watch your step with him. If he's had a sniff at what's going on and has sidled up to Gerrard it means that Sanderson's involved somewhere.'

'How d'you work that out?'

'Reason and the old man are like shit and a blanket. If Sanderson's smelt something in the undergrowth it's Reason he'll put in to winkle it out. Are you following me?'

'Not altogether.'

'If Gerrard and Reason are not working together then Reason could be doing a sniffing job on Gerrard. If he is, it means that Sanderson's on to Gerrard; and if Sanderson's on to Gerrard it won't take him that much longer to swivel his gunsight round to me!'

'So, what do you want me to do now?'

'Stick with the Frenchman. The important day is Tuesday. After that there really shouldn't be too much of a problem but, between then and now, and particularly on that day, I want you to keep as tight a string as you can on him. On Tuesday I want to know exactly what he does from the minute he opens his eyes to when he goes out of your front door. Once the door's shut you can relax. He'll have a team breathing down his neck so closely that he'll need a scarf to keep the cold out. All you have to do is watch him out of sight then pick the phone up and tell me that the show's on the road. In any case give me a call tomorrow.'

'Of course.' Audrey was about to replace the receiver but hesitated, then said quickly, 'Just a minute, Gerrard's got your name, you know.'

There was no immediate reaction.

'Hallo? Are you still there, Geoffrey?' she asked.

'Yes. What d'you mean, he's got my name?'

'He's got a piece of paper in his wallet with Brocklebank and a seven-digit number scrawled all over it.'

'Where did he get it?'

'Christ knows! Maybe Lambdon gave it to him.'

'Lambdon's not in far enough to have my name. Did Gerrard have this bit of paper the last time you played games with him?'

'I don't know. I didn't go through his pockets then. I didn't get the chance. Maybe Lambdon's daughter gave it to him.'

'What makes you think that?'

'She turned up at the restaurant last night and wrote things down for Gerrard. I wanted to know what it was and while I was looking I turned up this other slip, the one with you all over it. I suppose it's possible she gave him both at the same time, but I somehow doubt it. I watched from a distance and only saw the one exchange. It could have been two bits of paper. Christ knows why you would come into her act, though.'

'It's a funny old game! Do you know anything about somebody putting Lambdon's wife away the other night?'

'What do you mean by putting her away?'

'What it usually means – somebody killed her.'

'Oh my God – how awful! No, I hadn't heard. Why would anybody want to do that? What's Freddie doing about it?'

'That's another thing. He's vanished.'

'Vanished?'

'Sunk without trace. Another bloody thing for me to worry about with this sodding Irish business. Our people would have been better advised to have thrown their coins at a bunch of circus chimps – the profit would have been more predictable. Do you know where the Lambdon girl is at the moment?'

'She's here in London. I've got her address.'

'Good. Look after it, it might come in useful if Gerrard starts getting uppity. He wouldn't want the girl stepping on the ice, would he?'

'I don't know. He hasn't opened his heart to me about it.'

'Goodbye, Audrey.' Brocklebank had lost patience.

Audrey dropped the receiver on to its cradle and for several seconds stared at herself in the mirrror. She didn't seem too happy about what she was seeing. She pulled a face and blew a mouthful of cigarette smoke at her reflection, then swore. It was a very unladylike word she used. With that off her chest she stubbed out her cigarette, picked up the towel from the floor and, wearing only a smile, wandered into the bathroom.

CHAPTER 17

Reason put a pint glass in front of Gerrard and sat down beside him. He took a second swig from his own tankard, wiped his lips with the back of his hand, and said, 'OK, what did the man have to say?'

Gerrard looked around the pub. The only other white face was the barman's. It was Reason's local, not his favourite, but it was safe – safe until a black came in with an Irish accent and a face that nobody knew.

Gerrard tasted the beer. It wasn't as good as the Fusilier's. He put the glass on the table and lit a cigarette.

'He showed me an "eyes only" memo. Half a dozen designates; no extras. It detailed security arrrangements right down to the number of rounds being issued, the colour of the men's shirts and the pattern of their ties. It was beautifully drawn up . . .?'

'But?'

'But there's a distance gap.'

'What's a distance gap?'

'No long-range protection. They've got a police helicopter with a marksman on board but they've pulled his teeth; it's been ordered to stay out of the immediate vicinity. The order says: be up there, be unobtrusive, and don't make any noise unless we invite you over to join in.'

Gerrard drank again from his glass and pulled a face. It wasn't the taste of the beer that disturbed him. 'Your people ask for trouble, Reason.'

Reason sipped his beer quietly. 'What else?'

'Beaune has got his own people – US Secret Service, best in the world at this sort of thing – but your people won't let them perform the way they would like to. I wonder if our friend Brocklebank has anything to do with that.'

Reason raised his eyebrows but made no comment.

Gerrard went on, 'Beyond Beaune's immediate screen is British territory and, as in your wars, they're relying on luck to keep the man out of harm. I feel sorry for the American Secret Service, they must be pissing blood every time they think about it. OK, so the target's covered for close-up, but all the inner ring's got is a police launch cruising up the middle of the Thames. That's his escort, by the way, he's coming by water. That's the security trump. Only a handful know that. Everybody else thinks it's down the road in an escorted Rolls – everybody, that is, except the chosen few – the IRA, the INLA, and the hired rifle. And now you.'

Reason sipped his beer again, noisily, but still said nothing.

'From the other side of the river,' continued Gerrard, 'there's a clear stretch of open ground – open uncluttered water, no obstructions – ideal conditions for the man with the gun.'

Reason put his beer down. 'What about the police launch; wouldn't that get in the way?'

'No, because it would be a high-up shot, a pop from five to six hundred metres – two pops if you like, and all the time in the world to tidy up and go home. There's no immediate flak at that distance, all the bother happens round the target. It takes a few minutes for their hands to stop shaking and then they grab everybody in sight with warts, a red tie and a beard, or a harelip, and generally make an ants' nest of themselves. Then somebody says, "Hey, it's gone right through him!" and somebody else'll throw himself across the corpse and bellow, "High velocity – long shot!" and then they'll pick themselves up and look across the water – by which time the shooter's out on the street looking like the rest of the world.'

'You sound as though you've been through all this before,' said Reason. 'D'you want to go and have a look over there to see if your theory will work on the ground?'

'I already have – and it does. Malseed met me in his car. He handed me a couple of sheets of type and said everything you want's in there. It was! I asked him to show me the other side of the water – just to keep the conversation going – and off we went. I could make that contract without raising a sweat. It'd be a shame to take their money.'

Reason's face showed no expression other than mild interest. 'Did he let you keep those flimsies he showed you?'

Gerrard shook his head. 'He kept his fingers on the corners all the time I was studying them. When I said I'd seen enough he snatched them away, tucked them into an envelope and slipped them into his inside jacket pocket. He'd been warned. Whoever gave them to him told him how to handle them. By now they've either been shredded or burned and the ashes disposed of.'

Reason scratched his nose. 'Did you tell him the hit would be a doddle?'

'No. But I did tell him I'd do it at long range, hence our trip over the bridge. I had to tell him something to keep his interest warm, and don't forget, it'll be his invitation that puts me under the same roof with your mole.'

'And did you?'

'Did I what?'

'Make Malseed happy enough to invite you to the party?'

'He's very happy. It's all arranged.' Gerrard lit a cigarette and trickled smoke slowly down his nostrils.

'The shoot's down for Tuesday. I get to meet my employers tomorrow.'

'That's unfortunate.'

'Why?'

'You've just talked yourself out of that other beer. Unless . . .' Reason smiled sheepishly, 'unless your friend told you where the meeting was taking place.'

Gerrard shook his head.

'No. It's all being done properly. The professionals take over from here. Malseed and the others'll be shoved into the background now until the hard men decide it's safe for them to crawl out and start talking.'

'What's the form then?'

'I call a number at half-past ten tomorrow morning. It'll be a public phone box. I'll be told to go somewhere and wait; there I'll be picked up. There'll be somebody watching that box and he'll stay with me until I'm handed over. I'll be given the runaround – to shake a friendly tail, then dropped somewhere under guard probably with an Irish .45 jammed behind my ear until they declare the pick-up safe.'

Reason stopped grinning. 'I'm glad Sanderson didn't ask me to do this one.' He sounded quite sincere.

Gerrard ignored the remark. He flicked his lighter under Reason's cigarette and went on, 'There'll be a hard man conducting the tour and I'll expect to be taken apart at least three times before we get where we're going. They'll be very touchy about anything out of the ordinary and I don't think they'll take too kindly to a greaseproof packet under my arm.'

Reason stood up and finished the last inch of beer in his glass. He said to Gerrard, 'At least you've got something to talk to them about. It should hold them spellbound while you rub your flint and whatnot over

156

the fuse. I only hope the bastards don't do away with you after they've heard your story and pinch your idea and put one of their own in for the kill.'

'Thanks,' said Gerrard. 'That's quite comforting.'

'Don't mention it,' grinned Reason. 'But let's get a move on and go and see Archibald Williams.'

'The bombmaker?'

'S'rite.'

Archie Williams greeted Clive Reason like a long-lost brother.

Reason responded in kind. 'Archie Williams is the best explosive-gadget maker in the world,' he told Gerrard. 'He once made an explosive device out of a communion wafer and blew the tongue off a man who said unkind things about Margaret Thatcher's handbag!' He cleared a space on the corner of an old utility dining-table and gingerly lowered one buttock on to it. 'So you can tell him your problem, Michel. Be frank with him.'

Gerrard looked into a pair of shrewd brown eyes and said, 'It's a bit more than tongues, Mr Williams.'

'Call me Archie.' The Welshman smiled encouragingly.

'OK, Archie, I want something that will kill up to a dozen people in a room and allow me to walk out without a scratch.'

Williams's eyes smiled. He held his hand up. 'Let me take it from there, Michel. You won't, of course, be allowed to carry anything like a bag or a rolled-up newspaper into this room with you.'

Gerrard shook his head.

Williams nodded understandingly. 'Right. Empty your pockets.' He swept everything off the end of the table with his arm. 'And shove everything on there.'

Gerrard did as he was told.

Williams stood, arms folded, deep in thought, staring at the contents of Gerrard's pockets for several minutes. Eventually, without change of expression, he picked up the silver Dupont lighter and held it at arm's length. He turned it slowly, this way and that, studying every angle like a diamond buyer examining the facets of a newly cut gem until, after a full minute's inspection, he shook his head and dropped it back on the table.

'Too small . . . much too small. Superficial, an arm and leg job.' He looked up at Gerrard. 'That won't do you, will it?'

Gerrard shook his head again.

But Williams was already back amongst Gerrard's belongings. 'What about this?' He picked up the blue packet of Gitanes. He weighed it in his hand and looked hard at the outside before opening the flap and staring at the two rows of cigarettes inside. After a moment he raised his head, smiled at each of the two men in turn, and whispered, like a conspirator, 'Cigarettes. A packet of cigarettes.'

'Help yourself,' Gerrard told him. 'Everybody else over here does.'

But Williams wasn't listening. He emptied the cigarettes on to the table and peered at the emptiness inside the container. He measured it and scribbled a series of calculations on a scrap of paper, then, after another long look at the empty packet, placed it carefully back on the table and studied it from a distance. He glanced up again, first at Reason, then Gerrard, and allowed them to see the glint of satisfaction in his dark eyes. He pointed a finger dramatically at the blue packet.

'There's our bomb,' he said.

Gerrard and Reason exchanged glances. Then Gerrard pulled a face. 'Sorry, Archie, if you packed that with Semtex it'd make it as heavy as a gold brick – and it still wouldn't throw enough weight about for my purpose. And what happens if they open it?'

'One thing at a time, my friend.' Archie wasn't put out. 'Let's leave the questions till the end.'

Gerrard frowned. Reason said, 'They sound to me like the sort of questions that ought to come at the beginning, Archie.'

Williams smiled amiably. 'Let's go outside and smoke one of these cigarettes and I'll tell you what I have in mind.' He picked up three of the cigarettes and led the two men through a small back door and into a quiet cul-de-sac on the other side of his railway arch workshop.

He sat on the back garden wall of a derelict terrace house and pulled heavily on the French cigarette. After he'd stopped coughing he said, 'D'you always smoke these, Michel?'

Gerrard nodded.

'Good. So whoever searches you might have seen you smoking them before?' He didn't wait for an answer. 'They're sufficiently unusual – have a different smell too – for him not to be surprised to see a packet of . . . what d'you call them?'

'Gitanes. But I don't think that's likely,' said Gerrard. 'I doubt whether any of the messenger boys will have come into contact with me before. But I'm not worried about that, a packet of cigarettes never excites curiosity; the problem arrives, as I said before, when the sweep weighs it and decides to take a look inside the packet.'

'I've taken all that into consideration,' replied Williams. He inhaled and coughed again. 'I can cut them up and stick the ends back into place so that it'll look just like an ordinary packet of twenty cigarettes. I'll put cellophane around it so that it looks brand new and I can allow for a couple of whole ones for you to smoke. Do it in front of your man; strip the cellophane, take one out and when you light it it'll be a green signal flashing at him. He won't give it another thought.'

Gerrard looked stonily at the Welshman.

Williams emptied his nose of smoke and sniffed the quiet Sunday air.

'You're still worried about the weight?' He didn't give Gerrard time to reply. 'OK, then let's talk about the weight.'

'Let's!' said Reason. 'I'm interested too.'

Williams frowned at the interruption and addressed his remarks to Gerrard. 'What I have in mind is trinitrobenzene-fol.' He hurried on despite Gerrard's sceptical expression. 'I can squeeze into this empty packet about two ounces — maybe a spoonful more, but it should be enough either way. Let's say two ounces to be on the safe side.'

'Gerrard said he wants to kill these guys, Archie, not give them a bloody headache!' Reason didn't look happy either.

Williams took on the air of a patient professor. 'This mixture's not run-of-the-mill, Clive. Trinitrobenzene is, but the addition of "f.o.l." gives us a different character altogether — one gives us the bang, the other points it in the right direction. Instead of everything going all over the bloody place this combination condenses the force of the explosion so that it bursts outwards like a catherine wheel.' He ran his hand in a sawing motion just below his breastbone. 'That's where you want it — chest high. No point in having everybody thrown two hundred feet in the air when you can cut them in half on the deck.'

Reason stared at him blankly. Gerrard looked a bit more interested.

'In the form I'm going to put it in, it'll cut through anybody, and anything, within a fifteen-yard radius. It'll fringe off at about twenty yards, but anybody on the same level, and within eight to ten yards of the point of detonation, will end up in a bucket . . . Imagine it — a group of people in a room; a whirling, red-hot, four-foot-thick, circular saw going off in the middle of the table. It'll mince everything in sight!'

Gerrard made a dismissive gesture with his hands. 'How does the man carrying this packet duck out of the way of that lot?'

'It's all been taken care of,' replied Williams. 'I'm giving you fifty seconds to get out of range; and I'm giving you the wherewithal to make your exit feasible.'

'A bullet in the back of the head's the only wherewithal he's likely to get if he tries to walk out in the middle of a meeting with these people.' Reason was impatient. Williams wasn't going fast enough for him.

Archie Williams inclined his head towards the railway arch. 'I've got a lovely drop of stuff in there that'll make Michel look as sick as Auntie Ethel's parrot. Its effect is instantaneous. One little drop and you'll look like a dug-up Chinaman. But don't worry, it'll be only skin deep; inside you'll be as right as rain.' He stared at the dubious Frenchman. 'Take my word for it.'

'How do I explain this sudden loss of form?' asked Gerrard.

'You can say it's a touch of tropical clap, comes on sudden-like; malaria – anything exotic – and you make a gallop for the lavatory. Nobody'll have the heart to stop you when they see the state you're in. I'll make up a dose into a soft capsule and you can stick it to the back of your teeth. One chew and there you go. Happy?'

Gerrard shook his head. 'Far from it, Archie.' He spoke slowly. 'The place'll be guarded back and front and up and down. Clive's right, they're not going to let anybody out for walkies, not once the port's started moving round the table and they're loosening their buttons for the dirty jokes – not even for somebody who looks like a mortuary case.' Gerrard shook his head again and pulled a face. 'I'm afraid that's a no-go, Archie. They'd probably tell me to stick my head out of the window and take deep breaths. That's as near as they'll let anybody get to the street.'

'Or they might throw him out on his head,' suggested Reason with a grin, 'provided it's high enough off the ground to guarantee he doesn't get up and walk away.'

Williams smiled benignly at Gerrard. 'I wasn't working on their sending you out into the street to recover your health. I've got you out of the room looking as sick as a dog. Let's take it from there. I told you the action of this bomb resembled a catherine wheel. Well, think on those lines. Allow another three feet up or down and all you'll get is a gentle warm massage as it passes over you – or tingling toes if you're standing above it! Get it?' He leaned forward and looked directly at Gerrard. 'No need to leave the house. Get out of the room and get yourself six feet below the point of detonation – I'd prefer below rather than above,' he paused, and frowned at a hastily projected mental picture, 'and let's say ten feet to exclude any minor infraction – and behind something solid. Do all that, and you should be able to weather the bang.'

'Should?' Gerrard still looked sceptical.

'We're always striving for perfection,' Williams told him lightly.

As soon as the door closed behind Gerrard on Monday morning Audrey dropped her air of languid over-indulgence and leapt out of bed to the window to watch until he turned the corner at the end of the road. Once he was out of sight she sat on the edge of the bed, pressed the seven buttons on the telephone set and waited. She looked nervously at the small carriage clock on the mantelpiece, and then at the watch on her wrist as if doubting the staying power of the older timepiece – both made heavy going of the next minute. Then the ringing in her ear stopped.

'He left five minutes ago.' The high-pitched, almost hysterical tone of her voice surprised her. She swallowed to clear the dryness from her throat and tried again. 'He went towards Belsize Park.' This time the wobble in her voice was hardly noticeable.

'Doesn't matter where he went,' said the voice in her ear, 'just so long as he went. Thanks, Audrey, you can go back to bed now – you probably need a good night's sleep!'

'I've lost the funny part of this story, Geoffrey,' said Audrey, drily. 'Aren't you supposed to be a bit worried about Gerrard being out on the loose?'

'No. And he's not on the loose. He'll have had company when he staggered down the road this morning. They'll stay with him until the Irishmen move in and cart him off to the meeting. But I'm not worried about that part of it. Tell me about yesterday; where did he go – what did he do?'

'I don't know – I don't know!'

'Don't be clever, Audrey.'

'I'm not. I don't know where he went, he didn't invite me along. Do you want to know what I did yesterday?'

'This is bloody silly, Audrey! The whole idea of your playing grown-ups with the Frenchman was so that we'd know what he was up to and who he was seeing. Didn't he say anything to you when he got home?'

'No,' she replied, 'and I didn't ask. And just in case it's escaped your attention, Gerrard doesn't take kindly to people poking questions in his ear. You might care to remember that if you ever find yourself lying next to him in the same gutter.'

'Have you found out anything else about him?'

'Only that he's no Maurice Chevalier. He's a hard bastard and he knows exactly how many beans make five – English and metric. Don't make the mistake of thinking he's a passionate Latin with his cock in his

161

hand and a loose tongue ready to flap the minute the light goes out. I told you that at the Crinton.'

'That's all very descriptive, Audrey, but it wasn't what I meant. Has he said anything about what he's doing over here?'

'Nothing, he's like a bloody clam.'

The phone went silent for a moment, then, 'OK Audrey, don't try pushing him, but stay with him.'

'For how much longer?'

'Two or three days, say four days at the most.'

'And . . .?'

'And if everything goes remotely according to plan your horny Frenchman'll be popping back over the hill and you can have a rest. A couple of days out of bed and you won't know yourself!'

'Very funny,' said Audrey coldly. 'So what's happening in two days?'

'I'll tell you then. Better you don't know now in case he tweaks the wrong thing and you talk in your sleep. For the meantime just keep playing the generous hostess – keep the man happy.'

'Christ, Geoffrey, I'm not sure I can keep up with him that long.'

'Read a few books, maybe there are quicker ways of tiring a man out.'

'OK, Geoffrey, we've done the funny bits, can we cut it out now, or is that it? Can I get back to bed now? I've already told you I'm worn out.'

'Just a minute. What time did he get back yesterday?'

'About four.'

'What did he do then?'

'Don't ask.'

'I didn't mean that. Good God! As well as all night?'

'I've just told you, it's like a bloody honeymoon!'

Brocklebank didn't laugh. 'I meant, did he go out again? Has he been in touch with Reason since Saturday night?'

'I don't think so. He didn't say anything to me about seeing Reason. This morning he was up with the chickens and left ten minutes before I phoned you. He made no calls; just had his bit of toast and jam with two cups of black coffee and off he went.'

'I'm beginning to get feelings about that bloody Frenchman.' Brocklebank's thoughts worked their way on to his tongue. Audrey's nerves prickled.

'If your feelings are that strong why don't you buy him off – or disinvolve him, get someone else to take his place – whatever that is?'

'It's too late for shuffling around, Audrey. It can't be changed now. Everything's on the line. You're quite sure Gerrard didn't ring Reason this morning, or take any other calls?'

'Not from my phone he didn't. It was exactly as I told you; he just upped and went. Didn't even pat my bottom or say cheerio! But, about this meeting today? If you're not a hundred per cent about it can't you give it a miss?'

'Out of the question. Gerrard and I have to do a tap-dance routine – he does the main part and I fill in the gaps. I'm the only one who can tell whether his balls are hanging in the right place.'

'I could help you there.'

'Go back to bed, Audrey! I'm talking grown-up stuff now. Ring me tonight if you can slip Gerrard's leash and I'll tell you all about it.'

'Be careful, Geoffrey.'

Audrey replaced the receiver and went back to bed. She set the alarm to go off in an hour. Before closing her eyes she rucked the pillow up round her ears like a Dutch milkmaid's bonnet; it produced a heavy, cotton-wool-like silence but failed to deaden the rumbling of fear in her stomach. But it held her attention until the alarm went. She hadn't slept a wink.

CHAPTER 18

Gerrard left the telephone box, walked to the far corner of the road and waited.

The taxi drew up as they said it would – maroon, with the front door advertising multi-coloured toothpaste and the 'for hire' sign switched off. The driver wound his window down and stared at him.

'Your name Siegfried?' he asked.

Gerrard nodded.

'What number you just been ringing?'

'3651.'

'Get in.'

As he drew away from the kerb the driver slid the communicating window open to its full extent and turned his head. 'Empty your pockets on to the back seat,' he said. He spoke without taking his eyes off the road. 'Everything out, including shooter if you're wearing one. Are you?'

'No.'

'Blade?'

Gerrard looked stolidly at the unshaven half-face. 'Everything's on the seat,' he told it. 'Do you want to look under my coat?'

'No, mate, not me. But he'll want to, him over there.' The driver pointed with his chin at a solitary figure standing on the far side of an almost deserted roundabout. 'And a lot more besides if I know old Tou –' He bit the name off the end of his tongue guiltily and ventured a quick glance into the back of his taxi. 'But never mind abaht that; he'll 'ave his hands about you the minute he climbs through the door. And while I'm at it, brother, take a word of advice; don't move or touch anything when I stop – he's got a very nervous disposition, he has. Very nervous indeed! Just sit tight and do what he says, nothing more than that, or this bleedin' cab could end up a bleedin' 'earse!'

The cab went round the island once again before cruising up to the waiting man. He didn't wait for it to stop but yanked the door open and slid into the moving vehicle as if he'd been practising the manoeuvre all morning. The driver gave a sharp grunt of approval and shot away from the kerb. His right hand went out, almost into the open window of a nervous old Cortina and then he was back into the thin stream of traffic. He did another tour of the roundabout before catching the eye of his new passenger in the rear mirror. He winked ostentatiously, but kept his mouth closed. There was no answering camaraderie; no smile, no wink back – only a flat, blank, almost non-existent acknowledgement. There was even less for Gerrard.

The new arrival was a man of middle height, anonymous in a light-grey suit and black, slightly scruffy, unpolished shoes; he wore a tie, badly knotted, but his chin was cleanly shaven and his jet black hair, parted down the middle, was stuck in place with sweet-smelling bay rum. He glanced briefly at Gerrard through expressionless, close-set dark eyes then leaned forward and spoke into the driver's ear.

'Anybody with him?' His voice was quiet, as if he didn't want Gerrard to hear. 'Anything behind?'

The driver shook his head without looking round. 'We're clean, Touhey,' he seemed to have lost his earlier inhibition about mentioning names, 'and have been all along.'

'What about him?'

'Same.'

The man called Touhey turned his head and studied the road behind – nothing against the driver, it was instinctive. He watched the traffic for a couple of minutes – about three-quarters of a mile – then turned and had a proper look at Gerrard.

After a second he said, 'Go and sit over there,' and nodded towards one of the bucket seats on the driver's side of the cab, 'and don't move until I tell you to.' His voice was dry and harsh as if he smoked too much and hadn't had a drink for a week – it was the modern Irish accent; it came through unparted lips; conspiratorial. Reason would have pointed his finger to the north-west and said, Londonderry – they all talk like ventriloquists' dummies up there; ventriloquists' dummies with their mouths nailed together.

Gerrard picked up the packet of cigarettes from the seat beside him and moved across the cab.

'Leave that,' growled Touhey, and stared at the packet in Gerrard's hand. 'What is it?'

'Cigarettes,' Gerrard told him. 'French cigarettes – Gitanes,' and wondered whether he hadn't said three words too many.

Touhey's eyes pinched together as he watched Gerrard reach forward and place the packet back on the seat, then, with an abrupt gesture of his hand, said, 'All right, never mind about that. Sit back there and be quiet. And don't light one of those things until I say so.' Touhey knew all about smokers.

The gold Dunhill interested him. He picked it up, weighed it in his hand, then inspected the bottom; it didn't raise his temperature. The rest of Gerrard's possessions he spread out on the seat and merely glanced at them. He curled his lip.

'Is this all you've got in your pockets?'

Gerrard nodded.

Touhey held on to the lighter for another second or two, flicked the lid a couple of times with his thumb, then tossed it to Gerrard and said, 'OK, take your coat off and pass it over here.'

Gerrard did as he was told.

While he was waiting he opened the packet of Gitanes, took a cigarette out and left the open packet balanced on the edge of the other jump seat. Touhey never gave it another glance – he'd already started rummaging through the pockets of Gerrard's jacket.

He was diligent. He ran his hands over the inner lining, then shook the coat like a bullfighter making sure his cape was all there, and finally swung it several times against the cab door. It seemed to satisfy him. He threw it on the seat beside the rest of Gerrard's stuff, and said, 'Take your shoes off, stretch your legs out and put your feet on the seat here.' He tapped the space beside him. There was no impatience in his manner, he seemed to have all the time in the world. It was illusory. He stared at Gerrard's feet for a moment then looked up and spoke to the back of the driver's head. 'How we doing for time?' he asked.

The driver leaned sideways towards the gap in the glass. 'Twenny-five to,' he said out of the corner of his mouth, 'be at the park in another five. OK?' He turned his ear for the reply, listened to the silence for a second then straightened up and surveyed the inside of the cab through his rear mirror. When he was satisfied Touhey was still in control he dropped his eyes and went back to concentrating on the zig-zag route he'd chosen along the dingy, deserted backstreets that kept him away from the main stream of traffic through London's north-east jungle. He knew exactly where he was going.

Touhey came back to Gerrard. He stared into his face for a moment as if looking for something; some clue as to what was going through his mind; but finding nothing dropped his gaze again to Gerrard's legs and feet.

Gerrard balanced himself uncomfortably on the tip-up seat while Touhey ran his hands up and down his legs. Touhey was thorough. He'd done it all before; he knew the hiding places and he wasn't shy. He gave a quick glance out of the side window, then said, 'Kneel down on the floor.' He didn't bother with above the waist – Gerrard's thin linen shirt showed what was underneath and Touhey wasn't interested in it.

When he'd finished he said, 'Put your coat on and sit back there.' He picked up Gerrard's shoes and reached inside them, one after the other. He felt the heels and tapped them with the back of his knuckles then dropped them on the floor by Gerrard's feet. 'Put 'em on,' he whispered, 'and put the rest of this stuff back in your pockets. You can light that fag if you want.' He threw a box of matches on to the seat beside Gerrard. 'Your lighter's had it,' he told him, then narrowed his eyes. 'Smoke,' he said, 'but don't move or turn your head until I tell you to, and when I say out, get out, move quickly and do exactly as I tell you. In the meantime sit quiet and don't say a word.'

He sounded like a boxing referee with last-minute advice to two straining fighters and, to emphasise the warning, looked long and hard into Gerrard's unflinching eyes. Something he saw there troubled him, but he let it pass and moved to the far corner of the cab where he lit a cigarette himself and rested his head on the hard leather seatback. He gripped the cigarette between his teeth and closed his eyes. But Touhey was neither asleep nor relaxed. He was tired, he was mentally and physically tired. He hadn't had a decent night's sleep since August '71, when the Brits in Northern Ireland had finally taken the gloves off and gone bare-knuckle; and he knew he wouldn't until the Brits put him under, or they threw their hand in. And what were the chances of the bastards doing that?

'Vicky Park coming up, Touhey.' The driver's voice broke into his tiredness. 'Where to now?'

Touhey didn't open his eyes. 'Lido, Grove Road. You know Pat Connell?'

'Yeh,' the driver grunted. He didn't look round.

'He'll be sitting in a car outside the Lido. Drive past, make sure it's him, and pull up in front. We'll get out. You follow us in the cab for five minutes then clear off. OK?'

'OK, Touhey.'

*

Gerrard left the taxi and climbed into the back of the car. It was an ordinary car, nothing special; no smoked windows, no curtains – an ordinary, everyday, nondescript IRA staff car. He moved across to the far side and gazed out of the window.

The driver studied him through the rear mirror. His eyes were narrowed against the smoke of the new cigarette he was lighting from the glowing stub of the old one pinched between his forefinger and thumb. Still puffing on the new cigarette he said to Touhey indistinctly, 'Shouldn't we put a bag or som'at over his head?' He flicked the crumpled stub of cigarette through the open window. 'I don't think I fancy this bastard's eyes boring into the back of my head while I'm driving – I don't trust these fuckin' Brits, they give me the willies.'

'Drive the car,' ordered Touhey, settling into the back seat next to Gerrard. He spoke gruffly, without friendship, the executive addressing the part-time driver. Just another Belfast yobbo, he thought; a bone-head from the Clonard brickyard with his newly cleaned fingernails, polished shoes and a tie that didn't fit his face, working hard to get his ticket for a trip down the Falls Road in a pine box under a brand new unused Republican banner to the ever wide-open iron gates of Milltown cemetery. Just like me! Touhey's face remained expressionless. He glanced quickly at Gerrard and envied his composure, then turned his head nervously in all directions as the car pulled away from the kerbside.

'I'd have covered his bloody head, m'self,' the driver persisted. He didn't turn round but looked upwards into the oblong mirror. The two pairs of unsmiling Irish eyes met briefly then flicked away; one pair to the road ahead, the other, sideways and behind.

'I know you would,' agreed Touhey, tiredly, 'and I suppose you think it would be all right driving through the streets of friggin' London with a man sitting in the back of your friggin' car with a friggin' Tesco's shopping bag on his friggin' head? You'd be able to explain that, would you?' Touhey didn't wait for a reply. 'D'you know what you're doing, boy?' Touhey spat drily. 'You're making my friggin' arse ache, so shut up and drive the friggin' car.'

Touhey's cool had slipped a fraction, and he knew it. He avoided the driver's eyes in the mirror and looked hard at Gerrard to see how he was taking it. He learned nothing there, and turned to study the cars grouped around them at a traffic light; it was enough to release the pressure. He lit another cigarette and gazed blankly at the back of the driver's neck.

The driver watched him through the mirror. He was unimpressed. 'You could at least make the bastard lie on the deck,' he said over his shoulder. 'He could be looking at the carpet instead of where we're going.'

Gerrard smiled at an attractive woman driving an open Mercedes 350. She ignored him. Gerrard went back to his thoughts. His companion said, 'Fuck it, Connell! I told you to shut up and drive.'

'It's your neck, Touhey.' The driver spat the ash off his cigarette and moved off in the wake of the Mercedes.

Connell pulled the car up outside a detached two-storey Victorian monstrosity. It stood behind a chest-high red-brick wall and was partly concealed by an untidy cluster of tall shuddering fir trees and a miniature jungle of neglected ornamental bushes. It could have been an East End doctor's surgery or a dogs' hospital. It was neither. It was an empty house.

But there were signs of occupation. The front door was pulled to but not shut, and upstairs on the first floor a curtain parted, flickered nervously, and fell back into place.

Touhey caught the movement. He nodded, almost imperceptibly, and nudged Gerrard in the arm. 'Get out of the car and go up the steps,' he ordered. 'The door'll open when you get to it. Go inside and wait for me.'

After Gerrard had left the car and disappeared into the house, Touhey leaned forward and patted Connell's shoulder. 'Park the car in the street round the back and come in through the garden door. You'll find a Jew-gun and two mags, both full, in the cupboard under the sink in the kitchen. Bring it and take over the front door. And I don't want any bloody arguments or fancy ideas. Got it?'

'Got it, Touhey.'

Touhey opened the car door. 'Good. And on your way round you can tell those two silly bastards skulking in the bushes to take those bloody woolly faces off. Tell 'em they're in London, not fuckin' Armagh – nobody's going to clock 'em down here. And, Connell . . .'

The boy from Clonard refused to bow his head. 'Touhey,' he said with a cocky, know-it-all grin, 'you're beginning to sound just like old Micky McGann! You thinking of getting yourself made up to General or something? You're not puffing your head up so's his hat'll fit you, are you?'

'Never mind what's happening to my fuckin' head,' rasped Touhey. 'Just make sure you understand what I'm bloody telling you. Are you listening?'

The grin didn't falter. 'I'm listening, Touhey. Go on.'

'Tell your two friends outside to get themselves round the back and cover the rear. Tell 'em to keep out of sight, but stay in the garden. I don't want them wandering around inside the house. OK?'

'OK. But what about the front, who's going to look after that?'

'Don't worry about the front, it's none of your business.' Touhey took pity on the boy. 'But if it'll stop you wetting your trousers it's being done from up there.' He jerked his chin at the upper front window. 'And I'll be up there too, keeping my eye on the Frog. Now get on with it.'

'Frog, Touhey? I thought he was a fuckin' Brit.'

'He's a Frog.'

Touhey left the car and bounded up the three steps to the front door. It opened just as he reached it, then closed firmly behind him. Connell stared at the closed door for a second while he shrugged a cigarette from the packet on the seat beside him. Nothing happened. He lit the cigarette and drove away. The house went back to looking like a disused dogs' home.

Inside, Gerrard leaned against the wall with his arms crossed. He looked first at Touhey, then at the man who'd been operating the door; another Irishman, one with jet black hair that started an inch above his eyebrows and pale-blue eyes that refused to stay still long enough to focus on any one object. He'd managed the door with one hand; in the other he held what Touhey had called a Jew-gun – a small, oblong, metal-cased Uzi. The Uzi was pointed at Gerrard's stomach.

'Put your stuff there,' Touhey whispered hoarsely to Gerrard, 'and we'll do it again. Legs apart, hands flat against the wall . . . That's right.'

Touhey's hands ran over Gerrard's body like metal detectors. It was the second time in less than half an hour. Touhey had imagination. He imagined lethals being plucked out of thin air like a magician pulling fags out of people's ears. He'd seen it done. He'd seen men stripped, and taken apart by experts in the Bone and down the Falls; he'd seen them skinned and then opened, and after all that, and before you had time to blink, the bastards had turned round with a service Browning in one hand and a packet of 9-mms in the other. And that wasn't going to happen here. You don't get Micky McGann's place at the table by losing your parcel; and sitting upstairs, nodding their old grey heads like Kremlin yes-men, was a parcel and three-quarters – lose one of them and you might as well go and sit with your back against the wall and blow your own bloody leg off! Touhey set his face to the task – nobody was going to die today; nobody on our side – not while Tadgh Touhey was minding them. He stopped thinking and grunted with satisfaction as he straightened up from Gerrard's ankles; he felt pleased with himself, there was nothing to worry about, it was all clean.

'He might have a gun up his arse,' pronounced Touhey as he eased his shoulders back, 'but that's about the only bloody place he could have one. He sure to God hasn't got one anywhere else!'

'You talking to me?' asked the man at the door. He looked puzzled.

'No, I'm talking to my bloody self.' Touhey wasn't being smart, he hadn't taken his eyes off Gerrard's face. 'OK, Frenchie, that's it. Let's go. Pick up your fags and lighter. The rest stays where it is; you can collect it on your way out.'

Gerrard slipped the Gitanes and slim gold Dunhill into separate pockets and refolded his arms. He spoke for the first time since leaving the taxi, 'Is everybody here then?' He made it sound conversational rather than inquisitive.

It brought no reply from Touhey – only a long hard look that ended with Touhey slipping his hand under his light-weight jacket and producing a slim, long-barrelled automatic. It was fitted with a dull, matt-finished silencer. He fondled it lovingly for a second or two then held it out, flat in his hand, and showed it to Gerrard.

'D'you know what this is?' he asked.

'Luger,' answered Gerrard, '7.65.' Nobody was going to get up and sing after he'd been hit with that. He knew why he was being shown it.

Touhey nodded his head approvingly. 'They said you'd know all about these things. Just as well because it's going to be pointing in your direction all the while you're here – just in case you get some strange Froggy ideas about how to behave upstairs.' Touhey stopped for a second and stared into Gerrard's eyes. He didn't expect Gerrard to say anything. He wasn't disappointed. Gerrard stared back at him and waited for the rest of it. Touhey, the Londonderry Irishman with the stitched-up mouth, was enjoying himself. But it didn't show.

'Hair trigger,' he whispered hoarsely and moved his finger so that Gerrard could inspect it. 'It and me's coming everywhere you go. You wanna leave the room for a piss when we're up there? OK by me, but you piss with this stroking your backbone. You wanna tom-tit? You'll tom-tit with me sitting on your lap and this jammed up one of your nostrils! OK?'

Gerrard said nothing.

'Just so's you know the form.'

The man with the Uzi giggled. He shouldn't have. Touhey wasn't joking.

'Did I say something funny?' Touhey didn't turn his head.

The grin vanished. 'No.'

'Then step back out of the way while I take monsieur upstairs. Stand yourself against the wall over there, and when Connell appears tell him I've changed my mind. Tell him to come up to the landing and do the door up there. OK?'

'OK.'

'But be careful – he'll be coming through the back, from the kitchen. Don't make any mistakes. The front door's yours and my voice's the only voice that's gonna move you. Have you got that?'

'Got it, Touhey.'

'Good. Now, how about you, Frenchie? Have you got it?'

Gerrard said, 'Let's get on with it.'

Touhey stepped back another pace and wrapped his hand round the slim butt of the Luger. It looked very businesslike. Without taking his eyes off Gerrard he waggled it at the narrow staircase. 'Up you go then,' he said. 'Hold the banister rail on both sides so that I can see your hands all the time. And, Frenchie, don't fall – if you do, say your prayers, because the drop you make'll be a bloody sight longer than the bottom of the stairs.' Touhey glanced briefly at the man with the Uzi and relaxed his features – it was nowhere near a smile. 'You can laugh at that if you want to, Wheelie,' he told him.

Wheelie didn't laugh.

Gerrard stopped at the top of the stairs. It was a narrow half-landing. There was a banistered corridor to the right, a door at the far end and half-way down the corridor two more doors, both with glass fanlights.

'Next one up,' Touhey's voice murmured in his ear and Gerrard felt his gut turn over with relief.

In front of him was another short flight of six stairs that emerged into a narrow hall. There were more doors, and on the right a staircase which led up to the top floor. Gerrard stopped and gauged the drop between this level and the small landing below. He made it about eight and a half feet – say three metres at an optimistic outside; and hopefully those two doors with the fanlights were both lavatories, or a bathroom and a lavatory. Either would do according to Archie Williams, but it would be close – Gerrard's face betrayed no emotion – close enough to tingle, if tingle was the word for having your backbone ripped out like a half-eaten

172

kipper. He calculated the distance again. He wished he hadn't. It seemed a lot less.

'Move!'

Touhey's voice was one step closer. He came alongside Gerrard and touched the door nearest them with the knuckles of his left hand. It was opened by Malseed.

The room was big and airy. It must have been quite pleasant in the old days, the curtains drawn against the outside poverty, the fire blazing and the family, full and fat, sitting around listening to the eldest virgin playing the spinet.

She wouldn't have liked the present audience.

In addition to Malseed, who was standing by the open door, there were seven men sitting around the room; hard-faced men – a couple had taken their jackets off and opened the neck of their shirts, but the others hadn't noticed the sticky atmosphere and sat as if waiting to go in for dinner. They were all smoking, some talking, one, sitting by the empty fireplace, stared blank-faced into a large handkerchief that contained the product of a heavy bout of coughing. He didn't look up.

There were no greetings for the newcomers, no introductions – only the odd half-concealed glance of curiosity; but when the door closed behind Gerrard and the Irishman the conversation stopped and the man nearest the window quietly drew the yellow curtains.

Malseed murmured into Gerrard's ear, 'Sit down over there, Gerrard, where we can all see you.' He was pleased and eager and looked as if he were about to fluff up the cushion in the armchair he'd offered Gerrard. Then he turned to Touhey. His manner changed.

'Where are you going to sit, Touhey? I presume you're staying with us?'

'Too bloody right I am,' rasped Touhey, 'and I'll sit next to him if you don't mind.' He slipped the Luger back into its home under his arm and lowered himself on to the wide armrest of Gerrard's chair. He allowed his arm to slide along the back of the chair, but he wasn't relaxed – he looked as carefree as an Indian playing tunes to a basketful of unmusical cobras and his eyes remained steadfastly on the side of Gerrard's head.

'Everything all right out there, Tadghy?' Somebody felt he had to say something. It was an anonymous voice. Nobody turned his head to look at it.

'Cosy,' Touhey told him, 'but I'll feel happier when I've seen this one disappearing into the crowd.'

'Why, what's the matter with him?'

'He's a Frog. I don't fancy him. He worries me.'

'What's he done to worry you, Touhey?'

'Nothing. Just being a Frog's enough. I'm not into Frogs. I know what a Brit'll do when he's playing games, but not these buggers – I don't know how they bounce when they're on the job.'

'He's working for us, Touhey – he's a good 'un.'

'So's a fuckin' Brit – when he's dead!'

'I think we'd better get on.' Malseed brought the meeting to order. He sat down in a high-backed chair by the window and waved his hand in Gerrard's direction.

'Brief, and to the point, Siegfried,' he began pompously. 'We're busy men and we've a lot to do.'

Gerrard waited. He knew politicians.

Malseed wound himself up a bit more. 'So, what we'd like first is to hear the outline of how you propose to make the kill, and then, in depth, the minutiae of your operation. Is that all right with you, gentlemen?'

There was no chorus of agreement, but out of the silence a voice growled, 'Stop the fuckin' cackle and let the Frog say what he's got to say.'

Malseed pursed his lips and frowned his distaste, but conceded, and with another gesture at Gerrard slumped back in his chair.

Gerrard looked round the room. The eyes he met were hostile, impatient, and critical; they looked like men who'd paid a lot of money for a Turner to fill the gap on the boardroom wall and were not entirely convinced they hadn't got themselves a Keating. And none of them looked like a senior member of British Intelligence.

'It won't make any difference to the outcome,' Gerrard began; his manner was relaxed, comfortable, 'but there's one small point I'd like clarified.'

Silence.

'It's to do with the target's screen; it was something mentioned in the security brief.' Gerrard looked directly at Malseed, but got nothing back. Not from Malseed.

'What d'you wanna know about it?' The question came from another part of the room, the accent Bronx rather than Brit. American-Irish, undisguised. Gerrard turned from Malseed to the man who'd spoken.

'Are you the one who drew it up?'

Malseed interrupted quickly, 'He's not here. He probably won't be now.' He looked quickly at his watch and frowned. 'Is it critical, this small point, or can we by-pass it and deal with it later? I'd like you to get on, please.' Malseed had now joined the hurry-up brigade and allowed a note of exasperation into his voice. He needn't have bothered. The Irish weren't impressed, they weren't watching him, they were all looking stonily at Gerrard. 'Because,' Malseed finished tamely, 'we're wasting time.'

'I said it wouldn't affect the outcome,' said Gerrard. 'The target's dead from the moment you nod your heads and say go.' He straightened his body and brought out the packet of Gitanes. He held it up for all to see and raised his chin interrogatively. They didn't say yes or no – they were all busy puffing away themselves – another one wasn't going to make any difference. He pulled a small table to the side of his chair, removed a cigarette from the packet and took Archie Williams's Dunhill from his other pocket. He put the Gitanes on the table.

Touhey watched every move. It was all too normal for a heavy smoker, he wasn't disturbed by a bloke lighting a fag, neither were the others; Gerrard could feel it, he could feel the hostility in the room lifting to make way for interest. Even Touhey was interested. He liked the Frenchman's opening sentence. So did the others.

Gerrard flicked the wheel of the Dunhill; once, twice, three times. Nothing happened, not even a spark. Touhey threw a box of matches on to the small table. It made the only sound in the room other than a muffled smoker's cough from near the fireplace. Gerrard frowned at the lighter and flicked it once more. With Touhey's two testers in the taxi it brought the number up to six. Six times, Archie had said – *six clicks to prime it then scrape a fraction of an inch off the ribbing to give a contact. Rub your thumbnail down the centre rib until you feel the pinhead knob; depress it gently, you've got a detonator. Put it on the centre of the Gitanes packet and you've got a bomb. And you've also got fifty seconds to get yourself at least six feet below it.*

Gerrard rested the Dunhill on his knee and used Touhey's matches to light the cigarette. When it was going he worked the tiny capsule loose from the back of his mouth and crushed it gently between his teeth. The bitter taste filled his mouth. He swallowed quickly and followed it down with a mouthful of smoke, then looked up at his audience.

'. . . that I guarantee,' he continued.

'Brit Security's not silly,' a voice grudgingly warned.

'Neither's USSS,' said another.

'What's that?'

'American Secret Service. They'll have a protective screen round Beaune.'

'American Secret Service? Don't you mean CIA?'

'No. It's fuck-all to do with the CIA! These people . . .'

'You're right,' interrupted Gerrard quickly. 'The screen that's been drawn around the target is good, but they've overlooked one thing.' He paused for effect, and felt like smiling. He'd got them. They were as attentive as a trainee bomb disposal squad at a practical demonstration.

The man by the fireplace stopped coughing into his handkerchief and looked up. 'What's that?' he asked.

'They've overlooked the distance factor.' Gerrard singled him out and spoke directly to him. 'They've got the close-up fanatical gunman complex – the man in the crowd with the snub-nose .38; their horizon's about ten metres. They haven't covered the long-range shot. Maybe they don't think anybody can shoot over water. If that's the case they are stupid and deserve to have problems, because that's exactly what I intend to do. They've given me a hole at six hundred metres – I can shoot that with a glass of Beaujolais in my hand.'

'Good boy!' an anonymous voice growled. 'That's just what I came to hear.'

'Hang on a minute.' The man who'd stopped coughing lit another cigarette and said, 'This opening for a long shot sounds a bit fishy to me, a bit too providential. The fuckin' SAS know all about that sort of thing, they know all about long shots.'

'They're not involved,' another Irish voice broke in – pure Irish, south of Dublin – Wicklow. 'The Brit police don't like having them around – thank Christ! And besides, they're all away.'

'What d'you mean – all away?'

'Just that. Hereford's empty. The whole bloody lot slipped away on their bikes and haven't been seen since.'

'I don't think I like the sound of that.'

'I do! It means somewhere some other poor bastards are getting their balls kicked in while we get on with putting the boot in over here.'

'Who told you this?'

'I'll tell you when he's gone.' The man with the soft County Wicklow accent looked pointedly at Gerrard. 'But you're not going yet, are you? Tell us some more about this fancy shooting you're going to do.'

Gerrard stared back at him. *Why the hell isn't this stuff of Williams's doing something?* He felt normal – too fucking normal. *What next? Give it another five minutes and put your hand up and ask to go for a pee?*

Gerrard shook his head at the man and said, 'There's nothing fancy about it, it's a straightforward kill. If your inside man's as close to the security planning team as he makes out, and the information he's passed on is accurate, I'll have two bullets in the target's chest before the people around him hear the first strike.'

'Details?' The man from County Wicklow wanted his money's worth.

Gerrard glanced fleetingly at each face in turn; they wanted their money's worth too. He gave it to them, item by item, detail by detail, as he spelt out coldly and without emotion how the Vice-President of the United States was going to die in a couple of days' time on the north bank of the Thames. His audience didn't clap when he finished but there were several relaxed nods of grudging approval. It gave him time to study each face again. *Where was Brocklebank?* 'Is your agent as reliable as you think he is?' He stared hard at Malseed. 'And as close to the centre as you would have me believe?'

But they didn't bite.

'I'd have thought the information you were shown spoke for itself.' The man by the fireplace wanted it over and done with. He'd heard what he came to hear, now it was time to wrap it up and get back under the blanket. 'And while we're on the subject, what was it you wanted to ask about earlier on?' He stopped talking and looked quizzingly at Gerrard. 'Is there anything wrong with you? Are you feeling all right?'

The perspiration stood out on Gerrard's forehead like glass marbles. It was ten minutes longer than instantaneous but Williams's Revenge attacked with a vengeance. Gerrard bit his lip theatrically and ran the back of his hand over a dripping forehead. His face had turned a deathly yellowish-grey and, without shivering like a dying man, it was still everything Williams had said it would be – a magnificent imitation of an extremely sick man.

'I'm all right,' he croaked, 'it's only a touch of malaria. Something to do with the stuffy atmosphere, it goes as quickly as it comes. Is there any water I could have?'

'By the look of you it's not bloody water you want – it's a bloody coffin!' It was an unsympathetic voice. 'Go and get him some water, Touhey.'

Gerrard crushed his cigarette out. 'Don't bother bringing the water. Tell me where it is, I'll go and put my head under the tap . . . That'll do it. I don't want to waste your time.'

'I'll take him down,' said Touhey, reluctantly. It was a reluctance tinged with suspicion. Hot French contract killers didn't get sudden attacks of tropical illness in the middle of a briefing – not in Touhey's book they didn't. He stared hard at Gerrard and then looked across the room at the man by the fireplace as if justifying his earlier misgivings about the way Frogs bounced when they were on the job. He didn't say it, but his expression did it for him: See what I mean?

He stood up and flexed his shoulders and, without taking his eyes off Gerrard, caught the Luger as it slipped out of its holster. It was almost a party trick.

'Come on then, Siegfried,' he sneered, 'let's go and wash the sweat off your face.'

Gerrard picked the lighter up off his knee and ran his thumbnail down its centre ridge, praying no one would notice the tiny, barely perceptible movement. The tiny pinhead yielded fractionally. He placed the Dunhill on the packet of Gitanes, to show them that he was coming back, and stood up. He started counting as soon as he was on his feet. He could feel real sweat mingling with Archie's artificially induced globules and it was an effort not to grab Touhey and start running for the corridor. He reached for the door-knob and ticked off six seconds . . .

'Hey, Siegfried!' It was another transatlantic-tinged Irish accent.
Gerrard turned.
Seven . . . eight . . .
'Yes?' He tried to keep the dread out of his voice.
'What happens if you get taken with this disease of yours when you're looking down the barrel at your contract?'
Twelve . . . thirteen . . .
'D'you expect everything to mark time while you get yourself sorted out and pour water over your face?'
Seventeen . . . eighteen . . .
Gerrard searched for the voice through the sweat filming down from his eyelids. He tried to avoid staring at the packet on the small table. He had a mental vision of a cloud of black oily smoke circling round the gold lighter on the blue packet, and let his eyes drift casually over it. It looked as innocent as a cigarette lighter sitting on a packet of Gitanes.

'Do you want to get somebody else for the job?' he said quietly.

Malseed's voice cut through the sudden tension. 'Go and wash your face, Siegfried.' He glared at the Irish-American voice. 'I know we're all a little bit edgy. It's understandable, there's a lot at stake, but can we save the medical questions? He wouldn't have the reputation he does if it had ever been a problem on a contract.' He flapped his hand impatiently at the two men by the door. 'Get him out of here, Touhey, and let's not waste any more time.' The words were music to Gerrard's ear. He pulled the door open and went through it with Touhey in close attendance.

Twenty-eight . . . twenty-nine . . .

'What's happening?' Connell stepped back against the wall and raised the Uzi so that its short stubby barrel pointed at both Touhey and Gerrard as they came through the doorway.

'Don't point that bloody Jew-gun at me, you stupid bastard,' Touhey snapped, 'point it at him.'

'What's the matter with him?' Connell moved the tiny barrel half an inch while Touhey pulled the door shut. 'He looks half dead to me.'

'He's having a little turn. I'm going to help him cool down.'

'D'you want any help?'

'When I want help splashing water on a Frog's face, Connell, I'll give it all up and take up digging ditches.'

'Again?'

'Shut your mouth, you useless young bastard! Stay here and guard the door, but keep that fucking thing pointed at his back. Come on, Frenchie, I'll go first, you follow me down. Be back in a minute, Connell.'

Gerrard stared at the back of Touhey's head and reached *thirty-five . . . then thirty-six . . . Fourteen seconds left. Or thereabouts . . . Christ! I hope your bloody fuse's a bit more accurate than your medicine, Archie!*

Touhey stopped in front of the second of the fanlighted doors.

Gerrard followed Touhey through the door and congratulated himself that it took a wise and clever Frenchman to know a shit-house when he saw one! Except this was better, this was a bathroom, with a big solid old-fashioned Victorian tub filling half the room. Gerrard kept his expression blank. He closed the door with his back and sagged against it.

'Fill the sink,' he gasped, 'I'll put my head straight in it.'

Through half-closed eyelids he watched Touhey slip the Luger back in its holster before turning on both taps above the sink. Touhey's eyes flickered once into the mirror to inspect Gerrard's sagging frame then dropped to watch the sink fill with swirling water.

Gerrard made no sound as he moved.

Two paces was all it needed. Gerrard grasped Touhey's elbows and pulled his hands away from the taps. As the Irishman jerked forward Gerrard grabbed his head with both hands and smashed it with all his strength on to the edge of the sink. Touhey went down like a stunned bullock. Gerrard joined him, snuggled his head under Touhey's armpit, and pressed him against the solid side of the old cast-iron bath. He closed his eyes and said, 'Fifty!' and clenched his teeth.

Nothing happened.

'Fuck you, Archie!'

Then his eardrums closed up as if somebody had stuck their two little fingers as far as they'd go into his ears.

He felt the explosion before he heard it; a garden rake clawing across his back pulling at him and tearing and threatening to drag him upwards into the red-hot blast that whooshed through the bathroom. This was Archie's fringe; it whistled through at just below ceiling height. He hung on grimly to the unconscious Touhey, using him as an anchor and a shield, and holding him down as he bobbed about like a man in rough water. He kept his eyes clenched tight and his face pressed into the side of the Irishman's body, yet still the searing white flash almost blinded him. But it was quick. The bang and its aftermath followed the heat, and then it was gone, leaving an ear-shattering silence that was broken only by the tinkle of glass as something dropped, like an afterthought, from a shattered frame somewhere in another part of the house.

Gerrard opened his eyes and spat the dryness from his mouth.

Everything was white. The ceiling plaster had reverted to powder and hung like suspended dust leaving only the wooden laths to show where Williams's claymore had sliced its way through the house.

He turned Touhey on to his back and took the gun from under his jacket. Touhey's forehead was split from one side of his head to the other and a long sticky stream of thick blood ran down the side of his nose to join a faster stream coursing out of his nostrils. His eyes were wide open and when he coughed more blood gushed from the side of his mouth. He saw the Luger in Gerrard's hand and managed a bubbly, 'Christ . . . !' It might have been the beginning of a self-administered absolution, or the realisation that he was about to find out how Frogs bounce when they're on the job, but he got no further. Gerrard placed the bulbous suppressor under Touhey's chin and squeezed the trigger. He'd lost interest in Touhey by the time he'd crawled to the bathroom door.

The blast had pulled the door off its hinges and it hung drunkenly, at an angle, held in place only by the solid brass Victorian lock. Gerrard crawled through the gap into the corridor, and came face to face with Wheelie.

Wheelie had made it half-way up the stairs. His head was level with Gerrard's corridor and the two men stared at each other, like strangers, for a fleeting second. Wheelie's once jet black hair was flecked with the same dirty white dust that filled the house and his eyes, rimmed by fear-sweat, popped out of the grey mask like the startled eyes of a King Charles spaniel. He spat out a mouthful of dust and said, 'What the fuckin' . . . ?'

Gerrard's bullet hit him just below the eye. It shook most of the dust from his face and slammed him hard against the staircase wall. There he hung for several seconds, as if trying to work it all out, until his legs gave way and he crumpled into an untidy bundle further down the stairs.

Gerrard debated whether to go for Wheelie's Uzi, lying half-way up the stairs where he'd dropped it, when a movement in the corner of his eye brought him round, on his side, with the Luger pointed up the corridor.

The door at the far end had opened. The room overlooking the front of the house – the room where Touhey's Praetorians watched from behind closed curtains. Gerrard lay still and watched the door open wider.

The man knew what he was doing. The Armalite came first. Slowly it edged round the door, pointing straight down the corridor, then a foot balanced itself by the door jamb, and the rest came out with a rush.

He was looking everywhere at once, except at the carpet.

Gerrard's first shot took him in the ribs just above his left arm where it crossed his body to support the Armalite. The second was an inch higher, through the heart. The gunman continued moving forward with the impetus of his rush, but he was dead, with only a shudder left as he folded himself over the banisters and hung there like a rolled-up carpet waiting for the removal van.

Gerrard remained where he was and waited for the rest. But nobody came.

He moved towards the door on his knees and waited, briefly, by the door post for the second instalment. Nothing happened. He listened. There was no sound, no noise, no movement. He went into the room on his belly. No time to look anywhere else, just one eye round the corner quickly and the Luger moving as if attached to the eye's retina by a cotton thread.

He could have clumped in on stilts.

The second guard had lost interest. He'd done it the hard way. He was pinned to the wall by a triangular segment of heavy wardrobe mirror that had shattered under the blast and sent its fragments slicing through the room like shell splinters. This boy had won the largest piece. They call it the luck of the Irish; six feet long, three-quarters of an inch thick and shaped like Concorde. He'd known all about it. The expression on his face showed what he'd felt when he looked down and saw that his legs now parted a few inches below his breastbone. The other guard had been lucky, he must have known when to duck.

Gerrard looked away from the horror on the wall and back at the man draped over the banister rail, a quick professional glance, then leapt to his feet and doubled down the narrow corridor. He stopped at the short flight of stairs and waited for movement. Nothing happened. The dust was thicker here but the smell of explosion-mix overpowered almost everything else; everything except – Gerrard's nostrils widened and he inhaled deeply – except this, the abattoir factor; the smell of fresh blood coming through TNT. He didn't move. The sun's rays cut through the dust like powered searchlights. The sun shone from the right, where there was no window, it came from where before had been a solid internal wall and a heavy, thick oak door.

Gerrard mounted the six steps and saw Connell.

Connell had won his Irish tricolour. But he wasn't going to get his Milltown spectacular. He was pasted to the stairway wall that led to the top floor. He looked like a child's painting of Wurzel Gummidge; flat, but colourful, there was no depth to Connell, he'd taken the full blast and been crushed like paint into the wall. He'd been pulverised, his bones smashed flat – he was going to be for ever on that wall. His mother wouldn't have recognised him, not from his face, and the Jew-gun he'd cuddled so reassuringly was at the bottom of the stairs, near what used to be his feet, and, for all its lethal propensity, it now resembled a crumpled old bicycle mudguard. Gerrard pushed it away with his foot and turned to look into the room where the smell was coming from.

The sun came through quite freely. There was no outside wall any more, just a gap where the explosion had punched the window out and continued punching all the way round the room. Williams had been modestly right when he'd prophesied that two ounces of trinitrobenzene-fol would solve any number of small problems – provided those problems could be gathered together like a bunch of violets. Gerrard cast a professional eye around the room – there were no problems left here; far from it. He stared at the mess near what used to be the fireplace. The American had had his coughing problem solved for him – if everything was gathered together, along with the rest of his friends, there still wouldn't be enough body to fill a cigarette packet, let alone a box. Pity Brocklebank hadn't turned up. That would take some of the sun out of Sanderson's smile. Gerrard shook his head and went downstairs to retrieve his belongings.

Wheelie hadn't moved. He gazed upwards at the man hanging over the rail above him; Wheelie, with a small hole beside his nose, his dead eyes locked in reproach at the steady drip of blood coming from his dead mate's open mouth, ruining for ever his nice new navy-blue suit. Gerrard didn't disturb him. He stepped over Wheelie's body, collected the things he'd left on the sideboard and walked down the passage to the kitchen.

The back door was open, undamaged by the explosion but hanging precariously on two rusty brackets. Gerrard waited a second to adjust his eyes to the blazing sun, then, with the Luger held loosely in his right hand, walked out into the garden towards the two men standing at the edge of the overgrown vegetable plot.

They were studying the heavy green growth of a large patch of bolted rhubarb. It must have been very special rhubarb, the sort that didn't grow in the Divis Flats or a Turf Lodge back garden – it was something they'd never seen before; it absorbed them entirely. They didn't hear Gerrard's approach. But it couldn't last. The nearer of the two looked up slowly, as if nudged by premonition, but there was something not quite right, there was no urgency in his manner, no fear, his eyes had a flat glazed look as if he wasn't seeing, or what he was seeing he wasn't believing – and it was nothing to do with the man walking towards him.

Gerrard frowned as his finger tightened on the trigger, it was like shooting a dopey hare in the silly season. And then the Irishman moved. He swung his body round, sideways on, in a half-hearted effort to bring the Uzi round in Gerrard's direction. He made no cry, no warning to his partner and no attempt to squeeze the trigger on the machine pistol. Gerrard fired twice. The first bullet hit him in the neck; it made a sound like an egg splattering on a hard stone floor and brought the other man to life; the next took him high in the forehead, the force propelling him into his partner. Gerrard lowered the Luger to his side and watched the confusion.

The second man pushed the dead guard to one side and groped feverishly under his left armpit. But he knew he was going to be too late. He took his hand away quickly and held both hands, palms outward, for Gerrard to see. He gave a sickly grin. 'OK,' he said, 'I'm not going to argue.' Gerrard smiled sadly and fired twice. Both bullets hit the Irishman's heart – he was dead before his wrists dropped.

Gerrard walked towards the rhubarb patch to see what made it different from other rhubarb patches. It had to be something worth looking at. He grinned, unhumorously, as he peered into the tangle of leaves and red sticks. The grin vanished as quickly as it came.

It was as if the sculptor had thrown the bust away in disgust.

It lay grotesquely among the leaves in a liquid red mess; head and shoulders, a clean cut from elbow to elbow just below the breast, the face completely untouched – Malseed, sliced in half and thrown on the heap by a freak of explosion. Gerrard understood the two gunmen's preoccupation. He couldn't take his eyes off the monstrosity. When he finally did, something jolted him, he had to turn and look again, hard. He could have sworn Malseed's eyes had flickered.

Gerrard threw the Luger into the gunge in the rhubarb and walked quickly out of the back garden and into a side road. He made a half-hearted attempt at brushing the dust from his jacket and cleaned his shoes by rubbing them up and down on the backs of his trouser legs; then he walked casually in the opposite direction, away from the house. In the distance he heard the sirens. Everybody was coming to see what it was all about. When he turned the corner he stopped counting; he'd reached three hundred and sixty-two.

CHAPTER 19

'We've let the bugger off the bloody hook,' said General Sanderson. He dropped ice cubes noisily into two glasses and splashed whisky unevenly over the top of them, then, with the water jug poised threateningly over one of the glasses he looked up and caught Gerrard's eye in the huge gilt mirror overhanging the sideboard. 'Looks like we're going to have to start all over again. D'you think word's got over to Dublin yet?'

'I wouldn't be surprised,' said Gerrard. 'But they're probably still trying to work it all out – wondering why everything's suddenly gone dark.'

'They'll blame you, of course.'

'Not necessarily. They wouldn't know that I walked out of the place, and as I can't imagine anybody wanting to rummage around counting the number of fingers and toes in that room there's no reason why they should know.'

'What about all those dead soldiers hanging on banisters and littering the garden?'

Gerrard pulled a face. 'There's nothing to say a Frenchman killed them.' He stared hard at Sanderson. 'Unless you've already passed the word around.'

Sanderson's eyebrows shot upwards. 'That's an interesting thought. But go on about the way you think the Irish minds are working.'

Gerrard lit a cigarette and inhaled slowly. 'They'll still be sitting around in shock, they're disorganised, they've only had twelve hours to sort themselves out. But give them a bit longer – say another day, a day and a half – and the mist will lift and somebody will scratch his arse and say, "What about that bloody Frog? What happened to him?" When somebody tells them that "that bloody Frog" strolled out of the abattoir with nothing more than a headache they're going to want to talk about it. That will be the initial reaction. The next one will be, "I want that bastard." And somebody's going to come looking.'

Gerrard searched Sanderson's face for a flicker of expression – sympathy or interest, anything at all. He found nothing. 'But you know that already, General. Don't you?'

Sanderson smiled icily. 'Why, then, don't we offer them the head of the bloke who's just wiped out most of the Republican Army Council? It'll certainly bring Mr Brocklebank back to the card table. After all, he certified your purity – via Fred Lambdon, of course – and the way they'll interpret that is that he's partly responsible for the disaster. That's the way their minds work. He owes the Irish a debt – they'll order him to stick his head above the parapet again, provided,' he lowered his voice, 'we wrap things up in a manner that won't scare him off. I wonder if he realises that this whole bloody charade was set up basically to bring him out of his cubby hole?'

Gerrard took a long sip from his glass of whisky. He could still taste powdered distemper and Victorian dust. He grimaced and said, 'I doubt it. He has no reason to think the dogs have been turned on him. He hasn't made a mistake, not one that we know about; his name's intact and so's his cover. It means that this little operation of yours hasn't even partially exposed him. But you don't want him exposed, do you? You want him killed, so it's all back to the starting line. You know as much about him now as you did before, and he's no wiser either – he doesn't even know you're interested in him. He's not suspicious – unhappy maybe, and understandably worried about future dealings with the Irish, but suspicious? No. In his assessment he's still a highly placed mole who happened to get involved in some IRA activity and nobody pointed a finger at him. He can crawl back now. Nobody's marked him.'

'I agree,' said Sanderson, surprisingly, 'but without the Irish prodding him he won't move until he's sure the smoke has drifted somewhere else. He'll go back to sleeping and making sure he doesn't put a foot wrong. But, if we accept your assessment that he reckons he's still a virgin then there's always the possibility that he might take steps to protect that anonymity. D'you see what I'm getting at?'

'No.'

Sanderson closed his eyes. 'I'm going to pass the word around that I planted you among the Irish to kill Irishmen. The evidence shows you succeeded beyond our wildest dreams. The Irish wouldn't hesitate. An active role would be demanded of Brocklebank in helping to nail you for the wild boys across the water, bearing in mind what you said – that he thinks he's in the clear and nobody's marked him.'

'That was only an opinion, General.'

'It's the sort of opinion that appeals to me. I'm going to do what you suggested. I'm going to put your head on offer and see what happens.'

Gerrard didn't smile. 'And how do you propose doing that?'

'I'm not sure at the moment. I'll have to give it some serious thought over my mug of hot milk tonight. Where are you staying?'

'Somewhere no one'll think of looking for me – I've moved back to the Crinton. Reason knows I'm there.'

'Sounds a good idea. Erm . . .'

Gerrard got there first. 'Did you have any luck at the Fluters' Ball?'

Sanderson smiled and raised his eyebrows. 'Where did you pick up that description?'

'Reason.'

'I don't know why I bothered asking!'

Sanderson picked up his glass and carried it to his nose again. 'No luck required,' he said. 'When Irishmen embark on a butcher's holiday it usually ends up as either a major balls-up or something for the Sunday comics. This one was both; nothing lucky about it when the SAS is involved. Meticulous organisation, the best soldiers in the world – who needs luck?' He held his glass up to the light and stared at it; it was hard to tell whether he was toasting the best soldiers in the world or inspecting the strength of his drink. Gerrard watched without interrupting.

'The SAS moved out of Hereford on Sunday. One minute they were there, the next minute they were gone – just like smoke. They were all over the place and no one was any the wiser. They're the only people we've got in this country who can do that. Makes me wonder what on earth we did before the SAS . . .' Sanderson paused and closed his eyes to reflect and then he was off again: 'They'd been given a couple of days to move into position and when I dropped the flag they pounced. Three active service units hit and eliminated. It must have given Paddy and Paddy quite a shock to find themselves peering through the slits at real soldiers.'

'How many prisoners did you pick up?'

'A few,' Sanderson hedged.

'Do you send them back across the water?'

'No, it's too much trouble.'

'What do you do with them then?'

Sanderson looked Gerrard in the eye. 'We used to send them back to the dustbin. There they'd have a quiet chat with the RUC hard boys at Castlereagh, or the Strand in Londonderry, and then they'd be given their bucket and spade and tucked up in one of the holiday homes for captured heroes. We got a bit fed up with that, so we've now found a new way of dealing with them, a less complicated way than bottling them up in the Maze where they get bored and do mischief . . .'

It was Gerrard's turn to raise his eyebrows.

'We quietly drop 'em off the end of the pier and when the bubbles stop rising we know that particular problem's finished with.' Sanderson was serious.

Gerrard didn't doubt it. 'How many?' he asked.

Sanderson thought for a moment. 'Quite a lot,' he replied. 'Enough to make the little toes in Dublin twitch when they get the final score. I don't think we'll be having any more talk of targets in England for quite some time.'

'I didn't see anything about it in the paper.'

'You won't,' said Sanderson. 'And you won't hear a great deal about it either. The occasional bang here and there may get through, the odd goal flicked in past his own goalkeeper by twitchy Irish fingers, but no nationwide scare. We used to tell everybody what had happened but we don't do things like that any more, it plays into their hands – '

Gerrard stopped the General in mid-flow. 'How many people knew the SAS had taken to the streets before the round-up began?'

'Taken to the streets?'

'You know what I mean.'

'Why d'you want to know?'

'Because they knew about it.'

'Who?'

'The people at the meeting. They knew the SAS had left Bradbury Lines, they knew the place was empty. Somebody must have told one of them early this morning.'

'Did they know where they'd gone?'

'No. The discussion didn't get that far. But I don't think they suspected the exercise was to wipe out three of their active cells.'

'That's it then,' said Sanderson at length. 'Mr Brocklebank's exposed himself!'

'How?'

'He opened his mouth too soon. When I briefed him about the SAS movement out of Hereford I didn't mention how restricted that information was.'

'And how restricted was it?'

'Apart from those of us who drew up the operation only four others were brought in during the post-movement stage.'

Gerrard sat up slowly. His whole attitude changed. 'Only four?'

Sanderson nodded. 'And that wasn't until Sunday night. These four weren't briefed until after Bradbury Lines had been cleared and the SAS were out into the countryside. Sunday night was forty-eight hours after they'd left. One of those four passed the news on to his friends. If it had been one of the Planning Committee your meeting wouldn't have taken place. He would have told the Irishmen who the SAS was gunning for, and if that had happened you'd have been sitting in that house all on your own.'

Gerrard picked his glass up off the table but didn't drink. 'And that's the reason, General, why I asked you how many were in on the top briefing. But you amaze me when you say there were only four extras – I'd have thought a dozen or so; that would have been my idea of a restricted top-secret movement order.'

'That's all very well,' said Sanderson, 'but we're talking about four men – four highly trusted individuals in sensitive areas, each one of them stuffed up to the bloody eyeballs with enough secret matter to send us all back to the Stone Age. Irreplaceable – almost. And one of them's a shit-bag!'

Sanderson reached for his glass again, sipped from it, gave his mouth a little wash and swallowed. 'Their names are Fairfax, Brotherton, Roberts, and Harris, my number two. It's hard to believe that any of them could be Brocklebank, but it must be so.' He opened a locked drawer and pulled out four files, detaching a photograph from each and passing them across to Gerrard.

'You've no idea at all which of these four is the likely candidate, General?'

'No. I've used them all for my own ends at one time or another – plus another half-dozen lesser fish when the occasion demanded – particularly since Freddie Lambdon switched the red light on. I've dropped little hints all over the place in the forlorn expectation that something would end up in Dublin, or even Belfast, and that I could pinpoint the source, but this is the first time I've received a dividend. The trouble is I'm now likely to treat all four as if they were home-grown pariahs, and that's no good for me; neither is it for the three clean ones – or this country's security. I've got to move quickly. If you've got any serious suggestions I'd like to hear them.'

Gerrard lit another Gitane and settled back in his chair. 'Will they have had details of, and the results from, the explosion in Mile End yet?'

'Bound to.'

'All four?'

Sanderson nodded. 'Certainly, I've just explained their status. But it won't move beyond these four, not until I say so, and that won't be for several days yet.'

'Will they know about me?'

'Of your existence? Certainly.'

'And what I came to England for?'

Sanderson smiled crookedly. 'One of them thinks he knows. But he won't know who paid your fare – not unless I tell him.'

'Why don't you?'

'What?'

'Tell them.'

'What – everything . . . ?' Sanderson's voice tailed off as his thoughts collected round the suggestion and shaped it into a new approach – it mixed well with what he already had in mind. He tried it out in words, 'A little chat in confidence with each of them in turn? How, and why, I got you free-lancing over here? How I brought you to London and slipped you into Dublin's arms using Freddie Lambdon as the shoehorn?'

Gerrard nodded.

Sanderson continued, 'Something like "Not a word to a soul, but my Frenchman turned over a stone and found something underneath that makes him almost certain that the Irish have got a man on the inside – our inside. He's gone to Paris to confirm one or two things then he'll be back to pull the tooth"?' He paused in thought, then asked, 'What do you think?'

Gerrard almost smiled. 'Sounds a bit over the top to me. But it might work. At least it might frighten him into making a mistake.'

Sanderson nodded absently. 'We mustn't make it too easy for him. He's got to do some things for himself. He's got to be made to work for it, made to feel that he's in complete control, that every step he takes is an exercise of his own will and not due to any prompting of mine. Are you with me there?'

'I think I'm ahead of you.'

'As a matter of fact I'm quite sure it'll be the Irish who call the tune. They'll insist on going up front. They'd like to come at you like wild dogs in winter and with all the finesse of a Sumo wrestler, but they'll be made to take advice. Brocklebank? Now he'd do it differently. His only interest in having you put out of the way is to ensure his survival, but the Irish'll see it differently, they'll want revenge – they'll want a very generous pound of flesh – so they'll have to compromise. Brocklebank'll supply the organisation – the Irish'll supply the firing squad.'

'When are you going to break the news to the four?' asked Gerrard.

'Tomorrow morning.' He thought for a moment. 'He'll be stretched when he sees how close the finishing line is. I reckon he's going to need a cork up his arse to keep himself in the game long enough to know whether his cover'll last until the Irish bury you in Paris.'

Gerrard crushed his cigarette out slowly. 'How long do you expect he'll need that cork for, General?'

Sanderson didn't hesitate. 'Half an hour after I've finished with him he'll be burning up handfuls of tenpenny pieces on the phone to Dublin. Add on a couple of days while they kit their team out, then . . .' He closed his eyes to do his sums. 'Say four days to find you and a full day for games and the chop – let's say a week at the most.' He opened his eyes. 'That's what Mr Brocklebank'll plan for. If they haven't put you away within the week he'll pack up and go home. You want to know how long you've got before you start walking back to front?'

'Are you trying to put me off my dinner, General?'

Sanderson didn't laugh. 'You can expect a Provisional ASU to arrive in Paris when I said – in about forty-eight hours. They'll be the best they've got. They'll have money and they'll have contacts over there who'll point their noses in your direction. Don't take them lightly, Gerrard, they'll be at your door like a pack of sniffer dogs.'

Gerrard raised his glass and frowned at the nut-brown colour of its contents. He took a mouthful, swallowed, and felt his throat and stomach recoil and the strength of it. Sanderson's idea of water in evening whisky was none.

'Why Provisional?' he asked.

'They're the only ones likely to have people who know the difference between a muddy track and a Paris boulevard and also have a few of the basic skills. Any of the others are usually out of their depth beyond lighting the fuse on a bagful of sodium nitrate. So there you are! Beware of Irish accents inviting you for a stroll along the Seine. And talking of accents – take Reason with you. He'll know an Irish accent when he hears it – you might not. And besides, he can look after your back in the dark, they won't see him!'

Gerrard smiled politely. He made another attempt at the whisky, and coughed. 'Thanks for Reason,' he managed in between paroxysms, and after a pause for recovery said, 'It's only hypothetical, isn't it, that these Provo people will be directly connected to Brocklebank? It's pure supposition on your part. They might not be even related.'

'What are you getting at?'

'The Provos could chase me around Paris and half-way across France, and all we might end up with is another packet of dead Irishmen and nothing to show for it. Unless there's a bit more you haven't told me.' He looked Sanderson square in the eye. 'Is there?'

'No,' replied Sanderson, 'there's nothing more to go with that, but there is a little bit of advice, if you're in the mood for it.'

Gerrard raised his glass level with his chin and nodded.

'Right,' said Sanderson. 'Don't bother with the Irish rank and file when you come across them, they usually know bugger-all about what's going on. You can put them quietly out of their misery and drop them down the nearest drain. The bloke you want is the one with the mouth. You'll be able to tell which one that is because he'll have been taught how to shave and wear a tie – he'll also be able to count into double figures. Pick him up and have a quiet chat with him in a little corner somewhere. He'll know all about Brocklebank. If he doesn't he'll know someone who does and he'll put you on to him five minutes after you start tweaking his toes. That's my advice for what it's worth. But I've no doubt you've got a few ideas of your own, so let's just make sure the result's the one we all want.'

'Do you want me to keep in touch?'

'No. When you've got a name tell Maurice, he'll pass it on to me. Don't you ring me, I don't trust those bloody things.'

'What if I need some instruction, or more advice?'

'You won't. You've got everything you're going to get. When you know who Brocklebank is come over and kill him.' Sanderson put his empty glass on the table and stood up. He looked tired enough to be ready for bed. 'Anything else?' he asked.

Gerrard rose to his feet. He kept his unfinished whisky in his hand and ventured another mouthful.

'Are you going to tell your four friends about Lambdon?'

'Tell them what about him?'

'That he was planted on the Irish. That he was your man all the way from the beginning.'

Sanderson frowned. He obviously wasn't as tired as he looked – his brain was still ticking over. 'I'll let you know. After you tell me why you think I shouldn't – which is presumably what you're getting at. Isn't it?'

Gerrard nodded. 'I wouldn't like your man to think that it was any-body but me who pointed the stick in his direction. I wouldn't like to think of him troubled with the thought that Fred Lambdon had anything to do with his problems. I think it's better for Brocklebank that he has only one thing in sight at a time – it'll make things easier for us as well.'

'I'm sure Mr Brocklebank will be quite touched by your concern. But I don't follow you – Lambdon's dead, he's not going to worry about anybody breathing down his neck. So what's the real reason?'

'Brocklebank doesn't know that, does he?'

'No, neither does anybody else.'

'Don't tell him. Keep him in suspense. Let him think Fred has gone to ground to keep out of the way of your hatchet-men.'

'You still haven't told me the reason.'

Gerrard finished off the remains of his drink – it didn't even make his eyes water – he was getting used to it.

'I want Brocklebank to come for me,' he said. 'I don't want him distracted by any urge he might have to vent his spleen on Fred after you tell him it was he who started his sledge moving down towards the gap at the bottom of the valley.'

'That's a nice poetic turn of phrase. Reason again?'

'No. Gerrard,' said Gerrard impatiently. 'I wouldn't like to think of Brocklebank sending some of his Irishmen to go and argue with Lambdon's family. I said I wanted them in my direction.'

'You could have said that in the first place and I could now be sitting up in bed reading my book.' Sanderson frowned again but it was not in bad temper. 'What sort of family has Fred got?' He made it sound as compassionate as a question on an insurance claim form.

'He has a daughter.'

'I didn't know that. Strange, he never mentioned her. But never mind, leave it up to me, I'll see she's all right, we owe that to old Fred, don't we? I'll have one of our people make her his business; we'll get her buried nice and safe somewhere for the duration – just in case, eh? Now, where's she living? Didn't Freddie have a place down near the water somewhere?'

'I've no idea.'

'It doesn't matter. I'll have her looked up. And I'll bear in mind what you said about keeping our man on tenterhooks. But I can't promise to keep Fred Lambdon's share under wraps. You can never tell with these people, it might be politic to slip that bit under his left armpit during the discussion. I shall have to reserve judgement and play it the way it comes. But, as I said, as far as you're concerned have no worries about the girl, she'll be in good hands.'

'I won't.'

'Anything else?'

'You haven't got a hard-head by the name of Murray working for you, have you?'

'Murray . . . ?' Sanderson thought about it, but not for long. 'I don't think so.' His eyes were drooping like a slumbering lizard's, he was definitely ready for his bed. 'But ask Coney on your way out, he knows all about that sort of thing. Good-night.'

'Goodbye, General.'

'Do you know whether there's anybody on the General's books named Murray, Coney?'

'No, Mr Jerrud.'

'You mean you don't know?'

'I mean there ain't nobody named Murray, Mr Jerrud.'

'Just like that?'

'Just like that, Mr Jerrud. Er, Mr Jerrud . . .'

'What?'

'When you leave the 'ouse take the Cheyne Walk for a bit. It's down by the river, a pleasant walk this time of the night – you'll be able to see if you've got any company down there – much easier than the King's Road. Good-night, Mr Jerrud.'

Gerrard took Coney's advice.

He walked briskly along Cheyne Walk until he came to Chelsea Embankment. There he stopped, leaned on the Embankment wall and gazed at the flickering lights of the Festival Gardens on the other side of the river. He stayed in that position, like a man with nothing on his mind, just long enough for the couple behind him, and the giggling unisex threesome behind them, to pass out of sight. He waited another minute then turned back the way he'd come, crossed the road and strolled towards the telephone box he'd passed a few minutes before.

He dialled one of Clive Reason's numbers, then checked his watch. It was half-past eleven. He wondered whether Reason would be sitting up in bed like General Sanderson, sipping a hot toddy. The thought didn't bring a smile to his sombre features.

The phone started ringing at the other end. Nobody seemed in a hurry to answer it. Gerrard took the receiver away from his ear and stared out of the window at the night. It had been a long day, the sun had only just gone and above the yellow pinpricks of light reflected on the river the western reaches of the Thames still showed a thin grey line where it had slipped out of sight and into somebody else's horizon. He turned his

194

back on it and jammed the door open with his foot. The relief was imaginary. The telephone box clung tenaciously to its atmosphere of cabbage-smelling stuffiness, it stank like a garden greenhouse that had stood unventilated throughout the day. Gerrard wasn't enjoying his evening; his mood was edging towards bad.

The ringing in his ear finally stopped.

'Were you in bed?'

'Sort of,' replied Reason.

'Put her down – it'll make your eyes weak. Can you talk?'

'When I get my breath back,' said Reason. There was a pause while he cleared the room. 'I've been hearing about bangs and all sorts of strange things and happenings down in the East End. They can't make up their minds whether to blame the IRA or the gas board. Are you all right?'

Gerrard wasn't amused. 'I've got a headache. How long will it take you to get ready to go to France? You'll be there for three or four days, say a week at the outside . . .'

The humour died in Reason's voice. 'You've cleared it?'

'He suggested it.'

'OK. Give me fifteen minutes. Where shall I meet you?'

Gerrard relaxed the brittleness out of his voice. 'Just testing.' He smiled in the semi-darkness of the telephone kiosk. 'I had in mind tomorrow, some time before lunch. I think it's time you tried a French hamburger.'

'Very funny. D'you fancy a drink?'

'I've already had one, it's sleep I fancy at the moment. Why don't you meet me for a cup of coffee early tomorrow morning at the Crinton?'

'Just a minute, Michel. I think you'd better have a drink with me tonight.'

Gerrard's smile vanished. Reason hadn't tried to disguise the warning note in his voice.

'What is it?' he asked.

'I'll tell you over that drink,' persisted Reason. 'Where are you calling from?'

Gerrard told him.

'Go and wait on the opposite side of the road, on the river side. Light a cigarette; I'll be with you before you finish it.'

Reason led the way down a narrow flight of concrete steps to the basement and opened the door with a brass Yale. It wasn't the smartest drinking club in the land, he told Gerrard as he opened the door, but the whisky was honest and the membership unselective – twenty-five pounds a year and you got a key with your name on it and a licence to drink until the milkman came bashing on the door with the yoghurt and double cream.

He pointed Gerrard to an alcoved table just inside the door and strolled across the carpeted floor to the small bar occupying what, in the good old days, would have been the coal cellar. It had been cleaned out, washed and painted at least once since the last load of Derbyshire Household thudded down through the hole in the pavement above.

The half-dozen people drinking out of hours were hard to spot through the dim lighting, and the heavy pall of cigar and cigarette smoke was dense enough to form a secondary low ceiling. There was no music in the cellar. Only the chink of glass against glass as more tonic was added to gin, or more gin to tonic, and the low mumble of voices that filtered through the gloom proved that there were others in the room and that they were minding their own business. Reason didn't try to identify them.

He picked up two glasses of whisky and water from the bar in one hand and ran his fingers down the bare back of a large black female perched unsteadily on a fragile-looking rattan bar stool. She said nothing, but wrinkled her nose optimistically and laughed. The laugh followed Reason all the way across the room, but when he sat down opposite Gerrard his face was set to match the Frenchman's serious expression.

The room closed around them and the big woman at the bar drowned her moment of happiness with a long swig from a half-pint mug of black rum and coconut water and went back to her blues.

Gerrard stopped looking at her and slid his cigarettes across the table. 'Don't forget I'm a tired man, Reason,' he said, 'so don't start asking questions, just tell me what's troubling you.'

Reason helped himself to one of Gerrard's cigarettes and lit it. 'I went over to Highgate this morning.'

Gerrard raised his eyebrows.

'I was there at about the same time you were rubbing your flints together down the Mile End Road. I felt a little bit on edge so I decided to pass the time by having a good close look at your girl-friend. I wanted to satisfy myself she's worth all the fuss you've been making about her.'

Gerrard appeared almost disinterested. Reason wasn't fooled.

'Miller Street, bright yellow door?'

Gerrard nodded.

'Melanie Lambdon's a very attractive woman.'

Reason stopped talking to watch a man and a woman come through the door. He watched until they reached the bar. He stopped looking when the black woman on the rattan stool threw her arms around the man and kissed him – it looked as though he were going down the throat of a boa constrictor.

'Very attractive indeed.' He had another quick look to make sure the new arrival had survived. 'She's got nice legs and a nice body.' He paused. 'And she's got a watcher.'

Gerrard picked his drink up and started a Sanderson mouthwash routine with it. But it took too long. He wanted something into his stomach quickly to stop his gut lurching up into his throat.

'Tell me about the watcher,' he said.

Reason cradled his glass in both hands and propped his elbows on the table. He tipped the glass so that a steady stream ran into his mouth. 'Tall skinny lad,' he said, between swallows, 'in a little white BMW. He knew her movements; stayed downwind of her and when she went walkies he ducked out of sight down below the dashboard. He'll give himself a terrible hernia if he has to do that more than a couple of times a day.' Reason tilted the glass again. 'He stepped out of his little car once, stretched his long skinny legs as far as the end of the road, then came back again and carried on watching. He was wearing something under his arm.'

'How long did you stay there?'

'About three hours. Long enough to know he was on the job. I didn't touch him in case he was something you'd put there to look after her.' Reason waited a second. 'Was he?'

Gerrard shook his head. 'Did you see her come back? Is he still there?'

Reason emptied his glass and held his hand out for Gerrard's.

'Yes to the first question, and I don't know to the second. I watched her sail up the road and through the yellow door. Poetry in motion I believe they call it! I now understand why you want to bounce her up and down on your knee again. Anyway, that's the story. I thought you'd like to know what's happening up the road. When are we going to Paris?'

Gerrard ignored Reason's flippancy. 'That's not enough, Reason. How did you leave it?'

Reason wasn't put out. He continued smiling. 'Exactly as you would have left it yourself. There'll be a few people staring into sonny-boy's eyeballs if he takes half a step towards that yellow door after lights out. Relax. She's going to get more undisturbed sleep tonight than you are.

That skinny bugger doesn't realise it, but there are more eyes on him tonight than there are watching your average party political broadcast. OK?'

Gerrard said nothing for a moment, then nodded. 'OK.' He looked down at his glass. 'Can I buy us a drink here?'

Reason shook his head. 'Members only. Same again?'

Gerrard didn't reply. 'Why didn't you do something with his car number? You could have saved yourself all the waiting. Sanderson's friend Roberts? He could have sorted something out for you, couldn't he?'

Reason pulled a face. 'I don't believe in spreading things around too much. You drop a word here, and another word there, and before you know where you are there's a couple of hundred pointed heads peering around the corner in their new space-man's kit asking the poor sod for his driving licence. I don't mind having him watched – it's all good fun! Now, what about this Paris thing? You've got me all worked up – when are we going?'

Gerrard relaxed. He emptied his glass and slid it alongside Reason's. 'Make it a double.'

'What about Paris?'

'Change of plan. I want the girl in Paris.' He ignored Reason's raised eyebrows and toothy grin. 'I want you to bring her out tomorrow afternoon, preferably without disturbing the boy-friend. Put her on a plane, then go back and talk to him.' He reached over and tapped the back of Reason's hand with his lighter. 'And I'll bet you anything you like he'll be able to tell you exactly how many buttons ex-gunner Murray has on that navy-blue blazer he wears.'

Reason said, 'I wouldn't count on this being Murray's boy. He didn't look a bit like a bottle of Guinness to me; more like one of our girl guides – could even be one of Roberts's tracker dogs.'

'Roberts?'

'Why not? There's no reason why he shouldn't get in on the act. Commander Roberts could well have an interest in finding out why the good Colonel Lambdon has suddenly dropped out of the social whirl; or it could be Harris with the same idea, or a jealous boy-friend who doesn't like the way you keep stroking her bottom. It could even be her old man's Provo chums wondering . . .'

'Then you'll find all that out, won't you?'

Reason stared into his glass. 'Going back to Murray,' he said thoughtfully, 'd'you think he's still interested in knowing a bit more about you – even though the show's now over?'

'What do you think?'

Reason shrugged. 'I'm buggered if I can see what he's got to gain now. The girl's no longer any bloody use to him, and you're about as handy as last week's weather forecast.' He shook his head. 'It's not Murray,' he said definitely. 'It's got to be somebody else.'

Gerrard pulled another cigarette out of the packet and lit it from the stub in his hand. He continued puffing life into the new one as he spoke. 'Your skinny boy'll set your mind at rest tomorrow, won't he? But don't cross Murray out of your diary just yet . . . I've got feelings about him. There's always the chance that he's been away, saying his prayers or getting new orders and ideas, and maybe he hasn't heard that play ended this morning and there's nothing more for him to worry about. Maybe he's one of these intense young men who can't let go once they've started, or perhaps he doesn't connect Frenchmen with explosions in east London. Maybe he thinks the job Freddie Lambdon brought me over for is still on the cards and he's still interested. Do you want me to go on?'

'No thanks.'

Gerrard shrugged. 'OK. But while you're pulling teeth I want to know how they got on to her so easily.'

'You shall. Now, back to work. I pick her up tomorrow and take her to Heathrow. Then what?'

'Ring me at this number in Paris and let me know she's on her way.' Gerrard scribbled a number on the flap of the Gitanes packet, tore it off, and slid it across the table.

Reason glanced at it casually before slipping it into his shirt pocket. 'When are you going?' he asked.

'Tomorrow morning – early.'

'And me?'

'As soon as you've finished with the boy. Don't waste too much time over him, just milk him then tuck him out of the way somewhere. Don't bother chasing anything up. If he's Murray's *copain* he'll tell you where we can meet Murray and you and I can come back and castrate him at our leisure. The important thing is to sort out Brocklebank, not Murray, so getting to Paris is your second priority, OK?'

'OK.'

'I'll warn them you're on your way – they can start slaughtering the cows!'

CHAPTER 20

In the large Georgian house in Dublin Eugen Meier listened without interrupting as the casualty list was read to him over the phone from London.

Brocklebank stopped talking and waited. He almost felt sorry for the American. Almost – but he didn't let it prey on his mind. He sipped from his glass of whisky and stared at Audrey Gilling's knees, and listened to the silence.

Meier took the news philosophically. His expression didn't alter, his eyes remained flat behind their bottle bottoms and the only visible sign of his disappointment, if disappointment it was, was a slight tightening of the lips. He could have been listening to his broker telling him his Bank of America shares had slipped by three-quarters of a cent. After a short pause he said, 'OK, how did it happen? Where did we crack?'

'It would take too long to go into detail, Meier.' The voice from London was calm, matter of fact, as if losing the central command structure and three active cells was an everyday matter – something to get used to; something that time would heal. 'In a nutshell, it means that somebody was a bloody sight more shifty than we were. Either that, or somebody spoke out of turn – somebody in Dublin, or one of your dustbin-lid mechanics in America. Somewhere somebody shot his mouth off. I think Sanderson got in amongst us right at the beginning.'

'Who's Sanderson?'

'British General, controls a special department which includes the Irish Section. It's a very special section. You can call it the SAS of British Intelligence. He has direct access to them as well.'

'He controls the SAS?'

'Not quite. I said he can call on them. He's a no-holds-barred merchant, tore the rule book up when you were a little boy learning how to eat peas with a knife and fork at Harvard. But it doesn't matter now who he is, it's all over. I think you might as well pack your duffle bag and nip back across the pond – there's not going to be any more Irish offensive, not for a long time to come. Why don't you come back and see us again in a couple of years' time?'

Meier ignored Brocklebank's suggestion, and his invitation – his mind and his professional curiosity were on the meat of the matter. 'Are you quite sure about this demolition job? That it was done by the Frenchman on his own and not with a pack from one of the British anti-terrorist agencies? How can you be sure he was at the meeting and that he walked out in one piece?'

Brocklebank came back quickly. 'Take my word for it, Meier. It was a solo effort by the Frenchman. But it was certainly organised by Sanderson. The Frog walked out all right; not a scratch, everybody else – mincemeat.'

'But how can you be so certain?'

'I was given a special chums-only briefing by the man who put it all together – General Sanderson. It went the way he planned – no hitch, no slip, the perfect group take-out.'

'Hmmm . . . I thought you were supposed to be right in tight with the British security people? How come they didn't tell you what was going on?'

'Sanderson's a law unto himself. He didn't tell anybody until it was all over. Thank God he's only one among many running British Intelligence.'

'You ought to have been on to this Frenchman the minute he stepped off the plane.'

'I was. He didn't slip. This was an exception for the British, Meier. You can't fault them on it. They can be sloppy buggers nine times out of ten, but there's always the one that counts – this is that one out of ten; the one that counted – it was just our bad luck. But as I said, it's all water under the bridge; there's bugger-all you or I can do about it now except bang our heads against the wall – nothing is going to put Malseed and co. back in their boots.'

'I agree. But I think we'd better draw a bit of blood before we put the file back in the drawer. I think we'd better have this person Sanderson taken out – just to show that there's some ill feeling over here.' It was the nearest Eugen Meier came to lightening the conversation. But he didn't smile at his end of the phone.

There was a short pause, then the man in London said, 'I suggest you forget about that one, Meier. Unless, of course, you've got a spare battalion of kamakaze Irishmen who are prepared to fight their way past an SAS screen?'

The silence hobbled down the line. It didn't worry the man known as Brocklebank. He winked at the girl sitting opposite him and waved his empty glass at the well-stocked drinks trolley on the far side of the room.

The pause in Dublin was shorter than he'd expected.

'I thought you British were supposed to be masters of the understatement?'

'That's very perceptive of you, Meier. We are – and that *was* an understatement. Forget Sanderson, there's no way you can ever get to him. Concentrate on killing the Frenchman. That's the sort of thing the Irish'll appreciate – and understand.'

'I'm not with you.'

'The Irish understand only eyes for eyes and teeth for teeth. They're not into tactical killing.'

'Tell me what you want.'

'This game of Irish mastermind has put my head on the block. It's opened a crack in my cover that could prove fatal. I might have to move my tent. I need a bit of time, and I need a death to buy me that time. You can help me.'

'The Frenchman?'

'Yes. He's the one Sanderson will send after me when he puts the last piece in the jigsaw. With him out of the way I'm still in position.'

'Fair enough. Can the IRA make political capital out of a dead Frenchman?'

'The IRA can make political capital out of a little boy pissing up against a brick wall.'

'OK. What do you propose?'

Brocklebank looked relieved. He accepted the drink from Audrey Gilling, smiled and nodded at the receiver in his hand then raised his eyes to the ceiling. There was no reaction from Audrey, she could hear only one side of the conversation. She didn't smile, but sat down opposite him, crossed a long, slender leg and sipped her gin and tonic. Brocklebank took his eyes away from her knees and spoke into the telephone.

'I'd like you to get in touch with Michael McGann. He's the Provisionals' *Gauleiter*, if you don't mind the expression, in – '

'Never mind about that,' Meier broke in impatiently, 'how do I get hold of him?'

The interruption didn't upset Brocklebank. 'He'll have moved in from Armagh to take Donovan's place. He'll be on the Council now; one of those who can say yes or no. You'll find him in Dublin where you used to find Donovan. When you get hold of him ask him to give the okay to putting Sean into the field.'

'Who's Sean?'

'Sean's enough for you to be going on with. Mick'll know what I mean. Also ask him to pass the word over here to Phelan so that when I start tweaking his ear he'll sit up and take notice and do as he's told without his usual bloody-mindedness. Are you with me so far?'

'Go on . . . Just a minute, who's this Phelan?'

'He's number one Provo UK. He's my outside line.'

'OK. What else d'you want?'

'Fifty thousand dollars and whatever weapons McGann decides Sean'll want, dropped in Paris. McGann will organise the drop, but if he can't, I will. All you have to do is supply. Can you do that?'

'Sure.' But Meier had to ask in spite of himself, 'What's so special about this Sean guy? And why haven't I heard about him before?'

'You've just said it, Meier. He's special. Very special. If you want to know any more than that go and ask his brother.'

'Who's his brother?'

'Michael McGann.'

'Hmmm.' Meier became almost human again. 'So we've got an Irishman on our side who can walk down O'Connell Street and whistle at the same time. If he can manage that why haven't I heard about him until now?'

'I said he's special.'

'OK, tell me about this special Irishman. If he can count up to ten and crap without falling down the hole why wasn't he considered for the Frenchman's job?'

Brocklebank took a long drink from his glass before answering.

'Two reasons,' he said. 'One, he's not a technician. He's a shit-or-bust, close-in operator. Six feet distance, a stub nose .32 or .38 and a full magazine, and Sean McGann's your man. Secondly, he kills for fun – but don't call him a psychopath, they don't like being called things they can't spell. But that's what he is, a bloody psychopath – he can kill, but he can't think.'

Meier understood. 'OK,' he said lightly, 'I've got the message. Leave it up to me. You've got somebody he can talk to in Paris?'

'Yes. I'll sort that part of it out with Phelan. You get the go-ahead from McGann and arrange the packet in France and you can go home and pick corn-cobs until the Irish reckon they're ready for another go.'

'Are you still secure for the time being over there?'

Brocklebank sipped his whisky quietly. His expression didn't change. 'I'll be burned to a cinder in about ten days if the Frenchman's not put away,' he said, 'but if he is, and provided I'm not invited to any more Irish parties for some time, I should be able to pull my cover in around me and go back to sleep again. It all depends on how far Sanderson's bayonet has penetrated.'

They sounded like two old grave robbers discussing their next dig.

'You got somewhere to go if the wrong card turns up again?'

'Yes. It's all been taken care of.'

'OK, I'll put the McGann show on the road, then.'

Brocklebank dropped the receiver back on its rest, settled himself comfortably in the large armchair and quietly demolished the remains of his whisky. He closed his eyes for a second and thought about what the American had said, then opened them suddenly and stared at Audrey Gilling. It was a searching, wordless examination that went on for almost a minute. It made her shift uncomfortably.

'What is it, Geoffrey? What's the matter? Why are you looking at me like that?'

He didn't answer immediately.

'Geoffrey!' she repeated. Her voice edged a little higher, and she stood up to replenish his empty glass.

'I think it's time to go home,' he said. He continued to stare blankly at the chair she'd just vacated as if the answer lay there to whatever was troubling him; he barely acknowledged the new drink she placed in his hand. 'Even if McGann does find Gerrard, and gets lucky and shoves him down a hole,' he said slowly, 'I still think we've come to the end of the ball of string; I think the Irish have pointed Sanderson's nose in my direction.' He was speaking his thoughts aloud. Audrey frowned at him and moved out of range, and stood with her back to the drinks trolley; her own glass remained unfilled.

'I've stepped out too far,' he murmured, and looked across the room at her, inviting her agreement – or sympathy. 'And for what? For a bunch of snotty-nosed, raggy-arsed turnip-tops from Dublin. You wouldn't believe it, would you? Thirty-five bloody years of making a place at the table for Mother and it's all gone up the bloody spout. What a bloody waste!'

He sat up suddenly and shook the lethargy from his attitude. He'd made a decision. It cleared the doubt from his heavy features and, from a slow reflective drawl, his voice became brusque and decisive.

'We're leaving, Audrey. I'm going to wind up and clear out. I can feel the heat near my arse – it's time to go.'

'I'm glad to hear it. When are we going?'

'A week. Say a week today. If McGann wraps the Frenchman up we might squeeze a few more days, possibly a couple more weeks out of it – it'll depend what I see in old Sanderson's eye the next time we break bread together.'

'I'm worried, Geoffrey.'

'Trust me. Let's go to bed.'

Audrey's eyes widened and she glanced at the clock on the mantel-piece. 'What if Gerrard turns up?'

'We'll have a threesome!'

'I don't know how you can joke at a time like this.'

Brocklebank smiled the creases away from his face. 'It's not difficult, he's on his way home.'

'Gerrard's gone back to Paris?' Her mouth formed a perfect O, as if she was about to blow a bubble. 'How do you know?'

'Sanderson told me.'

She raised her eyebrows. 'Why would he tell you that?'

The big bald man frowned. 'That's a good question, Audrey,' he said slowly. 'Remind me to give it some thought.' Then he smiled wickedly. 'But in the meantime your friend Gerrard's on his way to France and, even if he isn't already half-way across the Channel, I doubt that he's going to whistle round here for a final quickie. It'd be like dashing over to South Wales with a bucket of coal for the town hall fire!'

'That's very unkind.'

'I didn't mean it to be. Come on, finish your drink and let's go upstairs and play games.'

'Sorry, Geoffrey, I've got a headache.'

CHAPTER 21

Heathrow Airport wasn't one of Reason's favourite places.

He leaned against the wall under one of the transparent bubbles in Terminal Two and whistled tunelessly into the receiver while he waited for the pips and squeaks to change into something definite. He was irritable. He scowled into the face of the diminutive sari-clad Sikh woman with a shoulder sack and a three-foot-wide broom who hesitated by the phone point. She was used to dark men scowling at her. She lowered her eyes dutifully and continued to push her non-existent broomful of rubbish across the broad expanse of shiny floor.

Gerrard's voice sounded hollow, and echoed as if he was bellowing down a rolled-up newspaper – the airport still hadn't got its acoustics right. Reason shrugged and turned his back on the ants' nest.

'She's on her way,' he said. 'You can collect her at Charles de Gaulle.' He paused for a second. 'There was a problem.'

Gerrard's voice gave nothing away. 'What was it this time?'

'The guy in the car, the one who was doing the watching.'

'Don't tell me!'

'He didn't fancy our company. Made a bloody nuisance of himself.'

'So you killed him!'

'No, didn't even scratch him. I warned my people I wanted him upright and healthy. They took me literally. I should have told them to shoot one of his legs off, I could have discussed the weather and other things with him while he was lying on his back bleeding to death. They were too gentle. One of them said boo to him and before they could tap him behind the ear he was out of that little white car like a raw egg. He cleared that friggin' great wall that runs alongside your Melanie's road as if he'd been training for it all his bloody life. I've never seen anything like it. Under different circumstances I'd have laughed. One of my clowns sent a couple of shots at his ankles but I think he jumped over them, or outran them.'

Gerrard didn't sound too disappointed. 'These things happen,' he said. 'Did he do, or say, anything interesting before your man frightened him?'

'Not a bloody thing. We didn't have time for a chat and his car gave us nothing at all, clean as a new suit it was – a complete bloody blank.'

'OK, that's it then – I can't see any reason for you to hang about over there now, you might as well come over tonight. Can you make it?'

Reason turned in his shell and looked in the opposite direction. His cover was leaning against the chocolate shop window. He grinned weakly at Reason and pulled himself up straight. Reason winked at him and continued talking to Gerrard. 'Let's do it tomorrow,' he said. 'I want to go back to Miller Street and spend a little bit of time there, just in case sonny-boy comes back for his car tonight.'

'Fair enough. Tomorrow then, what shall we say . . . Afternoon?'

'Evening.'

'Ring me.'

'Sure, about this time tomorrow. Cheers!'

Reason ducked out of the hair-drier and walked away without looking round.

CHAPTER 22

The little backstreet pub was Murray's idea of the perfect watering hole. Only him and Smithy, and a bored barman who sucked on a home-rolled cigarette and gazed moodily at the nude on the peanut card. Murray's idea of the perfect barman; uninterested, discreet, and a connoisseur of art – the perfect barman in the perfect pub. He emptied his pint mug and pushed it across the table towards Harry Smythe.

'OK, Smithy,' he said, 'go on from where you tried to put one between Percival's eyes. No – leave the beer for a moment .' He moved the empty glass fractionally away from Harry Smythe's reaching hand. 'Tell me what happened next.'

Smithy took his hand back and wrapped it round his own balloon-shaped glass. 'The bullet was as close as he'll ever want to be to one,' he said ungrammatically. His voice had developed a slight stammer in his hurry to get it over and done with. Murray didn't push him.

'He fell backwards out of the car and I left like a d-dose from the other side. When I looked round he was b-back on his feet with something black and nasty in his h-hands and he banged two off at me as I went over the wall. I reckoned I cleared it with about three feet to spare!' Harry Smythe sipped from his glass, swallowed, and blinked. The drink seemed to clear his stammer. 'I needn't have bothered though. He didn't follow.'

Murray raised his eyebrows. 'Why didn't he follow, Smithy?'

'Two reasons.' Smithy smiled weakly. 'He didn't follow because first of all he was too short-arsed to make the wall on his own, and secondly, as he was scrabbling around for a toe-hold, a voice bellowed, "Don't bother with him, he's probably five miles up the bloody north circular by now."'

Murray said, 'This voice you heard giving the orders. Did it mean anything to you?'

'Yes. It belonged to the big black who was having dinner with Gerrard in the restaurant on Saturday.'

'You could tell that from the other side of the wall?'

'No,' said Smithy patiently, 'I managed to haul myself up and have a look. He wasn't shouting, he was using his normal voice, but his tonsils, like everything else he's got, seemed to be double-sized. And he looked very cross. He had Melanie Lambdon with him. I didn't like the look of him at all – even with a bloody great wall between us! He bellowed at my bloke, "Get one of the others to mark that skinny bastard's car in case he's stupid enough to come back for it. You and Crispin cover me and the girl to the airport." At that point I thought it would be enough for the day and dropped back down my side of the wall.'

Murray shook his head. 'So they're all off to the airport – not for a cup of tea and a Chelsea bun, but to catch a bloody aeroplane. So, Smithy, where are they going, this bloody gang? And where does that leave the Frog?'

Smithy investigated the bottom of his empty glass. He avoided looking at Murray.

Murray scowled. 'I don't think he came here to pass the time of day with old Lambdon or to put his leg across the old man's daughter. I think he came for something specific, something to do with what he does best. I think he came here with a killing contract.' Murray pointed his finger at Harry Smythe then turned it and tapped himself on the chest several times. 'Now you and me, Smudger,' he said, 'are both old enough to know that men like Gerrard don't stoop to knocking off bookies' runners who've buggered off with the day's takings, aren't we?'

Smithy pulled a face and shoved his nose deeper into the brandy glass, but he didn't answer Murray.

Murray took it as read. 'Tell me who, in your humble opinion, you think is worth the sort of money you'd need to pay a man like Gerrard to have put out of the way? And who's putting up the wherewithal?'

Smithy shrugged his shoulders. He didn't look up.

'I don't know why I bother! Go and get the drinks, Smithy.'

'Talking about Frenchmen's friends,' Murray said when Smithy returned with new drinks, 'did you make any of them?'

Smithy tasted his brandy and ginger ale. It seemed about the right strength. 'I made the little snake who spent the evening rubbing herself up against him. Her name's Audrey Gilling.'

'Mrs?'

'Miss. She's clean. Lives in a nice second-floor flat in Rosslyn Hill and works for a travel agency in one of the streets off Piccadilly. She's got a large, elderly, bald-headed dad who calls round to see her.'

'Dad?'

'Sugar daddy, more like. Patted her bottom with the familiarity of a man who's been there before and knows what's under that tight little skirt. He had an expectant beam on his face as well.'

'How does this girl find her way on to Gerrard's knee?'

Harry Smythe was bored with Audrey Gilling, it was beginning to show. 'She's probably a friend of the coffee-coloured piece,' he said impatiently. 'Maybe they work the same street, or play in the same darts team. Christ knows! She probably got roped in the other night for a bit of light relief – I told you, she's clean.'

Murray sipped his beer reflectively. After a few moments he said, 'OK, let's scrub the scrubber. What about Sambo, have you got anything on him?'

'There's nothing to tell. He's a ghost.'

'Funny thing that,' said Murray, thoughtfully, 'mention of blacks and ghosts triggers off a little memory . . . Now let me think for a moment.' He straightened up in his chair, pointed the cigarette in his mouth towards the fireplace and blew down the side of it from the corner of his mouth. The ash shot off the end like a bullet. Murray stared at the fireplace for a second or two then turned back to Smithy.

'I've got it!' he said shortly. 'A couple of years ago, somebody talking about a spade doing a bit of specialising down there in Armagh . . . That's what I was trying to remember. This one was supposed to have been a big handy bloke, a bit like the one you've just described, someone who knew what it was all about. But he got taken. He got picked up and screwed.' Murray drew on his cigarette, closed his eyes, and looked back into the past. 'A Provo killer squad tapped him on the shoulder and took him in for interview . . . A boy named Sean McGann – nasty bit of work – was the one who conducted examinations down there for a while . . . They wrapped him up in a potato sack and dumped him outside the post office in Cullyhanna – that's just up the road from Crossmaglen. They left him alive – Christ knows why.'

'It's like I said, Murray, you're trying to tie up ends that don't exist. This has got bugger-all to do with the bloke who was having dinner with Gerrard the other night.'

Murray grinned. 'I agree with you. I've changed my mind, I don't think it's our black we're talking about – far too much coincidence there.'

'So what's our next move?'

'There isn't one. You can go home. I suggest you drop out for a day or two. Give me a ring when you wake up.'

'What shall I do about my car?'

'Don't go anywhere near it. Is it clean?'

'Yes.'

'In your name?'

'Yup.'

'Ring the police station and report it pinched. Let the old Bill go and pick it up.'

'Clever.' Harry Smythe stood up and drained his glass. 'What'll you be doing, Murray?'

'Don't worry about me, boy, I've got lots of interesting little things to keep me busy until Frenchie comes swimming back across our Channel.'

'You're still sure he's coming back?'

'Instinct, Smithy! Bet your hangover on it!'

CHAPTER 23

Sean McGann savoured the warm Paris air as he strolled under the trees shading the broad pavement of Boulevard St Germain. He turned into Rue Benoît and carried on walking, unhurriedly, until he reached the Hôtel Royale, St Benoît half-way down the narrow street. Before turning into the entrance he gave a cursory glance over his shoulder. Nobody had followed him off the boulevard. The street was empty. He was alone.

The Royale was a small hotel. McGann turned his nose up at it as he pushed open the door to the reception and walked across the tiny foyer to the reception desk.

It was a small desk. But he had a choice. There were two of them holding the fort; one would have pleased Charlie Phelan – a pretty young thing in a dark-blue suit who raised his eyes briefly from his paper, looked McGann up and down, then lowered them again. He wasn't interested. McGann didn't like him either. He chose his friend, a flat-faced, sallow-skinned, three-quarters Algerian.

'You've got a room booked for me,' said McGann. It was a statement, not a question. 'The name's Bridges.'

The Algerian's black eyes hooded for a moment then came to life. His accent was good, pure French, colloquial – the fourth quarter must have been *pied-noir*, or even Metropolitan.

'Room number 4,' he said. He slid a small key on a plastic fob across the counter and lowered his voice. 'There's a message for you, Monsieur Bridges.'

McGann glanced quickly at the pretty boy's bowed head then back to his Algerian. 'What sort of message?'

'This . . .' He reached below the counter and brought out a manila envelope. 'He said I was to hand it to you personally.'

'Anything else?'

'No, monsieur, just the envelope and, er . . . your room's been booked for seven days. It's been paid for.'

'Thanks. Have I got a telephone?'

'No.' They replied together, but the Algerian was helpful: 'You can use the one in the hall – day or night, it's quite private.'

'Thanks.' McGann left them looking at each other and went up to his room.

The room was nothing more than he'd expected; a large double bed, a wardrobe and in the corner of the room, stuck there like an afterthought, a small adjunct with a washbasin, a lavatory, and the essential bidet. It was a room for sleeping in, or for sex; but in a room like this love might pose a few psychological problems. None of these worried McGann at the moment.

He threw his bag on to the stool at the foot of the bed and poured himself a large measure of duty-free Teacher's. He added an inch of tepid bathroom water and sipped as he sat on the bed and opened the envelope. It contained only a key wrapped in a piece of corrugated cardboard; a luggage locker key, number 26 – nothing else on it, just the number 26.

McGann stared at the key as he sipped his whisky. Good old Paddy Phelan, he'd done him proud with this one – nothing on the cardboard; nothing on the envelope – left baggage locker number 26? There couldn't be more than a thousand different places in Paris where the bloody key would fit. And where do you start? McGann's eyes glazed over . . . Railway stations? Invalides? Orly? Charles de Gaulle? He curled his lip and swallowed a large mouthful of whisky. It made him cough. You could only think the worst of Phelan, it would be just like that icy-eyed bastard to have arranged the drop at the furthest point, like the one he'd just left – locker number 26, Charles de Gaulle Airport . . . That would have amused Phelan, except he hadn't got a sense of humour – he said so himself. McGann drank and coughed again. What a bloody way to start a game of soldiers! He tossed the key in the air, caught it and slipped it in his jacket pocket. He emptied the glass abruptly, grimaced at the warm strength of the liquid and sent the glass slithering to the far edge of the bedside table. Phelan must have known, he was just making life bloody awkward. McGann stood up and tucked his jacket under his arm. It was time to upset Phelan's other friend.

McGann dialled the Clichy number Phelan had given him. 'Emergency,' had said Phelan, 'in case you can't get started. Only the once, mind you, nothing else – he'd rather not know about you.'

McGann's lip curled. *And if he's as evil as you, Charlie, we've really got problems!* The ringing tone stopped. Somebody had picked up the receiver and was waiting.

Nothing was said.

McGann listened to the silence for a second, then said quietly, 'I'm the guy you left the key for.'

'Who sent you?' The voice was American.

'Charlie Phelan.'

'OK. Montparnasse.'

'What about it?'

'That's where the key fits, dum-dum . . . Don't call me again.'

The phone went dead in McGann's ear.

McGann decided to walk to Montparnasse station.

A quick look across the road, a casual backward glance and a stop at a shop window, then on again until he was satisfied there was nobody else going to try their keys out at the Gare de Montparnasse.

McGann was alone, and he made sure he stayed alone when he opened the metal door on locker number 26. He was still alone when he left the station but he now had a pale-blue Air France cabin bag hanging from his shoulder. It was heavy. He hadn't looked, but he had a good idea what it held.

He retraced his steps, back along the Rue de Rennes, and turned into a small bar in the narrow street at the junction of Boulevard St Germain.

The bar was cool and quiet and almost empty, like the chapel of a tourist cathedral in the height of the summer season.

'Can I use your phone, Patrice?' he called. He'd been here before.

'You know where it is.'

McGann dialled his number and looked out of the window. It gave him a funnel-like view down Boulevard St Germain and a panoramic aspect of the Café Boule d'Or which occupied the entire corner on the far side of the boulevard. The pavement tables were packed. He suddenly felt thirsty.

'*Allô?*' The phone came to life in his ear. It was only one word but it was enough for McGann.

'Is that Monsieur Monod?' he asked.

'*Oui.*'

'My name is Bridges. I've come from London. Mr Brocklebank gave me your number and a little present for you, he said you'd be able to help me with a small problem.'

There followed a long pause, long enough for McGann to think about repeating his message, then the voice said, 'Didn't Mr Brocklebank tell you to say something else to me?'

McGann raised his eyes to the ceiling. 'Brocklebank said to tell you that the thirty-first of June was recorded as London's hottest day so far this summer . . .'

'The thirty-first?'

'That's what he said.'

'Of June?'

'That's right.'

'Very well.' If M. Monod was happy with the exchange his voice didn't betray it. 'Where are you near?' he asked.

'St Germain-des-Prés,' McGann replied.

Monod said nothing for a few seconds; then, 'Do you know the Boule d'Or on Boulevard St Germain?'

McGann continued to gaze out of the window at the Café Boule d'Or. 'No,' he said, 'but I'll find it.'

'Be there at half-past four this afternoon. Take the corner table at the end of the terrace facing the square so that you're right opposite the church. You'll see what I mean when you find the café. Have you understood that?'

McGann could see what he meant. 'Go on,' he said.

'Buy yourself an English newspaper and leave it open on the table. I will address you by your name. In that manner you will know who I am, but I won't stop if there's more than one of you sitting at the table. Make sure that you're alone.'

'What if somebody gets to the table before me?'

'You'll sort that out before I arrive. I want to see only one person sitting there. Don't forget, Monsieur Bridges, sixteen-thirty.' Monod replaced his phone abruptly, leaving McGann listening to just the hollow echo of a dead receiver.

In the basement of the building below Monod's apartment two men sat in a stuffy little room watching a seven-inch sound-activated tape slowly unwind. It continued turning for several seconds after Monod had replaced his receiver, then stopped; a red light flickered, and hovered as if it were unsure whether to cut off entirely or hang on for another minute or so in case there was more to come.

The two men exchanged quick glances, then both stared back at the machine. Neither man spoke.

The shorter of the two sat on a long-legged stool propped against the wall. He raised a small bottle of Kronenberg to his lips and filled his mouth with warm beer. As he gurgled the beer down his throat he pulled a face at the machine and glanced again, quickly, at his companion, but his expression showed only mild curiosity – as if a show of enthusiasm was going to erase, or cancel out, what he'd just heard.

His companion was less phlegmatic. A taller man, he made no attempt to hide his excitement. His eyes were lit up. He waited until his friend had emptied his mouth of beer then leaned forward in his deckchair and tapped him on the knee.

'Martin'?' he said gruffly. As he spoke he grasped his left hand with his right and cracked his knuckles with a teeth-grinding explosion; it was a half-nervous, half-compulsive gesture that he claimed helped him with his thinking.

The little man was used to it. He didn't flinch.

'Yes?' he answered. His eyes never left the machine.

'I didn't know *Rosbif* had thirty-one days in their June.'

Martineau tilted his head back again and formed his mouth into a smile round the narrow neck of the small bottle. He swallowed two more mouthfuls, lowered the bottle and wiped his lips with the back of his hand. Then he belched noisily and grinned at his colleague.

'They don't,' he said. 'Fatso's just done the next best thing to shoving the pointed end of a Browning up his arse and squeezing the trigger.'

'How's he managed that?'

'Monkey talk over the phone. The fat bastard's gone and dropped an overweight bollock; he's just booked himself an appointment with the long nail.'

Pierre Martineau slid off the stool and walked across to the tape machine. 'Get Marc in here, I want him to listen to this.' He turned back to the machine and switched it on.

CHAPTER 24

McGann closed the bedroom door behind him and threw the Air France bag on to the bed. He stood for a moment deep in thought with Monod's oily voice still echoing in his mind, then shook his head and picked up the bottle of Teacher's and carried it into the bathroom.

He poured a large measure into the tooth glass and topped it up with lukewarm water from the tap. It tasted like a purgative, but he stuck with it and drank nearly half the glass before plunging his face into the warm water in the cracked washbasin. He felt marginally better when he surfaced and raised the glass to his lips again. This time, instead of drinking, he swilled the whisky round his teeth like mouthwash and spat it out. He inspected his teeth in the mirror, ran his tongue over them, then glanced up to meet the pair of cool grey eyes that stared back at him. They told him to get on with it. He threw the rest of the whisky and water down the sink and went back into the bedroom.

The Air France bag crooked its finger at him.

He joined it on the bed, pulled the zip all the way open and tipped its contents on to the bedspread.

Fifty thousand dollars made an untidy pile.

He stacked them up – twenty-five elastic-banded packets of US twenty-dollar bills, all second-hand with not a crisply traceable note amongst them. He shrugged the money aside and went for the bundle wrapped in a dirty red and white striped shirt. It was a heavy bundle and carried a smell that made his nose twitch in anticipation. Gun-oil. He flared his nostrils and inhaled like a hungry junkie. McGann was hooked on gun-oil. He unwrapped the shirt. He had a fair idea what he was going to find. He wasn't disappointed.

The 7.56 Sauer Automatic was modified to take a stubby 3-inch silencer – just enough weight in the wrong place to throw it fractionally out of balance, but still unblemished – nearly seven inches of uncomplicated death; loaded, cocked, and ready to go. McGann's satisfaction showed as he handled it; it was all there – the potent feeling of manhood – an erection in slightly worn blued-metal.

He stripped it and cleaned it, and put it back together again. It didn't need it, its last owner had been in love with it and it showed. He slipped the magazine out, checked the rounds. Full. He clicked it back. He emptied and reloaded the spare magazine and dropped that into the bottom of the bag, then scooped the wads of money in on top of it and closed the zip. There was no point in hiding it – McGann gazed around the small and sparsely furnished room – and even if there was, where the bloody hell did you hide fifty thousand dollars in a room with only a bed and a wardrobe? He smiled to himself – it was only money, and there was a lot more where that came from . . . St Patrick's Day was every day on the Eastern seaboard.

He carried the bag into the lavatory and slid it between the cracked bidet and the wall. He studied it for a few seconds, and, as an afterthought, tossed the damp towel on top of it and then the torn shirt. He could still smell the oil on the striped segment, but it didn't matter; what sort of silly bugger would leave fifty thousand untraceables lying around in a third-class hotel bog? He turned his back on it without another thought.

There wasn't much else to do. He picked the Sauer up off the bed, cocked it again and tucked it into the waistband of his trousers. It felt snug and comfortable, as if it had spent all its life there. He looked at his watch again. Three o'clock. One and a half hours to wait – so it was time to go. He closed the door quietly behind him and went out into the shimmering afternoon.

He didn't hang about. He crossed the Boulevard St Germain and went straight back to the bar on the corner of Rue de Rennes. He accepted a Ricard from the sleepy barman and wandered casually to the table by the window overlooking the corner of the Café Boule d'Or. He touched his lips with the cold glass but didn't drink; his mind, like his eyes, was centred on the table at the far end of the café's pavement terrace. He settled down for a long wait.

Five minutes after McGann had taken up his position in the bar, Martineau turned his Peugeot on to the Boulevard St Germain and sidled into the slip road outside Le Drug St Germain.

He didn't sit there long; a couple of minutes staring at the crowd, then he switched off the engine and turned to his two companions. 'OK, you two,' he said, 'wait here. I'm going to have a little chat with my old *copain*, Georges-the-mouth. Make yourself comfortable, it might take a few minutes.'

'Old pisspot?' Jaubert looked up from the sporting page of his newspaper and frowned. 'I thought that miserable little bastard was still chewing *boudin* in *Santé*?'

Martineau grinned over his shoulder. 'I turned the key for him. I was missing all that free beer!'

'Not to mention the words . . .'

'Not to mention those.' Martineau turned to the young man at his side. 'Marc, pass me a couple of those bug things; I might as well put one in place while I'm over there. Get your stuff fixed up so that it's ready for me to test.'

'Do you want me to set up for one or two?'

'One . . . No, just a minute . . . Make it two. And, Jau', I didn't mean make yourself as comfortable as all that. Get out and cover him from outside.'

Jaubert straightened up from the back seat and opened his eyes. He didn't say anything. He slid out of the back door, stuck the newspaper under his arm and walked across the pavement to lean against the wall of the drugstore. He watched Martineau jink across the boulevard, his stubby legs carrying him between the fast-moving traffic until he was swallowed up by the crowd on the pavement outside the café. Jaubert lit a cigarette, opened his newspaper, and made himself look like everyone else.

It took Martineau ten minutes and two cold *demi-pressions* to bulldoze Georges, the pavement waiter of the Boule d'Or, into playing with the grown-ups. Between them they planted one of Marc Legoubin's sticky micro-bugs to the underside of the end table chosen by Monod. Provided Georges didn't get ideas beyond his station and frighten them away Monod and his guest were about to give their first, and if Martineau had anything to do about it their last, public performance.

Martineau had good reason to look pleased with himself when he left the café. He strolled along the opposite side of the Boulevard St Germain and crooked his finger at Jaubert as he passed him. Jaubert dragged himself away from the wall and the two men joined Legoubin in the Peugeot.

'OK, Jau',' said Martineau, 'this is your bit of the game. At four o'clock on the dot I want you to sidle over to that corner table and if anybody's sitting there, empty it. But do it nicely. Persuasion, Jau' – I don't want to see any little arses being dumped in the road! You got that?'

'You worry too much.'

'One of us has to! That bastard Monod, or the other clown, is going to be hanging around out there somewhere just waiting for one of your little exhibitions, so, as I said, do it nicely. Be discreet, make it look natural – a quiet word, something like that.'

'I said don't worry.'

'You know what you're looking for?'

'A guy wandering around with an English newspaper under his arm and a stupid look on his face.'

'Don't underestimate him. As soon as you've made him, slope off down the road – but make sure he sees you go. He'll want to watch you out of sight, so whatever you do don't look around. I'll appear from the other direction to make sure he's happy and comfortable. OK?'

'OK.'

'Take a roundabout route and come back and look after Marc. But don't go to sleep because I want you to keep an eye on me as well. I suggest you grab the same bit of wall you had earlier – you'll be able to see us both from there, no problem. OK?'

'OK.'

'When I move after *Rosbif* take off like a cork. I want to know you're right behind me. Watch my signals.'

'Don't worry.'

'If you say "don't worry" once more I'll stick my finger so far up your nose it'll come out of your arse! Now listen. Did you manage to ring Mother while I was over there?'

'Yes.'

'And?'

'Bruno'll be here to take the wedding pictures.' Jaubert looked at his watch. 'He's probably here now.'

'He knows the target?'

'He knows Monod. Took the last lot.' Jaubert leaned forward and looked at the high buildings further down Boulevard St Germain. 'Could be in any one of those. Don't worr – !'

'Go to sleep, Jau'.'

Martineau picked up the tiny earpiece, wiped it free of condensation and jammed it into his left ear. He leaned forward, turned up the sound on the receiver and listened to a clear conversation between the two women sitting at Monod's table. He stared across the road and tried to see whether the one telling her guilty secrets looked as interesting as she sounded but the crowds effectively blocked his view. He listened for a few more minutes then switched the receiver off and settled back in his seat. He closed his eyes, but didn't sleep.

It was nearly time.

McGann crammed the remainder of the second egg into his mouth and washed it down with the bottom inch of his iced Ricard. It was mainly ice, but he hardly noticed. He ran his tongue round the inside of his mouth, cleaning up the odd bits of egg that had stuck to his teeth. His eyes remained riveted to the tall man in the red shirt who had appeared from nowhere and taken up residence at the corner table across the road.

He'd seen nothing sinister in Jaubert's appearance; nothing sinister in the combined efforts of the waiter and Jaubert to dislodge two twittering females. From McGann's vantage point it all seemed very normal. But it had to be watched. Red shirt had probably done him a favour and frightened the two women back to their husbands. He'd be easier to shift. McGann was happy with his own explanation – he had uncomplicated explanations for uncomplicated manoeuvres. Two women bolting from a man standing there with his cock in his hand was normal – McGann was looking for the abnormal; the unusual; and so far he'd seen nothing to make him nervous.

He glanced at his watch again. Twenty past four. Time to stroll across the road and pick up a paper from the kiosk on the corner. Time to wander past the rows of tables like a man with only thirst on his mind, and time for a man named Monod to clock him as his customer – wherever he was watching from . . . And he would be watching, McGann had no doubt about that. But what about red shirt? How much time to dislodge him? Five minutes? Four to make him uncomfortable and one to see him on his way . . . Sure, but how? Play it by bum and hope he's not one of those!

McGann grinned to himself as he slid out of the dark bar and into the shadowless noise of Boulevard St Germain.

Jaubert saw him coming. He didn't need an English newspaper tucked under an arm to transpose a voice on thin brown magnetic tape into a man calling himself Bridges – it was instinct. He'd have picked him out of a thousand.

He looked up at the church tower on the opposite side of the square and watched the large hand of the clock judder into the slot one minute after the number five. He waited a second or two, as if absorbed with the old clock's performance, then ostentatiously compared its time with his own watch. He made sure McGann was watching. He stood up, finished his drink while he looked around, consulted his watch again, then pointed a finger at the waiter.

Jaubert thrust a note into Georges' hand and managed to ignore McGann who squeezed past him and sat down at the empty table. He deliberately kept his back to him and, although he felt his eyes boring into his shoulder blades, Jaubert turned away without looking round. He stepped down on to the kerb, looked at his watch once more, shrugged his shoulders, and moved off slowly into the crowd.

McGann watched Jaubert disappear.

'Bring me a café cognac, *garçon*.'

'*Oui, monsieur!*'

McGann raised the small green coffee cup to his lips just as the large hand on the church clock jinked its way to the half-hour mark. The one solitary clang almost drowned the voice in his ear.

'Monsieur Bridges?'

The full cup remained steady at McGann's lips as he turned slowly to face the voice. He found himself looking at the ugliest man he'd ever seen.

Somebody had described Monod as a well-dressed pear on legs. He'd been flattering him. Monod's face was obscene – it had never needed a razor, the original baby's bottom. Smooth and shiny, with a blubbery mouth and flaccid complexion, the face was topped by eyebrows plucked into a thin straight line over watery-blue eyes. These eyes now stared at McGann with curiosity, but without expectation. He didn't improve on his opening gambit.

McGann lowered his cup into its saucer. 'That's right,' he said. He didn't smile or offer his hand. 'And you're Monod?'

'I'm *Monsieur* Monod. But no conversation,' he held up a thick forefinger as McGann opened his mouth. 'Not yet. Not until I say.'

He lowered his huge backside into a chair and glanced casually around him. It was a deceptive casualness. He missed nothing. When he'd done the full circuit he started again – this time a cursory inspection; and then, satisfied with the world about him and the company he was keeping, turned his shiny bald head back to McGann.

'How is my friend Mr Brocklebank?' he asked.

McGann shook his head and drank more coffee. 'I've no idea,' he replied.

'Pardon?'

McGann exchanged his coffee cup for the brandy glass and sipped delicately. He stared into the fat man's eyes. 'I said, I've no idea. I don't know your friend Mr Brocklebank.'

The plucked eyebrows rose half an inch and Monod's massive backside shifted fractionally on the seat as if he were about to stand up and take off. He held that position for a second or two without speaking, then lowered himself. The chair groaned.

'Explain,' he demanded.

'Charlie Phelan sent me. You know Charlie Phelan?'

Monod's head didn't move an inch; neither a yes nor a no. He stared at McGann. He was suspicious.

'What does your Phelan say it is that Monsieur Brocklebank wants?'

'A favour.'

Monod haunched his almost non-existent shoulders. 'What favour?'

'He wants you to put me in touch with a man named Michel Gerrard. A Frenchman,' added McGann unnecessarily. 'He lives here, in Paris.'

'And what does Michel Gerrard do? What's his position? Is he official?'

'Gerrard's a professional killer, a contract man. If he's on government books that's up to you to find out. Personally I don't give a fuck who pays his wages, all I want to know is where his front-door key fits and where I can find him tomorrow morning.'

Monod stared across the table for several seconds, as if seeing the young Irishman for the first time. After a few seconds he turned his head to look for the waiter and ordered a half-bottle of chilled Dom Pérignon. He made no offer to McGann. While he waited for his champagne to arrive he surveyed the scenery once more. He looked moderately content with the appearance of the afternoon and, as he turned back, extracted a long, thin and very expensive cigar from the inside pocket of his jacket which he lit with a small, gold, ladies' Dupont. He blew a stream of pungent smoke across the table and, once again, almost smiled at McGann.

'What else do you know about him?'

'He's known in the funeral trade as Siegfried.'

Monod poured himself a glass of champagne. He took his time. He avoided McGann's eyes as he reached down and carefully manoeuvred the bottle back into its clinking nest of ice cubes and water and gave it a final little twirl.

'Ahh . . .' he said and looked up. 'Siegfried. He's a very dangerous man is this Siegfried, Monsieur Bridges.'

McGann wasn't impressed. 'Is he a freelance operator?'

'He was a shadow until about six months ago and then it was mooted in selected circles that he'd become approachable. I presume that meant he'd become de-officialised and open to the market – freelance, as you call it.' Monod's eyes did an upward trip leaving only the whites staring at McGann. 'Do you want my advice, Mr Bridges?'

McGann stared at the two white orbs. 'No thanks. It's help I want – not advice.'

'Nevertheless I'm going to give it to you.' Monod looked strangely ill at ease; he seemed to have forgotten his chilled champagne. 'My advice, Mr Bridges,' he said quietly, 'is go home. Forget all about Siegfried. You're out of your class. We're all out of our class. This man Siegfried is death. He'll brush you to one side as if you were a tiny little nothing, an excrescence, an irritation up his nose on a hot afternoon. Go home, Mr Bridges and gain yourself a little more living time.'

'Do you know the English word bollocks, Monod?'

'No, what does it mean?'

'It means I'm running out of time. I want the information I've asked for – quickly. Thanks for the advice – you can shove it!'

Monod didn't take umbrage. He filled his mouth with cigar smoke and blew it out so that it deflected off the table and dispersed around McGann's head; he left his lips pursed as if he was waiting for a kiss and remained like this for several seconds staring at McGann's blank expression. When he spoke his reply was totally unexpected.

'Take my apologies to Monsieur Brocklebank,' he said carefully, 'through your Phelan, of course, and tell him I'm unable, in this instance, to help him; tell him I don't fancy swimming in the same pool as the likes of Siegfried.'

'What the hell are you talking about?'

'I'm talking about your death wish, your desire to meet Monsieur Gerrard. I don't want the results of your stupidity knocking on my door for a contribution, so you'll have to get some other source to put the gun to your head and pull the trigger. I don't want to be involved in this. It's not to my liking. Tell that to Monsieur Brocklebank.'

'The IRA's not going to like this.'

'I'm not concerned with what the IRA likes or dislikes – I'm concerned solely with the health of Philippe Monod.'

'Nevertheless . . .'

Monod waved McGann aside with a flick of his wrist. 'Nevertheless nothing! I piss on the IRA – and yourself as well! I cannot, and will not, help you.'

'There's thirty thousand dollars in it for you.'

'The money is of no importance.'

'Forty thousand.'

'Forty-five.'

'OK. How soon?'

Monod emptied his glass and replaced it on the table. He burped delicately behind a podgy hand and wiped his lips with a silk handkerchief. 'Give me until this time tomorrow afternoon. I might have something for you by then, nothing definite, but let us wait and see. You have that much money available? In American currency?'

'The money's available. Do I ring you?'

'No you don't! You don't ever ring me again. I will contact you tomorrow afternoon. Where are you staying?'

'You're a trusting bastard, aren't you?'

'I trust no one. Give me your phone number.'

'Same here – no deal.'

'How am I to get in touch with you? You're making things very difficult for me.'

'Tough.' McGann pulled the *Daily Mail* towards him and wrote Phelan's Canning Town phone number on the margin. He tore it off and slid it across the table so that it rested alongside Monod's chubby forefinger. 'Ring that number tomorrow afternoon at three and ask where Sean McGann is staying in Paris. Ring the number they give you and you'll find me on the end of the line. OK?'

'You being this Sean McGann?'

'Just ring the number. I'll be waiting for your call tomorrow. Don't let me down.' McGann stood up and squeezed round behind Monod's chair. He leaned forward as he passed, and said, 'Don't move until I've gone. Finish your cigar and your champagne – and don't forget that word I taught you.'

'What word's that?'

'Bollocks.'

It's a very special sense, a seventh sense – an ability to smell trouble, to sniff danger, to duck when others continue strolling along the parapet picking their nose and wondering what's for tea. McGann had this sense. It was working now; an itching sensation at the back of his neck; a feeling of eyes in the crowd; a feeling that made him touch the butt of the Sauer in a barely noticeable brush of reassurance as he half-turned, as if to go back to the table he'd just left. He saw it out of the corner of his eye – a movement, only slight, but it was there; a short man with crew-cut greying hair had lifted his rump no more than three inches off his chair and dropped back again. The movement in itself was not threatening. But it was enough for McGann – enough to set the bells ringing.

He continued as if nothing had happened and turned into Boulevard St Germain. He didn't look round. On the corner of Rue St Benoît he stopped, opened his *Daily Mail* and waited for the short man to catch him up.

But he didn't come. There was nobody following him.

It disturbed McGann that somebody didn't come hurtling round the corner hot on his heels; it disturbed him that somebody should want to. Something was happening. But what?

He refolded his newspaper and strolled down the road towards the Royale St Benoît. He stood for a moment on the steps of the hotel. The quiet backwater remained a quiet backwater. He waited another couple of minutes, almost long enough to convince himself he'd made a mistake – almost.

But the sense was still nudging – it refused to go away. He frowned at his distorted reflection in the dusty mirror on the side of the entrance hall as he turned into the vestibule. It was empty. He ran quickly up the stairs, turned the corner and stopped with his back edging against the closed door of room number 3 and waited.

It was hot and listless and very, very quiet – the first floor of a crowded funeral parlour – nothing moved. There were no fans to disturb the atmosphere, no breeze bubbling up and down the short corridor, and downstairs only a muffled hawking cough to show that somebody was minding the shop. McGann turned his wrist over and glanced at the time. It was twenty past five. That was why nothing stirred. *Cinq à sept!* It was bedtime in Paris! He put his ear to the door and listened to the faint, metronomic creaking of old, tired bedsprings – it helped pass the time while he waited for something to happen, it took his mind off what wasn't going on downstairs. He pressed his ear closer. Money or love? He frowned and listened but no clue came through the door; no words, no laughter, no giggles, no cries, no murmured happiness – only the tune-less bounce of springs groaning to a regular beat and the throaty laboured grunt of a man with still a long way to go.

McGann stopped listening and poked his head round the corner. The vestibule remained deserted. Nothing disturbed the silence. He tried to convince himself he'd made a mistake. But he didn't move, he continued waiting.

Jaubert stayed on his side of the boulevard and watched McGann through the traffic. When McGann moved, Jaubert moved, and Legoubin trailed along a few yards behind. But Jaubert made no attempt to cross the road. He moved into the shade of a plane tree by a bus stop and saw McGann stop, open his newspaper, wait, and after a couple of minutes move on confidently down Rue St Benoît. At that point he almost lost sight of him. Then through a gap in the traffic he saw McGann turn into the Royale St Benoît. Without turning his head he waggled his fingers for Legoubin to follow and moved at a leisurely pace across the boulevard and down Rue St Benoît.

He gave the lobby of the hotel only a cursory glance as he walked past. It was empty. He signalled Legoubin to wait on the other side of the road then retraced his steps and entered the hotel. The vestibule was still empty. He gave the hall and stairway a brief inspection then banged the bell on the reception counter.

'Come out from behind that bloody door. I'm in a hurry!' Jaubert wasted no time on introduction. 'What's the name of the man who came in here about five minutes ago?'

'Monsieur Bridges. An Englishman.' The reply was prompt.

'Room number?'

'Four. First landing, turn left.' The Algerian tilted his chin upwards in the direction of the stairs.

'Got a back way up there?'

'No.'

'Telephone?'

'No.'

'Anybody staying with him?'

'No.'

'OK, get back in your kennel. Don't try sending any messages up the stairs, and don't come crawling out until I send for you. Got it?'

The Algerian nodded. He dropped his lips like a curtain over his protruding teeth and walked backwards into his office.

'And shut that bloody door behind you.'

McGann straightened up against the wall and frowned. The conversation he'd listened to had told him nothing, except that somebody had followed him and watched him come into the hotel.

He tiptoed across the corridor and let himself into number 4. Inside, he moved quickly. He pulled the Sauer from his waistband and slipped it under the mattress at the foot of the bed. He stripped the counterpane and left it in a crumpled roll and for good measure threw his jacket on top of it. It looked all very casual. Nothing to disturb the tenor of a gentle quiz; the satisfying of a policeman's curiosity as to why an Englishman would be taking afternoon cocktails with a fat profit-maker – there was nothing to it, no need to call on a poetic imagination, a monkey ought to be able to sing his way out of this one. McGann washed his hands, rinsed them, covered them in soap again and rubbed it in before drying them with a towel. He was still in the bathroom when the knock came on the door.

'Come in!' He moved quickly into the room, stretched himself out on the bed and put his hands casually round the back of his neck – and waited for the door to fall in.

The performance was wasted.

The knock came again, louder, persistent, but no words.

'Hang on!'

He opened the door slowly.

Martineau tightened his grip on the heavy Webley as the door began to open. Pressed flat against the wall he held the automatic against the door jamb at face height. He gave a quick warning glance at Jaubert. It wasn't necessary. Jaubert was enjoying himself. He stood with his back to the wall opposite the door, both hands crooked round a short-barrelled .38 Special aimed at a spot on the door corresponding to the height of a man's breastbone. There was no pressure left on the trigger.

But McGann did things properly. It was as if he could see through wood. He opened the door fully and stood still with a smile on his face and both hands visible – one on the door where everybody could see it and the other open on his chest as if he were half-way through crossing a blessing on himself.

Jaubert raised the Special so that McGann could see down its barrel. He'd noted the look of recognition in McGann's eyes and smiled back cheerfully. The situation pleased him. He liked even more the brief hint of shock that flashed across McGann's face almost rubbing out his stiff set smile; and he liked the professional manner with which he managed to hold it under control. Like Martineau, Jaubert knew a dummy when he saw one. He winked at McGann over the barrel of the Special; no dummy, this – it was going to be an interesting half-hour.

McGann breathed deeply but remained stock-still. Things were dawning in his mind; things like set-up; and nobody sends lumps of heavy artillery for a routine chat. Something wasn't right, this evil-looking bastard didn't even look copper. He continued staring at Jaubert, his smile of recognition clamping into a set, muscle-aching mask.

The smile held, but only just, when Jaubert's eyes flicked briefly to a point near McGann's right ear. McGann got the message. He didn't move his head but accepted the invitation and swivelled his eyes to the right. It didn't need much of a glance. The muzzle of a howitzer was six inches from his head, rock steady, and behind it the unsmiling face of the short man with the iron-grey crew-cut hair. McGann's smile finally died.

'There must be some mistake.'

'Shut up!' Martineau's voice was clear and concise. 'Put both hands on top of your head and take two steps forward.'

McGann did as he was told.

'OK, Jau' . . .'

Jaubert moved away from the wall and slid past McGann. He went through the open door – straight in; a quick glance round the room and then into the bathroom. He didn't stay long. He came back into the bedroom and stood to one side of the wardrobe and, with just a thoughtful pause, lifted its catch and allowed the unbalanced door to swing open. The rusty squeak was the only sound in the room; it was the only sound in the hotel. Jaubert stared into the wardrobe, ran his hand over the upper shelf, then slammed the door shut with his foot and rejoined Martineau in the corridor. Martineau hadn't moved.

McGann felt Jaubert's hand rest lightly in the small of his back.

'Up against the wall!'

Jaubert's voice was close to his ear. But he was given no time to comply. He was propelled across the corridor and slammed hard against the wall opposite.

'Arms outstretched. Legs apart.' Jaubert followed him across the corridor, his hand still in the small of his back.

'Don't look at me, English!' Jaubert kicked McGann behind his kneecap and pushed his face hard against the wall. 'Keep your face where it is.'

McGann grunted as Jaubert's hands groped and prodded. Jaubert made it last, and to show he'd finished he slammed his fist into the base of McGann's spine, shoving him tighter against the wall.

'He's clean, Martin' . . .'

Martineau took over. 'OK, you! Put your hands down to your sides and walk backwards into the room – no, wait! Just a minute. Marc!' Martineau rested the barrel of his pistol on McGann's shoulder and called down the corridor. Legoubin's head appeared at the top of the stairs. 'Marc.' Martineau didn't have to raise his voice, it carried all the way down the corridor. 'Watch the stairs and this door. Nobody comes in, and nobody goes out. Got it?'

'Got it, boss.'

'I'll give you a shout when we've finished with Jules here – you can help carry him home.' Martineau tapped McGann on the shoulder again. 'All right, you – move!'

'Can I say something?' McGann tried again but gave up when he felt the weight of Martineau's automatic grind into the nerve in his shoulder.

'No, not yet,' said Martineau. 'Just do everything I say. Your turn comes in a minute. In the meantime, no questions – nothing. OK?'

McGann looked into Martineau's eyes and nodded.

'Good. Keep going backwards until your legs touch the bed, then turn round and put both your hands on the mattress – outstretched.' Martineau turned briefly to Jaubert, 'I'm not happy, Jau', I'm sure he was carrying something out there.'

'D'you want me to do it again?'

'Yeh.' Martineau kicked the door shut with his foot and leaned against it while Jaubert slapped and pummelled McGann's body again. When he'd finished, Jaubert straightened up and shook his head. 'Still nothing,' he said.

'What about his coat?'

Jaubert picked up McGann's coat and waved it about. He shook his head again, then leaned forward and looked into McGann's face.

'Where's your gun, boy?'

'I don't know wha – '

'Smell his hands, Jau'.'

'Turn round. That's it, now sit on the bed and hold your hands out.' Jaubert sniffed McGann's hands. 'Soap and water, boss. OK, what have you done with the gun, boy?'

'I don't know what you're talking about.'

'Shut up. On your feet again.'

McGann stood up slowly, his hands outstretched and well away from his body.

'Sit down there.' Jaubert waggled his pistol at the end of the bed. 'And put your hands on your knees. Don't look at me, boy, look at him.'

McGann did as he was told and looked at Martineau. He didn't like what he saw.

Jaubert went to the head of the bed, lifted the two pillows and bolster and inspected the underneath. He shook his head to himself and raised the duvet half-way before letting it drop.

'I think he's telling the truth, Martin'.' Jaubert curled his lip and stared hard at McGann. 'You'd better be.' He slipped the Special back into its small holster on his belt and pushed the luggage rack against the wall with his foot. As he sat down he cracked his knuckles loudly and, without taking his eyes off McGann, said gruffly, 'Because if you're not . . .' He left the threat unfinished and lit a cigarette.

'Do you want one of these, Martin'?'

'Not yet.' Martineau folded his arms, but kept the Webley out in the open where McGann could see it. Martineau's eyes hadn't so much as flickered from McGann's face since the Irishman had opened the bedroom door, but now there was an easier, less wary look about him and when he spoke to McGann it was in a soft, almost friendly voice.

'You look worried but not curious about two men pointing guns at you in a hotel bedroom.'

'Can I talk now?' asked McGann.

'Of course.'

'You're quite right about me being worried,' he said easily. 'Wouldn't you be?'

Martineau said nothing.

It gave McGann confidence to hear his own voice. 'You've made a mistake. But it won't take much to straighten it out . . . Let me show you my . . .' He reached for his jacket, but stopped when Martineau's hand came round with the Webley.

'Tsk, tsk!' chided Martineau. 'Just the lips, that's all you move, boy. And that's enough about your worries – tell us about your curiosity. Or the lack of it.'

McGann replaced his hand on his knee. 'There's nothing to say. I make it a habit never to be curious about what other people's policemen do.'

'You speak very good French.'

'Thank you.'

'Doesn't he speak good French, Jau'?'

'Hmm.'

'We're not policemen.' Martineau paused and watched McGann's expression. McGann offered him nothing except a raised eyebrow.

Martineau continued, 'We're Internal Security, Intelligence.'

McGann kept his fear under control and his face blank. 'I don't know anything about those things.'

'Of course you don't. But you won't mind answering a few questions?'

'Not at all.'

'That's good. It's good, isn't it, Jau'?'

Jaubert didn't answer. He looked bored but managed in response to coax a gentle crack from an overlooked knuckle. Martineau was still talking.

'So, let's start with what you're doing in France.'

McGann took a deep breath. He felt like a high diver. It seemed an awful long way down, but he jumped all the same.

'Having a short holiday, a sort of long weekend . . . I don't know anything about Security matters, or Intelligence – and neither do I want to. Like I said, you've made a mistake.' He gave Martineau a reassuring smile, but got nothing back. He kept it in place and offered it to Jaubert. Jaubert didn't want it either and gave him a flat inexpressive stare in exchange. McGann felt his act deserved better. He turned his head back to the short man and shrugged his shoulders. 'A case of mistaken identity.'

Martineau yawned, and seemed to come to a decision. He slipped the heavy automatic back into its holster and nodded to McGann – he missed the flash of surprise behind McGann's eyes; instantaneous – it was gone before it saw daylight. 'Good,' Martineau smiled back at McGann, 'then let's get this little mistake sorted out quickly, shall we, so that Jau' and I can go back to directing the traffic, eh?'

McGann laughed at the joke and nodded enthusiastically.

'What's your name?'

'Bridges,' replied McGann.

'Have you a passport?'

'In my coat pocket.' McGann took his hand away from his knee again to reach for the jacket.

'I didn't say move,' snapped Martineau. McGann's hand stopped dead, like a break-dancer waiting for the music to catch up. 'I said have you a passport?'

'Yes.'

'Put your hand back on your knee. Is the name Bridges on that passport?'

'No, it's McGann.'

McGann was disturbed. It had been a silly, unnecessary lie, but McGann's disturbance was not so much at his own stupidity as the complete lack of surprise shown by Martineau. Jaubert unwound himself from the luggage rack and walked slowly round the foot of the bed and stood in front of McGann. He looked bored and half asleep. He waited a second then noisily cracked his knuckles, first one hand, then the other.

'Stand up,' he ordered.

McGann stood up and Jaubert hit him. He didn't telegraph the punch. One hand came out of the other and he caught him with a downward chop, a blow that might have pole-axed a young bullock; but this was worse, it slammed into McGann's groin, exactly where Jaubert had intended.

For a brief fraction of a second the shock took precedence over the pain. But only for a brief fraction of a second, then McGann's eyes popped out of his head. The scream started at the pit of his stomach, almost where the blow had landed; it crawled up his throat just ahead of the hard-boiled eggs and Ricard, but as his tonsils moved to one side to let them out Jaubert slapped one of the large pillows across his face and pressed his weight down on it.

McGann prayed for death. His throat was filled with vomit and scream and his lungs flapped about in his chest like two punctured balloons – flat, empty and useless. He kicked out wildly and tried to pull the nightmare from his face, but Jaubert wasn't even trying; he held the pillow down tight and managed to find time to glance over his shoulder and wink at Martineau. By the time he turned back to McGann the only movement on the bed was a limp waving of arms; a pre-unconscious twitch.

But Jaubert had timed it like a senior anaesthetist. He lifted the pillow and tossed it to the head of the bed.

Martineau lit a cigarette and leaned forward to study the result.

McGann was still there – only just. Not quite dead, not quite unconscious, floating somewhere in between – red and blue; the scream had worn itself out against the pillow and there was nothing left to start another one. Suddenly McGann found he could breathe again. It was almost as painful as not breathing. The air seared like red-hot needles into the depths of his collapsed lungs and he choked and coughed and gagged as he tried to get more air down than his throat could cope with. He was oblivious of his surroundings. He couldn't give a damn about Jaubert; Martineau didn't exist, and Monod . . . Who was Monod? He couldn't even feel the pain in his groin – nothing mattered except getting vital oxygen into his lungs, and with his chest heaving like a blacksmith's bellows and heartbeats thudding like jungle drums behind his eyeballs he neither felt nor cared about the gentle slapping of Jaubert's hand on his cheeks.

He was still not there when Jaubert pulled him into a sitting position and replaced his hands for him on the two lumps of shaking jelly that used to be his knees. It wasn't finished. He opened his eyes and saw Jaubert's fist coming towards him again. He closed his eyes again and waited for the second explosion. But nothing came, nothing that hurt; only a light tap on the chin and a kind word – almost a kind word:

'The next one's the broken arm, English – and after that, over my knee goes your leg.' Jaubert spoke softly into his ear. 'Do you want to talk intelligently? If so, nod so that we know the message has gone home.'

McGann raised his bowed head by half a centimetre, looked into Jaubert's unsmiling features and let it drop again.

Jaubert seemed satisfied with the response.

'He's all yours, Martin'.'

Martineau blew a perfect smoke ring and watched it rise until it wriggled out of shape and vanished somewhere near the ceiling. He lowered his gaze to McGann. 'I hate violence,' he said. 'Don't you?'

McGann stared back at him. He wasn't ready for speech yet.

'So, now that we've got that out of the way tell me about Monod and all his English connections.'

'Who's Monod?'

'Jau' . . . ?' Martineau's smile vanished.

McGann collected himself quickly. 'You mean the fat guy who was drinking at my table in the café round the corner? Was that his name – Monod?'

'That's the one.' Martineau couldn't be bothered with another smile. He kept his face straight. 'And about Brocklebank, and . . .' he brought a small piece of paper out of his pocket, 'and Phelan.'

'Phelan?' There was a nasty suspicion forming in McGann's mind.

'Yes, but most of all I want to know about the German named Siegfried.'

'He's not German, he's – '

'Don't stop.'

'You bugged me!'

'No, Mr McGann,' said Martineau affably, 'we didn't bug you, we bugged your friend Monod. Just give me a brief outline on the people I've mentioned and we can go into small things like detail back in my office . . . A nice cup of tea and a pleasant little chat . . . Isn't that how they do it in London?'

Jaubert stood up and jerked his head to one side. Martineau nodded without taking his eyes off McGann.

Jaubert watched the Irishman sweat, then, satisfied with the effect, nodded his head and turned and vanished into the small washroom.

Martineau blew another smoke ring at the ceiling.

The lavatory flushed and Jaubert's head appeared round the corner of the doorway.

'Look what I've found!' He waved a packet of US twenty-dollar bills at Martineau. He riffled through the wad with his thumb and grinned. 'There's more. Loads more. A whole bagful!'

'Bring it out here.'

Martineau looked hard at McGann as if trying to read his thoughts, but there was nothing in the Irishman's face.

McGann suddenly grimaced back at Martineau. He straightened his back and brought his shoulders up. 'Cramp,' he said in reply to Martineau's warning frown; but he left his hands resting on the bed.

Jaubert came out of the primitive bathroom and gave McGann's shoulder a playful pat as he walked past him. But his heart wasn't in it – his interest was totally in the bag he carried under his arm.

'There you go, Martin'.' He held the Air France bag open for Martineau's inspection. 'I like the way these young *anglais* throw a bit of spare cash into a bag and come over here for a bit of French cunt! What did he say it was – a sort of long weekend? The cheeky little bastard!' He looked up at McGann then put his hand in again and brought out another wadge of notes and stared at them. 'How much do you reckon is in there, Martin'?'

The two men lowered their heads over the bag. For a second McGann was forgotten.

And that was all McGann needed – one second.

Martineau reached into the bottom of the bag. His hand went behind and below the wads of notes and when his fingers touched metal he knew exactly what it was. He didn't have to bring it out. There was no mistaking the feel and the shape of an automatic pistol magazine. It was heavy, loaded – they came in pairs. There was no need to feel around for the other one, he knew where it would be; it would be stuck in the butt of a pistol – and that pistol . . . He didn't look up. He threw the bag away from him – no time even to warn Jaubert – and reached across his chest for the Webley.

But he knew it was already too late.

McGann's first shot smashed into the side of Jaubert's head.

The thwack of the bullet's impact was louder than the silenced explosion – Jaubert died without realising he'd been shot.

The second bullet tore through the back of Martineau's hand and thudded into his chest; it deflected off his rib cage and ripped through his lung before flattening against his shoulder blade. His hand stayed where it was, useless and trapped in the folds of his coat. He remained for several seconds resting against the wall where he'd been propelled by the force of the bullet until his knees gave way and he slid painfully down on to his haunches.

There was anger behind the pain. Anger at his own stupidity, which quickly made way for sorrow; sorrow for Jaubert, curled up beside him like a puppeteer's wooden doll with a smile on his face and half his head splashed against the wall. But there was nothing else, no other emotion. He didn't flinch when he looked up and strained to focus on McGann still sitting where he'd been told to sit – on the edge of the bed. Martineau knew what was coming; he'd been expecting it for over thirty years.

McGann held the Sauer loosely in his left hand. He grinned cheerfully at Martineau as he brought the automatic up, then slowly shook his head. There was no triumph in his expression, no excitement, no feeling. It was all part of the game – he'd won, the little man had lost, and the shake of the head was one of reprobation, a rebuke for throwing away a winning hand.

Martineau didn't close his eyes.

The third bullet hit him just above the cheekbone, slamming his head hard against the wall and jerking his feet from under him like a Cossack dancer showing off at a peasant wedding. He stayed propped against the wall for a few seconds longer, no expression on his face, but one eye still seemingly focused on a point half-way between the end of his nose and the barrel of McGann's automatic. But Martineau was dead and seeing nothing; and then the little shivers that pulled and jerked his arms finally disturbed his balance so that he slithered sideways until he lay face to face with Jaubert. There was about an inch between them, their eyes staring into each other's like lovers' after the first frantic orgasm; Jaubert wouldn't have liked being that close to Martineau.

Martineau wouldn't have been too pleased about it either.

McGann waited a few minutes then went to the door and listened. There was still the man who short-arse had called Marc hanging about somewhere along the corridor, probably with his ear glued to number 3's door, but more likely near the top of the stairs.

McGann straightened up and opened the door a fraction.

'*Marc . . . ?*' he whispered through the crack. It was a fair imitation of Martineau's voice.

'*Oui?*' Legoubin was where McGann had guessed – half-way between the door and the top of the stairs.

'*Viens ici!*' McGann left the door ajar and stood to one side.

Legoubin came through the door and stifled a yawn. 'Christ! It smells like a gun shop in here! What have you two done to the poor bastard – shot his toes off?'

'Not quite, Marc . . .' whispered McGann as he slid in behind him, 'the poor bastard's standing just behind you, and if you remain perfectly still you'll be able to feel his gun on the back of your neck. Feel it? You do? Good! But don't do anything silly . . . Don't look round, and don't move your hands from where they are.'

Legoubin froze.

'Close the door with the back of your foot. Don't slam it. That's it. Now stand still again.' McGann ran his hand down Legoubin's left side and relieved him of the pistol in his belt holster. He slid the gun under the bed and heard it thud against the wainscot, then stepped back against the wall. 'Turn round,' he said, 'and say hallo to your friends.'

Legoubin turned slowly.

He fought to keep his stomach from erupting into his throat.

It couldn't be . . . But it was – it was a Grand Guignol tableau, with Martineau curled up like a sleeping midget making eyes at Jaubert who had only half a head. And this smiling bastard was the one who'd done it. But how . . . ?

Legoubin stared at McGann as he came out of shock.

McGann gave him no respite. He prodded Jaubert's body with his foot. The kick caused Jaubert's bended knee to straighten out, and as his foot slid on the loose carpet it set up a series of little jerking motions, juddering Jaubert's corpse into a more comfortable position.

Legoubin's stomach heaved again, but he couldn't look away.

'This guy thought he was tough,' grinned McGann. 'Let it be a lesson to you, Marc, if you've got similar thoughts about yourself.'

Legoubin's stomach finally erupted. He didn't try to hold it back. When he'd finished he wiped his mouth with the back of his hand and stared at McGann through watering eyes. 'Go fuck yourself!' he mumbled. It was an effort to say. It took everything he had.

'Goodbye, Marc!' McGann's finger tightened on the trigger.

Legoubin's stomach heaved again and he doubled up – it didn't seem to matter any more.

McGann watched him for a second, then he shook his head and said, 'I'll give you points for guts, Frog – even if you can't keep your dinner down.' He lowered the pistol and smiled grimly. 'OK, go over there and sit yourself down beside old short-arse. Squat down on your heels with your back to the wall. That's the way . . . Now put your hands on your knees and spread your fingers out. That's it, you've got it. Right, have you finished being sick?'

Legoubin didn't trust himself to answer. He bowed his head and found himself staring directly into Martineau's eyes. Martineau seemed to be smiling, but it was only from the mouth; a corpse's grin that pulled his lips to one side exposing yellow, nicotine-stained teeth. McGann's voice broke into Legoubin's communion.

'I said have you finished being sick? And you've got about five and half seconds to find your tongue, or you get Jaubert's problem.'

'What is it you want?'

McGann stopped smiling. 'I want some information. Why did I get star treatment – who decided I was blue-eyes?'

'Blame it on the company you keep. Monod – he was our target. We were cashing in his contacts as they came to the trough . . . You were just unlucky.'

'Was I? How were you into Monod?'

'We were wired into his phone.'

'And . . . ?'

'And the usual, the full-time visual.' Legoubin cleared his throat. He was feeling better now – it was all right as long as he didn't look down at Martineau and Jaubert. He swallowed, and gagged. The taste and smell of vomit was overpowering. It was enough for Legoubin. He stopped there. He decided he'd said enough.

But it wasn't enough for McGann. 'Where's the back-up now?'

'Martineau sent them home when fatso gave you the place and a time.'

'Why?'

'We thought we could handle it.'

'And how many had you made before me?'

'You were the first.'

McGann pulled a face. 'I might have known! OK,' he waved the pistol at Jaubert's body, 'so while this streak of piss was holding my table in the café and Shorty was watching from a distance, you, I suppose, were stuck on the other end of the line. Is that right?'

Legoubin shook his head. 'End of what line . . . ?'

Plop!

Legoubin hardly felt the bullet.

It went between his fingers and tore through the soft flesh above his kneecap. It missed the bone by a fraction of an inch and came out at the back of his thigh – clean, and uncomplicated, a surgeon couldn't have made a neater job with a scalpel and a local anaesthetic. Legoubin didn't believe it. For a second or two he watched the thick blood welling out from the hole between his fingers before deciding it was true. Then he began to scream and his leg collapsed and he tipped forward.

Then came the pain.

He clutched his knee with both hands and pulled it protectively against his chest in a vain effort to stem the blood – he had a vague idea that if he hid it from sight it wouldn't hurt so much. It didn't work. But the scream helped take his mind off it, and he went up a notch. But before it reached its peak and was ready to burst through his clenched teeth he felt the barrel of McGann's automatic rammed into his mouth and jammed hard over his tongue. It acted like the bit in a horse's mouth. The scream died to a gurgle, and in its place he heard McGann's voice hissing into his ear. 'I told you, you silly bastard, didn't I? I told you you were on a hiding to fuck-all? Didn't I tell you? Didn't I warn you?'

Legoubin managed to squeeze a groan past the steel bit. He wasn't listening. He kept his eyes firmly closed, but it didn't stop McGann.

'So why start trying to be clever at this bloody stage? You stupid bastard, little short-arse there told me all about the bug they'd laid on in the café, and I know what these two were up to while Monod was gargling champagne . . . So it stands to reason, doesn't it, that you were sitting at the end of the bloody bug. Well, doesn't it? Come on, nod your fucking head! That's right. Now tell me what you got down the wire, you stupid bastard! I'm going to take this out of your mouth. You get a few seconds to take a grip on yourself, and while you're doing that you can work out whether you think it's going to be worth it before you say it . . . And while you're at it,' McGann waggled the barrel about inside Legoubin's mouth, 'cut out the bloody girlie noises – you can have another scream when I do the other leg. If you've got all that nod your head again.'

When the automatic was removed from his mouth Legoubin opened his eyes and took a deep breath. He remained curled on the floor. McGann didn't seem to mind.

'Go on from where we left off.' McGann's voice now came from over by the bed.

'The reception was bad,' Legoubin lied. He spat out a mouthful of oily blood and spoke in gasps, in time with the sharp surges of pain coming up from his knee. 'There was a lot of interference. I missed most of what was being said . . .'

'Fuck all that! I asked what you got.'

'It sounded as if you'd bought Monod to dig out a French contract killer who's gone to ground over here. Something about the English wanting to interview him . . . The guy's name was Siegfried, or Michel something or other. I didn't get the rest of it.'

'It's Gerrard. Monod said he might be working for French Intelligence.'

'I didn't get that bit.'

'Well does he?'

'Does he what?'

'Are you looking for another sore knee? I asked you if this Gerrard works for one of the Firms. Don't try and be smart about it, just answer the question. Do you know anything about him, does the name Siegfried ring any bells?'

'No,' said Legoubin emphatically. He didn't have to lie. 'There are no Siegfrieds in G, not in my bit of it anyway, and none in Six as far as I know.'

'Wasn't worth it then, was it?'

Legoubin pulled himself up and turned his head so that he could see exactly where the voice was coming from, but he knew, even before he looked, that there were going to be no chances on offer today. McGann had got it all under control. He sat comfortably on the edge of the bed with the pistol, rock steady, resting on his thigh. It pointed a fraction above Legoubin's line of vision – about half-way between his eyebrows and his hairline – and he could see McGann's finger gently caressing the trigger in tiny crescentic movements, like a man absently smoothing a hardening nipple. It mesmerised Legoubin. He spoke without taking his eyes off the finger.

'What wasn't?'

McGann motioned to the two bodies with his free hand. 'That. It wasn't worth two dustbin bags to find out that I'm looking for a Froggy kill-man, was it? Well, was it?'

Legoubin continued watching McGann's finger; he didn't reply.

'OK, how did you take it, tape or notes?'

Legoubin lowered his head again. The heat had gone out of the bullet wound and it was sharp and cold now; he could feel shock setting in. He groaned and left it at that.

'Do you want the other knee done?'

The threat worked. 'Notes,' he grunted, 'just names and places.'

'Where are they?'

'Gone. Agency postman was waiting in the Drug'. He'll have collected them and taken them in for processing, but as I said, it was only names and places.' It seemed necessary to Legoubin to lie as much as possible. He didn't know why, possibly a forlorn optimism that something might be done to redress the balance; but he wasn't convinced, all he could see at the moment was: goodbye Martineau, and goodbye Jaubert – and where did you get that limp, Legoubin? McGann was speaking again. Legoubin gritted his teeth.

'Did you get my name?'

'I had you as Bridges, and query Sean McGann.'

'Uhuh . . . And you got Brocklebank, Phelan and Gerrard. Right?'

'Did I?'

'That's what you told short-arse.'

Legoubin kept quiet.

'And I don't believe you about the notes. I don't think you're as stupid as you're trying to sound. I think you're the only one left with enough in his nut to have me nailed to the wall. Am I right?'

Legoubin stared at him.

'I think you're going to be a bloody nuisance, Marc.'

Legoubin raised his head. A tiny knot of suspicion was hammering out a message, it made his mouth dry and put a rough edge on his voice. He hoped it didn't show.

'So we're going to have to do something about it.'

'Like what?'

'Like goodbye, Marc.'

The realisation was slow coming. Legoubin frowned as he tried to work it out, and then he noticed McGann's finger – it had stopped caressing the nipple. He watched it tighten. He didn't hear the plop, or feel the soft-nosed bullet plough into his forehead. He was dead before he understood. He died with a look of curiosity, almost disappointment, as if dying at the age of twenty-three deserved a few more preliminaries.

McGann searched the bodies for notes or tapes, but found nothing. It took a matter of moments to put his few things together and sling the Air France bag over his shoulder. He stopped at the door and looked at the three bodies. There was no expression on his face – just a look of professional interest. He sniffed. It was all there, the killer's opium, the adrenergic smell of blown cordite and already, faintly, the cloying sweetness of dead man, and somewhere in amongst it the heavy pungency of Martineau's last cigarette. It didn't improve the mixture. But there was no time to linger. McGann wrinkled his nose and opened the door.

McGann didn't hurry. He turned into the Boulevard St Germain and strolled casually eastwards towards the Boulevard St Michel. He went with the crowd and stayed on the same side of the Boulevard until he reached the Métro. He didn't look right, or left, or behind as he descended into the cool, anonymous, overcrowded world of the Paris Underground. He was as conspicuous as another bee in the nest. He looked like a well-behaved Left Bank student; a student with fifty thousand dollars in his bag and a 7.56 Sauer tucked neatly into his waistband. McGann was on the loose again and running free.

CHAPTER 25

Gerrard stood on the balcony of his flat, six storeys above the shimmering rooftops of Paris, and gazed at the glistening white beehive of the Sacré Coeur on its mound in the distance.

He lit a cigarette and looked at his watch. Five to six. Reason was due at seven – half an hour to clear Charles de Gaulle and another half an hour to the Quai de Conti by taxi, plus extra for a black Englishman with no French. Gerrard was bored with waiting. He blew smoke into the damp atmosphere and watched a *bâteau-mouche* crawl round the far side of the Île de la Cité – the activity was painful; it looked as if Paris was struggling to keep its eyes open until the sun went down. He stared across the jumbled roofs in the direction of Maurice's flat.

No question about what Maurice would be doing on a sticky evening.

Maurice – codename *Maurice*; spymaster, the President's man – he'd have lost control of the afternoon; pushed it aside until the evening and half a dozen full-sized Macallans brought him back to life. Crises or no, Maurice's priority was Maurice. But there were no crises, not today, not in Maurice's world. He'd made that very clear this morning, but the welcome had been genuine – by Maurice's standards . . .

'Richard says he's not finished with you yet.' Maurice could have been talking about the lawnmower.

Gerrard lowered himself into the comfortable leather armchair on the opposite side of Maurice's desk and loosened his shirt collar. Maurice hadn't heard of air-conditioning. Gerrard raised his eyebrows.

'Richard?'

'Richard Sanderson. General Sanderson to you. The man you've been working for for the past seven days.' Maurice leaned forward, placed his elbows on the table and grasped his hands together. They were badly deformed hands – the fingers had no nails. They ended in misshapen blobs half-way between the top joint and where the nails should have been. They'd been like that for over forty years – he no longer missed them. He pointed one of the blobs at Gerrard. 'He said you were quite enthusiastic about being pegged out as bait for a bunch of Irish knifemen.'

'Enthusiastic's putting it a bit strong.' Gerrard didn't smile. 'Are you happy about it?'

'No, I'm not. Converting it into currency it seems a damned high price to pay for an unseen card. It's only a nod and a wink at the very outside, with the possibility that the only thing to come out of it is your hide stuck on somebody's lavatory wall. I wouldn't like that.'

'Thank God we agree on some things!'

Maurice bared his teeth, but didn't allow it to develop into a smile. 'I can see the way Richard's mind is working, but it seems a bit forlorn to me. I can't somehow seee a gang of Irishmen booting their way up and down the Champs-Elysées looking for a Frenchman with jam on his fingers.'

'The Irish have a reputation for vindictiveness – they enjoy debt collecting,' interrupted Gerrard.

Maurice shrugged the interruption aside. 'Even if they did set up an expedition I can't see one of them being primed with the name and address of the man who's causing old Richard all this lost sleep. It's much too risky an undertaking, particularly if they took a wrong turning.'

'That's what Sanderson is banking on their doing.'

'I know that. But it's not a straight line, there would have to be a cut-out, and if your Brocklebank is holding the sort of cards Richard thinks he is – a double cut-out.'

'Sanderson has all that worked out,' said Gerrard. 'He reckons Brocklebank will be organising the party, so one of the boot boys, at least, will have to be in contact with him one way or another. It doesn't, according to Sanderson, have to be direct contact but somebody in his pipeline; somebody he reports to. That somebody will be the one we go for; he'll be the one who points us in the right direction – Sanderson's theory! He thinks all I've got to do is roll the Irishmen up, sort out who's giving the orders, take him to one side and discuss his chain of command – which he reckons will bring us to the cut-out man.'

'The one with the pointing finger.'

'That's right. It doesn't matter how many cut-outs there are – double cut-outs, double-doubles, treble-doubles, once you get it going it becomes the domino principle – each one knocks the other one down.'

'And that's your theory too, is it?'

'No, all Sanderson's. Black and white, nothing in between. Is there anything in this for us, Maurice?'

'I'm getting some very rare Macallan, fifty years old – I don't know about you.'

'That's not what I meant.'

'I know.'

'Then it's unofficial?'

'I'm returning a favour. Are you off now?'

Gerrard nodded and stood up.

'Good. Keep me in touch, and be careful.'

Gerrard shook the old man's hand across the desk and grinned crookedly. The grin vanished abruptly when Maurice, without change of expression, said, 'Where are you keeping that young woman you snatched from under Richard's nose?'

Gerrard raised his eyebrows. 'What young woman is that, Maurice?'

'You know very well what young woman. Her name's Lambdon. Richard wanted her kept in England. What are you doing with her over here?'

'Are you watching me, Maurice?'

'I was. Now I'm not. Answer my question.'

Gerrard relented. 'She's staying at my place. She's better off over here where I can keep an eye on her.'

'Oh, is she? I don't see her standing here beside you. How do you know she's not having a conversation with these people who are supposed to be coming to look for you? She could be a liability, Michel, you should have left her in England. Richard's people would have taken care of her – he was quite upset about it. Where is she now?'

'I dropped her in the Rivoli to do some shopping. She'll be all right – she's not stupid.'

Maurice's eyes gleamed. 'Pretty girl, is she?'

'Yes.'

'And you've let her loose in Paris on her own?'

'No, I got Lili to go with her.'

'You two getting together again?'

'No, Maurice, she's married to someone else.'

'Pity. But I don't understand you modern people. How the hell can you send your mistress out shopping with your ex-wife?'

'Slow down, Maurice. She's not my mistress, she's just a girl – the daughter of an old friend. I owe it to him to keep an eye on her until the smoke drifts away.'

'That's a joke?'

'No joke.'

'Then you must think old equals stupid, Michel! Looking after an old friend's daughter? You've just voiced every dirty old man's ambition – I'll bet you a case of decent Scotch you'll be admiring the dimples on her little bottom within the week . . . Looking after an old friend's daughter! Don't make me laugh!' But Maurice didn't laugh. He stared at Gerrard's sombre expression and abruptly changed the subject. 'This man Richard gave you – where is he now?'

Gerrard looked at his watch again. It was only half-past eleven – half-past ten in London. What Reason was doing at half-past ten in the morning was anybody's guess. 'He's tying up a few loose ends in London,' he said. 'He'll be here this evening. Goodbye, Maurice.'

'*Au revoir*, Michel. How old did you say your friend's daughter was?'

Gerrard smiled. 'I didn't, Maurice. I'll be in touch.'

He got as far as the door.

'You're staying in Paris for a few days?'

'Yes.'

'Then I'll know where to find you if a bunch of noisy Irishmen arrive and start making a nuisance of themselves.'

Gerrard crushed his cigarette under his heel and turned away from the balcony. As he stepped into the cool drawing-room the tinny chimes of a backstreet church clock rang out across the Seine. Seven o'clock, and as the final chime faded the phone rang. It was as if somebody had waited for the noise to die down before ringing.

CHAPTER 26

It took twenty-five minutes for the news to shuffle its way across Paris.

Twenty-five minutes, and like a hot potato it was held briefly, breath sucked in through closed teeth, and passed on before the fingers felt the heat. Nobody fancied this one.

Twenty-five minutes after Martineau's body had been turned over and searched by a white-faced gendarme the Deputy Director of Operations sat in the Director's office and stared at him across his desk. The potato had arrived home.

Gregoire de Puy-Monbraque, Director of Department G, French Internal Security, seemed to be having some difficulty in digesting the bare facts given him by his deputy. 'One man you say?' The ridge above his nose, pinched into a deep ravine of doubt, pulled his heavy grey eyebrows together like an angry, bristly caterpillar. 'You're trying to tell me that Martineau, Jaubert and the other one . . . What's his name?'

'Legoubin.'

'Legoubin, allowed themselves to be bundled into the sack by one solitary person? Is that what you're trying to tell me, Claude?'

The Deputy Director nodded. 'The girl in the hotel room opposite confirmed it. She said only one man came out of the room. She's still being talked to.'

'Who found the bodies?'

'Reception clerk. He said the room was booked for only one person, and that's all he saw – just the one. His buddy on the desk confirmed it. The buddy's a fairy.'

'I don't believe it! Three so-called professionals from this department meekly lining themselves up in front of a one-man firing squad . . . And what the hell's this rubbish?' Puy-Monbraque picked up Legoubin's shorthand notes and stared at the indecipherable squiggle for a few seconds before allowing the sheets to drop from his fingers on to the desk. 'Where did this come from?'

'Martineau's car. They'd got a wire going in the café across the road. Legoubin left the notes under his seat – he must have gone after the other two as back-up. The car was marked by the clean-up people after they'd turned over the bodies. It had been seen anyway – it had been there too long.'

'What do they mean, these doodles?'

'There's a translation in the pocket of the file and a tape's on its way over.'

'A tape of what?'

'Talk in the café. It's routine procedure. A couple of metres of voices to go with the words . . .' Claude hesitated at Puy-Monbraque's raised eyebrows, 'like fingerprints.'

'Whatever next!' Puy-Monbraque took out the sheets of transcript and riffled through them. 'Have you been through this?'

'Briefly.'

Puy-Monbraque settled back in his chair. 'In that case you know what it's all about?'

Claude nodded, and covered his tracks. 'I did say briefly.'

Puy-Monbraque finished reading the typescript and threw the sheets on the desk.

'There's fuck-all in there that tells me anything more than I already know. Three men get themselves killed and nobody knows why – let alone by whom. There's something missing.' He seemed to be talking to himself, but Claude knew better.

'So where's that tape you were telling me about, Claude?'

Claude leapt to his feet. He was glad to be doing something other than staring at Puy-Monbraque's choleric eyebrows. He opened the door and barked down the corridor, then stood aside as a sombre-faced young man came into the room carrying a portable cassette player.

'Plug it in,' Claude told him. 'And don't go away. I'll have another job for you in a minute.'

The young man retreated out of range, rested his back gratefully against the wall and listened to the hollow distorted voices of Sean McGann and Philippe Monod making their introductions and trading their first insults.

The conversation was over almost as soon as it started.

The suddenness of its end took Puy-Monbraque by surprise. He raised his heavy eyebrows and stared hard at the small machine. 'Is that it?' he growled. 'A pansy Frenchman and a *raton* scratching at each other's arses in a pavement café? Is that all there is to it? Where did you say this bloody café was?'

'Boulevard St Ger – ' Claude began.

'Yes, all right! I know where the bloody place is.' Puy-Monbraque pointed his finger at the now silent machine. 'That's told me nothing, or at least nothing that makes any sense to me! In fact, according to that – and these . . .' He picked up Legoubin's notes and dropped them back on the desk, 'what it all boils down to is that Martineau got himself and two others knocked off for fuck-all! Is that a reasonable assumption?'

Claude choked into his handkerchief. It was easier than trying to think up a reply, and while he recovered, Puy-Monbraque turned his attention to the young man by the wall. 'What do you make of it?'

The young man straightened himself up and looked Puy-Monbraque in the eye. 'I haven't read Legoubin's notes, sir,' he said with a trace of truculence. 'But from what I've heard so far there appears to be only one thing left to do.'

Puy-Monbraque raised his chin. 'And what is that?'

'Pull in this bastard Monod and screw him until his eyes pop out. When he's cooked we'll get him to fill in the gaps – he should be able to tell us more than that thing's done.' The young man nodded disdainfully at the tape machine. 'Or what, presumably, you've found in there.' He flicked his eyes briefly at the notes and the file on the desk beside Claude's hand. 'If not, we'll invite him to make a few guesses before we push his eyes back in and flush him down the lavatory.' He stopped and waited for Puy-Monbraque to rap his knuckles, but all he got was a pair of unflickering eyes from under the bushy eyebrows. He took a deep breath.

'And while that's going on we'll turn the dogs loose to look for the one called Bridges. He'll be shacked up in Paris somewhere. By tomorrow morning he won't be able to use a backstreet *pissoir* without being kicked in the balls by one of our people. And when we've racked this one up alongside Monod we'll know exactly what Martineau knew when the lid was dropped on him. When we've got that lot, sir . . .' He hesitated, as if he suddenly realised who it was he was giving advice to, and his voice lost some of its confidence. 'We should then be able to go back and start at square one again, and . . .'

'Thank you,' said Puy-Monbraque drily. He turned his attention back to his deputy. 'Do that, Claude. Do what the boy suggests. Bring Monod along to see us – he can have his last supper downstairs before we nail him to the cross!'

'You heard the Director!'

'Just a minute!' Puy-Monbraque wasn't finished. 'Let's make the bastard miserable as well as unhappy.'

'Sir?'

'Take a couple of men and watch his house until bedtime. Let him get ready for a good night's sleep. Wait until he's drunk his whisky, taken his sleeping pill and put on his silk pyjamas, then, when he's crawled between the sheets and the bedroom light's switched off, march in and drag the bastard out. Don't say a word to him; shove him into the back of your car and throw him into the surgery.'

Puy-Monbraque waited until the door closed.

'In Legoubin's notes,' he said to Claude, 'this Bridges was reported as saying he was of the IRA. Am I expected to believe that?'

Claude shrugged his shoulders. 'What does it matter?'

'It matters,' snapped Puy-Monbraque, 'because I don't like tribal wars overlapping into my territory. The IRA's an English problem, it's nothing to do with us, and I want it to stay that way. If somebody's trying to involve us in it I want to know who that somebody is, and I want to know why.'

'I'll make it my personal responsibility.'

'Now, this name Bridges, Claude? Is that Irish?'

'I couldn't tell you.'

'McGann?'

'No idea. They all sound the same to me over there – their names don't mean a thing, Scottish, Irish, English . . . I don't like any of them, never have, but I try not to let it worry me.'

'Well, you can start bloody worrying now, Claude, and tell me when you last heard of a mad dog screaming his origins from the rooftops.'

'What do you mean?'

'This man who can't make up his mind whether his name is Bridges or McGann – doesn't it strike you as peculiar that he's telling everybody he comes into contact with who he carries a gun for? You normally have to pull that sort of thing out of them with a dentist's drill. The man's either a loud-mouthed fool or he's been told to come and make a noise.'

'Don't you think you're complicating a straightforward issue?'

'No, I don't. I know the English. It's just the sort of smart trick I'd expect of them. Send somebody over here calling himself IRA, kill a couple of Frenchmen, the sort that hurts us most, and where do your sympathies lie if a bowler hat pops in for a cup of tea and a biscuit and a request for us to take sides? That's not complicating the bloody issue, Claude, that's understanding it. But enough of that; you said Martineau had organised a camera crew?'

Claude nodded.

'So? Did they get there? Is anything happening?'

'They're working on it now.'

'Good. Apart from that I suppose everybody's sitting around with their thumbs up their arses waiting for me to tell them what to do?'

'Not quite. I've clamped airports, ferries, ports and all frontiers – official and unofficial. Nobody's – '

'You've done all that on what?' interrupted Puy-Monbraque.

'On the name, of course – Bridges or McGann. I was about to add that until further notice nobody will be leaving France without a more than thorough passport check. By morning all exits out of the country will have a picture to go with the name.'

'Anything else?'

'No – apart from that we're all sitting around with our thumbs up our arses waiting for you to tell us what to do.'

'Are you finding this amusing, Claude?'

'No, sir. Shall I go on?'

'I thought you said there was nothing else.'

'Nothing else I can do, but there is something for you.'

'Go on.'

'From here on it's going to have to be top-level stuff, eyeball to eyeball on your part to get everybody else involved. All I've done is the basics – the switchboard operator could have done it while she was painting her toenails.'

'Get on with it, Claude.'

'The Prefect has to be persuaded to mobilise the *Sûreté* and the *Gendarmerie* to beat the undergrowth for us. That's urgent. When do you want to see him?'

'Tonight. Arrange it, please. What else?'

'That's a priority – I'll prepare a list of the other things.'

Puy-Monbraque stared blankly at his deputy for a second or two then picked up the file and rummaged among the sheets of typescript. He found the sheet he was looking for and frowned down the page until he came to the paragraph that gave him the name he required. He stuck his finger on it, looked up, and said, 'Brocklebank? What sort of name is that?'

Claude pulled a face and shook his head. 'No idea – you're the one who knows the English.'

Puy-Monbraque dropped the sheet back into the file and shuffled it across to Claude. 'Go through this lot again,' he said, 'pick out all the names and see if any of them mean anything to British Special Branch in London, or MI5.'

Claude raised his eyebrows in surprise. 'In spite of what you just said about possible British involvement?'

'Yes, in spite of that. It'll show them how naïve and trusting we are.' Puy-Monbraque didn't smile. 'And while you're at it send them a photo of Bridges – if he's genuine IRA they might know him by sight, although I doubt it, and I doubt even more that they'll tell us if they do, but you might as well give it a try.'

'Why do these matters have to be made so complicated?' Claude looked quite unhappy. 'We don't have the same problem with the *Boches* or the Italians – do we? Or is it just my imagination?'

Puy-Monbraque smiled contentedly. 'It's the English nature, Claude. They can't do a thing without twisting it round like a Danish pastry – they're not simple-minded folk like us! And by the way, don't tell them the reason for your query. Say it's a routine matter – your curiosity about a strangely familiar face wandering in and out of our Paris *chiottes*. But be careful with them – if you give them half a finger the bastards'll take your arm off right up to the shoulder and we'll have the fucking place swarming with bowler hats and umbrellas. I don't need that. I'm going to have enough on my plate with the Admiral and his fucking DGSE boilermen at the *Piscine* getting in my way! And one more thing – the Press . . . I want them kept in the dark.'

'I'll have a word with the *Sûreté*, they can invoke NS/12 – '

'I wouldn't do that,' said Puy-Monbraque quickly. 'That's been known to get them more steamed up than the reason for it. Tell them it's drugs – or money – or women – or all three, and then shut up; let them use their imaginations, that's what they're paid for. And while I'm on the subject . . . If you haven't done so already get somebody with a big hand to slap the hotel people across the mouth about speaking out of turn. Better still, put them away for a day or two, let them sample the waters over at Vincennes.'

'It's already been done.'

'Good.'

Puy-Monbraque sat back in his chair and emptied the glass of whisky that had been standing on his desk. He held up the empty glass and rested it against his lips, then sighted across the rim at the man opposite. 'And coming nearer home.' He bared his teeth so that through the glass's convexity they were distorted into an arc of discoloured piano keys. Claude's mind drifted as he regarded the novelty, and he almost missed the next sentence.

' . . . the bastard who's responsible for all this local unpleasantness.'

Claude pursed his lips, then drooped them like an aged bloodhound. 'I thought we'd covered just about every aspect of Bridges-McGann . . .' he began, then realised his gaffe and stopped in mid-sentence.

'You haven't been listening, Claude.' Puy-Monbraque let him off lightly. He pushed himself forward and grimaced when the sciatic nerve in his back complained at the sudden change of position. 'I'm not talking about Bridges, I'm talking about Siegfried.' He replaced his empty glass on the table and waved his hand at Legoubin's shorthand notes. 'I want you to go and dig the bastard out of the swamp and bring him here so that I can talk to him.'

Claude shook his head. 'I don't think we need bother ourselves about him, sir. I think he's a tangent; peripheral – he didn't kill Martineau and his crew. The one we should be going for is the Englishman, McGann – he's the one we should point our stick at. Pick him up and wring him out and I think everything else will slot into its proper place. That's how I see it. I recommend we concentrate on him.'

Puy-Monbraque stared at Claude's wobbly chins for a second or two, then said firmly, 'No, Claude, the person *I* want is the one who calls himself Siegfried. No arguments. Go and dig the bastard out – now! I want him here,' he pointed to the floor on the other side of the desk, 'on his knees, on that carpet with his head bowed and a tear in his eye explaining to me why, at the mention of his name, three men from this department end up hanging from hooks in a butcher's shop on the other side of the river. And I want this happening in hours, not days.'

Claude stared at him.

'But what you can do first is put all that stuff together.' Puy-Monbraque pointed to the file. 'Wrap it up with that earlier Monod bumf and send it under cover to Interior. Put a blue tab on it so that it goes direct to the Minister. I don't want it floating around every other department in the building, or being used as a table mat for somebody's bowl of olives. I want him to get it tonight, and I want him to be the one to open it. I want to hear some fireworks going off in both Interior and Defence at about croissant time tomorrow morning. Is that clear?'

'Don't you think we ought to send a copy to the *Piscine?*'

'I said direct to Interior.'

'The Admiral won't like that.'

'Fuck the Admiral! If the Minister wants him to see it he can tear the tab off and send the bloody thing back to whoever he likes. Same applies to *Maurice*. Do it right away.'

CHAPTER 27

Gerrard glanced at his watch as he walked across the room. By the time he'd poured himself a large whisky and lit another cigarette the ringing had stopped. He stood beside the phone and sipped his drink until it rang again. This time he picked it up before the bell got into its full stride. 'I was just thinking about you, Maurice,' he said.

Maurice grunted. It sounded uncomplimentary. Then, without preliminaries, he said, 'Your dancing troupe's arrived from Ireland.'

He sounded like a man in a bad temper; a man who'd been rudely nudged out of an early-evening nap and offered a large dose of bad news before he'd rubbed the sleep out of his eyes. Gerrard recognised the symptoms. He sipped again from his glass and waited. The chink of ice cubes and the gurgle must have travelled down the line.

'Did you hear what I said?'

'Yes. How many?'

'One.'

'It's a joke?'

'Hardly. He sounds like a one-man Panzer group. He killed three Special Group people this afternoon over on the Left Bank. Apparently he was looking for you.'

Gerrard crushed his cigarette out. 'Where can I see you?'

'My place. Be here in fifteen minutes.' Maurice didn't say goodbye; goodbye was the sound of the receiver being dropped into its cradle.

Gerrard finished his drink, frowned at himself in the mirror then opened the drawer in the telephone table and took out a .38 Walther PPK. No need to check the magazine – the small pistol was loaded and cocked. He tucked it into his waistband and closed his coat over it. It felt snug and comfortable, and familiar, like an old friend.

Maurice sat deep in his armchair and stared thoughtfully at Gerrard's bowed head. He'd already read the contents of the folder – twice, after a first glance of disbelief. Now it was Gerrard's turn. Gerrard's head told him nothing. He thought about Martineau again. The rethink didn't make it sound any better.

Maurice looked away from the top of Gerrard's head, still bowed over the file with the blue tab, and continued his thoughts aloud.

'The President's not going to like it,' he said.

'The President's not going to like what?' Gerrard looked up from the file and studied the old man's face.

Maurice grimaced. 'He's not going to like what's in that file.'

Gerrard tapped the open file with his finger. 'Can we get back to this?' he asked.

'Certainly.'

'These three – Martineau, Jaubert and Legoubin – were they average for *Six*?'

'You could say that. Why?'

'It doesn't say much for the rest of them!'

Maurice wasn't amused. 'They were good men those, Michel. Top operatives, or at least two of them were.'

'Who are you quoting, Maurice?'

'Puy-Monbraque. Martineau was about to become number two at G.' Maurice pointed a stumped finger at the file. 'It's all in there, at the back of the file. Puy-Monbraque's old woman, what's his name, Claude something or other, has filled in the gaps for us. It sounds to me though as if he's washed his hands of the affair, or would like to. But Martineau was good stuff, no comparison, he was top drawer according to his record outline, and so was Jaubert. The third one was the boy, new, inexperienced and expendable – but not this expendable – he still had a long way to go.'

'He's not going to get there now.' Gerrard was unsympathetic. 'So what does that make the Irishman?'

Maurice sniffed noisily. 'Something special, I'd say. Or very lucky. Or we've been misled and there's more than one of him. What do you think?'

Gerrard didn't have to think too long about it. 'He'll be one of the élite. You should know the type, Maurice – one of a kind, a lonely operator, a good one who knows what he's doing. And probably lucky as well.' Gerrard picked up the file again and glanced briefly through Claude's summary, then looked back at Maurice with a thoughtful expression on his face.

'I see what you mean about them washing their hands of it. Can't we take – ?'

'Just a minute,' Maurice interjected, 'I didn't say anything about Puy-Monbraque trying to duck out of it. He's not the sort of man to wash his hands of trouble, least of all the sort of trouble that results in a visit to the mortuary. I was referring to his fancy number two.'

'It doesn't matter who,' said Gerrard, deliberately. 'Why don't we do that? Why don't we take the thing off their hands?'

'Because Puy-Monbraque won't stand for it.'

'He'd have to if you slapped a Presidential K notice on it.'

Maurice frowned and shook his head. 'I'd rather not. Ks are guaranteed to make everybody sit up and pay more attention than they otherwise would, which is not the object of the exercise. I want this thing to have the appearance of a routine murder hunt, Michel, not a declaration of war, and above all I don't want the media to pick up an IRA angle.'

'Puy-Monbraque agrees with you,' said Gerrard. 'According to this he's put it about that his men were involved in a drugs undercover operation. An operation with international implications.'

'Thin,' said Maurice, 'and very unlikely.'

'Which is irrelevant.' There was a trace of impatience in Gerrard's voice which was not lost on Maurice.

'Quite! Which is why I said no K notice. So let's try it another way. On the assumption the Irishman hasn't bolted back to a cooler climate . . .'

'An assumption based on what?'

'Instinct.'

'Your instinct's out of date, Maurice. They don't hang around any more to see whether the fire's burning brightly. Nowadays it's in, out and away – and if it goes wrong come back and finish it off some other day.' Gerrard drew heavily on his cigarette. 'He's bolted for the coast. He'll get as close to home as possible and jump across at the first clear opportunity. I reckon we're going to have to wait for another visit. Try a different assumption.'

'No. I disagree,' Maurice said firmly. 'He's going to stay here, in Paris. He's going to stick it out and have another go at finding you. People like him don't frighten easily, nor do they panic. This one's not going to do either, and he's not going to be put off by a hiccup. He didn't come here to kill a handful of Intelligence Officers, he came here to kill you. Don't lose sight of that. You're his target, Michel – they'll give him another contact to replace the one he's blown and he'll be back sniffing along the track like an eager Dobermann with a flea up its arse. He's staying around until he finds you. That's what he'll do – unless, of course, his masters over in Ireland or England get a touch of cold feet and pull him out.'

'You're adding to the problem, Maurice.'

'Life's full of problems, Michel, and here's another one – Puy-Monbraque's people are going to want a long undisturbed conversation with this Irishman when they get their hands on him, so we're going to have to persuade Puy-Monbraque to let you have first word.'

'Half an hour is all I need – after that they can paste him to the wall. Can you arrange it?'

'Of course I can arrange it. We'll make you the Presidential Agent for the duration. But in doing so I must ask you not to forget where the axe stops.'

Gerrard smiled gently at the old man.

'Where does the axe stop, Maurice?'

'Half a centimetre above my neck!' Maurice didn't share Gerrard's sense of humour. 'This letter I'm going to give you,' he said seriously, 'don't abuse it, and don't flash it around unless absolutely necessary, and above all, keep my name out of it . . . You'll want to go and talk to this Monod person of course?' The change of subject was abrupt. Maurice was warming up for dismissal.

Gerrard nodded. 'Where are they holding him?'

'I'll let you know. Leave it till morning, by which time I'll have the President's signature on some paper for you. Call in at Neuilly first thing. Puy-Monbraque . . .' Maurice stopped and almost smiled.

'What about him?'

The smile continued. 'He's not going to like being told you're taking charge of his circus. He's not going to like you either.'

'Aren't you going to prepare him for it?'

'No. It's all yours now. You'll have the authority, just drop in on him. And the very best of luck to you! Now, is there anything else I can do for you before you go?'

'Can you let me have a Department note for Reason?'

'Who's he?'

'Clive Reason. I told you about him – Sanderson's Irish expert. And I think he'd better have a piece of our equipment if we're dealing with bad-tempered Irishmen – something fairly heavy, he's a big lad.'

Maurice nodded. 'I'll warn the armourer you'll be down to make a nuisance of yourself in the morning. Make it early. Half-past seven – don't be late.' It was goodbye and close the door quietly behind you.

Gerrard ignored the invitation. 'Has DST shown any interest in this?'

He picked the file up from where he'd dropped it on the floor and opened it again as if to remind himself of the cast, but thought better of it and threw it carefully on to one of Maurice's leather-covered armchairs. 'Or more to the point, have they seen it yet?'

Maurice yawned and shook his head. 'No. Puy-Monbraque sent it direct to the Minister's office. It came on to me – unopened.' He pointed to the file. 'Blue tab – Minister of the Interior for direct transmission to the President. Why do you want DST kept out? I presume that's what you meant?'

Gerrard nodded. 'They're too political.'

'Fair enough. Leave it to me,' said Maurice, imperiously. 'But a word of warning about Puy-Monbraque.'

'OK.'

'Don't be flippant with him, Michel. Puy-Monbraque's not your friend, he's not going out of his way to do you any favours. If he does anything at all for you it'll be on the strength of the President's letter, so keep that in mind in your dealings with him. You will, of course, hand the Irishman over to Puy-Monbraque when you've finished talking to him?'

Gerrard smiled coldly. 'How would he like him, dead or alive?' He was serious.

'I hope that's a joke?'

'It's not.'

Maurice stared at Gerrard for several seconds. 'Sort that one out with Puy-Monbraque,' he said. 'Is there anything else?'

Gerrard shook his head and stood up. 'I'll see you in the morning,' he said.

Maurice watched him as far as the door, then said, 'Michel, whatever happens I'm not in any way involved in this operation – particularly if it goes wrong.'

Gerrard stopped with his hand on the door-knob and turned to look hard at the old man in the armchair. 'I understand, Maurice,' he said. 'In that event, who am I working for?'

'Like I said – you're the President's man. It's just you and him. I'm not in it.'

'Good-night, Maurice.'

'Good luck.'

CHAPTER 28

'Close your eyes, Melanie, there's a man with no clothes on disappearing into the bedroom.'

'Bother, I missed it!'

'You didn't miss a lot – it was nothing special, only Michel by the dimples in his cheeks! But what's this?' The tall, beautiful, dark-eyed woman raised her chin to meet Reason's ready appraisal. 'And why aren't *you* dressed like Michel?' Her accent was very French. Everything about her was very French. She smiled flirtatiously into Reason's eyes and held her hand out. 'My name's Lili.'

'Put him down, Lili!' Gerrard reappeared, dressed in a white towelling bathrobe. Still barefooted he carried a frosted bottle of chilled Krug in each hand. 'His tribe eats people if they get the chance.'

Lili continued staring into Reason's eyes. 'I think I might enjoy being eaten by you.'

Reason didn't smile. 'If your stomach's in the right place I'll tell you where I usually start.'

Lili almost blushed, but not quite. 'Naughty!' she whispered. 'Should I be frightened or excited?' She wasn't allowed to know. Reason grinned when Gerrard put a glass of champagne in her hand and directed her to a chair by the window.

'Go and sit down – I have a favour to ask.'

'Thank you, Michel – champagne, yes, chair no.' She was serious. 'I can't stay long enough to sit down. I'm off first thing in the morning. I only came to deliver Melanie to you.'

'Thanks,' said Gerrard, reverting to French, 'but now I want you to take her away again.'

Lili shook her head. But before she could voice her objection, Gerrard picked up two cigarettes, lit them both and placed one between her lips. It was an automatic gesture from the past. 'Lili, I'm not begging – I need a home for this girl for a couple of days.'

'Michel, I'm going away!'

'Take her with you.'

'To Buenos Aires? Don't be silly! Why don't you take her with you, she'll keep you amused.'

'I don't want to be amused, I want her tucked away, somewhere where I don't have to keep looking over my shoulder and worrying about her; I want her out of the way, Lili, I can't afford to have her getting tangled in my feet. Can't you suggest something?'

'No, I must go. Why don't you leave her here?'

Gerrard shook his head. 'Don't be stupid!'

'Jealous?' Lili patted him affectionately on one cheek while she kissed him on the other. 'Take her with you, Michel,' she said softly, 'otherwise that's just what you will be doing – looking over your shoulder all the time!'

The room seemed quiet and empty after Lili had left, and Melanie had gone for a bath. Reason stretched himself full length on the settee and held up his empty glass for Gerrard to refill. When the full glass was back in his hand he looked up at Gerrard and said, 'I don't think I like the sound of your new playmates.'

Gerrard recharged his own glass from a giant bottle of Famous Grouse. 'They'll grow on you,' he said, without looking up.

'No they won't.' Reason sipped from his glass and pulled a face. 'Where d'you reckon this guy is now?'

'He could be anywhere. The last word we had was of his strolling out of a Left Bank hotel into the crowd. Whether he's put his head down and scrambled for home, or gone to ground here while he waits for new instructions, is as much your guess as everybody else's. You might as well throw in your ten francs' worth. You can start by telling me whether any of those names mean anything to you.'

'Phelan's a common enough Irish name,' Reason suggested. 'On a par with Murphy and potato. If it's the Phelan I'm thinking of, though, he's a nasty evil bastard. Got the mentality of an SS concentration camp stoker – you need to pull a pair of leather gloves on when you hit him in case something unpleasant rubs off.'

'Sounds a charming fellow.'

'He's Ireland's favourite son in London, pulls the strings and lights the touchpaper. It's got to be him, I don't think there's another Phelan who could start wheels turning over here.' Reason sipped again from his glass. 'And if it is, he's your link, but whether you'd get anything out of

Charles Phelan this side of the grave is another matter. You want to know about the other one?'

'McGann?'

'If it's the McGann I think it is I'm glad I came! It's a name worn by the IRA's up-and-coming Chief of Staff. This military genius is one Michael McGann. He has a family who help out in the business. Your butcher could be his brother Sean, or he could be just a run-of-the-mill hot-shot who's been given the name to make the earth tremble. But by the sound of the way he went about his work I'd put my money on family. The only thing that really surprises me is that this guy's running naked.'

'We don't know that. He could have friends round the corner.'

Reason pulled a face. 'Possible . . . But it reinforces my suspicion. If it's the McGann I'm thinking of, a back-up crew would be a hindrance to him. He's a lone runner – enjoys his own company.'

'Have you run across him?'

'It's a long story. I'll tell you about it some time, but not now.' Reason swung his legs off the settee and sat up. 'What's next?' he asked. Some of the humour had left his eyes.

'We're going to have a little chat tomorrow morning with McGann's contact, the one who started this ball rolling.'

CHAPTER 29

McGann changed trains four times before surfacing into the evening sunlight at Place Félix-Eboue.

It was unplanned, spur of the moment – a last-second dash as the doors of the train closed. Nobody else fancied Félix-Eboue; nobody joined him on the deserted platform. But he waited, just in case, and when the train pulled away leaving a silent, deserted station he wandered upstairs and waited again at the Métro entrance. He studied the underground map, but briefly, then shrugged the two bags into a more comfortable position on his shoulder and moved out of the shelter of the station entrance and turned left into Avenue Daumesnil.

He took his time. He knew what he was looking for. Not the brightly lit café with its restaurant bulging out on to the pavement, nor the dingy bar with its silent drunks, but the one on the corner – clean, quiet, the family café – the Café Daumesnil, original name; no restaurant and the outside almost deserted – a haven for the bored or lonely.

McGann spotted her before he reached the café.

She was sitting alone at a pavement table, a woman of about thirty reading a paperback book and sipping cloudy yellow liquid from a small glass. Alone, because there was no other glass on the table, and definitely bored, probably lonely, hopefully both. McGann slowed down for a better look. It was exactly what he wanted. He wasn't too particular about her appearance – she could have had warts and a faceful of smallpox scars for all he was concerned – but what she had to have was a bed, and four solid walls to keep the militia at arm's length. McGann smiled to himself. It might turn out to be her lucky night . . .

He squeezed between two tables and sat down with his back to the café window. He was within touching distance of the woman. She looked up briefly, smiled hesitantly, and returned to her book. The smile was enough for McGann.

Ten minutes later she had a new *pastis*. Three-quarters of an hour later, and three more *pastis*, they were having dinner in a small bistro on the Boulevard Poniatowski near Porte de Dorée. At half-past eleven she opened the door of her small studio flat, and at eleven thirty-five McGann lowered her gently on to her bed, slipped the tiny white briefs over her firm, tanned thighs and entered her willing body.

CHAPTER 30

There were about thirty of them. Good clear pictures of two men sitting at a café table with their backs to a dark curtained window. There was no attempt at artistic presentation – they were all taken from the same angle and varied only in expression and gesture. There were several full-faced enlargements of McGann.

Puy-Monbraque riffled through the photographs as if they were a pack of cards. He split the pack in two and sent a wadge sliding across the desk to Gerrard, then shuffled his own pile again and spread the prints out in front of him like a man about to start a session of patience. Nobody spoke as he pored over them.

Gerrard did the same with his own pack.

'Which one's Monod?' he asked Claude. 'As if I couldn't guess.'

'The fat one with the smug expression and all the chins. We've managed downstairs to cure him of the expression but we're having a bit of a problem with the chins.' Claude looked over Puy-Monbraque's shoulder at the rows of pictures to remind himself of what Monod had looked like yesterday, then shook his head. 'He doesn't look quite like his picture at the moment. It's been a long night for him. But he is, erm . . . beginning to bend towards our point of view.'

Gerrard was no longer listening. He turned in his chair and looked at Reason.

'Did you understand any of that, Clive?'

'Not a bloody word . . . What have you got there?'

'Pictures.' Gerrard split his pack in half. 'See if they do anything to you.'

Reason glanced at the top picture, then back at Gerrard and pulled a face. 'His name's McGann, and like I said last night you can forget the Bridges bit, it doesn't mean a thing . . .' He broke off for a second but continued staring at McGann's likeness. Then he looked up. 'You've got a problem here,' he said.

Puy-Monbraque raised his head from the photographs and stared at Reason. His eyes were almost hidden under his bushy eyebrows. 'You talk as if you know this man,' he said. He spoke in English – perfect, upper-class-accent English.

Reason stared back at Puy-Monbraque and jabbed his long finger at the full-face photograph of McGann on top of the pile on his knee.

'This man,' he said, 'when he was not much more than a boy, was master gunner of an IRA execution squad. He was very, very good at his job. He enjoyed his work. He enjoyed it so much that they sent him off as an exchange student with the PLO. That was when they had their military academy at Rashadiya, in South Lebanon. They arranged a tour for him with the Baader-Meinhof before it became the Red Army Faction, so he knows how to kill in German as well. He's your university of terrorism graduate – a double first in bloodlust and honours in unpleasantness. But it doesn't show to any marked degree. Walking along the street he looks like anybody else, but if you see him coming towards you, get on to the other side of the road quickly. He's not unintelligent – quite the opposite. He's no fool and, as you can see by the picture, he's quite a pretty boy. He has a lot of charm and he likes the ladies – and he seems to have something they like; they throw themselves at him, so I'm told.'

With that, Reason stretched back in his chair and placed a cigarette between his lips. He didn't light it but gripped it between his teeth and looked down again at McGann's portrait. There was none of the usual humour in his eyes.

After what seemed an eternity of silence Puy-Monbraque brought his eyebrows together again and said, not unkindly, 'That's most enlightening. You seem to have made a study of this man, it's a pity you didn't tell us about him before.'

'Before what?' said Reason.

The old man shook his head. He didn't apologise, or explain. 'This McGann? Does he work with a team? How many men will he have brought with him?'

'None, he's a loner,' said Reason. 'He came here on a one-man hunt. He won't go back until he finishes the job, unless . . .' Reason broke off and watched the old man's eyes narrow.

'Unless what?'

'Unless his people at home decide he's too valuable to provide a monkey for a French security exercise.'

'I wish I saw this in the same light-hearted vein as you do, young man,' growled Puy-Monbraque. 'Unfortunately I view three dead men as a

266

trifle more than a security exercise.' He looked hard at Gerrard as if withdrawing any forgiveness he might have felt earlier, then realigned the big black man in his sights. 'Is that all you want to tell us about this person?'

Reason smiled unrepentantly. 'What else do you want to know – the colour of the hair on his balls?'

'I thought I made it clear that this wasn't, in my opinion, a matter for lightheartedness.'

Gerrard moved in on tiptoe and eased the fuse out of the ticking bomb. 'Clive – the Director, like myself, is curious to know how you came by all this stuff. It sounds as if you've been peeking into the boy's personal diary.'

Reason said, 'He told me himself.'

'What's the man talking about?' Puy-Monbraque was not amused either. He'd had enough of the Irishman McGann, and the black man was getting on his nerves, as was his French friend. But curiosity got the better of him. He continued, speaking in English, 'Is he trying to say he has been in contact with this person?'

'Clive?' Gerrard stared at Reason.

Reason slowly uncoiled from his armchair and stood at his full height. He seemed to fill that part of the room, even though by any standard it was a huge room, and wordlessly, as if he were thinking of something else, tugged the pale-blue shirt out of the waistband of his trousers and unfastened the buttons and the top part of the zip to expose his flat, muscular stomach. The Frenchmen looked on, fascinated.

Reason had three navels.

Perfectly symmetrical, the line of navels could have been drawn with a draughtsman's instrument. The gap between them was a micrometrical inch and a half. The centre one was the real one, the one by which he'd been attached to his mother, but those on either side bore the puckered scars of bullet entry holes. Reason lowered his eyes and studied his stomach for a second or two then looked up into the startled faces of his audience. He smiled grimly. 'We're that close, McGann and I. He told me all about the interesting life he'd led while he was setting me up as a shooting gallery. When I got over my gut-ache I thought I owed it to him to keep up to date on his progress.'

Reason dragged heavily on his cigarette and exhaled slowly. 'So, now that you know all about McGann you can toss a coin up to decide who gets second word with him.'

Puy-Monbraque stopped staring at Reason and looked to Gerrard for guidance. 'What's he talking about?'

Gerrard frowned a warning at Reason before shrugging his shoulders at Puy-Monbraque. 'It's the English sense of humour, Director, there's nothing significant in it.'

Puy-Monbraque was still not happy. He reverted to French.

'Just as long, then, as these words don't turn into anything more drastic than loose teeth and a sore crotch. I wouldn't like you to forget that my men received considerably more than holes in their stomach. I want the last word, and I want the man intact – not in bits and pieces. I hope that's clearly understood?'

Gerrard looked the old man straight in the eye. It was a good job Reason didn't understand French. 'Of course, Director, there was never any question about it. After I've spoken to McGann he'll be dropped on your doorstep. All I want from him is conversation; I'll leave the screams to you.'

Puy-Monbraque nodded contentedly. 'Excuse me, just one moment.' He turned to Claude.

'Claude, take the English conversation off the tape and have it transcribed into French.' He jerked his chin at one of the wall cabinets and smiled disarmingly at Gerrard. 'You understand . . .?'

Gerrard smiled back. He understood.

Puy-Monbraque returned to Claude. 'And run it into the profile. Get something on the wire to Mossad or Shin Beth, they might have him on their list – they seem to have extraordinarily long memories for those who have touched foreheads with the PLO. And while you're at it send a picture to the Germans and mention a B-M connection. Do that now, and on your way out tell somebody to wait outside the door to take these two gentlemen downstairs.'

When Claude had gone he turned back to Gerrard. 'That seems to be just about everything for the time being – ' He broke off and stared hard at Maurice's envelope still lying in the middle of the desk where he'd pushed it. 'Unless there's anything more you require of me, or my department?'

Gerrard said, 'Just the one thing, Director.'

Puy-Monbraque raised his eyebrows. He needn't have worried.

'Assuming the inevitable, that McGann breaks cover, I'd like your assurance that there will be no attempt made to collect him by force, no matter where, and no matter how many men you've got near him.' Gerrard picked the envelope up off the desk and held it in his hand for a second or two before slipping it carefully into his inside pocket. The gesture wasn't lost on Puy-Monbraque.

'You have my word,' he said. 'Instruction will go out within the next quarter of an hour that, when located, McGann is to be followed only – nothing more than that. He'll be taken solely at my discretion – following discussion, of course, with you.' He placed his fingers together, pursed his lips and waited for Gerrard's sign of approval. He accepted a curt nod as the sign and continued, 'Agreement has already been reached with the Director of the DGSE, and the Prefect of Police, that the entire operation will come under my direction, so all directives will originate here.' He tapped the desk several times with his finger to show exactly where. 'And I stress again – nothing will bear my signature that differs in any way from what you and I have already agreed. All senior officers involved will be informed that you reflect, exactly, my strategy in this matter and written instructions will be issued to that effect. Your orders will not be questioned.'

'And if they are?'

'They won't be, because I shall assign one of my senior aides to liaise on your behalf; it'll also save you and me from having to meet again,' he bared his teeth in an imitation smile, '. . . except, of course, in happier circumstances. Is there anything else?'

Gerrard shook his head. 'I'd like a word with Monod now. Is he expecting us?'

Puy-Monbraque almost smiled again. 'Expect is not quite the description I'd apply to Monod's social programme. I think for him it's more a state of what's going to happen next. At the moment he's living life by the second, but he's not bored – new experiences can never be boring, can they? I'm looking forward to meeting Mr McGann in similar circumstances.'

Sitting shivering on a hard kitchen stool in a windowless room, sometimes in the dark, sometimes in the stark brightness of the single high-wattage bulb suspended a few inches above his head, Philippe Monod was desperately unhappy.

He'd lost count of how much time had elapsed since they'd dragged him from his fluffy comfortable bed and thrown him, clad only in pyjamas, into this stone-floored cupboard of a room. How many hours ago was it – or was it only minutes – since the supreme humiliation: the degradation of the first onset of real fear that took him unaware and pressed like a stone on his overloaded bladder. Nobody took any notice when he asked for the toilet so he relieved himself in the corner of the room. They were waiting. They let him feel the first sweet tinge of relief, then they pounced, two of them – burly, muscular, stony-faced young men who timed it perfectly. Silently, and in unison, one kicked his legs from under him and the other stood on his back, rocking his weight from one leg to the other, balancing with his arms outstretched, like a circus juggler on a large soft ball. Neither spoke or made a sound – not even an absent-minded whistle. It was too much for Monod. He lay and whimpered, then sobbed like a baby, the sobs punctuated with barklike groans each time the man on his back shifted his weight, and all the time he could feel the warm liquid continue to run down his legs drenching his cream silk pyjamas. When his bladder had finally emptied the young man stepped down from his back.

They'd picked him up roughly. One cuffed him round the ear, not hard, but enough to bruise, just enough to sting – the way an angry father slaps the boy who wets his trousers. In time with the slaps the other healthy, clean-cut young man repeated over and over again, 'You dirty fat bastard – what are you? You dirty fat bastard – what are you?' until they jammed him back on to the hard wooden stool.

Those were the last words he'd heard. Now he wanted to sleep, but the light burned into his eyeballs and he knew that if he slept he'd fall off the stool and they'd come in and stand on his back again.

It was at this point Monod wondered whether death really was as unpleasant as it was made out to be.

'On your feet!'

Monod started guiltily. He jerked his head up from his chest and nearly fell off the stool. He'd been dozing, he had no idea how long, but he knew it was a punishable offence and braced himself.

The two young men who burst into the room were not the same pair as earlier. They were no less unfriendly than the last two; but more enthusiastic – they'd probably had a very restful night's sleep and a good basketful of hot buttered croissants for breakfast. They grabbed Monod, one on either side, and ran him down a semi-dark corridor, up a flight of rough concrete stairs and into a room similar in size and shape to the one he'd just left.

But compared to that this was a palace. There were several wooden slatted chairs dotted around the room and a table set in civilised splendour in the centre of it; the light was softer, subdued, and gentle on the eyes and the bulb was covered by a chiffon tasselled shade. Luxury! And more . . . ! Monod's bare feet touched, and enjoyed, the comforting softness of the man-made fibre carpet that covered the room throughout and when the hands released him he stumbled in a daze towards the table and lowered himself gratefully into the chair beside it. He closed his eyes and his aching mind turned the simple act of resting his head in his arms on the table into the ultimate pleasure – the most wonderful thing in the world.

At least it would have been if it had lasted longer than a fraction of a second.

'What the bloody hell do you think you're doing?'

One of his new guards, leaning casually against the wall, brought Monod back to sitting attention.

'I didn't say sit. Did you hear me tell Monod he could sit, André?'

André shook his head and took over. 'Stand up,' he said. There was no menace in his voice; it was just a simply spoken command, but it frightened Monod. He leapt to his feet and stood swaying from side to side with his fingers resting on the wooden haven in front of him – it looked more inviting than any bed he'd known. Would he ever know a soft bed again? He shook his head and said, 'I'm sorry.'

The first man said, 'I didn't say talk. Sit down!'

He sat.

'Stand up!'

'Sit down!' They took it in turns.

'Stand up!'

And suddenly there were no more commands, but through the mist he saw another two men enter the room. He remained standing.

'Is he being sociable?' asked Gerrard.

'Very! Little finger up in the air, blowing on his tea like a *vicomtesse*,' the first young man said. 'He can't do enough for us. Willing's not quite the word, but we're getting there. If he lapses in his manners give us a shout, we'll be just outside.'

'Thank you.'

'Did you hear that, Fatty?' The guard named André put his head back round the door. 'Don't disappoint the nice gentlemen or we won't let you come and play feeties with us again.'

'What's feeties?' asked Gerrard.

'It's a new game, sir. He played it with our colleagues. He'll tell you all about it. You'll tell the gentlemen how to play feeties, won't you, Monod?'

When the door closed behind the guard, Gerrard lit a cigarette, passed the packet to Reason and said to Monod, 'Sit down, and tell me about feeties.'

Monod collapsed gratefully into the chair and rested his arms on the table.

'I said sit down, not lie down.'

Monod shot into an upright position. He rearranged himself and sat with his back pressed hard into the chair rungs, then set his face into an expression of eager humility. Anxious to please, he almost wobbled with obedience – like a half-trained gun-puppy.

'Do you speak English?'

'Yes, sir.'

'Then tell us in English about feeties.'

Monod looked into Gerrard's face for encouragement, for a sign that reprieve was not too far away, but he saw nothing – no pity, no sympathy, not even malice or mild disapproval – nothing. It was more frightening than the angry young men. He looked away from the face and down at his hands, trembling on his silk-covered thighs.

'They throw me to the ground and walk up and down on my back.'

'You enjoy it?'

'No, sir.'

'But you prefer it to the more sophisticated methods of persuasion?'

'I don't understand.'

'Yes you do.'

'Yes I do!' parroted Monod, quickly. 'But please, sir, I don't need any sort of persuasion. Please ask your questions.'

'Would you like a cigarette?'

Monod shuddered. Would he like a cigarette? He was being invited back into the human race – civilisation, a cigarette, a kind word – it was like absolution to a dying Catholic. 'Thank you, I'd like a cigarette very much, please.'

Gerrard passed one across the table and lit it for him. He watched Monod inhale deeply, like a man surfacing from a sunken submarine, and waited for the euphoria to dilute. He didn't give him a chance for another pull.

'Tell me about McGann.'

'I know of no one by that name.'

'Bridges?'

'I've told them all I know.'

'Tell me.'

'He came recommended from an official in London. He was of the IRA.'

'The official was?'

'No, Bridges. He claimed to be a representative of the IRA.'

'And the official's name?'

Monod shot a quick glance at Reason. It was wasted. Reason was busy studying smoke rings. He brought his eyes back to Gerrard.

'Brocklebank.'

'Anything else?'

'No – just Brocklebank.'

'What's this official position he occupies in London?' Gerrard leaned forward and took the barely touched cigarette from Monod's fingers and crushed it out on the table-top. Monod felt like crying.

'I don't know,' he said reluctantly. 'I believe it was something to do with British Intelligence, but I'm only guessing.'

'What did he do to make you believe he was British Intelligence?'

'The manner of his play. Since he's been concerned with the IRA he's never asked for British target movements; nor for plans of British VIP security screening or any of the files that would be of interest to a terrorist organisation like the IRA.'

'In other words,' joined in Reason, still gazing at his smoke rings, 'he knew all about those things before you did?'

'It seemed that way.'

'How do you get in touch with him?'

'I don't, he usually sends someone to see me.'

'But what happened when you wanted him at short notice; like when you had something that was burning a hole in the paper?'

'He gave me a number in London to ring.'

Gerrard exchanged glances with Reason as he took a slim gold Parker from his inside pocket. He pulled the cigarette packet towards him and said, 'What's the number?'

Monod looked as if he were about to burst into tears. 'I don't keep things like that in my head.'

Gerrard didn't look up from the cigarette packet. 'Clive,' he said quietly, 'go and give those two fellows outside a nudge, will you.'

Reason didn't have to move.

'Please!' Monod's voice almost dried up with fright. 'I have the number hidden . . . I can get it if you'll allow me to go home.'

'We'll talk about that later. When did you last see Mr Brocklebank?'

'I haven't seen him since our initial meeting. Everything was done through a go-between . . .'

'A permanent go-between?'

'No, they varied. As long as they had the correct sentence for me I accepted them as bona fide emissaries from Mr Brocklebank.'

'What does Brocklebank look like?'

'I'm not sure. I'm not very good at faces. It *was* a long time ago.'

'Try,' Gerrard said firmly.

Monod closed his eyes and looked back to the beginning of his end.

'A heavy man, but not fat, he looked as though he did quite a lot of exercise and kept himself fit. He didn't smoke. He might now, but he didn't then. Clean, well-dressed, but not expensive clothes. Age between fifty and sixty.'

'Ten years? The gap's too wide. Try again.'

'I can't get closer, he wore a wig.'

'A wig?'

'Yes. Nice fair texture, no grey in it at all. It makes it very difficult to judge a man's age accurately when he's not being honest.'

'Was he bald underneath?'

Monod hunched his shoulders.

Gerrard said, 'Does that sound like anybody you know, Clive?'

Reason was intently studying his fingernails. He didn't look up. 'Sounds like every bus queue at the top of Whitehall Place round about five o'clock on a weekday afternoon!'

Gerrard turned back to Monod and flicked the half-full packet of cigarettes across the table. They came to rest beside Monod's podgy hand. 'Put them in your pocket,' he said, 'and tell me who Mr Brocklebank was working for when you first met him.'

'Didn't I say?' Monod stood up painfully and dropped the cigarettes in his pyjama pocket. Under the thin material they stood out like a large oblong name tab with the logo on the packet as clear as if he'd hung them round his neck. He wouldn't keep them for very long, he knew that, but hanging on to a packet of cigarettes was going to be the least of his worries.

Gerrard shook his head.

Monod looked up and tried to smile, but nothing came. He was never going to smile again – ever. 'He was working for the Russians. Quite high up, probably an honorary colonel, maybe even a real one. I do recollect him appearing during our first meeting with a man he introduced as Irektsivin.'

'Piotr Irektsivin?'

'Yes.' Monod's face lit up. 'You know him?'

Gerrard ignored Monod's question. 'Brocklebank was working for

Irektsivin?'

'The other way round, I think. Irektsivin is head of the KGB assets protection bureau in Western Europe. He treated Brocklebank with great respect so Brocklebank must have been at least a colonel . . . But they're good at that, the English, aren't they? High-ranking Intelligence Service officials working for their enemies – half the British Secret Service must be honorary Russian colonels – at the very least.' Monod wasn't joking. 'May I have a match please, sir?'

He stuck what was probably going to be his last cigarette in his mouth and leaned towards Gerrard for a light. He kept it glued between his thick pursed lips and had to wrinkle his eyes against the smoke that fluttered around his hairless eyebrows. It gave him an expression of curiosity, almost of surprise. 'You didn't mention your name, sir,' he said from the side of his mouth. 'Just in case . . . happier circumstances perhaps . . . ?' He left the sentence unfinished – there weren't going to be any happier circumstances, and he knew it.

Gerrard almost smiled but held it in check. 'That's Mr Reason from England,' he said. 'And my name's Gerrard, Michel Gerrard.'

He got no pleasure from the look of horror that suffused Monod's flabby face and he turned his back before the fat, hairless little man lowered himself on to the chair and buried his head in his arms. As he followed Reason out of the room he heard Monod crying – it sounded like a distraught woman opening up her heart. Gerrard closed the door quietly behind him. There was no need to say goodbye.

CHAPTER 31

McGann was fast asleep. But his eyes opened the moment the key touched the door.

The Sauer was out of the bag and resting on his stomach under the sheet before the key turned in the lock. As the door opened he eased the cocking lever back gently as far as it would go.

Pascale did all the wrong things.

She opened the door slowly before putting her head round the corner, then closed it quietly and tiptoed towards the bed. McGann smiled as she leaned over him. Had it been dark, or dusk and gloomy, or a badly lit room, Pascale de Foure would be dead. Instead she leaned over him and kissed his mouth and slipped her hand under the bedsheet. Her aim was six inches too high. She didn't recoil from the warm metal. McGann placed his other hand over hers and kept it trapped in that position. She didn't object. She gave a little wriggle that brought her body down on to McGann's, and continued kissing him. After a moment she removed her lips a fraction away from his and breathed huskily into his open mouth, 'Very hard, the right shape, and warm. What are you playing with down there?'

'You wouldn't like it if I told you.'

She bit his lip very gently. 'Tell me.'

'It's a gun.'

She ran her hand over the warm metal again. She didn't believe him. It was a joke. It took a full second for the disbelief to evaporate and then her eyes popped out.

'Oh my God!'

She tried to snatch her hand away but McGann tightened his grip. 'Don't have hysterics,' he whispered calmly, 'and don't stop what you're doing, I like it!'

'*Sean!*' Her voice rose in her throat but it came out as a muted scream. McGann put his free hand over her mouth, gently but firmly, then pulled himself off the pillow so that his head rested on the headboard.

'Shhh!' he whispered soothingly and took his hand from her mouth. She caught her breath but her eyes refused to settle down.

'If this is not a joke, Sean, tell me what's going on. Why are you hiding a gun down there? Why do you have a gun at all . . .? Sean – *what's going on!*' The hysteria was on its way back again.

McGann had his story ready. All it needed was the telling – and a gullible, non-hysterical listener. 'Listen!' he whispered urgently.

He needed a friend for the next few days, somebody who trusted him, somebody who would hide him until the pack stopped baying; somebody who wouldn't wet her knickers when she read about dead agents and saw photofit pictures of Sean McGann splashed all over her evening paper. Pascale de Foure was about to be briefed on the McGann version. If she didn't like it she'd find herself rolled up in a blanket under the bed; if she did she had about three more days left in which to broaden her neglected horizon. Three days, or thereabouts, for the dogs to exhaust themselves – three days, Pascale de Foure, and you become dispensable. McGann smiled reassuringly into her troubled eyes.

'This might take a minute or two.'

'Sean, I'm afraid.'

'No you're not. Listen to what I'm going to tell you, and if you don't believe me when I've finished you can pick up the phone and ring the police.'

She shook her head furiously – a wise decision.

McGann slid the pistol back into the bag. It was still fully cocked, no safety – Pascale de Foure was that fraction of a second away from dying. McGann pulled himself up into a sitting position and slipped the pillow down behind his back. He adjusted the crumpled sheet around his waist and grinned encouragingly into Pascale's eyes; he was about to sell an apple to a dying boar.

'Do you read books?' he asked.

She shook her head. 'What's that got to do with it?'

'Do you?' he persisted.

'What do you think I was doing when you first set eyes on me?'

'Then you know the sort of things that go on all over the world in the name of national security. Things like espionage, counter-espionage, intelligence, undercover agents, spies – all that sort of stuff? You read about it all the time, don't you?'

'James Bond?' She smiled nervously and parted her small white teeth allowing a tip of pink tongue to nip out and run quickly over dry lips; it was a set smile, with a tiny tremble of fear hovering just below the surface.

'Yes, that sort of thing,' said McGann, easily.

'You . . . ?' she began. The doubt was no longer hovering – it was out in the open; Pascale de Foure was smiling herself into the family vault in Ploubalay cemetery.

McGann gave her another chance.

'I told you you could ring the police if you wanted.'

She bit her lip and stopped smiling.

McGann said, 'I'm an agent of the Irish Secret Intelligence Service. I'm here on an undercover operation with French Intelligence.'

'Honestly, Sean!'

'I asked you to listen.'

'Go on then. But don't make me laugh.'

'I promise you anything but a laugh when I've finished. Just hear me out.'

'I'm listening.'

'And don't interrupt, OK? Your government believes that the English have infiltrated the French Intelligence network. As an expert on British Secret Service methods and organisations I've been loaned to your government to work in conjunction with the DST, but, last night, three DST agents and myself were ambushed by British operatives in a hotel off Boulevard St Germain. They killed my three friends. I got away. But I have to stay out of sight.'

'What is the DST?' The doubt had vanished from Pascale's eyes. It was replaced by interest, curiosity, and, McGann hadn't missed it – concern. 'I've never heard it mentioned,' she said huskily. 'Is it something to do with the police?'

McGann uttered a silent prayer. Thank God for gullible women! 'The DST?' he said seriously. 'There's no reason why you should have heard of it. It's a counter-espionage agency – highly secret; it's the *Direction de la Surveillance du Territoire*. It's better you don't know too much.'

'You said your friends were killed?'

'Killed so that I could get away. Three good Frenchmen killed by the British.'

'How awful. What do you have to do now?'

'Keep out of the way for a few days. The problem is that the British have friends in high places here in France. They've infiltrated everywhere . . .' McGann was beginning to enjoy himself. 'They've infiltrated the newspapers, the radio, maybe even the television . . . Nothing's safe from these people. I wouldn't put it past them to stitch up a picture to look like me and write a load of guff to suggest it was I who did the killing. Don't shake your head, Pascale, they've done worse things than that! They're capable of anything, and there are people who'd believe such things. The English are evil, they're cunning, they spend a lot of time trying to drive wedges between friends like us – the Irish and the French. Do you like the English?'

'I can't say I've ever given it a thought.' She arched her eyebrows at him. 'But I am very, very fond of the Irish!' To prove it, Pascale leaned forward, put both hands on McGann's shoulders and forced him backwards. She stared into his eyes for a second then lowered her head and began kissing, very gently, each of McGann's tiny hair-covered nipples. She'd had enough of politics. It was time to change the subject.

But not for McGann. He put his hand round the back of her head and took hold of a handful of long blonde hair. She squealed, half in delight half in pain, as he pulled her firmly upwards until her face was level with his. 'There's a time and a place,' he said roughly and kissed her hard on the mouth. She squealed again, louder, to show that she was ready, but McGann had other things on his mind. Like Charlie Phelan for one. He let her go and, ignoring her disappointed pleas, slipped out of the bed and into the bathroom. The Air France bag went with him.

'What are you going to do next?' she called through the door.

McGann stepped under the shower but left the curtain open so that he could hear what was going on.

'I'm going to make a phone call,' he shouted back.

'I know that,' she said. 'I mean what are you going to do about these English spies? Won't they come looking for you?'

'They don't know where I am, and they won't find me here, will they? Not unless you run up and down Avenue Daumesnil telling everybody what you're doing to me in your bed.'

'And I'm not likely to do that while there's a chance of more! Perhaps I could blackmail you.'

McGann ignored her flippancy and kept things serious. 'They lost me last night on Boulevard St Germain. They'll expect me to run for Ireland.' He opened the door and poked his head round the corner. He carried on shaving as he talked. 'But they'll be mistaken, won't they?'

'Will they?'

'Of course they will, because instead of standing in the queue for the boat to Cork I shall be tucked away here in Avenue Daumesnil, snuggling up to the beautiful Pascale de Foure! And when they get bored

279

looking for me we'll crawl out of our little nest and I shall go back and finish what I came here to do.'

'Say it again.'

'What?'

'The bit about what you're going to be doing, and who you're going to do it with.'

'Come in here, then.'

'Take that stuff off your face first.'

'The shower'll wash it off.'

'You've just had a shower.'

'Come here!'

'What about your phone call, Sean?'

'Christ! What's the time?'

'Twenty to eleven.'

'I'm late! Quick, while I'm drying myself, get me a pair of jeans out of that bag . . . and a T-shirt.'

'You only have to walk across the room.' Pascale de Foure, pretty, naked, and wet, her hair plastered to her head and face, leaned weakly against the glass partition and watched the powerful jets play pins and needles on her body. 'I don't mind you using the phone without clothes – or is that against your religion!'

'Out!' McGann reached into the shower and took one full-budded wet nipple between his finger and thumb and led her gently out of the bathroom.

'Oh, that's cruel . . . Ouch! Stop it, Sean, it hurts!'

'Do as you're told.'

'All right. Let go and pass me a towel.'

'Later. I've just told you, I'm in a hurry.'

'I'm soaking wet.'

'Dry yourself while I'm out.'

She stopped in her tracks. 'What do you mean, while you're out? You're not going out! You can't, I won't let you!' She ran her fingers between the mask of wet hair that hung over her face, parted it down the middle and pasted half on each side of her head. She stared at McGann in disbelief. 'After what you've just told me? Sean, you must be mad! Somebody'll see you . . . They'll come for you . . . Why do you have to go out?'

McGann got his own clothes from the bag. As he pulled on a pair of faded blue jeans he said, 'I've got to get to a telephone, and I've got to get to one by eleven; now, for Christ's sake get out of my way!'

'You don't have to go out.'

McGann ignored her. He pulled a white T-shirt over his head and slipped a grubby pair of trainers on his feet. 'Give me your key,' he demanded. 'I'll knock before I come in. If anybody comes while I'm out don't open the door – pretend you're not in.'

'Let me come with you.'

McGann shook his head and picked up the Air France bag. He threw it over his shoulder. 'I'll be about half an hour, it shouldn't be any longer than that. Why don't you get us something to eat?'

'Sean, I'm afraid.'

'There's no need to be.' He put his finger under her chin, raised it and smiled. 'You have nothing to worry about, beautiful de Foure.' He ran the finger lightly up and down her neck, then down through the water-splattered valley between her breasts; he zig-zagged across her stomach and stopped where the damp curly blonde hair began. He spread his hand out. Before she could react, he squeezed and said, 'You're wet. Inside and out! Go and dry yourself. And don't forget to put some clothes on – just in case I bring the local *bonze* back for coffee and doughnuts.'

He was gone before she had time to ask what a *bonze* was.

McGann strolled casually along Avenue Daumesnil until he came to the café where he'd met Pascale.

It was almost a replay of the previous evening. Only two or three of the tables on the pavement were occupied. None of the occupants showed any interest in Sean McGann. Like the paranoiac, McGann wondered why.

He walked to the far end of the café and sat down. He had plenty of time in spite of what he'd told the girl. He ordered a coffee and a large brandy and drank half of each before looking at his watch again. Eleven-ten. He glanced over his shoulder and peered through the window at the clock inside the café; it almost agreed; eight minutes past eleven – about a quarter-past ten in Canning Town.

He left his unfinished drinks on the table, shouldered the Air France bag and went into the gloomy interior of the café in search of the telephone. It was as he expected; an old-fashioned cabinet with a half-glazed door in the corner next to the lavatory; a sensible arrangement – two sound-proofed non-essentials for a café catering for an incurious clientele with strong bladders. He went in, closed the door and made himself comfortable.

Phelan sounded as if he were speaking from the shop next door. 'You're a stupid, inefficient, incompetent bastard!'

McGann grinned at the wall of the phone box. He'd have grinned into Phelan's face if Phelan had been standing beside him – it always had that effect on him, the bouncing Adam's apple and the groin-straining falsetto.

'And good morning to you too, Charlie.' Phelan's pause for breath allowed McGann a toehold into the conversation. 'And if you'll calm yourself down for a moment you'll be able to think up a few new words – you're going to need them. I've got a bit of bad news.'

Phelan brought himself down, but his voice remained high, higher than usual – it always did when he was agitated. 'You don't have to tell me,' he squeaked. 'Everything about you is fucking bad news, you incompetent, big-mouthed bastard!'

McGann bridled. 'Are you going to let me say my piece, Phelan, or do I give you half an hour to kick yourself round the garden and ring you back again when you're ready to listen?'

'You go too far, McGann. One of these days . . .'

'Sure, Charlie, whatever you say. But make up your bloody mind because I'm not prepared to stand here listening to you scratching your tonsils when I could be outside doing something constructive. D'you want to hear my bad news or don't you?'

'Let me tell you mine first.' Phelan's voice was much calmer, as if he'd taken a long drink, or had a premonitory view of McGann lying on his stomach with the back of his neck bared for the Irish kiss.

'You're in trouble, McGann. Big trouble.'

'Get to the point, Charlie. It's bloody hot standing in this cupboard. What trouble are you talking about?'

'Mouth trouble, McGann. One of your big failings. There's a bit of paper being tossed around over here with your name on it. Does that mean anything to you?'

McGann frowned but said nothing.

'Struck you dumb has it?' Phelan strove for his highest note. 'It probably doesn't worry a stupid bastard like you, McGann, having the British Intelligence people getting little notes from the French about your secret and confidential balls-ups over there?' He paused for a brief half a second to let that bit get across the Channel, then screamed at the top of his voice, 'No, I don't suppose it bloody does! It doesn't turn me over all that much either. So what am I worried about? I'm worried because my fuckin' name's on that bit of paper too, McGann – that's what I'm fuckin' worried about! And so's Mr Brocklebank's – and he's fuckin' worried as well! That's my bit of bad news. Now what's yours?'

McGann wished he'd brought his brandy in with him. The phone box had suddenly become a coffin; it was hot and stuffy and oppressive – he wanted to get out and start running. The delay was too long for Phelan.

'I said, what's your bloody bad news?' Phelan reached his highest note yet.

McGann gritted his teeth against the onslaught on his eardrum and allowed himself a rapid glance over his shoulder. Nobody out there was taking any notice. 'We were blown, Charlie,' he said. There was no truculence in his voice now, no apology either. The excuse was valid, a good one – the best possible excuse – it was exactly what had happened. But try and get that through Charlie Phelan's inbred antagonism. 'It was a set-up from the word go.'

'What d'you mean, a set-up?' Phelan was no longer screaming.

'They'd got your man Monod on a lead. I joined him on it when I made contact. They'd even got the meeting place wired for sound so we were on a loser at square one. When I'd finished talking with Monod they waltzed in and rolled me up. They've probably got Monod nailed to one of the struts of the Eiffel Tower by now.'

'Just a minute! There are one or two things I don't follow here.' Phelan's voice was now calm, cold and analytical. 'Who's this "they" you're talking about? And were they expecting you or just screwing anybody holding hands with Monod?'

'They were security people – official. DGSE I think, or a room in it called Section Six, but it's not important. The important thing is that they stopped my movements.'

'That's the next bit I don't understand,' broke in Phelan. 'If these people took you in, what are you doing talking to me now on the phone?' Suspicion slowed his words down and brought the agitated trill back into his voice. 'You're not . . .? Christ, McGann, you're not bloody stupid enough to . . .?'

'No, Charlie.' McGann smiled to himself, he preferred an agitated Phelan to the cold calculating model. He knew where he stood when he was shrieking. 'I'm not. And I'm not stupid either. I was about to tell you, and if you don't keep interrupting every other word I say, you'll know as much about it as I do in half the time it's taking. And Charlie, I don't like standing around in the open so put your middle finger up somewhere that'll calm you down so that I can get out of this place and back under cover.'

'I've warned you once, McGann!'

'So you have, Charlie! OK, listen to this. Right in the middle of rapping my knuckles one of the gorillas found the bag with the money in it – the fifty thousand I picked up from the station, and – '

Phelan couldn't restrain himself. 'The bastards took the money and let you go? McGann, you're not worth that fuckin' much . . .'

'Charlie, I asked you not to interrupt. And no, the bastards didn't take the money – they don't need money where they've gone.'

The silence from Canning Town was like a bubble thundering around inside a spirit level – it seemed to go on for ever. 'Are you still there, Charlie?' McGann was anxious to get it over with.

Phelan was still there. 'We're talking about more than one, are we?' he said finally. He sounded as if he didn't want to believe it.

'We're talking about three, Charlie.'

'Holy Mother of Christ!' It really was a shriek this time. 'You must be fuckin' mad! Are you trying to tell me you've killed three agents of the French Intelligence Service? Is that what you're trying to tell me, McGann?'

'That's right, Charlie. It was them or me.'

'Holy Mother of . . .! What the bloody hell were they, blind men? Cripples? Never mind, hang on a minute.'

McGann heard him talking faintly to someone else in the room. He strained, and heard Phelan say, 'The mad bastard's stiffed three bloody Frog security men. D'you want . . .' Phelan must have put his hand over the mouthpiece. Everything went dead until, after a minute of sweaty, impatient waiting, the falsetto burst into McGann's eardrum again.

'Did you get anything out of Monod about Gerrard before you were hooked?'

'Only that Monod was petrified of him. Reckoned he was official at one time or another but didn't know what his status was this week. Have you got anybody else for me?'

'You must be bloody joking! The word, McGann, is that you're to get your arse back here as fast as possible. Christ knows how you're going to do it, it must be like a bloody ants' nest over there at the moment. Somehow you've got to put the water between you and the Frogs. I suggest you go for the ferry. Give it a couple of days for the novelty to wear off and make for the busiest ferry, or the nearest. Just a minute.'

Phelan was being bounced up and down on somebody's knee, he was being manipulated and prompted. McGann pulled a face at the wall, then looked again over his shoulder. *Old Charlie Phelan was no different to anybody else in Karno's Army – he was like the rest of us, somebody was telling him what to do – everybody had somebody to tell what to do. Fifty pence each way on Brocklebank* . . . McGann opened the door of the telephone box a fraction of an inch to let in some of the wine-laden, smoky air – it was worse than the stuff he'd already got. He closed the crack quickly, just as Phelan arrived back.

'You can use some of the money to buy yourself out of a fix, but for Christ's sake from now on start using your head instead of your bloody gun. No more killing, McGann, and if they pick you up again you're working for the English. You're a bloody Englishman, and don't you bloody forget it! We don't want to upset the few friends we've got left over there. D'you understand that or d'you want me to repeat it?'

'Spare me that, Charlie! I understand. See you in a couple of days then.' McGann was now in a hurry.

'Just a minute.' Another jab in the side – a bit more gratuitous advice on its way. 'No more mention of Mr Brocklebank. Forget all about him, forget the name – he doesn't exist. OK?'

'OK, Charlie.' *And say goodbye to Mr Brocklebank for me – whoever he is* . . .

'One more thing, Sean.'

It's Sean now, is it? Get ready, here comes the knife! 'What's that, Charlie?'

'Have you an address, in case we need to get in touch with you during the next couple of days? You did say you had somewhere to tuck up, didn't you?'

You mean, Charlie, that when Brocklebank's had a chance to think this one over, he'd like to know where to send the man with the cheese-wire to cut his name out of my throat? That's what you mean, isn't it, Charlie?

McGann grinned to himself. 'I didn't actually, Charlie, but don't ring me, I'll ring you! You know how it is, I've got to keep moving. I'll be in touch.'

'McGann, just a – '

'*Ciao,* Charlie.'

He drained the small glass and slid it on to the nearest table. Time to see if Pascale'd dried herself off. He moved away from the café with the bag over his shoulder and a thoughtful look in his eye and, as he walked down Daumesnil towards Porte de Dorée, he committed the cardinal sin – he forgot to look behind him.

Detective Robert Megnier was tired and bored. He sat at a table outside the Café Daumesnil and sipped his Pernod. Without thinking he added more water, sipped again, turned his nose up at the dilution and continued reading the centre page of his newspaper. What he read put him in a worse mood. Detective Megnier was not only tired and bored, he was also in a bad temper. He looked at his watch. Too late to go home and catch up on lost sleep; too early to go back to the pig-pen, and not enough time for a meal. What a life!

He looked over the top of his newspaper at the sound of clicking heels and watched the pretty shop assistant with the big breasts and no bra trip past the café. She saw him out of the corner of her eye, tossed her head with satisfaction and gave an added emphasis to the swing of her tight little bottom. It was instinctive – she would have screamed for a policeman if he'd gone for her with his hands outstretched. Megnier didn't smile. He watched her until she turned the corner by the *tabac*.

At that point her place was taken by a young man in a white T-shirt who ambled across his line of vision.

Megnier went back to his newspaper. He looked up again, briefly, when the young man stopped at the farthest table under the café's awning and called for the waiter. Idle curiosity – Megnier brought his paper up and tried to concentrate on what he was reading. But the face was vaguely familiar. Someone he knew. Or deceptive – a face from the small screen. A footballer? Rugby? A singer? Possibly, but someone nearer. An old friend? It niggled into Megnier's memory bank while he read the same sentence several times over. When all his options had been rejected he moved the paper to one side and looked again, a fleeting glance – unobtrusive.

It took him like a blow between the eyes.

Actor? Football player . . . ? You stupid bastard, Megnier! You're sitting ten metres away from the Englishman half the French police force is looking for!

Megnier finished cursing himself behind the newspaper that he'd drawn protectively round himself. Under its cover he carefully eased the small photograph from the pocket of the open-necked shirt under his jacket. No doubt about it. He held it in his right hand on the edge of the newspaper and studied it, surreptitiously, against the real thing.

Megnier casually folded the newspaper and placed it on the table. As he reached for his glass he felt a slight tingle in his fingers. A tremble? He lit a cigarette. It helped. He continued looking intently across the avenue at nothing. It was a strain not to stare down the row of tables and make an indelible mental sketch of McGann – even more of a strain not to run at him and scream, 'Got you, you bastard!' But his self-control won, and he contented himself with the odd, and accidental, oblique glance. He wasn't all that impressed with what he saw.

Megnier stretched his legs out in front of him and tried to look non-chalant. He glanced along the tables again and nearly had a heart attack. He was just in time to see the Englishman disappear into the café. He called the waiter and ordered another *pastis* – for the nerves – and asked if there was a back entrance.

'No, just a lavatory and a telephone kiosk.'

Megnier relaxed. He sipped his drink, lit another cigarette and considered his options. *Obey orders and instructions and you'll let someone else get the credit – and the promotion. The bastards'll be falling over themselves to get in on this one. Disobey the orders and bring him in under your arm. Good, that's more like it – but what if it goes wrong? It won't. And in any case there are worse things in life than directing traffic for the next twenty-five years . . . Grab the chance – you'll never get a better one . . .*

And if there's a balls-up?

There won't be. But if there is you're covered – you drop back on to the instructions and follow them to the letter. It's called initiative!

McGann continued walking in the morning sunshine as if he hadn't a care in the world.

When he turned off the Avenue Daumesnil into the narrow street that led to Pascale's apartment block it was with barely a cursory glance that he surveyed the world behind him. That was a mistake. It wasn't long enough, or serious enough, to register the heavily built young man on the opposite side of the road.

Detective Megnier did his stuff well. He looked like everybody else on the Avenue Daumesnil; hands in pockets, jacket open, a cigarette in the corner of his mouth and a rolled-up newspaper under his arm, he stood in the bus queue and watched McGann's progress. He waited discreetly on the far side of the broad avenue until McGann disappeared into the entrance of the newly-sand-blasted apartment block.

He hitched the short-barrelled .38 Police Special closer to his right hand and buttoned up his jacket before crossing the avenue. He'd carried out the first part of his self-imposed bargain – he'd followed instructions; no balls-ups, he'd found the hole. He could now stand here and watch the entrance or he could go inside the building and put his toe into the water – nothing dramatic, just a quick look over the killing ground, a discreet chat with the concierge and a check on the exits . . . Nothing wrong with that. No rules broken so far. Nothing more than an intelligent interpretation of instructions – nothing to bolt the rabbit even if he did pop his head out of the hole.

Megnier glanced up at the prosperous-looking building as he strolled across the road and wondered how a skinny Englishman who'd frightened the balls off the people at d'Arcole had managed to get his feet on the mantelpiece somewhere up there. But he didn't dwell on it. He stuck his thumb on the button on the wall, pushed the door open and went into the cool entrance hall. It was larger than he'd expected.

The old concierge had his back to the door when Megnier entered.

He was standing at the foot of the carpeted stairs glaring upwards where McGann had disappeared a minute or two earlier. He turned when he heard the hall door click shut, but remained where he was standing. He needed only the one brief glance to know exactly what had walked through his front door. He pulled his gammy leg away from the stairs and raised his chin enquiringly.

Megnier thrust the photograph of McGann under his nose and rasped in a theatrical whisper, 'This man came in here a minute ago. Where did he go?'

The old man glanced at the picture of McGann. 'He's with Mademoiselle de Foure – flat five, third floor – it's the door on the left. The other one's empty, they've gone away. What's he been up to?'

But he was talking to himself. Megnier had gone.

Megnier climbed up to the third floor and pressed his ear to door number five. He could hear nothing. He waited and debated ringing the bell.

On the other side of the door McGann and Pascale sat opposite each other at a round, grey marble-topped table finishing off a first course of tomato salad.

The shutters on the main window were pushed back and the thin curtains drawn to soften the harsh glare of the sun, now almost at its midday peak and already threatening a sweltering afternoon.

McGann glanced quickly at Pascale. He cupped his chin in his hand and stared moodily at the tiny globules of oil that rolled around his plate as he mopped up the last of the vinaigrette with a piece of bread.

It was half-way to his mouth when the doorbell rang.

Pascale's sharp intake of breath was the only sound in the room.

McGann replaced the soggy piece of bread on his plate and with great concentration manoeuvred it carefully around the rim, first to one side, then to the other, until he was satisfied with its final resting place. He continued staring at it for another second or two then looked up slowly into Pascale's eyes. She stared back.

'Go and open the door!' McGann's command broke the spell.

As soon as her back was turned McGann got up from the table and slipped noiselessly into the kitchen. He partly closed the door, leaving just enough gap to allow a narrow view of the room, and waited with one eye glued to the crack.

He could have kicked himself.

The airline bag glared at him from where he'd thrown it when he came in. Careless? Bloody stark stupidity! McGann's eye didn't blink. The bag rested in full view, no apology for what it was, propped against the foot of last night's bed – the playground – now converted into a divan, its guilt blushingly concealed by a patchwork cover and a pile of multi-coloured cushions. The Air France bag stood out like a trade mark – McGann could have written the description for them: '*last seen carrying* . . . ' He swore under his breath, but made no attempt to go out and re-trieve it.

The indistinct mumble of voices from the doorway suddenly became clearer as Pascale moved into his narrow strip of vision. She was leading somebody into the room and her head was turned as she spoke to him over her shoulder.

McGann knew it wasn't the concierge. His eye was riveted on the man's orange-coloured sports shirt with the white collar. It didn't matter about the jacket, except that it took some of the pain away; it was the thatch above, the carroty red hair that made the wearer look like a Derry boy banner-waver.

McGann had marvelled at the combination when he'd seen it sitting outside the café in the Avenue Daumesnil, and now here it was again, unmistakable, dropping in to pass the time of the day. McGann curled his lip. Stupid bastard! All that was missing was the red ball on the end of his nose. McGann almost smiled. Police? Cheer up, Sean – he might not even be police!

'Sean, it's the police!' Pascale was staring at the crack in the kitchen door. There was a deep frown on her face and a puzzled note in her voice. 'Are you there, Sean? It's a special census. Can you come and show the officer your passport, please?'

McGann picked up the short thick-bladed kitchen knife that Pascale had used for cutting tomatoes and ran his thumb from its needle-sharp point to its haft. It was like a razor. He held it in his left hand and pushed the door open.

'Coming, *chérie*!' he called.

The smiling face from the photograph took Megnier by surprise.

McGann came smoothly round the door with his right hand out-stretched and a greeting on his lips. The Frenchman reacted auto-matically. He accepted the hand offered him and immediately regretted it, but, before he could withdraw he felt his hand gripped as if in a vice and he was pulled off balance. He had no opportunity to use his strength and as he fought to control the pressure that was forcing him round he watched helplessly as McGann came inside his outstretched arm and brought his left hand, underarm, into his exposed chest. The whole in-cident had taken no longer than the flash of a second.

Megnier actually felt the sharp knife slit his shirt and prick through the skin between his ribs. There was nothing he could do. He didn't feel the blade slide through the layers of fat and flesh as McGann, smoothly and expertly, guided it into his heart.

Megnier was dead. But it hadn't reached his brain. His eyes refused to unfocus from McGann's smiling mouth, slightly stiff from effort as he slid the blade across the heart – first an inch to the right, then an inch to the left. Megnier's knees buckled and he felt himself lowered gently to the floor by the hand still grasped firmly in a handshake. But he refused to go. He still hung on until his lifeless hand, released by McGann, flopped heavily across his face like an empty glove.

As the darkness started to close in he looked across an out-of-focus strip of carpet at a pair of unmoving feet, surprisingly crisp and sharp; so sharp that he could almost read the name on the shoes; it was an English name – he wanted to laugh but nothing happened. And then, through dead ears, and as he fought against the tiredness that dragged his eyelids together, he could hear the woman screaming. He strained to listen; a high-pitched, monotonous female scream: 'No! No! No!' repeated over and over again until, like an axe falling on an unprotected throat, it was cut off, to vanish, along with his world, into a whirlpool of silent dark-ness. And then nothing.

McGann left Megnier to his death throes and turned his attention to Pascale.

She was out of control. Not quite on her knees, she was doubled up from the waist almost in a posture of prayer, and with her legs pressed tightly together she shook and chattered like somebody just dragged out of an Arctic dip. She tried to block out the horror at her feet by covering her face with both hands. But, as if in disbelief, she still managed to stare boggle-eyed at McGann through the gaps between her fingers. And all the time she screamed. A continuous, unbroken, high-pitched, re-verberating scream. It was shock turning into hysteria and filled the room like a medieval torture chamber – it was a hideous noise – but she couldn't hear it.

McGann could. He reached across the dead policeman's body and pulled both her hands down from her face. He hit her without warning – a brutal open-handed slap delivered with all his strength.

His timing was perfect. The blow caught her cheek with the sound of a heavy fish being dropped on a wet slab. It brought with it an instant and deathly silence and the force of it threw her across the room in a bundle of arms and legs. She made no effort to break her fall and collapsed in an untidy heap beside the divan where, silent except for a broken, choked sob, she buried her head in her arms and tried to shut out the nightmare. McGann turned back to Megnier – he'd already lost interest in Pascale de Foure.

He knelt beside Megnier, turned him over on his back, and went systematically through his pockets.

It was a pathetic yield; hardly a thing to identify Megnier as an in-dividual, a man of taste – dubious or otherwise – a personality different from other men; Megnier could have been a candidate for the insignifi-cant – the almost unknown detective. Apart from a Police Department authority card in a cheap plastic holder, and the short-barrelled .38 Special tucked into the holster on his belt, Megnier stood out like a tree in the wood; he was Monsieur Ordinaire – he could have been an off-duty bus conductor.

McGann brought a plastic shopping-bag from the kitchen and dropped Megnier's possessions into it one by one – the scruffy wallet, a crumpled packet of Gauloises, sun-glasses, a half-empty envelope of condoms, a comb and a bunch of keys. He pushed up the sleeve of the dead man's jacket and slipped the expanding metal watch-strap over his floppy, lifeless fingers and, as he did so, glanced with professional in-terest at the large bloodstain still forming over Megnier's colourful sports shirt. The tiny bubbles of blood had found a narrow outlet beside the knife's haft and oozed gently, like spilt ink on blotting paper, towards the shirt pocket. McGann slipped the soggy photograph out of the pocket. He stared at it for ten seconds – then uttered one word: 'Fuck!'

He straightened up and gazed thoughtfully at the dead detective. Apart from rolling him up and shoving him under the bed, or in the bath, there wasn't much to be done with him. And why bother? Who was going to come looking for a stiff, an anonymous stiff at that, in the flat of a girl who's gone to see Mummy in the country for a week or two? And, in the unlikely event that somebody did fall over him, who was going to connect it with S. McGann Esq? But, thanks to this silly bastard, bang went the couple of days in the shade – the stupid bastard had forced forward the sailing time. Pity. But it didn't matter all that much. By the time the Frogs sorted out this clown and worked out that he was one of their own, S. McGann'd be sipping cooled Guinness in Canning Town. And who was going to help him find his way down to the water's edge? McGann smiled into Megnier's flat eyes then looked across the room at Pascale.

She was no longer on the floor. She'd dragged herself on to the covered bed and, with her back to the room, had curled herself up like a frightened snail. She'd buried her head under two of the coloured cushions and although her body was still and unmoving, a strange, muffled, almost silent moaning came from beneath the cushions. Her feet were bare and her short skirt crumpled like a concertina round her thighs. McGann could see a tiny glimmer of white silk where her legs were drawn up and joined tightly together. He moved towards her, his lips pursed in a silent whistle, and sat on the edge of the bed. The sounds from under the cushions stopped when she felt his weight next to her and her body stiffened, but she made no other movement.

'Pascale,' he hissed.

She shook her head and dislodged one of the cushions. 'Go away,' she sobbed, indistinctly, and buried her face deeper into the bed. When McGann touched her she shuddered, briefly, and tried to move out of range of his hand but there was nowhere for her to go. She brought her knees up to her chest and clutched them to her as if protecting herself from a frontal assault and, with another choking sob, placed her hands over her ears.

But McGann persisted. 'He's one of the people I told you about,' he whispered urgently. 'Are you going to listen?'

She kept her face buried in the bed-cover.

'OK.' He moved his hand to the back of her thigh and stroked gently upwards, towards her hip. 'You're going to have to listen one way or the other.' He stood up and quietly undressed.

He lay beside her again and when she felt his body against her back she half raised her head and in a choking hoarse voice moaned, 'Don't . . . Please leave me alone . . . Go away. Don't touch me.'

He put his hand on the side of her head and pushed her face back into the cushion. He held her there, in spite of her frightened whimpers, and moved his other hand back to her hip. He ran his fingers over the smooth, taut fragment of white silk and tugged it down over her clenched thighs. Without a word he entered her from behind, brutally and fiercely, while she sobbed silently into the cushion.

When he'd finished he remained in position, pressing into her back, his mouth close to her ear. She had stopped crying; but made no movement or sound when he reached up and drew the mask of disarranged hair to one side of her face.

'Will you listen now?' he said, and gently bit the lobe of her ear. His voice was heavy and breathless.

'Are you going to tell me some more lies?' Pascale's voice was surprisingly clear, even though it came from the depths of the bed-cover. But the tremor of fright remained. It was going to take more than acquiescent rape to erase that.

McGann ignored the accusation. 'Would you be happier if it was me lying on the floor instead of him?'

'Don't tempt me!'

'Pascale, that man came to kill me. He was one of the men who trapped me and my friends yesterday . . . He's an English agent – a trained killer. And it wouldn't have stopped with me.'

She caught her breath on a half sob, half choke. 'What do you mean?'

'You . . . You'd have been next. These people don't leave loose ends hanging around.' McGann stopped talking and studied the side of her face – he saw no sign that she was taking it all in. She hadn't got much longer to make up her mind. 'That's what you'd have been to him – a loose end. He'd have had you too. It wasn't a question of him or me – it was him or us. I was protecting you as much as myself.'

Pascale swallowed contentedly. The painful slap was fading into an erotic memory and McGann's words were the ones she wanted to hear. It made it all right. She straightened her legs and stretched against McGann's body, then turned her head towards his and allowed him to kiss her mouth. It was soft and salty.

'But he was French,' she said hesitantly. 'He showed me his card. He said he was police. He had no accent . . .'

McGann pressed into her again, but kept his mouth close to hers; it made his neck ache, but it was winning the war. 'Don't be silly,' he breathed, 'these people are professionals. They're highly trained, they leave nothing to chance.' He ran his tongue across her top lip, and allowed himself a snigger. 'Did you think the British would send a high-grade killer over here speaking French like Winston Churchill? How many times do I have to tell you – we're not dealing with fools.' McGann knew he'd won. He brought his arm over her body and gently stroked her breast. She didn't struggle, or object.

'How did you know about him? How did he find you? I thought you said . . .'

McGann kissed her again. Her wet mouth was responsive.

'I recognised him by his shirt,' he said truthfully, 'but I don't know how he found me here. They've got contacts everywhere . . .' He tailed off, then said absently, almost to himself, 'I'm going to have to move quickly now.'

'Oh no, Sean! Don't . . . Surely they won't send more . . . Maybe he was just lucky . . . He can't tell them where you are now, can he?' She paused for a second, surprised at her callousness. 'He is dead, isn't he?'

She didn't need a reply. She didn't get one. McGann ignored her questions and continued, 'And I want you to come with me.'

'But, Sean . . .'

'Please. I can't leave you here alone, not now. You've become too precious to me.'

'I'm afraid!' She turned her head awkwardly to look into his eyes. 'Why don't you go to the police and tell them everything? I'll come with you.' She sounded like a little girl offering safety in numbers. 'They can't all be working for the English,' she stopped and blinked tears from her eyes, 'can they?'

'I've been through all that with you,' said McGann, impatiently. It was time to go, with or without Mademoiselle de Foure, preferably with – two young people on a trip to the seaside – far less worrying to the French fuzz. They wanted a mad Irishman running from a close-mesh net around Boulevard St Germain – a mad bugger all on his own with an Air France bag over his shoulder and a pocket full of 7.65s – not a young man with bags under his eyes and the reason for them sitting beside him. 'It'll do you good, a nice little trip to the coast. I might even take you as far as Dinard. Anyway,' McGann glanced over his shoulder at Megnier; he was still there, 'you can't stay here with that lying on your carpet.'

She stiffened again. He'd brought her back to reality. 'Oh, God! What are you going to do about . . . about . . .' She tailed off, unable to bring herself to say the word.

'You don't have to worry about him,' said McGann, quickly. 'As soon as we get on the road I'll give our people a ring and they'll come and clear it up. When you get back from Dinard there'll be no sign that anything has happened here. OK?'

Instead of replying she arched her back away from him, removed his hand from her breast and wriggled her bottom against his bare loins. McGann knew he was home and dry.

McGann emptied everything from the Air France bag into a plain canvas hold-all. He placed that, the other hold-all containing his clothes, and the plastic bag with Megnier's meagre effects, on the floor at the foot of the bed. He checked the Sauer, inspected the magazine, recocked it and slipped it into the hold-all where it lay concealed but easily accessible just below the half-open zip. Then he sat on the bed and waited for Pascale.

She took her time. When she emerged from the bathroom she was wearing a pair of faded blue jeans and a white brassière with a tiny ridge of lace along the upper edge of the cups. She tried to smile as she tripped once again round the mound on the floor but all that developed was a sickly grimace.

McGann watched her come, then shook his head. 'Take them off,' he said.

She stopped dead and stared at him, then her eyes widened and the grimace vanished into a loud suggestive giggle – it sounded out of place, like laughter in the crematorium, and she put her hand guiltily over her mouth. But the giggle remained in her eyes.

There was no amusement in McGann's eyes. 'I said get them off!' She missed the undertone again. He was serious.

'How romantic,' she smiled, 'and energetic!' But she did as she was told and peeled the skin-tight jeans over her thighs and, with a little provocative wriggle, stepped out of them and stood, legs pressed together, smiling her willingness at McGann.

'Now the bra.'

She removed the brassière and hooked her thumbs into the tiny lace-work resting on her hips.

'Not those,' snapped McGann. 'We've no more time for games. Now get dressed again.'

'What?' She gave a little moue of disappointment, but when she saw the serious glint in his eyes it changed to a puzzled frown. 'Sean, I don't understand . . .'

'Put on a skirt. A short skirt – very short, and a top, thin, something like this . . .' He flicked his own T-shirt. 'No bra – let's give 'em something to drool at.' He smoothed his hand over a hard, out-thrust breast then got up from the bed and patted her lightly on her almost bare bottom. 'Come on! Get a move on – do as I say!'

She shook her head slowly, like a hurt child. 'I think you're making fun of me.'

'I wouldn't do that,' he said smoothly. 'I want people to look at you, not at me – and the more you offer them the more they'll look. Simple?'

She blushed and raised her head. 'I still don't understand. What sort of people?'

'Oh, come on, Pascale, wake up! Think of horny young policemen. Or horny old policemen if you like. Think of anybody who wants to stop us and hand me over to their friends the British. I want them to look at you till their eyes pop out like gob-stoppers – and while they're looking at you they won't have time to look at me. OK? Now come on!' He leaned forward and kissed one of the hard pink nipples, then stood back quickly as the other one was presented. 'No time for that.'

'You're using me, Sean McGann.'

She covered her body with a clinging, skimpy red T-shirt and stepped into an above-the knee tight denim skirt. The skirt buttoned up at the front – there wasn't a lot left for the imagination.

McGann closed the flat door quietly, locked it and followed Pascale down the stairs. When he caught up with her he dropped the key in her shoulder bag and took her hand – they looked like a young married couple who were still happy about it.

The old concierge watched them from behind his curtained window. McGann saw the movement and locked eyes for the briefest second with the toothless old man. They both knew what was going to happen. The concierge waited until the door slammed, gave a long perceptive glance at the stairway, then picked up his telephone.

McGann was way ahead of him. He took Pascale by the arm and led her into the blinding hot sun towards the Avenue Daumesnil.

'Where do you keep your car? Quick!' he muttered once they were clear of the building.

'Charles de Foucauld,' she replied breathlessly. 'Across Poniatowski – it's parked by the Bois. What are we going to do now?'

He was back in control. 'I thought we'd go and have a little picnic by the seaside!'

He took her hand to stop her running blindly across the road. Nobody looked twice at them; no pounding feet on the pavement behind; McGann relaxed – he was in the clear again.

CHAPTER 32

Clive Reason awoke with a start, and searched with his eyes for the alarm that had brought him out of an uncomfortable ten minutes' sleep. The bell wasn't far away, or difficult to locate – the unmelodious, continental clang of the telephone sitting on the small table at the foot of the *chaise-longue*. He sat up, swung his feet to the ground and watched the telephone ring. It seemed to go on for ever. He closed his eyes against the noise and waited for Gerrard to do something about it.

Gerrard heard it and felt the same way. He waited in the bathroom, but it didn't stop. The telephone won. He wrapped a towel around his waist and squelched across the carpet leaving a trail of wet footprints behind him. He lit a cigarette before picking up the receiver and tossed the packet into Reason's lap.

'Go and make some coffee,' he said. 'I don't like the way this phone is ringing – it sounds like bad news.'

He listened to the voice on the other end of the line without interrupting, then spoke rapidly and crisply for about half a minute. He replaced the receiver and joined Reason in the kitchen.

'Our boy's been on the warpath again.'

Reason looked up from the two mugs of coffee and raised his eyebrows. 'Sugar?'

'Two.'

'Did you know that too much sugar reduces your performance in the bedroom?'

'Just put the sugar in and stir it. He's killed a detective on the other side of town. Daumesnil – Porte de Dorée, that's out in the Vincennes direction.'

'How do they know it's McGann's work?'

Gerrard crushed his cigarette out and drank some more coffee. 'Nosy concierge. Found the detective where he shouldn't have been. He identified McGann from a picture. He'd already had one look at it – the dead man showed it to him before he went marching up the stairs to invite McGann to help him with his enquiries. Stupid bastard!'

'And got shot for his troubles?'

Gerrard shook his head. 'No. He knifed this one. Versatile little fucker, isn't he?'

Reason finished his coffee with a gulp and refilled his mug. 'Sounds as if he had a spare hole to bolt to. I wonder if he's got another one? It must be nice for him to have all these friends in Paris. He could be anywhere now, I suppose?'

Gerrard stretched his arm out and punched the big black man lightly on the arm – it was like hitting the trunk of a healthy oak. 'He could be. But it's not all bad. He's been drawn – he's out in the open again and on the run. There can't be much wrong with that. He's going to have to play our game for a day or two, and personally I reckon he's had enough. He can't keep on knocking off every policeman who gives him a second look and then duck into a convenient hole. Even Irishmen run out of convenient holes some time or other. Anyway, ducking for cover doesn't always work. It's just been proved. He'll be on his way home now, heading for the coast as I said. He's going to take the ferry.'

'You said that yesterday!'

'And I'm saying it again now. Go and get yourself a brandy. Take your time, there's no hurry.'

'There isn't?' Reason tried not to look sceptical.

'No. We've got all the time in the world. As I said, McGann's out in the open again, and, as Puy-Monbraque's man, Violle, was pleased to remind me, there are about ten thousand eager policemen anxious to show him that there's a lot of hard feeling about.'

Gerrard poured himself a whisky. He looked up when Melanie joined them with a glass of champagne but paid her no attention. As he turned to leave the room he stopped at the door and said to Reason, 'Look after the baby while I'm changing. There's more champagne if she wants it. Just make sure she doesn't drink too much.'

Reason smiled at Gerrard's back as he left. Melanie didn't. Her sense of humour seemed to have taken a slight knock. 'Did you understand what Michel and Lili were talking about yesterday?' she asked.

'No. I don't speak French. I didn't know you did.'

'Why should you? It was about me. He was trying to find a baby-sitter and a nursery so that I could be shoved out of the way while you two go jaunting off on some fancy fun and games. But I'm not staying here on my own, that's definite – wherever it is you're going, I'm coming too!'

The smile vanished from Reason's lips. 'I think he's right. You'd get in the way. Anyway, it'll be much more pleasant, and safer, to stay in Paris than run around the countryside with a bad-tempered Gerrard.'

'I'm coming with you.' She smiled softly and passed a bowl of cashews to Reason. She stared at him while he took a handful of nuts. 'If I can persuade him to let me come will you back me up?'

'You're expecting an awful lot for a cashew nut.'

'I knew I could count on you! Let me pour you another drink. What is it, whisky?'

'Putty . . .'

'What sort of drink's that?'

'It's not a drink – it's me. All a girl has to do is flicker her eyelids, smile nicely, and I'm all hers – putty, that's what I am.'

'You've forgotten the cashew nut.'

'I'll have a whisky please, make it a strong one.' Reason stopped smiling. 'Melanie, why d'you want to stick your nose into his business?'

'I want to be with him. Have you ever been in love?'

'How long's this been going on for?'

'For ever. But this is the first time I've said it aloud.'

'And you have, of course, discussed it with the lucky fellow?'

'Certainly not! And for God's sake don't tell him – he'd break into a sweaty canter before I could even start getting a halter round his neck.'

Gerrard's anger showed.

He emptied his glass and scowled. 'And that's exactly what I was afraid of – some silly young hero who thought he could round up a man like McGann on his own and win everlasting fame and fortune – the stupid bastard! What the bloody hell do they think this is – the bloody Wild West? Melanie, have some more champagne.'

'No thank you.'

Reason glanced at her out of the corner of his eye. She looked very prim. He managed to keep a straight face.

'I wonder what sort of story the evil little bugger told this girl-friend?' he asked Gerrard. 'Do we know anything about her – apart from being a gullible little bi – ?' He stopped, but they knew what he meant. 'And are we sure she went willingly and not with something hard shoved into her kidneys?'

'According to the concierge – quite willingly,' said Gerrard. 'The two of them, he said, looked a well-established couple. But they're not – they're newly-weds. The concierge had never seen McGann before, but the girl he sees every day. Her car is missing as well, but that might be in our favour.'

'Unusual make?' Reason put the refilled glass back in Gerrard's hand and returned to his place at the corner of the sideboard.

'No. It's the most common vehicle on French roads – a Renault 4.'

'OK, but what about its colour?' Reason didn't smile.

'Metallic grey. It's the most common colour, too.'

'Wonderful! The most common car in the most common colour. And that's in our favour?'

Gerrard drank a large mouthful of whisky. 'If McGann's girl-friend had loaded him into a car that stood out on the road he would have ditched it at the first set of traffic lights. Makes sense, doesn't it?'

Reason stared blankly at him.

'As it is, every other car he looks at is going to be the same as the one he's in, so he won't bother – he'll stick with it. We know what he's travelling in, we know what to look for – and so does everybody else in the hunt. They'll find him all right, but this time it'll be done properly – Puy-Monbraque's promised a public castration for the man who even thinks about trying the same stunt as that clown tried over at Daumesnil. One look is all they want. They'll stay with him until he's bedded down for the night, wherever that may be – but, before he puts his head on the pillow, they'll give us the word and we'll join the procession. From that moment it'll be our show. All we'll have to do is roll him up in his blanket and bring him home. In the meantime I've got something else for you to play with,' grinned Gerrard.

Reason looked askance but refused to be drawn. The ice cubes continued to rattle.

' . . . the phone number Monod used to get in touch with Brockle-bank.'

Reason perked up at the mention of Monod's name and put his glass down beside the decanter. 'I'd forgotten about him. Is he still being co-operative?'

'He's having a heart attack.'

'What brought that on?'

'I don't know, he's not having it until tonight.'

'Is that a joke?' asked Melanie. She knew it wasn't.

Gerrard stared at her over the rim of his glass. He didn't answer her question. 'Talking about jokes,' he said, 'it's time for us to sort out what we're going to do with you while Clive and I are out earning our wages.'

'I've already done it,' she said calmly. 'It's decided.'

300

Reason slid his buttock off the corner of the sideboard and stretched his arms. 'Why don't I go and try that telephone number you were talking about.'

'Just a minute.' Gerrard held his hand up to Reason; to Melanie he said, 'What do you mean it's been decided?'

'It means I'm coming with you.'

'No you're not.'

'Yes I am. I don't intend staying here on my own. Like I said, it's been decided!' She glanced quickly at Reason who saw what was coming and shook his head in warning. But she was now unstoppable. 'Clive agrees with me. He said it would be all right for me to come.'

'Oh, did he?'

'Yes. Didn't you, Clive?'

Reason nodded.

Gerrard stared at him for a moment then shrugged his shoulders. 'OK, you can go and make your phone call now. It's a London number.' He seemed to have washed his hands of Melanie Lambdon. 'It's 229 6412 – say you're a friend of Monod's, speaking on his behalf – that's probably all you'll have a chance to say before they slam the phone down or tell you to fuck off! I don't hold out much hope for it.'

Reason took the piece of paper Gerrard had pulled out of his pocket, but didn't move.

'What about Melanie?' he said.

'What about her?'

'Is she coming with us or not?'

'I thought the two of you had already made that decision.'

'You mean you agree?' asked a surprised Melanie and without waiting for a reply said, 'I'll be ready in ten minutes – you won't regret it!'

Reason dropped his finger sharply on the cradle of the telephone and looked across at Gerrard. He kept the receiver in his hand as if he were about to use it again.

'I don't suppose there's a chance that your friends in that funny office have a sense of humour?'

Gerrard shook his head. 'None at all. Why? What did you get?'

Reason passed the slip of paper back to Gerrard. 'The bloody Russian Embassy!'

The two men stared at each other. Gerrard was the first to speak. He was quite calm. 'You can screw up that piece of paper and forget all about it. Now I think of it I really can't imagine anybody trusting a clown like Monod with the key to the door. It's strange, though . . .' He frowned at Reason for a moment. 'I seem to recall somebody whispering Ivan's interest in the Brocklebank game quite some time before Monod spoke it out aloud. I wonder what the Russian is for Brocklebank?'

Before Reason could answer, the phone jangled under his finger. He looked at the receiver in his hand, then handed it to Gerrard.

The conversation was one-sided, and short, with nothing from Gerrard except the odd grunt; then, just before he replaced the receiver, he spoke urgently for several seconds. When he handed the instrument back to Reason he said casually, 'Violle. McGann's been sighted. They've got him on the lead and they're going with him to see where he spends the night.'

'Got a cigarette?' Reason asked.

'You don't sound too thrilled.' Gerrard threw the packet of Gitanes at him. 'Something you don't like about it?'

Reason stuck a cigarette in his mouth. 'Sounds like the beginning of an old record.'

'Not this time. They've got the professionals on to him. Special people, they're like glue.'

'Good. Got a light?'

Gerrard tossed his lighter into the big hand. 'Looks like he's going for Dieppe.'

'They're quite sure he's going for water?'

'I don't think there's any doubt about it. Violle favours Le Havre or Dieppe. Dieppe is favourite – there's more traffic there and that means more people and more chaos. McGann will only have to put on a pair of dark glasses and comb his hair on the opposite side of his head and he'll slip through like a raw mussel.'

'In the daytime.'

'Oh yes, it would have to be then – peak crossing time, queues, children, cars, the lot. McGann's not going to be silly enough to try a night crossing. He'll find somewhere to sleep, then nip out when everybody's thinking about what they're going to have for lunch . . . But it's all being taken care of. They'll do nothing more until you and I move in.'

Reason smiled icily. 'You can kick my arse off the jetty tomorrow afternoon if and when it's all been neatly wrapped up, but for the time being I'm going to try to curb my excitement. Maybe one day things will work out as smoothly as they're supposed to – maybe not. Try me again this time tomorrow. In the meantime, buckets and spades and the muddy waters of Dieppe?'

'That's right, and in your case a little baby-sitting problem. You could be lucky – she might want to paddle!' Gerrard stopped at the door. 'By the way,' he took a small wallet from his top pocket and removed a slip of paper, 'while I was reading that number out to you just now it suddenly occured to me that this could be another one.' He held the piece of paper out to Reason. 'Put a gap after the first three, and you've got a London telephone number with Brocklebank's name next to it.'

'Where did you get it?'

'I found it on the back of an envelope that Fred Lambdon gave me.'

Reason raised an eyebrow but Gerrard didn't elaborate.

'Give it a ring, see what happens. Be funny, wouldn't it, if it was Brocklebank on the end of the line this time? Save us the bother of chasing over the countryside for McGann.'

Reason frowned at the number on the piece of paper. 'Personally, I wouldn't find it funny at all – I'd hate for this bit of paper to deprive me of the pleasure of a conversation with Paddy McGann.'

He looked down at the phone and dialled the number. It didn't take long. He listened, put the receiver down without speaking into it and turned and grinned at Gerrard.

'It's a betting shop in Limehouse.' He looked at the number again. 'But don't burst into tears just yet – Lambdon wouldn't be hiding that around unless it had something to do with the name underneath it.' Reason continued studying the numbers as he emptied his glass. 'It's a coded number, a simple juggle. I'll have another go at it when we get back to England – assuming, of course, that McGann hasn't already shown us where the door-knocker is.'

'I'll meet you downstairs. There's a bottle of Grouse in that cupboard, bring it with you . . . You never know.'

Gerrard climbed into the car and threw a heavy bundle on to Reason's lap. He said, 'Hook that around you some time, it ought to fit, it was made for King-Kong when he worked for the DGSE. The other thing's been done over – Browning .45, throwing fractionally to the right.'

'Thanks. How fractionally?'

'A whisper – aim at the middle of his forehead at twenty-five metres and you'll hit him between the eyes!'

Gerrard eased his shoulders into the back of his seat and switched on the engine. As he pulled out on to the Quai de Conti he said, 'And the two of you can save the chit-chat and the funny remarks until we get out of this traffic.'

'Yes, *Bwana*!' The voice came softly from the back seat.

'That sort of thing!'

Reason tightened his seat belt and closed his eyes – he hadn't forgotten the last time he'd been driven by Gerrard.

CHAPTER 33

McGann closed his eyes and tried to relax his tingling nerves as Pascale manoeuvred the nippy Renault through the bustling traffic of the Périphérique.

But relaxation didn't come easily. The photograph had thrown his plans out of gear. He'd underestimated them. He should have realised. If they were bright enough to put down wires at the café they would hardly have overlooked the camera. He kicked himself for his own complacency. No wonder the man with the funny shirt had picked him out – how could he avoid it with a picture stuck on the end of his bloody nose?

McGann opened his eyes briefly at a stop-light and put his hand just above Pascale's bare knee. She liked it and smiled but said nothing as she gunned the small car into the next section of the race circuit. He closed his eyes again but left his hand where it was so that he could feel the gentle movements of the smooth muscle as she stroked the accelerator to keep in touch with the faster-moving traffic. But it didn't take his mind off the problem – a simple problem from whatever angle he approached it. Simple? Is that what it is? That just about every bloody copper in Paris, and probably in France, now had not only his description but a bloody picture to go with it? But it solved another problem – it eliminated any thought of a gentle stroll on to the ferry. Unless . . .?

He squeezed the leg under his hand, opened his eyes again, and turned sideways to study Pascale's profile. His steady gaze unnerved her. She tightened her grip on the wheel causing the car to veer a fraction too near to the path of a howling Porsche. Its screaming horn did nothing to help.

'Why are you looking at me like that?' she asked, nervously.

McGann's answer was glib, and almost sincere: 'Because you've got a nice face. I like looking at it. Do you carry your passport everywhere you go?'

She glanced sideways, quickly; puzzled, then back to the road. 'Why?'

McGann continued staring at her. He didn't answer.

She hesitated for a second; then, 'Erm . . . Yes, it's in my bag.' She frowned at the overhead direction gantry, and forgot about her passport. 'Where do you want to join the motorway?'

'I don't,' said McGann sharply. 'Keep away from the *péages* – they'll be crawling alive. They're the first places the searchers start checking. Get on to the N2 before St Denis and head north. You've got a road map?'

'Yes, of course . . . But why north? I thought you wanted the Channel?'

McGann scowled to himself. 'Just drive the car, sweetheart, you're not equipped to both think and drive at the same time.'

It was unkind, but she laughed – she was getting used to the Irish sense of humour. 'That's exactly what I have been doing since you put your hand on my leg.'

He moved his hand higher.

She giggled. 'Now that really is dangerous!' She forgot that she wanted to know why they were heading north.

McGann threw the Michelin map on to the back seat and said, 'Head for Soissons, take the D1 then the 937 to Péronne.'

'And then?'

'I'll tell you when we get there. Where's that passport you were talking about?'

'That *you* were talking about,' she corrected.

'Where is it?' McGann's tone changed abruptly. She had a sudden, vivid recollection of his telling her back in the flat to shut up, and a sharp stinging blow that almost took her head off – it was the same voice.

'In my bag,' she replied quickly. 'On the back seat.'

He took his hand off her thigh and stretched over the back of the seat to collect the bag. She watched him open it from the corner of her eye, but said nothing until he removed the wad of official documents.

'I thought it was my passport you wanted to see?' she ventured. 'That's my life history you've got there in your hands.'

'Nice!' McGann smiled condescendingly at Pascale's passport photograph. 'It's my other hobby.'

'What is?'

He looked up and grinned. 'Studying official photos.'

He kept the passport open on his knee and compared the photograph in it with the one on the pink driving licence. There was little difference between the two; they had the same mass-produced appearance; the same flat, character-destroying image churned out in strips of four from a while-you-wait booth. She was younger, probably in her teens, her

beautiful shining hair mutilated into a permed frizzy monstrosity to con-
form with the teenage fashion of a few years previously. The photographs bore no resemblance to the attractive woman sitting beside him.

'Why aren't you laughing?' she asked, without taking her eyes from
the road. 'Everybody laughs at passport pictures.'

'These aren't funny,' pronounced McGann, seriously. 'You ought to
burn them and get some more. Don't the Immigration people say anything to you when you go abroad?' He tapped the dark-blue passport
with his finger. 'This could be any girl with fuzzy hair. It's certainly not
you. When did you last use it?'

'February. Skiing in Austria. And no, nothing's ever been said. Have
you ever seen a passport being queried? I don't think they look at the picture. As long as you've got a passport they seem happy enough.'

McGann agreed with her. But he was only half listening. He was seeing himself wearing a frizzy blonde wig, powder and make-up and a pair
of artificial tits, smiling provocatively over the page of Pascale de Foure's
French passport at a busy ferry terminal police check – a police check
where they were looking for a dark-haired Irishman travelling on a
British passport in the name of Sean McGann. It appealed to his sense of
humour and the girl's words of assurance fell on his ears like golden
raindrops.

'You're not listening,' she pouted.

'Say it again.'

'I asked you what happens after Soissons.'

'I told you, head for Péronne. We'll join the N29 and cut across the
autoroute to Amiens and see what the temperature's like over there.'

'I thought you were going to take me to Dinard?'

'That comes later. Let's see first what's happening around Amiens. If
it's clear and we slip through we've got the whole of the coast all the way
from Calais to St Malo to choose from.' He rested his hand lightly on her
bare knee again. 'What do you say to staying the night somewhere, and
decide what we're going to do in the morning?'

She wriggled her shoulders into a more comfortable position and
stretched her arms and legs with a sigh. 'I say, yes . . .' she murmured,
'but I'm hungry.'

'What's the time?'

She glanced at her watch: 'Fifteen twenty-five.'

'We'll buy something in Amiens. Don't hurry, just take your time, and
if I go to sleep pick a supermarket on the outskirts and wake me there.'

'How can you sleep at a time like this?'

McGann smiled. He moved his hand higher up her thigh, tightened his grip and closed his eyes. 'Watch me!'

McGann awoke with a start when the car stopped and the engine died. He was wide awake but kept his eyes closed as he half-reached towards the canvas bag and the automatic. His hand hovered just short of the bag.

'Why have we stopped? Where are we?' he hissed.

'About eight kilometres from Amiens.'

He blinked at the monstrous neon name of a hypermarket then turned his head and casually studied the surrounding car-park. Not full – but enough vehicles standing around in their little oblong islands to render one Renault 4, colour metallic grey, almost invisible.

McGann had considered changing cars. If it was to be done this was the ideal place, but he decided against it – the disguise couldn't be improved upon. But he was in no hurry to move – he sat and waited, and watched. Nothing happened. After a few silent minutes he said, 'I'll go and do the shopping. You stay here. Don't get out of the car. How are we off for petrol?'

She switched on the ignition and checked the dial. 'A quarter full. I think I'd better fill it up . . . Where are we going next?'

McGann stared at her, then smiled. 'I haven't made up my mind yet. We'll work it out when I get back. Look, take this and go and fill up over there,' he dropped a small pile of notes into her lap and jerked his chin at the petrol bay, 'and check the oil while you're at it.'

He slung the canvas bag over his shoulder and climbed out of the car. He looked around once more. It was still nothing more than a car-park; nobody staring or waving their arms. He poked his head back in the window. 'Wait for me on the other side of the pumps. Don't go out into the road until I get there.'

'Don't be long!'

McGann didn't look back.

Leading off the feeder road from the petrol bay was a narrow tree-lined avenue. The crowns of the trees that lined both sides of the avenue were heavy with dark-green summer foliage, the branches of which met overhead and turned the narrow road into a dark tunnel. In this dark tunnel, shaded from the heat, and partially shielded from observation, a small blue and white police patrol car shimmered in the dappled shade of the trees.

The driver was fast asleep. His seat was adjusted to a comfortable sleeping angle and he'd tilted his cap forward so that its visor, propped on the end of his nose, shielded his eyes from the sun – and anything else that might jog his conscience. He dozed contentedly.

The second man in the car remained awake. It would be his turn to sleep tomorrow. He was younger by several years than his sleeping mentor and still retained the sharp pinched look of an ambitious policeman. At the moment his ambition was in the doldrums as he gazed moodily across the road. But he wasn't bored; he'd got a sexily dressed woman, who was busy pouring petrol into her small silver Renault, to watch.

He puffed reflectively on his cigarette, trickling the smoke out of the side of his mouth and watching it dragged by the almost non-existent draught through his side window and out into the soft evening air. In between puffs he concentrated on the woman, some twenty metres away, and savoured her trim figure and pretty legs as if she were lying on the bed beside him waiting for the light to go out . . . He tried not to get too carried away when she lifted the bonnet to check the oil. When she leaned over into the engine her dress rose just high enough to be erotic, and Marchand could feel himself straining his groin against her nicely rounded, inviting little bottom.

Every so often his eyes left the woman and switched to the road to survey the rare passing car, recording in his mind the make and colour, followed by a brief mental exercise on the registration number. After each vehicle his eyes went back to Pascale's hips and legs. But he knew the distraction wasn't going to stand there entertaining him until it was time to go home. He sighed noisily, but it didn't disturb his companion. He continued staring, putting as much of Pascale's appearance as he could into his memory bank to help him over the next half-hour.

He took a last long pull on the stub of cigarette and flicked it through the window where it exploded in a shower of sparks on the concrete road. He looked back across to the petrol bay just in time to see a nice show of tanned thigh as Pascale ducked into the driving-seat. He felt a tinge of regret. But it was a short-lived regret.

Instead of pulling out of the exit gap after paying for the petrol at the window of the brick pay booth, she reversed the car to one side of it and stopped the engine. Marchand sat up in his seat for a better, closer look.

She was quite attractive – he hadn't realised that, he'd been concentrating on the moving parts – and she had long blonde hair. Marchand liked blondes, real ones, and this one was real – he could almost feel it – be nice sitting in that other seat with your hand between those legs . . . Plenty of room with the seat tilted back . . . He ran his eyes casually over the car: Renault 4 – the roads of France are littered with the things. Silver-grey – no imagination, must be the husband's choice, she would have imagination, sure to have with a body like that . . . He gave an automatic glance at the number plate. A Paris number – pity, not likely to see her cruising around Amiens . . . He slid another cigarette from the packet on the dashboard and placed it between his lips. He struck a match and watched it flare. But his eyes didn't focus on the flame – they swung back to the Renault's number plate, and as he absorbed the number again he suddenly hissed with pain as the cardboard match burned down and reached his fingers.

'NOT TO BE STOPPED UNDER ANY CIRCUMSTANCES . . .' with 'any circumstances' underlined. 'SIGHTING TO BE REPORTED IMMEDIATELY . . .' – underline 'immediately'. 'DO NOT APPROACH, DO NOT ATTEMPT ARREST . . .' – two heavy lines under the 'do nots'. 'FOLLOW VEHICLE ONLY ON INSTRUCTIONS . . .' Instructions? Whose bloody instructions?

'Marc!' He punched his sleeping partner on the arm. 'Sit up and look across there, by the petrol pay booth. There's a car with a blonde sitting in it.'

'Very nice!'

'Look at the bloody registration number!'

'So?'

'Look on the board!'

The older man took his time. He stared at Pascale's car and compared its registration number digit by digit with that on the clipboard. It seemed to take for ever. Far too long for Marchand.

'Well?'

'No question about it, boy – that's the one.'

The older policeman pronounced his verdict without enthusiasm. It was the wrong time of the day to be sitting in the sun looking at a grade 'A' bollock-dropper. He could smell trouble. After twenty-eight years of problem-free, promotionless decision-dodging he didn't need to smell trouble – he could almost reach out and touch it. If he'd been alone he'd have gone back to sleep.

'Ring it through exactly as you see it,' he grunted.

Marchand did as he was told and within seconds, through a squawk of atmosphere and crackle, a voice cut into the tense silence of the patrol car.

'This is Commissaire Bourdon,' the voice said. 'Don't take any action. Don't move from your present position. Keep the car under observation but don't show any interest in it, or its occupants. Confirm that there are two people sitting in it now.'

Marchand clicked the button on the hand-set. 'Understood, Commissaire. Only one occupant visible – a female aged between twenty-five and thirty . . .' He described Pascale's appearance with the accuracy of a man who'd spent a good five minutes lusting after her. It went down well with the Commissaire.

'There should be a man as well.'

'Negative, Commissaire.'

'*Merde!* Are you sure? Perhaps in the back, lying down?'

Marchand would have given his skin to oblige, but kept his head. 'Negative again, Commissaire. Without closer inspection the report is: only one person occupying the vehicle.'

'OK. Keep watching. There's a surveillance group in unmarked cars on its way. If the suspect car leaves its position before the senior officer makes contact with you you're cleared to follow. But use the utmost discretion, and break off contact the instant the control car makes radio contact with you. Acknowledge.'

'Understood, Commissaire. Over and out.'

Marchand let go of the hand-set and sat back in his seat and took a deep breath. He found his hands were shaking.

His partner regarded him with interest.

'Commissaire Bourdon, my young friend,' he said, 'has just made sure that it'll be your balls that go into orbit – not his, if anybody cocks this one up!'

Twenty minutes later McGann left the hypermarket through one of its side exits. He threaded his way down the maze of parked cars and cut at an oblique angle towards the petrol service area. Under his arm he carried a small cardboard box. In it were jammed the two halves of a broken stick of bread, a packet of cheese, butter, pâté, a large bunch of grapes, apples, a plastic bottle of milk and four cans of German lager. His other purchases were packed into the bottom of the canvas bag under the money and guarded by the coiled-up Sauer. These were: a frizzy near-blonde wig, a brassière with stiff cups, a large wad of cotton wool and a selection of lipsticks, nail varnish and make-up. The bag swung comfortably on his left shoulder, with the pistol just under the partly open zip, loaded, cocked, and ready to go back to work.

He spotted the Renault as he cleared the front of the last row of vehicles nearest the exit – and almost missed the poacher . . .

Beyond the Renault, distorted by the shimmering heat rising from the macadam surface of the car-park and floating like a desert mirage, was the unmistakable snub nose of a police car partially concealed in the shadow of the leafy avenue.

The shock lasted a numbing half a second.

McGann made no sudden movement. He stopped naturally, and without taking his eyes off the police vehicle took an unhurried, almost casual step sideways and backwards to regain the security of the row of parked cars. He ducked behind a large Mercedes, drew the Sauer from the bag and tucked it into the waistband of his jeans as he studied Pascale's Renault and the police car from behind the protective bulk of the heavy German car.

Remaining still, he watched for several minutes, covering every possible angle and every likely ambush position, and only when he was sure that he could cross the dead ground between himself and the petrol pay booth unobserved by the occupants of the police car did he move from the security of the Mercedes.

He straightened up and walked casually towards the Renault, keeping the brick building solidly between himself and the patrol car. Before reaching it he stooped and, as he went through the motions of tying a loose shoelace, managed to ease his head round the tail of a Peugeot Estate. It gave him a perfect view of the police car. He glanced quickly over his shoulder, then back to the car. Just the one. No back-up visible in front or behind. No support vehicles, no navy-blue heads ducking up and down among the trees. And nothing up there . . . He looked briefly into the sky, then to the roof of the hypermarket and finally back to the blue and white vehicle again. His eyes covered the entire area, inch by inch, for the second time. Then he started all over again. After the third time he was sure – this was no ambush . . . His eyes went back to the patrol car and for the first time studied its occupants.

There were only two of them and one was obviously asleep. McGann looked hard. No doubt about it, his head thrown back and his *képi* pushed forward over his eyes he was out to the world. He might have been dreaming about McGann, but one thing was certain – he wasn't looking for him. McGann almost grinned to himself as he studied the other one. He was no better. Another live-wire. This one was smoking, his head bowed – half asleep. McGann relaxed, but only superficially. He was still on the balls of his feet and his hand hovered nervously, twitching just above the pistol grip in his waistband, but he'd made up his mind – it was coincidence. A narrow coincidence he allowed, but one thing it wasn't – it wasn't a high-grade special group crew keyed up on a knife-edge surveillance operation.

He eased back from the Peugeot's rear and moved without stealth along the side of the brick booth until he reached the corner of the building. He now had only Pascale's Renault to conceal his advance over the last few yards of open ground. He looked carefully round the corner at the two heads in the police car again. They weren't interested. He nipped out of his cover, ducked behind the Renault, jerked open the door and slid into the right-hand seat.

'Did you see that, Marchand?' Marc spoke from the corner of his mouth. He made no movement. His cap visor still covered his eyes and his head remained set on the back of the seat.

Marchand stuck his hand out of the window and flicked the ash off his cigarette.

'Did I see what?'

'Somebody's been watching us for the last fifteen minutes. We've been given a bloody good going-over.'

'*Merde!*'

'Don't look at the car! A young guy with a box under his arm and a bag over his shoulder has been crouched on his knees in the car-park watching us for well over a quarter of an hour. He's just walked round the side of the pay booth there and ducked into the Renault.'

The man in the driving-seat pushed himself off the back of his seat and stretched as if he were just waking out of a pleasant afternoon nap. It wasn't a difficult act for him to perform, he'd been waking out of pleasant afternoon naps on this spot for years. He pushed his *képi* back into place and prised the microphone from Marchand's fingers. He held it between his knees as he spoke to Commissaire Bourdon's operator. When he'd finished talking he kept his finger on the 'speak' button until he was satisfied the Renault was not going to make a dash for it. Only then did he flick the switch and say, 'Over . . .'

As he did so a new, louder voice cut through the crackling speaker. 'This is Inspector Leclerc, surveillance control one. You've been told about me.' It was a statement not a question. 'Is the car still in the same position. Do you still have it in sight?'

'Here, you talk to them.' The microphone dropped into Marchand's lap. 'Keep your voice low and your head bowed – Al Capone's still got his eye on us!'

Marchand flicked the switch. 'There's no change.'

'OK, they've got to pass me to get on the main road. Stay there until

313

they move. Don't follow. Buzz me the minute it starts rolling. OK?'
  'OK.'

McGann and Pascale stopped for their dinner in a lay-by just the other
side of Amiens.

Six kilometres ahead of them, in another lay-by, Inspector Leclerc sat
in his Citroën smoking and enjoying the pre-dusk scenery, while behind,
about three kilometres on the other side of Pascale's parked Renault,
another car of Leclerc's team slumbered through the evening and waited.

It was a long wait.

Leclerc stared at the illuminated clock on the Citroën's dashboard for
the eighteenth time and flicked his half-smoked cigarette out of the open
window. Without turning his head, he said to the back of the car, 'How
long since you spoke to Louise?'

'Ten minutes.'

'They can still see McGann's car?'

'Just – but it's a strain, she said.'

'Everything's a bloody strain! OK, have another word with her now.
Confirm that the Renault hasn't moved, then talk on the phone to that
man – what's-his-name? the one from *Six*, or *G* – or whatever it is . . .
You've got his number?'

'Yes, boss.'

'Tell him our target's holed up somewhere between Amiens and Poix.
Tell him I haven't got a clue where he's heading for. He could turn back
to Amiens or Abbeville and then go north, or he could cut across country
and finish up at Dieppe. It's anybody's guess until he moves his arse out
of that lay-by. Tell Monsieur – what did you say his name was?'

'Violle.'

'Tell Monsieur Violle that if he wants to get his super-bogey out on
the road now he can do just that, because when it's dark . . .' He turned
to the man at his side. 'When'll it be dark here, Paul?'

'Hour, hour and a half.'

'Whenever it is, the guy in that car's going to want a bed for the night –
he's not going to fancy shacking up on the roadside in that biscuit box.
When he moves that's the time I recommend these hot-shots should be
on call to move in. Have you got all that?'

'Yes, boss.'

McGann leaned forward and stared through the windscreen at the sky.
It was quite dark. The sun had dropped through the hole at the end of

the road and all that was left of it was a vague yellowy pink strip being rapidly pushed downwards by a relentless blackness.

'We can go whenever you want,' he said to Pascale. 'We'll head straight for the coast, direct route, it's not far away. When we get to the sea we'll find a hotel.'

'What sort of hotel?' asked Pascale. 'What can we afford?'

McGann laughed. 'We'll charge it to the Company! Let's go for the best – the biggest – the most expensive – I think we've earned it!'

'Are you sure, Sean?' Pascale sounded doubtful.

She had every reason to.

CHAPTER 34

Inspector Leclerc stared gloomily through his windscreen as he listened to the woman sitting in the passenger seat.

The Citroën was tucked into a small cutting off the main Le Tréport–Dieppe road and although shielded by trees, and invisible from the road, its occupants had a clear, unobstructed view of the hotel opposite.

The huge five-star hotel they were watching stood in its own spacious grounds set well back from the road. It enjoyed a commanding view of the sea across its own lengthy strip of white sand beach. It was a minor paradise – if you had the money.

Earlier in the evening somebody had pulled the switch and flooded the building with orange light. The grounds, with their own concealed floodlighting, were bathed in a white, fairy-tale glow; it was as bright as the middle of day. McGann couldn't have chosen better; he had his own personal security perimeter clearly defined.

Inspector Leclerc saw it in a different light.

Following the Renault out of Le Tréport earlier he'd called in more teams and spaced them on the main Le Tréport–Dieppe road. Others he'd parked in the grounds of the larger hotels so that wherever McGann decided to spend the night, somebody would be nearby to cover him. It had all gone very well.

The girl sitting in the car next to Leclerc had watched McGann and Pascale arrive. She'd checked their room number and, after a brief phone call to Amiens Control, had joined Leclerc among the trees.

'Number 23?' queried Leclerc. 'Is that on the first floor?'

'Yes, André – with a large balcony. You can't quite see it from here. It's on the far side, just above the front car-park. But there are quite a few cars scattered about. Immediately below McGann's room is a grassed area with shrubs and flowerbeds.'

'You saw all this in the dark?'

Chantale sighed. 'André, when I left the hotel the place was lit up like the Arc de Triomphe. You could sit on the grass over there and read your telephone directory. And in answer to your next question: no, there's absolutely no way your spooky friends are going to get into that room via the balcony without being seen crossing the grass.'

Leclerc said drily, 'You must have a very uneventful bedroom life, young lady.' He wasn't smiling, he was concentrating on the next move.

'How's that, Inspector?'

'If you can read my mind you can read anybody's. It can't be much fun for you if you always know what's coming next.'

'I didn't realise I was an exception.'

Leclerc wasn't listening. 'Tell those people,' he said to the radio operator, 'that their target's crawled into a hole for the night. Tell them where we are and how to get here. And wake me up when they arrive.'

Gerrard reversed down the narrow lane and squeezed in behind the dark-green Citroën.

Leclerc detached himself from the shadows, pulled open the back door and slid on to the back seat beside Melanie. His eyebrows rose fractionally but otherwise he showed no surprise at seeing a woman curled up on the seat beside him. He missed Melanie's answering smile when the closing car door shut off the light. He leaned forward and pushed his hand between the two front seats.

'Monsieur Gerrard?' he asked. He didn't waggle the hand around but left it there and waited for one of the two men to shake it.

Gerrard turned in his seat. 'McGann's in that hotel over there, is he?' he asked.

Leclerc raised his eyebrows again then rested his elbows on his knees and cupped his chin in his hand. 'McGann and his woman,' he said, 'have been tucked up over there for about three-quarters of an hour. They have a room on the first floor. I sent an agent to have a look around. She tells me the windows are wide open but the curtains are drawn and all the lights on. They came directly to this place – whistled through Le Tréport as if they knew exactly where they were going, then dashed into the hotel as though they'd both got something red-hot between their legs that needed putting out. Beg pardon, mam'selle . . . They went straight up to their room without bothering about food, or anything else. My agent reckoned they seemed to have only one thing on their minds so I think it might be an appropriate moment . . .?' He left the suggestion in the air.

Gerrard's eyes pierced the gloom of the car looking for Leclerc's expression, but saw only a pale featureless image. He said to it, 'How well do you know this hotel? Do you have any authority in this region?'

Leclerc's teeth flashed in response. 'The answer to your first question is, I don't know it at all. Never seen it before in my life and never been inside – couldn't afford it for one thing . . . As for the second,' Leclerc took a deep breath and grinned in the dark again, 'my authority is a bit like yours, it goes slightly beyond knocking off tarts for soliciting. As far as this place is concerned, though, the manager knows all about my authority – I can inspire in him all sorts of co-operation – or fear. It depends which emotion is required! Do you fancy a stroll across the road?'

'You read my mind.' Gerrard grinned back at Leclerc. He'd taken an instant liking to him. 'What do you think – the simple approach?'

Leaving Reason in the car with Melanie, the two men walked casually across the road and turned left at the corner of the building. Leclerc walked openly across the foyer to the reception area. As he passed it he gave a cursory, almost uninterested glance up the wide stairway that led to the bedrooms; then a longer, more detailed but discreet inspection of the occupants of the small balcony lounge at the far end of the foyer.

Gerrard delayed his entrance until Leclerc reached the reception desk then moved casually in his wake, inspecting the restaurant and bar before joining him from the opposite direction.

Leclerc pressed the button on the desk. The young man who answered the buzzer was despatched to find the manager. He wasn't too happy about the chore. Neither was the manager when he appeared.

Diminutive, immaculately dressed, with tight narrow lips and a carefully trimmed hairline moustache he was everybody's idea of a French hotel manager. He stared unsmilingly at the two men as he approached the desk and began talking before he reached them.

'If you haven't made a reservation, gentlemen, I'm afraid . . .'

He wasn't allowed to finish. Leclerc raised his eyebrows, then his finger, and with a sad little smile placed a white folded card on the counter.

'Have you seen one of these before, monsieur?' he asked, in a soft, friendly voice.

The manager glanced briefly at Gerrard, received an affable smile in return then fussily arranged a pair of gold-framed half-moon glasses on the end of his nose. Leclerc slid the card two inches towards him. The little man looked hard at Leclerc over the rim of his glasses, then down at the card, and back to Leclerc's unsmiling face again before stretching out his hand to touch the card.

'Open it,' ordered Leclerc. 'And read what it says.'

The man did as he was told. He took his time studying the photograph of an unsmiling young Leclerc on the inside of the cover, then compared it with the unsmiling older version standing in front of him. He closed the card and politely held it out to Leclerc. Leclerc left it on the desk then placed his elbows on the counter to bring his face level with the manager's.

'Monsieur . . .?' he said.

'Beaucaire. Henri Beaucaire,' responded the little man hastily and offered Leclerc a hand. Leclerc touched it lightly with the tips of his fingers.

'My colleague,' said Leclerc, moving his hand in Gerrard's direction, 'will require some assistance and co-operation from you.' He stared into the little man's eyes for a moment to make sure the words were going in. 'Particularly co-operation.'

'It goes without – '

'I haven't finished yet,' cut in Leclerc. 'What he's come for is to re-move one of your guests. Nothing to worry about.' He nearly smiled at the look of horror on Beaucaire's face. 'It will be done with the utmost discretion. There will be no upheaval, no unpleasantness or disruption and your other guests will remain totally ignorant of what's going on.'

M. Henri Beaucaire said nothing. He looked as if he'd gone into a trance.

Leclerc picked up his card and stowed it carefully in an inside pocket. He pulled a pad of hotel stationery towards him and scribbled on it a series of digits in large clear figures.

'If you want to confirm my authority you can do so by ringing this number,' he said. The tone of his voice told Beaucaire that it would be a very unwise thing to do.

Beaucaire took the hint. 'Totally unnecessary, sir!' He tried to smile but nothing happened. 'I welcome the opportunity to help the police, particularly members of your er, um, Bureau.' He tore the strip of paper into small pieces and dropped them into the waste basket on the business side of the desk. The gesture evidently cleansed his soul of animosity. His attitude became as relaxed as the paper flakes fluttering into the bas-ket and he managed to smile at Leclerc with honest, hotel-manager hypocrisy. 'Now, sir.' He gave his hands a quick, vigorous dry wash. 'Please be good enough to tell me exactly what you require of me and of my staff. The entire hotel administration is at your service.'

*

Reason was almost invisible. He sat on the grass talking quietly to Melanie through the open window of Gerrard's Citroën. Beside him sat Leclerc's ever-curious Chantale listening fascinated, while the rest of Leclerc's crew kept themselves out of complication, voluntarily entombed in their smoke-filled cocoon.

Leclerc sat down on the grass on the other side of Reason and offered him a cigarette. Leclerc rarely smoked, when he did it meant something was troubling him. A match flared in the darkness lighting up the policeman's serious expression before he dimmed it with the end of his cigarette. When he was alight he gave a brief nod to Reason, raised his head and blew out a mouthful of smoke.

'I think I'd better hang around a bit,' he said to Gerrard, and puffed on his cigarette again. 'Just in case.'

'Just in case of what?' asked Gerrard.

'I can't put my finger on it,' said Leclerc uneasily. 'Something doesn't feel right.'

Gerrard put his hand round the end of his cigarette while he pulled on it. The faint glow lit up his face. He wasn't smiling.

'Thanks for the offer, Leclerc, but I can't see anything going wrong at this stage.'

Leclerc shook his head. 'You're probably right. I must be getting old!' He pulled himself up off the bank and held his hand out to Gerrard. 'Some other time perhaps . . .?' He gave a brief nod to Reason, flicked his cigarette away into the darkness and climbed into the front of the waiting car. He closed the door quietly, but with a muffled cough and a curse. Two half-smoked cigarettes hurtled out of rapidly opened rear windows as the car slipped away and disappeared in the direction of Dieppe.

Gerrard remained where he was, staring silently at the floodlit hotel through the screen of trees and leaves. Leclerc's disquiet had left an echo. But it was only an echo. Gerrard shrugged it aside, and after a couple of minutes finished his cigarette and climbed into the car.

As he started up the engine he said to Reason, 'I can't see any point in creeping through the trees again. I think we'll drive up as if we've come to spend the night. I'll point out McGann's room to you when we get there, not that it'll do you any good, I think we're going to have to go in by his front door.'

Reason's teeth gleamed momentarily in the dark. 'That sounds like a major demolition job?'

Gerrard grinned back. 'That's what we're going to take a look at. I don't think Monsieur Beaucaire would be too happy about having his nice hotel turned into something like Libya's London embassy.'

'Who's Monsieur Beaucaire?'

'You're going to find out in a minute or two. Are you ready for a whisky?'

'And champagne for the lady?' suggested Melanie.

'I knew she was going to be a nuisance,' said Gerrard.

'And I'm hungry too.'

'I did tell you, Reason, but you wouldn't listen, would you?'

CHAPTER 35

Reason sat in Beaucaire's swivel chair with his feet on the corner of the desk and aimed the big Browning automatic at the bracket lamp on the wall. 'I think,' he said to Gerrard, 'we should wander up to room 23, bang on the door and when McGann opens it drag him out by the scruff of his neck and kick his little Irish arse all the way down the stairs and out into the car.' He raised the Browning off the lamp and, still aiming, brought it slowly down again and fired an imaginary shot – it was good shooting.

Gerrard shook his head. 'Let's be serious.'

Reason nodded. There was no humour in his eyes. 'OK, we bang on the door. When he opens it we shoot him in the groin, take his toys away, then jump up and down on him until he starts making sensible noises.'

Gerrard picked up his glass but didn't drink from it. He nursed it between his hands and stared at Reason over its rim.

'And while all that's going on who's going to keep de Foure out of the firing line?'

Reason stopped killing light bulbs. He lowered the automatic, placed it on Beaucaire's desk diary and reached for his glass. His face showed no change of expression, his voice remained on the same even plane.

'If she gets in the way she dies or gets hurt – I'm not particularly worried about her. She volunteered for the party – she takes her chance with the rest of us. Is that serious enough for you?'

Gerrard sipped from his glass and smiled drily. 'She's supposed to be sexy.'

'I don't give a bugger!' Reason didn't smile back. 'And neither will McGann. If she gets in his way he's just as likely to blow her legs off if it means giving himself a five-minute start.'

'So if it's she who opens the door, we shoot our way through her to get to him. OK?'

'Fair enough,' said Reason. 'Let's go.' He picked up the Browning again, looked at it closely and slid a round into the breech; then, holding the hammer with his forefinger and thumb, he squeezed the trigger and gently lowered the hammer as far as it would go. He slipped the pistol carefully into the waistband at the back of his trousers and stood up, helping himself to a handful of tiny triangular-cut sandwiches. He stuffed them into his mouth three at a time before holding the plate out to Gerrard.

Gerrard shook his head. 'Just a minute. Slow down. Go and ask that boy out there to fetch Beaucaire. I have a better idea.'

Monsieur Beaucaire refused to sit down. He stood politely against the wall and stared nervously, first at Reason, and then at Gerrard. He had good reason to be nervous – he didn't like at all the look of the picture the questions were painting.

'. . . You say that each floor has an independent electrical system?' Gerrard didn't let up.

'That's right.'

'So, if, for example, you wanted to cut off all the power from the first floor it could be done without affecting any other part of the hotel?'

Beaucaire nodded. 'There's a junction box in a cupboard under the stairs at the end of each corridor; each room has its own set of fuses. The cupboards are locked at all times, except when the cleaners are working, but I hold the master key.'

'Thank you.' Gerrard held his hand out for the key. 'You know how to work the hotel switchboard?'

'Naturally – but . . .'

'Good. You personally will man the reception switchboard during the period when the lights are out on the first floor.'

'You didn't say anything about putting lights out.'

'I have now. And when it happens I want you to reassure the residents on that floor that a fuse has blown, nothing serious, and that everything is being taken care of. At this time of the night not many of them will be awake to notice that the electricity has failed.'

Beaucaire's lips twitched with protest, but he contained the unspoken words and guarded his helpful expression.

'But our man will notice it,' said Gerrard. 'He'll ring reception the minute I pull the plug. He'll probably be the first to notice the lights have gone out. You're going to tell him that everything is under control. He'll believe you because you're the hotel manager. Make sure you tell him who you are. At least he'll be a little more relaxed having spoken to you.'

'He will?'

Gerrard sipped from his glass and stared into the little man's eyes. 'That's how we want him – nice and relaxed. And when you've got him that way you'll confide to him that the electrician is on his way to remedy the fault and will be checking each room.'

'Is that all?' There was no trace of sarcasm in Beaucaire's voice.

'For you, yes. But first I want you to come with me to the first floor and point out the cupboard and the electrical switches.'

'Now?'

'No, shortly, when we start throwing the dice. You go and look after your hotel now, I'll send your boy for you when we're ready to go.'

'What was that all about?' asked Reason.

Gerrard lit a cigarette and threw the packet on to the desk. He waited while Reason lit up, then said, 'In about ten minutes I shall extinguish all the lights on the first floor – McGann's floor. When McGann wonders why he's gone blind he'll call reception and get Beaucaire, who will tell him there has been an electrical failure on the first floor affecting all rooms, and that repairs are in hand. The first thing McGann will do is dart for the balcony to make sure his neighbours have got the same problem. They will have. That will slow his pulse down to about a hundred and twenty and quiet any suspicion that he has been singled out for something special. Are you happy with that so far?'

'Go on,' said Reason. He looked neither happy nor unhappy.

'We'll give him a few more minutes' darkness to get him quivering for the sight or sound of an electrician then I will bang on his door and tell him I have located the fault and I've come to check one of his plugs or switches. When he opens the door you'll tap him on the ear, pick him up under your arm, and drop him gently off the balcony. We'll load him into the car and whistle off down the road to Paris.'

'What about the girl? Even if McGann doesn't make her open the door, won't she be screaming her head off while I'm doing a blacksmith's job on McGann's face?'

'We've already discussed that. Do what you have to do.'

'I suggest that you stick a pillow over her face,' said Melanie. She'd sat quietly curled up in an armchair, drinking Beaucaire's private stock of champagne and nibbling tiny triangles of smoked salmon sandwich, listening without comment. Now she had decided to join in. 'It's the only thing that's going to stop the woman's screams waking up the whole hotel – if she does that you'll have the corridor full of chattering spectators! Is that what you want?'

The two men stopped and stared at her.

'I wouldn't like her nursing me when I'm sick,' said Reason.

'Thanks. You can go back to sleep now,' Gerrard told her.

Gerrard, Reason and Beaucaire climbed the thickly carpeted stairway in single file. They stopped on Beaucaire's signal in front of a narrow door set under the slope of the next flight of stairs. Beaucaire peered nervously along the empty corridor before giving way to Gerrard at the cupboard door.

Reason, lacking Beaucaire's reservations, stood casually on guard at the top of the stairs; he passed the time glancing alternately down to the mezzanine landing and, shielded from view by the stairway wall, along the corridor as far as room number 23. It looked no different to the other nine doors in the corridor. Wrong! Room 23 wasn't like the others; he felt a twinge of memory and the beginnings of a slight flutter in the middle of his stomach but he controlled it and dragged his eyes back to the stairs.

Beaucaire's powerful torch cut through the cobwebbed blackness of the cubbyhole like a laser and lit up the wooden cabinet on the far wall. The beam lingered only briefly, then began to dance to the trembling of Beaucaire's hand as he tried to point it at the trip switch on one side of the cabinet and the main supply junction box on the other.

But it was enough for Gerrard. He removed the torch from Beaucaire's hand and backed the little man towards the stairway. He gave him a quick pat on the arm and whispered the words Beaucaire had been waiting for.

'Go and wait by the telephone.' He pointed to Reason. 'He'll come with you and wait on the landing at the turn of the stairs. Give him a wave when number 23 picks up the phone. We're not interested in anybody else who can't find his way into his girl-friend in the dark. Only number 23. I'm going to count to fifteen then throw the switch.'

Gerrard counted to seventeen in deference to the little man's nervousness, then pressed the button on the trip switch. The cut-out dropped with a muffled thud. He switched off the torch and moved out of the cubby hole into the corridor. It was in complete darkness. He felt his way to the top of the stairs and waited, his eyes quickly adjusting to the faint glimmer of light that crawled up the stairway from the ground floor. But there was no noise. He strained for the sound of a door opening, a telephone ringing, a bellow of surprise from behind one of the doors – something alive somewhere, but there was nothing, only a deafening silence, and dark, like the inside of a coffin.

It lasted five minutes. It seemed longer. The sudden movement almost took him by surprise. Silent and unseen and with the quietest of warning whispers Reason was there beside him at the top of the stairs – and he hadn't felt a thing. It was like meeting a shadow.

As he reached out to touch the movement, Reason said, 'He rang.' His voice was an almost inaudible whisper which he spoke into the side of Gerrard's head. Then his teeth gleamed in the dark – they were the only part of him that showed. 'Two others rang as well – both men! Haven't they got any fingers?'

Gerrard waited three more minutes by the luminous dial of his watch, then touched Reason's arm.

'Come on.'

They walked soundlessly along the corridor, their footsteps muffled by the thick-pile carpet, until they stood outside room number 23. Gerrard transferred the torch to his left hand, quietly eased the Walther out of its holster and moved to one side of the door.

Reason's Browning had a flat gleam to it; it was almost hidden in his large fist. He showed it to Gerrard, held his other hand out for the torch, then pointed both pistol and torch at the door to show he was ready. Gerrard nodded and pressed himself against the wall on the other side of the doorway. He touched Reason's arm with the barrel of his automatic and made a knocking gesture towards the door. Reason's teeth gleamed again, briefly, and using the hand holding the torch he knocked firmly on the door.

In the dark silence it sounded like a rifle shot in the jungle. It echoed up and down the corridor as if, in the darkness, it was unable to find an exit before vanishing into silence. But the two men weren't interested in echoes.

They listened for a sound behind the door.

Nothing.

The silence resumed, unbroken for a few more long seconds. Then Reason prodded Gerrard and pointed to the door.

'L'électricien, m'sieur ... S'il vous plaît ...?' sang out Gerrard.

The edge of the torch beam caught the beginnings of a smile on his lips as he pressed himself back against the wall and aimed the Walther, at arm's length, at the closed door.

Reason brought his ear away from the door panel. He glanced quickly at Gerrard and placed his pistol barrel across his lips in a gesture of silence.

Then the silence was broken.

'Just a minute, I can't find the lock.'

McGann's voice, only two inches away on the other side of the wooden door sent a memory coursing up Reason's spine. He braced himself. The lock clicked free and McGann, finishing the sentence, pulled the door open.

'Sorry to keep you wai – '

He got no further.

The bright torchlight flashed into his eyes. He was blinded. But there was no time to think about it.

Immediately behind the first flash came an even brighter, blinding light; one that nearly took his head off as Reason hit him a tremendous blow with the flat of his pistol.

It caught him cleanly, with a soggy thwack, and opened up the side of his face like an over-ripe mango.

McGann didn't feel it immediately. Shock, surprise, fear – pain . . . One after the other, and then all together; but by the time his brain had sorted it out he was almost gone. He stood still for a moment, a bemused look on his face that slowly vanished under a red mask as blood gushed from the gouge made by Reason's hammer blow.

Reason studied the result for half a second. His features showed nothing except a cool appraisal of his handiwork. He looked moderately content.

McGann's face was almost split in two, but the injury was only superficial. Deepish, the cut ran from the corner of his eye to the centre of his mouth, and the edge of his nostril, where the automatic's fore-sight had sliced inwards, was shredded like a piece of chewed celery and hung in little tatters like the edge of a segment of torn lace. McGann's eyes had vanished somewhere into his head. He was seeing nothing and for a brief moment looked like an image in a surrealistic painting as he slowly subsided on to his haunches. Then he tried to make a sound. It was a subconscious attempt, a warning to nobody, but when his mouth opened for another try Reason pulled him upright by his hair until he stood wavering on his jelly legs. Bending him from the waist he held him steady for half a second, then brought his knee up and rammed it into McGann's chin with a sickening crunch. The blow would have felled a bullock.

McGann dropped senseless to the floor of the small hallway where he lay, face upwards, his legs and arms twitching like a dead man's.

But he wasn't dead.

Reason's eyes were still without expression when he directed the torch on to McGann's bloody face. He stared for a moment longer into McGann's unseeing eyes then, without looking up, whispered urgently over his shoulder, 'Michel! The lights! quick – !'

But Gerrard was already on his way. He crashed into the cupboard at the end of the corridor and after a scrabbling, banging assault on the unfamiliar, unlighted cubbyhole his hand, to his relief, found the switch and with a sharp flick the corridor was bathed in light.

He ran blindly back down the corridor, struggling to adjust his eyes to the new brightness. He caught sight of the time on the clock on the end wall . . . Two minutes. Christ! Is that all it took? Perhaps the clock had stopped! He didn't dwell on it – there was something else his brain was trying to tell him; something nagging at the forefront of his mind as he rushed back down the corridor; something obvious; something missing, something was wrong.

It came with a rush. McGann's girl-friend wasn't screaming.

And then it started.

'Sean!'

BANG! BANG! BANG! BANG!

Four sharp reports – lightweight – not heavy Browning .45 . . . Then the scream and the name over and over again; the noise was horren-dous as the explosions and screams reverberated along the silent corri-dor – Sean!

BANG! and after a slight pause, BANG! again.

Then a BOOM! And the screaming stopped.

Pascale had never fired a gun in her life. She pointed it through the bedroom door at where the black man was kneeling over Sean's body with a gun jammed into his stomach. She stood shaking and shivering fifteen feet away and just kept pulling the trigger. The bullets showered around the room hitting the ceiling, the wall, the door, and, before he had time to react, two, in quick succession, hit Reason. The first thud-ded over his collar-bone and down into his neck, and threw him across McGann's almost naked body. His right arm was useless. He searched with his left hand for the Browning and throwing himself on to his back brought it painfully across his body. A fraction's fatal hesitation because it was a woman and, as he squeezed the trigger, Pascale's seventh wild bullet caught him just above the left eye, gouging into the skin and slicing across his skull.

Reason collapsed over McGann as his bullet ploughed into her chest.

And then Gerrard was through the door, the Walther steady in both hands pointing into the bedroom.

He almost tripped over Reason's body.

Pascale was leaning against the far wall where she had been thrown, the top half of McGann's pyjamas rapidly dyeing a rich red as blood flooded from a .45 bullet hole below her neck; her face was contorted with terror and fear. McGann's Sauer was still in her hand and she looked at it with horror as she waved it in Gerrard's direction. But she hadn't the strength to squeeze the trigger. Gerrard fired once, killing her instantly. She crumpled, without a sound, against the wall on the far side of the room and, without a second glance at her, Gerrard went down on his knee beside Reason.

For a brief moment Reason stared up and tried to say something but nothing came; he tried again but his mouth wouldn't work and his eyes refused to focus and slowly Gerrard's face, staring angrily down at him, faded into a gentle, airy black mist.

The explosions had brought the hotel awake; it was like a disturbed bees' nest.

Gerrard picked out a white, frightened face, puffing with the exertion of an unaccustomed scramble up the stairs, peering round the corner of the door. Henri Beaucaire.

'Get in here!' snapped Gerrard. 'And shut that door! Quick! The phone – '

Beaucaire took in the carnage in one terrified glance and almost passed out – 'What . . .? W-what . . .?'

'Get on the phone – as quick as you can. Ring that number Inspector Leclerc gave you and tell him you want an ambulance – quickly . . . And tell him to get himself here as well . . . Go!'

Beaucaire hurled himself at the door, happy to get out of the room. 'And tell somebody to get all those people back into their rooms.' Gerrard looked up from Reason's body. Beaucaire was out of the door. 'Send the woman up here!' he shouted to the retreating manager's back.

By the time an ashen-faced Melanie arrived Gerrard had made Reason as comfortable as he could. There had been no sound from him. His eyes were loosely closed and an ominous trickle of frothy blood was trickling steadily from the corner of his mouth. But he was still alive – just.

Gerrard rolled the semi-conscious McGann on to his back and bound his hands behind him, tightly, ignoring the added groans forced out of the mutilated face. He wrapped one of the hotel towels round his head then bound his feet together with another. He dragged him into the bathroom, lifted him and dropped him face down into the empty bath. He switched off the light and closed the door.

When he came out of the bathroom Melanie was kneeling beside Reason, staring into his grey face. 'There's an ambulance on the way,' she said calmly and then, authoritatively, 'Get some blankets – quickly!'

She hadn't been into the bedroom. Fortunately. Gerrard swept the undersheet from the large double bed and threw it, unconcernedly, over Pascale's huddled body. He grabbed the duvet and joined Melanie in the small hallway. As she draped the quilt over Reason he leaned against the wall and lit a cigarette. 'When it arrives go with the ambulance, Melanie,' he said when she straightened up.

'But . . .' she began.

'Don't argue with me!' he snapped. His anger, hidden from sight, was waiting for the opportunity. 'Just listen and do as I say! Get him into hospital; I'll sort things out with Violle as soon as I've finished here. Stay with him until the morning. I'll arrange for a car to fetch you to Paris. We'll meet at the flat. I want to go back to London before lunch – OK?'

'OK. What about McGa – ?'

'That's none of your business.'

'What will you be doing?'

Gerrard didn't have to reply. Leclerc didn't knock. He looked grim but efficient and with him was a team of paramedics who, without fuss, checked Reason's wounds and rushed him out of the room and into the ambulance. As the siren faded along the Dieppe road Leclerc sat on the edge of the bed, lifted the sheet and stared at Pascale's body.

'Pity,' he said absently and picked McGann's Sauer from her dead fingers. 'What do you want to do about the Irishman?' he asked as he accepted a cigarette from Gerrard.

'I want to talk to him,' replied Gerrard. 'In private – no interference.'

Leclerc understood. 'Will it be noisy?'

'It might.'

Leclerc smiled grimly as he swung his legs round to the other side of the bed and picked up the phone. After a brief conversation he stood up and said to Gerrard, 'That was a man called Voisin. He's an Agency part-timer and has a small boat-yard between here and Dieppe. He has a place you can use.' Leclerc studied the end of his cigarette, then flicked the ash off on to the carpet. 'You can make all the noise you like, there's no one around him for miles. I'll drop you off on my way back and introduce you. Do you want me to talk to your people in Paris – tell them it's all over and they can disband the troops and go back to bed?'

'Thank you.'

'Er . . . I will be asked – did McGann survive?'

'I don't think so.'

CHAPTER 36

Under a dim yellow overhead light a long twin-screw motor-launch rocked gently alongside the reinforced wooden jetty. The man leaning against the superstructure threw his cigarette into the water and walked across to meet Leclerc's car as it pulled into the yard. Gerrard and Leclerc carried McGann along a narrow rutted path that ran through an abandoned orchard and into a rusting-metal Nissen-type shed. 'It was left here by the Germans in '44,' explained Voisin. 'I often wondered whether it was ever going to be useful.' His face gleamed in the light of the portable flood lamp that he carried under his arm. He was a big man, over six feet, well built but carrying no surplus weight. His almost white hair looked luminous in the artificial light and his unruly blond beard made his age indefinable. The wrinkles round his eyes showed that he had a good sense of humour. But he wasn't curious. He barely gave McGann's wrapped-up body a glance.

'Give us a shout if you need any help,' he told Gerrard. 'I'll be on the boat. Come and have a drink when you've finished.' He left with Leclerc after a brief handshake.

Gerrard finished his cigarette, ground it into the dust on the doorstep and went back into the hut.

He bent over McGann and checked his bonds again.

'Are you awake, McGann?' he asked.

McGann felt and heard, but he couldn't see.

He lay face down on the dusty concrete floor. His eyes were open but all he had to look at was a grey, out-of-focus mass, something like a badly finished, ridged and ruckled carpet – but without the softness. This grey mass was hard and unyielding. He felt and tasted a powdery dust that had worked its way up his nose and infiltrated his tightly closed lips; it was bitter and unpleasant and he tried to spit his mouth clean but there was no saliva there; his mouth was crusted, and tasted of salt and blood.

He closed his eyes when he felt the return of almost forgotten child-hood nightmares – the dreaded claustrophobia. It didn't mess around creeping up on him, it came back with a vengeance to gnaw at his self-control. It started with his inability to move – or see; he needed a wider angle of vision otherwise he was going to start screaming.

He grazed his chin painfully on the rough floor as he tried to turn his head for a better view. But it didn't work – all he got was an extra surge of blood from the cuts in his head that trickled across his eye and down to his mouth.

When his eye cleared there were new things to look at; a trousered leg and a foot – a poor dividend for the added pain, but it took his mind off the claustrophobia. He stared with one eye at Gerrard's scuffed shoe, covered with the all-pervading white powder and grotesquely distorted by its nearness to his face. He pulled his eyes back as far as they would go and concentrated on the shoe's brogue pattern. It wasn't much, but it helped to relieve the panic that clawed and spidered around in his mind.

There was another nudge on his shoulder and the voice addressed him again. This time the words were in French.

'I asked you if you were awake. If you can't speak, nod – but do one or the other.'

McGann tried to speak. It sounded like a dog worrying a bone. And then, out of the corner of his eye he saw a head come into his vision; a head pointed and elongated in distortion. It stared into his eye and spoke again.

'Ah, good, you are awake! I'm glad to see you've come back to us. I was quite worried about you a few minutes ago – I thought your candle had gone out.' Gerrard touched him with his foot again to make sure he remained awake, then strolled to the end of the hut and checked outside once more before slamming the metal door shut with his shoulder.

On his way back he picked up a discarded, rickety, old-fashioned wooden beer crate and placed it beside the body. He lowered himself on to it, moving his bottom experimentally until he found the most secure position then, lighting another cigarette, addressed the back of the Irish-man's head.

'Are you ready for conversation, McGann?' he asked, in English.

McGann had managed to turn his head to one side and, with an accu-mulation of hard-earned blood and spit, had cleared most of the dust from his mouth. His voice came out of the mask quite clearly.

'I can't talk in this position,' he said hopefully. 'You're going to have to take my face out of this muck. Until then – get stuffed!'

'I see.' Gerrard leaned over and tested the strength of McGann's bonds. Satisfied, he picked him up bodily and dropped him with a crunch on to his back. He waited until the yell of anguish had died away, then said smilingly, 'You only have to ask, boy!' He settled himself back comfortably on the beer crate and looked down at McGann.

McGann's bare chest was covered with a mixture of grey dust and ordinary black dirt and his face had acquired the added feature of a raw, skinless nose and an open grated chin; both stood out bloodily against the unhealthy torn and dirty visage. McGann's eyes, however, were un-damaged and unsubdued. He looked stonily at Gerrard; there was no hint of fear on his face; only a searching curiosity, a mental summing-up, and an appraisal of an opponent's capabilities – or cruelty. He could see some of that in this man's eyes as he searched deeper for the sign of weakness or give; everybody has their weakness, but if this Frenchman had one he wasn't showing it – there was nothing there to give McGann either comfort or reassurance.

Gerrard knew he was being assessed and drew slowly on his cigarette. He hoped McGann had made the correct assessment – it would save him a lot of misery later on. He rested his elbows on his knees and smiled down at McGann.

'I know what you work for and what you are supposed to be good at,' he said conversationally. 'But tell me, who winds you up in the morning and points you along the road?'

'What's that supposed to mean?'

'Who tells you to come to Paris and kill people? Who directs you?'

McGann gazed blandly up at the ceiling. A Frenchman, a soft touch, speaking English in a voice like the bank manager – this was going to be OK! He'd forgotten what he'd seen in the Frenchman's eyes.

'Bloke called Smith,' he replied.

Gerrard's expression and voice didn't change. 'Where does Mr Smith call you from? Where and how do the two of you make contact, and what other names does he have?'

'I don't know, I don't know, and I don't know! That's those three questions answered. What's the next one?' McGann grinned at Gerrard, but it wasn't a success.

Gerrard drew on his cigarette again, blew a thin stream of smoke towards the tin roof and looked down at the Irishman.

'Who and what is Brocklebank, and where can I find him?'

'Never heard of him. Sounds like some sort of cabbage!'

'I think we have the act going round the wrong way, McGann. What's your first name?'

'Sean,' replied McGann, slightly puzzled, but with a smile.

Gerrard smiled back. It was a friendly smile that showed his teeth. 'Well, Sean, answering those few simple questions intelligently was your chance of breaking even in this little bit of unpleasantness. Pity – you've just blown that chance.'

McGann laughed into Gerrard's face. But the laugh didn't last long. It disappeared like a blind being drawn across a lighted window when Gerrard, still smiling, leaned forward and undid the buttons on his thin cotton pyjamas.

'Hey! What the bloody hell do you think you're doing . . .?'

Gerrard stopped and looked into McGann's eyes and winked. He stood up from his box and eased the pyjamas carefully down over McGann's squirming hips until they concertinaed in an untidy heap around his ankles. McGann stopped yelping. He lay in embarrassed nakedness. He tried to raise his knees upwards in a half-protective, half-modest reflex gesture, but Gerrard smiled wearily at him and cracked the barrel of the Walther smartly across both kneecaps. McGann screamed once and straightened them out again.

His eyes never left Gerrard's – his assessment of the Frenchman was rapidly changing. Unless he was a sadistic bastard indulging in a bit of bluff . . . That was it – bluff . . . The bastard was bluffing! But he looked serious – a hard bastard with a stupid grin on his face, and McGann had known some hard bastards. This one looked a bit nearer granite.

He stopped thinking and stared in disbelief as Gerrard cocked the automatic. The round slid into the breech with a clunk like a dungeon door closing and, holding it at arm's length, Gerrard sighted casually along the flat barrel casing. The cigarette in the corner of his mouth forced him to squint over the thin spiral of smoke. McGann didn't know what to make of it. He frowned into Gerrard's eyes. Then looked down.

The Walther was aimed directly at his groin.

'You're bluffing,' he rasped. But he pulled his stomach in, just in case, and tried to get the important stuff out of the way. As a last resort he squeezed his thighs tightly together. 'You're fuckin' bluffin,' he said again and almost began to believe it until he looked up and saw Gerrard's finger whiten against the trigger. 'You wouldn't bloody dare!' McGann heard the words coming from his mouth but he didn't recognise the voice – it sounded like Charlie Phelan's. For a brief second he looked deep into Gerrard's eyes. Gerrard winked at him over the gun barrel and

McGann started screaming – even before Gerrard squeezed the trigger.
BANG!

The heavy lead bullet seared a groove between McGann's tightly clenched thighs; it bounced off the concrete floor and, screaming like a banshee, thwacked with a dull thump into the far wall.

Gerrard screwed up his face and gently massaged his eardrum with his finger. The tingling from the reverberation of the explosion took a few seconds to subside. But Gerrard was in no hurry. He crossed his legs and waited, at the same time sniffing appreciatively the addictive aroma of blown cordite. When he'd had enough he looked down and smiled at the man on the floor.

McGann lay still with his eyes tightly closed, and his lips, white where he'd bitten the blood from them, were drawn back over his clenched teeth. A large uncontrollable tear forced its way through his screwed-up eyelids and coursed erratically down his cheek, cutting a miniature channel through the grey and black grime to join the sweat round his neck.

'Holy Mother of God!' he wept. 'You're mad! What sort of fuckin' madman would do a thing like that?' He caught his breath and slowly raised his eyelids to look into the cool, grey, expressionless eyes of the man sitting watching him.

Gerrard smiled – it was only a mouth smile, nothing to do with friendship, and when he saw McGann's eyes open he raised his eyebrows to show him that he was interested, but said nothing.

'You're mad!' repeated McGann. He found that talking didn't hurt too much – it took his mind off something that he daren't think about. But he knew he was going to feel it, in just a few seconds – when the heat wore off. 'D'you know that? You're stark, staring, bloody mad!' McGann shook his head incredulously. 'You're a fuckin' maniac!' He dare not look between his legs. The whole region was numb, there was no feeling, not even pain – not yet. He knew he'd have to look, but he didn't want to. His voice broke into a half-sob again. 'What the hell have you done . . .? You didn't even give me a chance.'

Gerrard pulled on his cigarette and shook his head slowly from side to side. 'You're repeating yourself – and you're beginning to whine. Be quiet while I inspect your balls.' He stopped and drew on his cigarette again and smiled broadly, this time with his eyes as well, 'How's the voice – feel any change yet? Let's have a look.'

McGann sobbed quietly as Gerrard leaned forward and stared critically at his naked thighs.

There were identical twin weals, no more than a centimetre deep on either thigh. They looked like little channels gouged out with an old-fashioned marrow scoop and as Gerrard studied them they bubbled up and filled with good red Irish blood. But they looked far worse than they actually were. Shortly they would become excruciatingly painful. At the moment they were still numb. Gerrard looked up into McGann's startled, protruding eyes, and nodded seriously.

'Very close that . . . Why don't you have a look?'

McGann looked, and nearly fainted.

'You dirty, underhand, Frog bastard!' Shock had taken control of his tongue – he'd forgotten already who he was dealing with.

Gerrard reminded him. He leaned forward again and touched McGann's quivering thigh with the barrel of the pistol.

'Do you know the trouble with you, McGann?' he said. The smile had gone now. There was nothing to look at but blank granite. McGann ignored him. He was mesmerised by the channels of blood on his thighs and the ugliness of the cold barrel of the Walther too near the thing he treasured most. 'The trouble with you is that you've not been exposed to the no-holds-barred set. You're not yet ready for the realities of this war you've been enjoying. You've been spoilt. The British have been up to their pathetic little games again, playing by the rules, getting their balls kicked and slapping your wrists in return. That's how it's been, McGann, hasn't it? Rules for them, and the dirty tricks manual for you – and all the howling and whining from your lot when one of the poor bastards turns on you and kicks you back. That's your trouble, McGann. That's why you're whining now.'

McGann stopped contemplating his new wounds and looked up into Gerrard's eyes. He decided to chance his hand again.

'You talk a lot of balls about something you know fuck-all about, Frog!'

'And that's your second mistake. I think you've got a funny little idea at the back of your mind that you're talking to a Brit. Am I right?'

McGann curled his lip in reply.

Gerrard wasn't put out. 'I can see I am. OK, here's a little something for you to mull over before we move on to the next phase of our interview. I suggest you digest it well, and don't speak again until you've given it a great deal of thought . . .'

'Piss off!'

'I'm not a Brit, McGann. I don't play cricket and I don't have rules or fancy morals . . .' Gerrard pointed to his open neck. 'No tie either – so no scruples about kicking a man in the balls when he's down. Got all that, Sean?'

'Fuck off, windbag!'

'You sure about that?'

'You heard me.'

'Do you want to have another go at those questions?'

'You're getting on my tits.'

Gerrard smiled gently again. He sat back on his box and raised the Walther so that it was pointing once again at McGann's groin. He gazed down the barrel, frowned, then brought it up to his face and carefully puffed a tiny fragment of cigarette ash off the front sight. Then he aimed it again.

McGann almost laughed out loud. He couldn't believe that the Frenchman would do it again – he was too theatrical . . . Typical bloody Frog – all fuckin' talk . . . !

Gerrard squeezed the trigger again.

BANG!

The second bullet hit two inches higher and McGann screamed again – much louder. And longer.

Gerrard winced against the shattering roar which, for the second time in a few minutes, echoed and bounced around the tin hut. He gently massaged his ear again as he watched McGann's face. When the noise finally rippled away it left an intense vacuum of silence, hollow and un-real, broken only by McGann's uncontrolled sobs.

'OK, Sean, you can stop crying now – we've come to the end of the games. Here in France we call those the openers. What we call the next phase is the rough stuff.'

McGann's eyes opened reluctantly and immediately filled with un-stoppable tears as the excruciating shafts of pain rocketed to the nerve centres at the back of his brain. He stared blindly in Gerrard's direction, like a child seeking solace from its mother, but no words came from his half-open mouth. He tried again, but Gerrard stopped him with a wave of the automatic – he was quite unmoved.

'Do you want me to repeat those questions I asked, or can you remember them?'

McGann breathed deeply, his damp sweaty chest rising and falling with the effort, but he took his time.

Gerrard stopped smiling. 'We haven't got all day. And before you say something stupid, that last shot was only that much away from your little prick.' He held his thumb and forefinger about an inch apart for

McGann to gauge the distance. 'The next one will have the girls queuing up to laugh at it. And the one after that will allow you to tell them how it happened in your new squeaky voice. That is my last piece of advice to you, McGann.'

'There's nowhere in the fuckin' world you'll be sa – '

Gerrard stopped him with a gentle tap on the side of the head with the barrel of the automatic. McGann squealed and clenched his teeth, but finally got the message. He bit back his next bout of swearing.

Gerrard merely smiled again. He shook his head and raised the pistol so that McGann couldn't help seeing it.

'The questions?' he suggested, gently.

'OK, OK, OK!' McGann said hurriedly. 'There's no need for any more of that,' then added slyly, 'How about loosening my hands, they've gone dead on me?' He looked up appealingly, but without expectations.

There was no mercy forthcoming. No sympathy either. 'Get on with it!' Gerrard allowed a little impatience to edge into his voice and brought the Walther up in to the aim again. He hit the roof of his mouth with his tongue. It made a loud popping noise like the sound of the cork coming out of a good bottle of wine.

'Pop!' he said seriously. 'The next one's the bull's-eye – no prick! Don't keep me waiting. Do you remember the first question?'

'Give it me again.'

'Who arranges your errands for you?'

'His name's Charlie Phelan.'

'Where can I find him?'

'You can't. He . . .'

Gerrard tut-tutted and moved the pistol fractionally.

'Once a week, usually Saturday,' said McGann quickly. 'At 42 Donovan Place, Canning Town. It's an active-service unit HQ.'

'OK,' said Gerrard reluctantly. 'This Phelan, what does he look like?' He wondered for a moment whether he wore a navy-blue blazer with a little embroidered cannon on the breast pocket, and had a second name – like Murray.

He was disappointed.

'Tall, thin guy,' said McGann willingly. 'Black hair, got the beginnings of a beard. It's never been anything but the beginnings since I've known him. Speaks with a high-pitched squeaky voice.'

'OK, that's enough about Phelan – let's move on to the one called Brocklebank.'

'I don't know anything about the man. Nothing at all. Well – nothing more than I've heard.'

'What have you heard?'

McGann considered for a moment, then said, 'Brocklebank's not his real name. He's supposed to be a fairly big potato in Brit Intelligence circles . . .' He stopped and Gerrard raised his eyebrows. It was enough to get McGann going again. He looked down and studied his injuries as he spoke. 'That's all I know about him.' He shot a quick glance upwards at Gerrard's face. He didn't like what he saw there and looked down again, hopefully out of range of the eyes. 'God's honest truth,' he whispered. 'That's all I know about him.'

Gerrard lit another cigarette. A few seconds passed before he spoke.

'OK,' he said. 'You've won me over. I'll accept you don't know much about Brocklebank. I ought to have known better, asking the shit-house cleaner for anything more complicated than another sheet of lavatory paper. So, as *you* don't know – tell me who does.'

'Phelan's in contact with him.'

'Squeaky voice?'

'Yeh.'

'So, if I go knocking at number 42 – what is it? Donovan Place – and ask for Mr Phelan, he'll oblige me, will he?'

'He's a hard bastard.'

'They said you were! How close is this Phelan to the man we're talking about?'

'Phelan is Brocklebank's touch with the IRA in England. But I don't think even he could take you to his front door. You'd be wasting your time.'

'You're a funny little fellow, Sean. A few minutes ago you were howling that you didn't know Brocklebank from a bar of soap – and yet here he comes again. You could be his bum-boy the way you're talking about him. But before you unburden yourself again, tell me, do you know a man named Murray? Dresses like an English gent, ex-soldier, probably Royal Artillery?'

McGann looked genuinely curious – and interested. 'Murray?' he frowned. 'I don't know the name. Is he one of ours?'

'You tell me!'

McGann shook his head. 'It doesn't do anything to me. What's he supposed to be?'

Another Murray dead-end. Gerrard kept the exasperation from his face. He could see McGann was telling the truth.

'Forget it,' he told him. 'You were going to say something more about

Brocklebank.'

'No I wasn't. It's like I said, I don't . . .'

Gerrard cut in before McGann got into his stride. 'No – like you didn't say!' He tapped him on the head with the pistol barrel again. 'For example, you didn't say how you knew that Brocklebank was doing his turn for Irish money.' He tapped McGann's head again to emphasise the point. 'And you didn't tell me how you knew that Phelan was the only friend he had in town. You seem to know an awful lot more than where the shit bucket's emptied, McGann, which is the impression you tried to give to me. In your position that's the silliest so far. Do you want to think a little more about the consequences before we start answering those questions again?'

McGann kicked himself for walking into the Frenchman's ambush – he'd underestimated the crafty bastard again. He tried a little diversion.

'I wish you'd stop banging that bloody thing on my head – it's giving me a headache.'

'Good! Tell me some other things that Phelan let drop about Brocklebank.'

'He's got a woman who cuts out.'

'Who, Phelan?'

'No, the other one, Brocklebank. She's also in the game.'

'Do you mean on the game?'

'No, in the game. She works for Brit Intelligence too. She's very close to Brocklebank, does a lot of dealing for him.'

'Are there any Brits in British Intelligence?' Gerrard ground his cigarette into the dust. He wasn't smiling. 'What is the woman's name?'

'I'm not sure, I think it's Audrey something or other.'

Gerrard frowned. Too much of a coincidence. 'How can I meet her?'

'Through Phelan. I said she cuts out. Brocklebank's an old hand, he knows how to keep himself warm. And clean.'

Gerrard shifted his weight on the beer box. It groaned in protest but remained intact and upright. He crossed his legs into a more comfortable position.

'Tell me why you came to France.'

'To look for a man who killed a roomful of the IRA Planning Committee. He owes us a few pounds of flesh.'

'What is he doing in France?'

'He's a bloody Frenchman – bought by the British. A contract hitman by the name of Siegfried. Ever heard of him?'

Gerrard looked blankly at the sweating Irishman.

'Brocklebank was supposed to have vetted this Siegfried. Apparently he was quite upset about the guy turning his hat inside out – took it very personally by all accounts.'

'Whose accounts were they?'

'Who else's? Phelan's, of course. He said Brocklebank assured them that he'd got this Siegfried character wrapped up so tight he couldn't have gone for a crap without him knowing about it.'

'What did he mean by that?'

'He'd got somebody in the Frenchman's camp watching everything he did. That was his story, and I gathered from Phelan that that's the story he was sticking to. But you know the result – I just told you – somebody blinked and half the bloody Committee got pasted to the wall. Phelan said that Brocklebank missed getting his by only a few minutes. Lucky bastard some say! Others? Well ...' McGann tried to shrug his shoulders but stopped short when it started everything hurting again. He felt he was getting on quite well – all that was needed now was a couple of pints of bitter to cement the friendship. And there was bound to be an opportunity for a well-trained boy to exploit a fraction's lowering of the guard. Keep it up, Frog, turn the music up – let's get really friendly! He brought his mind back to what he thought the Frenchman wanted to hear.

'It was Brocklebank who put out the contract on this French guy. Not much else he could do, was there?'

Gerrard inclined his head in agreement.

'So he drew up papers for the best of our bunch – and here I am.' McGann almost managed a smile but his torn lip wouldn't let him, instead he winked and jerked his head in a little knowing nod.

Gerrard nodded back, reflectively. 'What did he say to you – go to Paris and kill everybody there named Siegfried?'

'Not quite. Brocklebank knew what else he was called.'

Gerrard smiled encouragingly. 'And what was that?'

'Gerrard. Michel Gerrard. They gave me a contact in Paris who was going to point me towards him. The contact brought half the French Security Services along with him to our meeting. That was all it needed. Talk about the shit hitting the fan!'

'Their friends are all looking forward to seeing you back there.'

McGann shook his head smugly. 'Then it's just as well we're going to do a deal about sending me to Ireland, isn't it?'

Gerrard pulled a face. He lit another cigarette from the smouldering tip of the old one and flicked the used stub across the room.

McGann watched the sparks shatter on the concrete, then strained his eyes up to study Gerrard's face. 'It's no skin off your nose. I'm wanted in Ireland; they'll be grateful.'

Gerrard raised his eyebrows.

'Besides which, I'm a known member of the IRA. What I did in Paris was political – you wouldn't want all your friends to know that your government's dancing to British music. Your people wouldn't thank you if the war suddenly moved to the Champs-Elysées – would they? So why don't you slip me on the ferry to Rosslare and save yourself a lot of unnecessary aggravation?'

Gerrard wasn't listening, but to McGann his silence was promising. He managed to work his lips into the semblance of a smile. 'It's like I said earlier, some you win, some you lose – nobody's going to blame you, Monsieur – what is your name by the way?'

'Gerrard.'

McGann's smile locked into place. 'Coincidence?'

'No.'

'You're Siegfried?'

'That's right.'

McGann was speechless for some time. Then he closed his eyes – it was his way of showing he'd just seen what the end of the road looked like. After half a minute or so he spoke. The new-found confidence burst like a soap bubble and his voice went hoarse with fear. He kept his eyes closed to hide the message.

'You've been on to me right from the word go, haven't you? How did you do it?' He didn't expect a reply. He didn't get one.

Gerrard turned his wrist over and looked at the face of his watch. 'Time to go,' he said and nodded at McGann's bleeding legs. 'Bit of a shame getting yourself hurt like that, wasn't it? Waste of my time as well. You haven't been much help to me. In fact all you've been is a nuisance if we're honest with ourselves.'

'Do you want me to apologise?'

Gerrard smiled to himself. 'If I untie your feet do you think you'll be able to walk?'

'What have you got in mind?'

'I thought a little boat trip.'

'Where to?'

Gerrard shook his head as he stripped the binding from around McGann's feet and threw it to one side of the hut. 'I won't spoil the surprise. But first things first. Here, kick your feet about a bit, it'll get the

343

circulation going again.' He moved back, well out of the way of McGann's flailing legs.

'Ker-rist Almighty ...!' McGann's voice echoed round the hut. Gerrard allowed him a couple of minutes' swearing and hissing before he moved back and stood over him.

'What now?' asked McGann when he'd got used to the feel of his damaged legs.

'A gentle stroll through a French wood,' Gerrard told him, 'and then a nice breezy little boat trip.'

'You'll never get away with it!'

'We'll see.'

Voisin sat in the cockpit of his launch smoking Gauloises and drinking from an unlabelled litre bottle of wine. The overhead lighting cast gentle shadows and he showed no surprise as he watched the two men approach. He stood up but said nothing; there were no greetings, just the briefest of nods between two Frenchmen. It was as if Voisin had read Gerrard's mind; the engines were ticking over.

McGann shuffled to a halt. He didn't look surprised to see Voisin or the motor cruiser riding gently at the jetty. He didn't have long to study it.

'Lie down.' Gerrard's foot thumped into the back of his knees and he was sent sprawling on his face in the soft gravel.

'Shove his hands in his pockets and put a rope round him,' Gerrard said to Voisin, 'and throw him aboard – there's no need to be gentle with him.'

They propped him up against the raised side of the cabin so that he had a good view of everything that was going on around him, then left him on his own while the cruiser edged its way from the jetty and out into the harbour. After a few moments' discussion, Voisin opened the throttles of the powerful engines and swung the boat in a gentle arc to head out to the open Channel.

'What have you got in mind for me?' asked McGann, shouting to make himself heard over the roar of the engines and the crashing of the hull as it bounced across the white crested water.

Gerrard crossed the deck and sat down beside him. He lowered his head until it was close to McGann's face, and shouted into his ear, 'You sure you want to know, Sean?'

McGann grinned at him bravely. 'Sure. Go on, surprise me.'

'OK. I'm going to take you out there and bury you at sea – like they do with sailors.'

McGann looked into Gerrard's eyes for the trace of a smile, but found none. He curled his lip and snorted, but it was only a half-hearted snort and was cut short by a small tic that began to jerk the muscle under his left eye. He continued to stare into Gerrard's face.

'I don't think that's very funny,' he said finally.

'It wasn't intended to be.'

'You're joking,' he shouted into Gerrard's eyes.

Gerrard shook his head. 'No joke, Sean.' He stood up on the bucketing deck and hung on to the brass rail to keep his balance while he gazed around at the moonlit open sea. He shaded his eyes with an outstretched hand and after a few moments nodded to himself, then waved to attract Voisin's attention.

'This'll do,' he shouted. 'It looks reasonably consecrated.'

McGann knew it was a joke. He began to laugh.

Voisin closed the throttles until the engines barely ticked. The silence was suddenly overwhelming. Apart from the gentle slapping of water against the hull there was no sound, except an ecstatic popping from the rear where the exhaust bubbled erratically into the light swell that nudged the boat's stern. None of this interested McGann, who, from his raised position on the deck, kept his eyes fixed on the two Frenchmen and tried to follow their conversation. His lip reading wasn't very successful.

After a moment Voisin left and went below. Gerrard waited at the top of the companionway, called out something softly, then pulled himself out of the cockpit and joined McGann on the deck.

He stood looking down at him for some time without saying a word.

A few minutes later Voisin staggered back on deck with a bulky, fifty-litre metal barrel.

McGann stared – he didn't know what to make of it.

Voisin secured a long length of nylon rope to the barrel and heaved it over the side. It filled within seconds, an audible gurgling of green sea water that rushed through the open nozzle; it took a muscle-bulging haul to pull it back on deck. Voisin grimaced with the strain. The container sloshed to the deck with a wet thump, spraying water noisily and liberally around his feet.

The sound brought McGann out of his trance. He raised his eyes from the container and scrutinised the bearded man's expression for a clue. There was nothing there. He had a quick glance at Gerrard's face. Nothing there either.

Voisin dragged the heavy barrel across the deck until it stood solidly on the boat's gunwale. He tied the other end of the rope round McGann's ankles and tested the strength of the knots. He nodded reassuringly to Gerrard, then turned the bright spotlight so that it shone on the water just to the side of the boat. The two Frenchmen moved across the deck to where McGann was sitting and stood staring, wordlessly, down at him. They looked like two undertakers working out how much timber the coffin was going to take. After a moment Gerrard looked across the deck at the water-filled barrel.

'Is that going to be heavy enough?' he asked Voisin. 'I don't want the bastard bobbing up and down for ever like a mooring buoy.' There was no humour in Gerrard's voice, he was making a matter-of-fact statement; the bound man on the deck could have been a sack of potatoes for all the consideration he gave his feelings.

But Voisin was different – he could see the funny side of it. He answered with enthusiasm, 'Don't worry about that.' He kicked the barrel, which answered with a solid clunk. 'This'll take him to the bottom like an upside-down rocket! He'll be down there for ever. Probably longer! The only thing that's going to give way eventually will be these.' He tapped McGann's feet with his shoe. 'His ankles – they'll be the first to go. But that's a long time away.' He looked down into McGann's bulging eyeballs and smiled. 'Not a bad way to go really – no pain.'

McGann found his voice.

He screamed.

Gerrard and Voisin exchanged glances, and Gerrard nodded hurriedly. Voisin lowered the container into the water until it disappeared under the green, white-flecked swell, pulling the rope tight round McGann's ankles.

They picked him up by his armpits, holding him firmly against the strain of the taut line, but as their hands went under him he tried to struggle from the grasp and arched his back and bent his knees in an attempt to hold his ground. He no longer felt the pain in his wounded thighs and tried to squirm his way back to the safety of the deck, but it was like straining against steel hawsers. It was remorseless, and in his terror he finally let go and felt his bladder empty itself. The two Frenchmen looked at each other as they lowered him over the side. Neither said a word.

The tight rope first pulled his legs straight, and then strained against his body. As his feet touched the water the screams got louder.

'I'm a prisoner of war!' he screamed at the top of his voice. 'The

Geneva Conv – ' His last word was cut off as Gerrard and Voisin, simultaneously, released their grip on his armpits. He went under like a ton of lead with hardly a splash, and the two Frenchmen stood studying the foaming bubbles that scurried to the surface until, too deep, they dispersed before reaching the surface and were lost in the gentle swell.

Voisin was the first to look up. He offered Gerrard a cigarette, lit one himself and inhaled luxuriously. Gerrard did the same. He stared grimly at McGann's grave for several seconds then shook his head and flicked his unsmoked cigarette into the water. He looked at his watch.

'Let's get away from here, Voisin. I'm suddenly tired of this place. Make a call for me as soon as you can. I want my car sent to London. Diplomatic – I don't want it looked at. They'll understand.'

'Consider it done.'

CHAPTER 37

'You still interested in that Frenchman, Murray?'

'Could be . . .' Murray held the telephone loosely under his chin while he fumbled first for a cigarette and then for something to light it with. 'Where is he?' There was no surprise in Murray's voice; Murray was never surprised by certainties any more than he was surprised by the stuff he was watching on the box. With the sound turned down the news was almost watchable.

'I couldn't put my finger on him at the moment, but I'm reliably informed he's gone to ground somewhere in London.'

'Where'd he come from?'

'France. A bird named Melanie Lambdon came with him.'

'Was there a big black guy around anywhere?'

'No.'

Murray's eyes narrowed while he digested this. He pulled heavily on his cigarette again and watched a scruffy bearded youth with a dirty towel round his head shoot off a whole magazine of Kalashnikov down an empty street in Beirut. He was doing it for the TV camera. Murray stared blankly.

'The Lambdon girl – where'd the Frog take her?'

'They were followed to London. They said you'd know where her front door was. What's it all about?'

'She's this week's prize – a maggot to catch a Frog! We thought we'd take her down the river to our workshop and then ask him to tea. The theory is that he'll come on his hands and knees to the bloke who's bouncing her up and down in his lap. They're like that, the Frogs – think a lot of their women.'

'Let's hope you haven't found the exception. You know where she lives then?'

'I do. Anything else?'

'I'd have thought that was enough for one day.'

'OK, good-night.'
'Good-night, Murray.'

Murray pretended to be reading his newspaper as Melanie came out of her door and turned towards his car.

He was parked discreetly down the road between a white BMW and an orange Renault and had an almost unrestricted view of her front door.

He raised his eyes from the paper as she drew level and followed her progress through his rear mirror to the corner of the street.

'Melanie Lambdon's going to do a bit of early shopping,' he told the girl with the big tits on page three. 'Probably run out of cornflakes or Guinness, or the Frog's eaten her reserve of fresh snails. No make-up; bit splodgy under the eyes – could be nest work. It's all very promising. She'll be back, she's not dressed for Bond Street or Harrods, no need to panic off after her. Let's find out first whether she's been having the French connection! If she has, it's a doddle, he'll come for an interview on his fingertips. But where the bloody hell is he now?' Murray's blood pressure had just begun to move into the start position when Melanie re-appeared in the narrow confines of the mirror. She carried an awkwardly swinging transparent polythene cover which, suspended from a wire coat hanger, swayed backwards and forwards as she moved briskly down the shaded tree-lined street.

'Bingo!' said Murray cheerfully to his paper girl-friend as Melanie walked past and he identified the contents of the plastic wrapper. 'If that's not a Frenchman's Sunday suit I'll go and eat a bucket of snails! The bugger's in the house all right, probably getting his legs straightened out after bending them up and down over her all night!'

Murray shook his head in admiration as he watched Melanie open the yellow door with her key and swing inside. *That bastard Frog's got the luck of O'Reilly's mongrel bitch if he's had his leg over that all night – and by the look of her, half the bloody morning too!* He grinned to himself. *And there's old Smithy – the poor gullible bastard – who reckons she's never studied the shadows on the ceiling from under a pair of hairy shoulders! Never mind, Smithy Boy – I did warn you – it only takes the tip of a tongue in the right corner to persuade them to hand it over. Even to you! But enough of the erotica . . . I think we'll give this horny bugger another half an hour to put his clean trousers on and then we'll decide on his future.*

Murray settled himself down with a cigarette and returned his concentration to page three and the red-hot but untouchable nipples of the busty brunette. Some of the interest had gone out of it, though; she

349

looked a little bit coarse now – a bit tarty; more like the short end of a thirty-bob touch after two and a half minutes of the Melanie Lambdon show.

Gerrard sat on the edge of Melanie's rumpled bed and dialled Sanderson's private number. Coney answered.

There was no social chit-chat. Gerrard said, 'Coney, I can't get a reply from the General's reserve number, do you know where I can find him? It's urgent.'

'You've been in France wiv Mr Rason, 'aven't you, Mr Jerrud?'

'What's that got to do with it?'

Coney wasn't answering questions. ''Ow long you bin back 'ere?'

Gerrard gritted his teeth. 'Since last night – why?'

'Because I'm surprised you didn't see 'im. He's bin in Paris since the day before yesterday. Staying wiv 'is Frog friend – beg your pardon – staying wiv 'is French friend, Monsoower Maurice.'

Gerrard's eyes narrowed. What the hell were the devious old bastards playing at? He heaved on his cigarette before smashing it out in the tiny porcelain dish on the table beside Melanie's bed.

'What's the best way to get in touch with Colonel Harris? David Street?' He took a shot in the dark: 'Or the other place?'

'Ring 'is 'ome. It's XD, the number's – 'ang on . . . 240 1012. It's a clean line.'

'Goodbye, Coney.' Gerrard replaced the receiver and took out Brocklebank's jumbled-up telephone number. There was no comparison between the two, but he rang the number Coney had given him all the same. There was no reply. He pulled a face – life was never going to be that easy. It was time to invoke Roberts's support. He dialled the number for Scotland Yard. Commander Roberts was not available. No, they didn't know where he was. No, there was no home number for universal consumption . . . try again tomorrow . . . leave your number, and no, don't ring him again, he'll ring you. Gerrard gave them the number of the Russian Embassy in Paris.

Who are we left with? Gerrard lit another cigarette and reached down into the bottom of the barrel.

'Michel, what are you doing here?' Audrey Gilling was breathless, as though she'd been running – or lying down. Gerrard smiled to himself, it was all the same to Audrey, even sitting on it seemed to make her eyes water – she sounded as throaty as she did in the early hours when the moon was glancing across the crumpled bedsheets.

'I've got a problem. Can I talk?' he asked.

'I'll ring you back in about twenty minutes,' she whispered. 'Where are you? What's your number?'

He gave her Melanie's telephone number.

'Where's that?'

'Highgate.' He could have bitten his tongue off.

'Staying with the Lambdon girl then, are you?'

And just how the hell would you know that, Audrey?

'Mind your own business, Audrey! And don't be long.'

'Is Audrey the blonde with the oysters?' Melanie kicked her shoes off and lay on her tummy across the bed. She propped her chin in her hand and regarded Gerrard critically. She didn't wait for his confirmation. 'I didn't hear you tell her you were spoken for.'

But Gerrard was dialling his next number.

'Maurice, I've got a problem.' The bubbles and squeaks of the international exchange died down after his opening sentence, and then it sounded as if he was talking to the man next door.

'The whole of life is a problem, Michel . . . It always has been.'

'That's another argument, Maurice. Listen, this may sound stupid, but is General Sanderson staying with you?'

'No.'

'His man disagrees,' said Gerrard caustically. 'He says General Sanderson has gone to Paris. He's staying with his old friend Monsieur Maurice!'

'Forget Richard. What's your problem?'

'Without Sanderson I've no incentive. I'm left without a right marker – I've no base and nothing to turn to. I might as well come home.'

'Don't do that,' said Maurice, quickly. 'Stick with the target. Take it to its conclusion. This Brocklebank will start running when he realises how close you are to him. Richard's probably let him know in a roundabout way that he's been singed.'

'The term is "burnt", Maurice!'

'Do you want to hear the rest of this theory?'

'Please.'

'Then don't interrupt. Richard would have passed the news round his table that you were on your way back to London. He's probably moved out of the way deliberately to make this Brocklebank person feel he's got a clear run to wherever he wants to go. He's probably putting stuff together now for his retirement fund. I suggest you play the card you drew from the Irishman.'

'You've seen Voisin?'

'Yes. Interesting life you lead! Puy-Monbraque is furious. Now, listen – when you meet Mr Brocklebank ask him if he's got any friends on the Quai d'Orsay, the *Piscine*, or even, heaven forbid, *Le Château*.'

'*Le Château?*'

'L'Elysée – Château Mitterrand.'

'You think Brocklebank's international?'

'His masters are. But you never can tell, he might speak French as well as Irish.'

Gerrard nudged the conversation back to the starting point. 'Maurice, without Sanderson I've no friend here. I need somebody to point for me, all I've got is fifth choice and she doesn't fill me with confidence.'

'Smart lad like you shouldn't need friends. Try it out on your own – don't mess around with girls. Call on Colonel Harris, we're pretty sure he's clean. He'll guide you if you come to a right or left fork. He'll know who you are. But don't mention me. I'll make my name with him when, and if, he moves into Richard's seat. Anything else?'

'You mean apart from the nothing this call's brought me?'

'Don't be funny, Michel, this is a serious business. Ring me when it's finished and let me know where to send the wreath. *Au revoir.*'

Gerrard replaced the dead receiver with a wry smile. All he'd learned was that Sanderson had moved out of the way to give Brocklebank a free run; that Brocklebank could be the spider for more than one European agency; and that Maurice didn't altogether trust Harris, presumably reflecting his old wartime buddy's misgivings.

Audrey left her office, cut up David Street into Oxford Street and darted down the steps of Bond Street Underground. It was a busy time of day. She waited impatiently in a small queue for the telephone.

The familiar, unhurried voice failed to calm her down.

She didn't say hallo. 'Michel Gerrard's here. He's here in London.'

'How d'you know?'

'He just rang. Wants to see me – says he's got a problem. What's it all about, Geoffrey?'

'He's come to kill me.' The silence seemed to go on for ever.

'I don't understand. What are you talking about?'

'Just that. I should have realised earlier. McGann must have fucked up, and Gerrard has killed him. I've been expecting him back. Sanderson let something drop the other day and then it all slotted into place

– Gerrard was imported to scrub my slate clean. It's been that all along. Everything else was secondary.'

'I thought . . .?'

'I know what you thought – the Irish thing. So did I. But, intentionally or otherwise, Sanderson's stuck one between my ribs, and we're not hanging around to find out whether he knew something definite or was just probing.'

'What are we going to do?'

'We're going to bugger off! What exactly did Gerrard say he wanted?'

'He wanted to talk on a clean line. I said I'd ring him back.'

'What hotel's he staying at?'

'He's not, he's with Freddie Lambdon's girl at Highgate.'

There was a longish pause. When the voice came back it had a new, interested note in it. 'Is there something going on with this girl, Audrey? Is Gerrard taking care of both you and her?'

'Don't be crude, Geoffrey.' Audrey paused for thought. 'You might be right. The signs were there last week when I met her in the restaurant. Signs from her, that is.'

'So you think he's doing her a favour?'

'That's one way of putting it. Why d'you want to know?'

'It could lower the temperature. If your diagnosis is anywhere near the mark, Audrey, she could guarantee me an extra couple of days.'

'I'm still not with you, Geoffrey.'

'You will be. Get in touch with Phelan – right away. Tell him where the girl lives and what she looks like. He's to go there and move in with her – quietly, without fuss. And for Christ's sake drum it into his thick Irish head that we don't want her buried. Not yet. Explain to him in as many three-letter words as you can think of exactly what we want her for.'

'Certainly, Geoffrey! And what do we want her for?'

'I can see this is not your best time of day, Audrey! Wake up! I want the bloody girl as bait for Gerrard who, if we can take your word for it, is having all the pips dragged out of him! These bloody trigger-men ought to be castrated – the stupid bastards leave themselves wide open to being drawn in! Make sure Phelan knows what the bait's for, I want her kept in one piece until we've sorted Gerrard out; that means I want a woman to dangle under his nose not a bloody rag doll with a broken neck. Explain that to him. You know what the mad bastard's like, particularly if she gets up his nose.'

'Poor kid!'

'She might enjoy it.'

'Nobody enjoys Phelan, Geoffrey.'

'OK. When he's got her wrapped up and pliable, tell him to wait by her phone until we ring. Tell him I want her awake and in a fit state to coo into the mouthpiece – I don't want her spitting teeth and coughing blood while Gerrard's trying to reassure her that all is well. When that's been done Phelan's to get her out of London and down to Suffolk and wait there until we arrive.'

'You've forgotten something.'

'What's that?'

'You've forgotten Gerrard. He doesn't usually stay around women for long, so this one must mean something special. Isn't he going to object to Phelan walking in and messing around with his little play-mate?' There was an edge to her voice that had nothing to do with tension.

'Ring him back. Tell him you're ready to hear about his problems – invite him out for a cup of cocoa and a slice of cake while he bares his soul. That'll leave the hutch door unbarred. All Phelan has to do is invite himself in. Any more silly questions?'

'What if Gerrard decides to bring the girl with him?'

'Dissuade him. You'll think of a way. Incidentally – he's going to ask you for some help in looking me up.'

'Why me?'

'Because he hasn't got anybody else here. He won't get any joy from our friend; Sanderson's deserted ship; and I've made myself incommunicado. If my guess is correct the only person Gerrard knows who has any connection with anything over here is Audrey Gilling. You're going to let him persuade you to bring him to our front door.'

'You're joking, of course?'

'*Au contraire!* I want him at my place. I want him under my nose while I'm packing my books – I want him where I can see him, not hanging around in the shadows pulling faces at me in the dark.'

Audrey interrupted. 'Geoffrey, this man Gerrard's like a bloody razor blade! He won't be pulling faces – he'll be blowing your bloody head off! You underestimate this bastard and you'll be lying on the carpet kicking your life away before you've even had time to say "how d'you do"!'

'Calm down, Audrey. I don't think your friend Gerrard's going to want to do anything more violent than stroke my back after he's had a word with Charles Phelan Esquire and heard the young Miss Lambdon whimpering in the background.'

'You're a clever bastard, Geoffrey.'

'We need twenty-four hours, possibly forty-eight, for a clear run and this girl is going to supply that, provided, as I said earlier, that you've read the signs correctly. Let's hope that he didn't make a pig of himself last night and left nothing worth dying for!'

'Goodbye, Geoffrey.'

Audrey replaced the receiver and glanced quickly at the tiny watch on her wrist – fifteen minutes had passed since her conversation with Gerrard. It seemed much longer. She dug into an expensive crocodile-skin handbag and unearthed a small brown leather-covered address book. She left it open on the ledge while she dialled a number. Phelan's squeaky voice jarred into her ear.

She went straight into her act. 'The Frenchman – Gerrard, the one you know as Siegfried – has just arrived back in England. He's come to settle his account with Brocklebank. We want you to hold an end down while he's being dealt with . . .'

'Just a minute! Is there more than one Frog named Gerrard in this game?'

'No, just the one.' Audrey contained her surprise – and patience. She knew how to talk to Irishmen.

'Then I'm not with you,' squeaked Phelan. 'Somebody's feeding you sponge. I've got an operation mounted against this Frog in Paris – if he's here now then my man'll be here with him. The Frog's been marked by one of the best men in the business. If there's any end to be held down forget it. The Frog's dead – or as good as.'

'I don't know how I'm going to break this to you, Charlie – '

'Break what?'

'I think it's the other way round. Brocklebank thinks your little cowboy stumbled over the grown-ups' feet and has been put away.'

'Is that definite?' Phelan didn't sound too disappointed.

'I think you'd better assume it is. They do say that Siegfried hits the ball awfully hard when he's playing for money. I'd scrub your lad off the list if I were you. Can I go on with your instructions?'

'Where's the bastard holed up?'

'Charlie, I was told to tell you what's expected of you, not start you off on a one-man Macnamara. Are you going to listen intelligently or . . .?'

'Or what?'

'Take my advice, Phelan, this is a bit out of your league, stick to choir practice and leave the brain work to the people with brains.'

'You ought to think yourself lucky there's a few miles of wire between me and you, Gilling! Bloody lucky!'

'Or would you rather have a word first with the Managing Director about how serious it is?'

Phelan took his time. Over the silence, Audrey heard a match being struck, followed by a heavy exhalation of smoke – it calmed Phelan down and his voice pitched less painfully on her eardrums.

'I'm listening,' he grunted.

When she'd finished she added, 'And if you get it into your head to have a go at taking the Frenchman out yourself you might like to know that I'm taping at this end.'

Phelan made no comment on the warning – he wasn't stupid. 'Where's the Frog at this minute?'

'I'm going to get him away from there now. The girl'll be on her own. Treat her gently. Goodbye, Charlie.'

'Just a minute . . .'

'Be quick.'

'I want that Frog. When you bring him down to Suffolk your game'll be over. When you go I want the bastard handed over to me. With no conditions.'

Audrey paled at the thought, but didn't hesitate. 'Of course, Charlie. You have my word on that. D'you want me to tie him up myself?'

'Get stuffed, Gilling.'

Audrey laughed out loud. 'No thanks!' The chuckle died in her throat. 'Don't speak to me like that, Phelan.'

Audrey replaced the receiver with a shudder and left it sitting there for a few minutes while it cleansed itself of Phelan's nastiness. After she'd lit a cigarette she looked at her watch again and dialled the Highgate number.

Gerrard picked up the telephone at the first ring.

'Are you alone, Michel?' asked Audrey.

'Can we talk?' he responded coldly. 'And don't say anything clever – just answer yes or no.'

'Yes, darling! Tell Audrey all your problems.'

'What do the names Sanderson and Harris mean to you?'

Audrey was silent for a moment. Then, 'Not on the telephone, Michel. Can we meet somewhere?'

'Where?'

'Let's have coffee at the Ritz,' she said quickly. 'In . . .' she paused to look at her watch, 'how about forty-five minutes?'

'Forty-five minutes will be fine.' Gerrard was very definite. Audrey heaved a sigh of relief.

Gerrard replaced the receiver and strode across the thick white carpet. Melanie saw his feet approaching but kept her eyes on the open page on her lap. The feet stopped and her chin was gently raised by a firm hand. Gerrard kissed her mouth softly.

'Say it,' he ordered.

'Say what?'

'That you're not jealous.'

Her eyes flashed but she didn't pull her chin away from his hand. 'I am jealous!' she hissed. 'I hate that woman! I detest her.'

He kissed her lips again, and lingered.

She said huskily, 'Where are you meeting her?'

'It's better you don't know.'

'Better for whom? Oh, stop it, Melanie!' She suddenly smiled. 'There you are, you see, that's what happens when you trifle with a woman young enough to be your daughter!'

Gerrard grinned. 'Don't change.' He kissed her again. 'I like trifling with you.'

'Don't let it go to your head!'

CHAPTER 38

Murray threw another half-smoked cigarette out of the window and watched it roll slowly back down the pavement to join the small pile already collected on the kerb.

It was developing into one of those stifling, airless mornings – the aftermath of the storm that never was – sticky, heavy and bad-tempered. Murray had all the windows wound down but the featherlike breeze that trickled into the Scirocco did nothing to relieve him of the feeling that he was a jacket potato being crisply done in the Aga for lunch. He wiped his face and hands with a large handkerchief then stuck two fingers into the collar of his shirt to ease it away from his sweating neck. He loosened his tie and studied the effect in the rectangular rear mirror. As he straightened it back into position something made him look over his shoulder.

He was just in time to see the taxi turn slowly into the tree-shaded road behind him.

He turned back to his front and watched it through the mirror as it crawled towards him, the driver's head bobbing backwards and forwards as he looked for a number – or, as Murray fervently advised him under his breath, a yellow door?

The driver must have heard. His face relaxed as he passed Murray's parked car and his eyes alighted on the yellow door.

Murray blew a cooling sigh of relief over his sweating top lip and reached for another cigarette. He touched the end of it with the car's lighter, threw the newspaper off his knees and turned on the ignition. The engine purred silently into life. Murray listened to it for a few seconds, then eased himself into a comfortable driving position and gazed with new interest at the door to Melanie Lambdon's house.

The taxi stopped and the yellow door opened. They must have been waiting. Murray watched Gerrard walk towards the taxi. Alone? Where the bloody hell was the girl? Murray frowned at the small house and lowered himself a few more inches behind the wheel. He could still see

Gerrard holding the passenger door open as he spoke to the driver.

Then Gerrard turned his head briefly, raised a hand to the open yellow door and disappeared into the cab. Murray heard the taxi door close with a thud and watched it crawl towards the other end of the road. He relaxed and sucked contentedly on his smouldering cigarette. *That's the Frog out of the way. Now all we have to do is roll the girl up and when we're ready for him invite Froggy into our parlour for a conversation. Shouldn't be any problems there, provided they've struck up a reasonable friendship! But first things first – let's get sleeping beauty up on his feet and out into the world to earn his keep.*

It took Murray ten minutes to find a telephone; ten minutes while he was doing it to worry about Melanie Lambdon pulling on her trainers and jogging round the park – she was a quick little mover when she made up her mind, so Harry said. As if Harry knew anything about the way little movers moved. Must have been wishful thinking on Harry's part, unless he was talking about the way she played hockey!

He pulled open the heavy, spring-loaded door, lit a cigarette to kill the odour in the kiosk and dialled Harry Smythe's number. It rang steadily and boringly, and to pass the time he watched the local traffic warden giving himself a thrill staring at a 'C'-registration Sierra, its front wheels just intruding into two yellow lines. A rep's car. Murray grinned. He must be worried sick! The warden shook his head at it contentedly; his luck seemed to be better than Murray's.

Murray stared at the black receiver and let it ring ten more times before dropping it back into its cradle. He studied the face of the expensive watch on his wrist then dialled the number again. He held the receiver several inches from his ear and listened to the same monotonous flat ringing tone. The box was getting hotter and Murray's temper shorter, and his foot was beginning to ache from holding the door open. He wrinkled his nose in disgust at the overwhelming stink of the mixture of piss and unwashed sweat that riddled the phone box as he wiped the moisture from the phone's earpiece on his trouser leg. The buzzing changed to frantic pips. He waited another second then tapped the tenpenny piece into its slot and listened to the silence he'd bought.

'Anybody there?' he asked sharply.

Harry Smythe swallowed the foul taste in his mouth and said, 'Good morning, Murray.'

'How did you know it was me?'

'I don't know anybody else who'd ring me at this ungodly hour. What's the time?'

Murray grinned into the little cracked mirror. 'It's the end of night as far as you're concerned, Smudge. A lovely warm summer morning. Go and put your head in a bucket of lukewarm water and brush your teeth and meet me in Miller Street.'

'Miller Street? Highgate?'

'Ten out of ten, Smudge! The jet set's returned – they've all come back to see us and we're going on stage again. Don't take too long over it, you and I have got work to do. And, Smudger . . .'

'Softly, Murray, I've got a bit of a head.'

'Oh dear!'

'What were you going to say?'

'Before you put your coat on, strap that spaghetti-maker's tool under your armpit, will you, we're moving up into the trenches.'

Murray had added only two more smouldering cigarette ends to the pile in the gutter before a tall figure in a light-grey checked suit turned the corner and moved into the distorted oblong of the Scirocco's wing mirror.

Harry Smythe slid with difficulty into the passenger seat. His bony knees rested uncomfortably against the low dashboard but he smiled as he turned to Murray and helped himself from the packet of cigarettes on the ledge.

'And in response to your sympathetic enquiry,' he drawled, 'I don't feel at all well – I've got a mouth like a puppy's basket and a head like a wet coconut.' He lit his cigarette, turned a paler shade of green, coughed, and thought about stubbing it out, but changed his mind. 'So, what's going on, Murray? You've got a very serious look about you.'

'It's that bloody Frenchman again, Smithy. The bastard's back, as I prophesied a few days ago you'll remember, and he's moved in there with your girl-friend.' Murray pointed his cigarette at Melanie's house. 'Mademoiselle Lambdon's in there now. She's alone. The Frog's gone bounding off in a taxi somewhere.' He turned his head and looked at Harry Smythe. It brought a happy smile to his face.

Harry Smythe's cheerful expression had disintegrated. It reflected the true state of his head. He looked at the yellow door with the same serious expression that Murray had worn earlier.

'What do you want me to do, Murray?'

'Not a lot, Smithy,' grinned Murray. 'I just want you to go in there, talk to her nicely in the old Sloaney vernacular and persuade her to go on a little trip with you to Richmond. You know the house at Richmond?'

Smythe nodded pensively.

'Good,' continued Murray. 'Now, I've worked all this out while I've been sitting here in this bloody tropical paradise and you've been lying flat on your back, and I've decided there are two ways. Way number one – you go in and give Miss Melanie Lambdon a little peck on the cheek and tell her Michel Gerrard sent you to collect her because he's caught up in something important and he needs to see her urgently – something like that. You can roll it up into an acceptable package; something that an impressionable bird can nibble on, particularly one who's just spent the night lying on her back in the nest with an energetic Frenchman teaching her how to tango.'

Harry Smythe kept his own counsel. He pulled on his cigarette and looked hard at the yellow door. 'You said there were two ways. What's the other one?'

The grin vanished from Murray's face. 'You go in there and close the door quietly behind you. "Hallo Melanie, sweetheart," you say, then your rap her smartly across the knuckles with the barrel of that Italian thing you've got tucked under your armpit, and tell her that if she doesn't get her arse out of that house and into her car in record time you'll blow a hole in her foot.'

'And if that doesn't do the trick?'

'You blow a hole in her foot.'

Harry Smythe winced, as Murray knew he would. 'I think I'll give the first method a whirl,' he said weakly.

'I thought you might! The choice is yours. But don't let me down, Smudge. Whether she comes out with a smile of anticipation on her face or hobbling on one foot I leave entirely up to you – just so long as she comes out. D'you know which is her car?'

Harry Smythe nodded without enthusiasm. He leaned forward to stub his cigarette out in the ashtray and without a word unfurled himself from the front seat and quietly closed the door. He edged his thin frame between the Scirocco's nose and the rear of the orange Renault and gave Murray a finger shot as he passed the windscreen. He almost smiled at Murray's serious grin, but he let it go, he wasn't in the mood for smiles at the moment.

He pushed the button on the side of the yellow door and stepped backwards to look up and down the narrow street. It was like any other day in Miller Street, not a lot of movement and an almost unbroken line of vehicles parked along the kerbside. The leafy trees gave an impression of shade and tranquillity, but the shade was illusory, it was as hot here as anywhere else in London.

He turned back to the door when it was opened.

Melanie smiled at Harry Smythe, tentatively at first, then in surprise, but not disappointment. She'd changed into a lightweight navy linen dress which showed her figure exactly for what it was and highlighted the soft, almost blonde hair that fell in a controlled sweep across her forehead. She held the door open with her knee and stood balancing on one leg while she continued attempting to fasten a small diamond brooch to the knot of a silk scarf tied loosely round her neck. Harry studied her with approval. It was difficult in his state of health to keep the look of guilt from his eyes.

'Harry?' She smiled quizzically. 'At this time of day?' She made a pretence of studying her watch. 'I didn't think you normally left the party until this time! And you don't look well. Green about the gills and a funny look in your eye. You're not in love or anything, are you?'

Harry shook his head and returned a sickly smile. 'Had a bad night. Well, it was a good night actually but the effect is bad – I've got a monumental hangover. It needs coffee, hot and black – have you got any?'

'Of course. Come into the kitchen. But I haven't got a lot of time, Harry. I'm not trying to be unkind but I want to be in Bond Street by eleven. Why don't you come with me, the air'll do you good?'

'Ugh! It's too fresh for me at this time of the morning. And anyway, Bond Street's off your itinerary for this morning. But don't stand around, there's a good girl, go and put the coffee on.'

'What are you talking about, Harry?' Melanie turned sharply. 'What do you mean – off my itinerary?'

'Er, no Bond Street,' he repeated. 'I come bearing messages from one Monsieur Gerrard . . .'

'Michel?' Melanie's smile vanished like the sun behind a heavy cloud. 'How do you know Michel? You only met him briefly. What do you mean you've come from him? Come from where? He's only just left here. There's nothing wrong, is there?'

'Good God, no! Nothing like that.' Harry Smythe beamed cheerfully, but her knees had already gone. She sat down quickly on one of the kitchen chairs. 'Don't sit down,' he ordered. 'Go and get that coffee.' He pulled a chair out and sat at the end of the table near the door and lit a cigarette. 'I don't really know old Gerrard.' He pulled on his cigarette and coughed. 'But the people I work for have rather tenuous connections with him. We're all in the same pudding bowl so to speak – nothing sinister – just a little exercise.' The lies seemed to be sliding out quite well. Harry patted himself on the back and prepared a few more. 'So, if you'll pass me that cup I'll tell you what Monsieur Gerrard expects of you.'

Melanie poured him a large cup of coffee and one for herself and sat down opposite.

'Harry, I didn't know you were in this business.'

'What business is that, Melanie?'

'Don't play silly buggers with me, Harry. You know what business I'm talking about . . .' She stopped and stared at him. 'God, Harry! You of all people! Isn't there anybody left in London who does a normal job of work? Everybody I know seems to have taken up with the spy game. Really, Harry, you might have told me.'

Harry smiled sheepishly but before he could reply the front-door bell rang.

When the yellow door closed behind Harry Smythe, Murray lit another cigarette, loosened his tie, and relaxed back into his seat. He arranged the headrest so that it jammed uncomfortably into the back of his neck and settled down to watch the minute hand of the dashboard clock jerk its way round the small dial.

He felt a tiny touch of cramp intrude into the other aches. He eased one buttock off the seat, leaned as far as he could towards the passenger side, and waggled the offending leg around until the cramp disappeared. As he straightened up he saw the Royal Mail delivery van moving slowly towards him from the opposite direction.

Nothing to get excited about. Murray watched it incuriously as the driver manoeuvred the heavy van into a narrow gap and parked it with the two nearside wheels high up on the kerb.

Murray frowned. He continued to watch the van even after it had juddered to a standstill.

Murray slid down in his seat and lowered his head slowly until only his eyes showed above the dashboard.

The van driver moved across the front seat of his van and slid out of the cab on the pavement side. He clutched a small brown parcel, about the size of a shoe-box, under his left arm.

'Definitely not pillow games – not this one,' observed Murray to himself in a whisper as he watched the postman make his way unerringly to the popular yellow-painted door. *Because if I'm not mistaken we've got Volunteer Charlie Phelan of Her Majesty's Irish Republican Army strolling down Miller Street, Highgate, as if it was Springfield Road, Belfast, and Guin-*

ness time at O'Flaherty's! Murray's eyes hardened. He blinked to keep the perspiration from running down his eyelids as he watched Phelan turn into Melanie Lambdon's concrete garden. Phelan didn't hesitate; straight in and rang the bell as if it were the front door of Sinn Fein HQ.

Murray's thoughts came back from the realms of speculation to cold reality with a stomach-jarring thud. He slipped the .45 Browning out of its holster and began to unwind himself out of his seat; then he hesitated, grimaced as if in agony, and slowly subsided back out of sight.

Phelan hadn't moved. He was still standing on Melanie Lambdon's front doorstep looking every inch the conscientious postman. Murray continued to stare at him from below the dashboard. His eyes hardened. *Sorry, Harry – you're going to have to sort this one out yourself. Try one of your nice smiles and Phelan might pat you on the back and send you home. But I wouldn't count on it.*

Harry Smythe started guiltily at the sound of the front-door bell and looked fleetingly at his watch. Just like Murray to get itchy and want to push the ball down the bloody hill . . . No bloody patience that man, none at all – he's probably come to do the knuckle-cracking himself. Harry glanced quickly at his own knuckles and felt a gentle sweat break out somewhere between his shoulder blades. Melanie looked at him curiously as she got up to answer the door. He tilted his chair back on to two legs so that he could see out of the kitchen. When she opened the front door he saw the postman standing there with a parcel in his hands.

Harry let his breath out in a slow silent whistle of relief and allowed his chair to drop forward on to its four legs. He lit another cigarette, and drained his cup, grimacing as the bitter taste of coffee grounds hit his tongue. When he heard Melanie come back into the kitchen he looked up. The grimace froze. It wasn't Melanie. He was looking into the round tube attached to the end of the long barrel of a Luger.

Harry just had time to register the postman's pale-blue expressionless eyes before he died. His eyes remained focused on Phelan for a fraction of a second after the bullet tore through his brain. But it was only for an imagined moment and then the shutter came down and the brightness flicked off like a power failure, leaving a fixed, sightless stare. Harry Smythe didn't even realise he was dead.

And Phelan couldn't have cared less.

He left Harry Smythe twitching his life away on the kitchen table and turned back into the drawing room. He stepped over Melanie's crumpled figure and quietly shut the front door. He came back, opened the door to the stairway and stood listening. Satisfied with the silence upstairs he moved noiselessly on to the landing and checked each room, looking under the beds and in the wardrobes before moving back down the stairs. The ground floor took less time. He poked his head into the garden and closed and locked the french windows.

It had all been too easy.

He turned Melanie on her back. The side of her temple was already turning purple where he'd whacked her across the side of the head with a pocket sandbag. She'd gone down without a whimper. He didn't give it a second glance. He dragged her across the room and threw her roughly into one of the armchairs. Apart from an unconscious moan she looked as dead as Harry Smythe.

He ran briskly upstairs and came back with a handful of nylon tights. He shook out two pairs, tied her hands tightly in front of her, then her legs and feet and stood back, staring into her face. He seemed not quite happy with what he saw. He reached forward and slapped her twice across the face. Another moan came from between her lips, then a slight movement of her head. It was enough for Phelan – she'd be able to moan down the telephone. He turned his back without another glance and left her. She looked like an abandoned rag doll, finished with for the day, crumpled, unwanted and thrown into the armchair.

He half-filled a glass tumbler from a bottle of Teacher's and pulled up the other armchair. He looked neither happy nor content. He didn't look at the woman again; he rested his dirty boots on an expensive rosewood coffee table, closed his eyes and sat back and waited for the phone to ring.

CHAPTER 39

Gerrard walked through the main door of the Ritz, passed through the foyer, and spotted Audrey Gilling immediately in the tea room opposite.

As he pulled a chair out she smiled comfortably and peered into his face. 'You look dreadful, darling. Haggard – as though you've been up all night! Or did the young Lambdon take exception to the French rules and fight you off with her hockey stick?'

Gerrard's answering smile was tight. 'Pour the coffee, Audrey. The way I feel at the moment you stand a good chance of looking just like this before the day is finished!' He passed her a lighted Gitane then sipped his coffee. She had a feeling he meant what he said.

'About those names you mentioned over the telephone,' she began.

'Forget them. It was something else I wanted to talk about.'

She blew smoke delicately up to the ceiling and regarded him out of the side of her eye. 'But what do you know about General Sanderson?' she persisted. 'He's supposed to be quite – er, well . . . you know what I mean.'

Gerrard shrugged his shoulders. 'He told me all about himself when he took over paying my wages.'

Audrey's eyebrows shot up. 'I don't follow. Since when have we taken to paying Frenchmen to come over here and do our screwing for us?'

'Would you like to rephrase that, Audrey?'

Audrey didn't smile. 'You know what I mean.'

Gerrard nodded. 'Since somebody moved into your top-security echelon and made it impossible for a kill to be mounted against him by one of your own people. Sanderson called in a favour from his friends in Paris and I came over to help him out.'

'Old boy network? London and Paris? I don't believe it!'

'Try.'

Audrey reflected for a moment then widened her eyes. 'Why, the wily old sod! I can see it now. When you killed all those Irishmen at Mile End you were doing it for Sanderson? And hoping, presumably, to land his fish for him as well. Is that it?'

Gerrard didn't answer.

She frowned at him and, on a change of tack, said, 'The Irish know about you, Michel. They're very cross with you. They're planning to run you through a blunt bacon-slicer and send little bits of you all over the world in those tiny wedding-cake boxes. You've made them very, very angry, Michel.' She looked around the elegant surroundings, then pursed her lips and shook her head. 'Do many people know you're back in England?'

'Only you, Audrey.'

She thought about that for a moment, then said, 'What are you doing back here then? And what help do you need from me?'

'I've already told you. Sanderson's rabbit should've been in one of the plastic bags on the lawn at Mile End, but his luck went on a high.' Gerrard stared at her from across the table. 'I've come back to finish the job.'

'You know who he is?' Audrey lowered her gaze from Gerrard's eyes and crushed her cigarette out.

'Sanderson's flushed him out into the open. But I've lost Sanderson – he's vanished.'

'That's strange.'

'I agree. That's why I've come to you.'

Her expression betrayed nothing. She continued pounding her cigarette into the ashtray until it concertinaed like a Chinese fire-cracker. 'I honestly don't see how I can help you, Michel,' she said at length, and looked up. 'I'm no substitute for Reason, I'm not a field agent. If it's strong-arm stuff you want you'll have to look elsewhere. You know what my strong point is!' She managed a small smile. 'Administration, that's my forte.'

'I know your strong point, Audrey – and your forte. And neither of them's administration.' Gerrard smiled back at her. 'But you can relax, it's not muscle I want from you but two little bits of ferreting.'

'Ferreting?' Audrey tried to smile but her lips refused to move. 'You didn't say who this rabbit was that you're gunning for. Do I know him?'

'Gentleman who calls himself Brocklebank.'

'I don't know anybody of that name,' said Audrey, quickly.

'You said that almost without thinking.' Gerrard's smile remained in place. 'But there's no reason why you should know the name. It's not a real one but it's effective; it hasn't spun off anywhere – except to Sanderson and, recently, to me. But Sanderson's not around to pull the bits of thread for me – I've no access to British files.'

'So what *have* you got?'

'Two introductions to Mr Brocklebank's private auditorium. But they're roundabouts – I want you to pull them straight for me.'

'Let's try them one at a time.'

'OK. The first is an Irishman who goes by the name of Phelan. I've got an address – I want you to confirm it for me.'

'Where did you get it from?'

'It doesn't matter. Do you know the name?' Gerrard frowned at her, suspiciously.

'No,' she replied hastily. 'It's a common Irish name. It might be a face to the filers. I'll get them to run it through. What's the other cover?'

Gerrard sat back in his chair and lit another cigarette. He blew smoke at the ceiling while Audrey watched in silence. After a moment he leaned forward, scribbled the Limehouse bookie's number and printed the name BROCKLEBANK on a piece of paper, and passed it across the table.

'I want that number messed around with until it comes up in the right sequence. Then I want a name and an address put to it. Which do you want to do first – the Irishman, or that?' He tapped the piece of paper with the end of his cigarette. 'Or both?'

She shook her head and smiled weakly. 'I'll let you know.'

Audrey sat in the ladies' room for ten minutes and smoked two cigarettes. When she decided enough time had passed she slipped out of the main door, into Piccadilly, nipped down Arlington Street and back into the hotel through the other entrance. She stopped at the telephone in the hall and made a brief call. She listened for a few seconds, made no notes and after a brief glance over her shoulder, said, 'We'll be with you in about an hour – but expect us in less.'

When she got back to the table there were two large gins and tonic standing where the coffee cups had been.

She smiled gratefully and picked one up. She needed it. The ice cubes rattled cheerfully against the side of the glass as she brought it up to her mouth. Nothing was said. Gerrard looked very comfortable, patient, like one of the ambush party – the one at the pointed end who could see movement along the track. Audrey had the same feeling; but hers was the vulnerable feeling of being the one wandering into the ambush. But she couldn't quite make out why. She kept her eyes away from his and let the ice touch her lip as she took a tiny sip from her glass. It had a delicious numbing effect and helped move the sincerity screen into place across her eyes. She swallowed a little more, and put the glass down.

'Very nice,' she told him. 'Very thoughtful.'

Gerrard smiled evenly. 'Any luck?'

She touched her lips with the crisp white napkin and looked straight into his eyes.

'The address of the number is 16 Hillman Court, St John's Wood.'

'And the name?'

'Brocklebank. As you'd written on the paper.'

Gerrard drew slowly on his cigarette but didn't stop her.

'And the other thing – what was it? Oh, yes, Phelan . . . He doesn't live there any more. He was last seen with his brown cardboard attaché case, waving his grubby handkerchief from the deck of the ferry at Fishguard. You can forget him.' Audrey picked her glass up and sipped again, grateful for the opportunity not to have to look into Gerrard's eyes.

'Thanks, Audrey.' Gerrard raised his glass, 'Cheers!'

He listened to the ice cubes clunking solidly against the side of her glass, but she refused to meet his eyes, instead continued to swill the gin and tonic around nervously until it rose dangerously to the rim. When she'd got it over-excited she sipped again, delicately, and said softly, 'Michel, I can't let you go to this address on your own . . .' She looked up from the glass into Gerrard's eyes. 'I know that part of London very well. You'll need back-up. If this Brocklebank's as good as you say he is he'll have contingencies. I might be of help. Please let me come with you.'

'It might be dangerous.'

'Please?'

'I don't know what to say, Audrey!'

Audrey smiled modestly.

'That's Hillman Court, next on the left,' said Audrey and guided Gerrard down the wide tree-lined avenue. 'You can pull in and park anywhere down here.'

'I'm glad you came along, Audrey.' Gerrard gave Audrey's thigh a friendly pat. 'I'd never have found this place on my own.'

He pulled the Citroën into the kerb and switched off the engine. He looked up and down the road and saw that it was empty of passers-by. He turned in his seat and smiled, then, without warning, leaned across Audrey's knees and tugged fiercely at the panelling on the offside door. Audrey stifled a shriek. It died in her throat when Gerrard's hand emerged from behind the door panel clutching a snub-nose South African 9mm Mamba Automatic. He pushed himself away from her knees and cocked the weapon. It gave a solid and reassuring clunk.

Gerrard smiled sadly at Audrey's expression. He slipped the hand holding the pistol round the back of her head so that it dangled by the side of her face.

'Stretch your legs out and open them wide, there's a good girl,' he said quietly.

She stretched out as far as she could go, arching her back off the seat while Gerrard ran his free hand up and down the front of her body; then he urged her forward and gave her back the same treatment.

'If I wasn't so bloody scared I'd be enjoying this,' she said through clenched teeth. 'And if you've finished perhaps I can restore my lost decorum. You've made me feel like a five-quid tart, you bastard!'

'I'll pay you when it's over,' said Gerrard, coldly, and pushed her back into the seat. He wasn't rough, but it was enough to convince her the games were over; that somehow she'd wandered into the barbed wire. She looked hard, but could see no amusement in Gerrard's eyes when he reached under her outstretched legs and lifted her handbag on to his knees.

'Sit quietly, Audrey,' he warned her. 'Whatever you do don't move. This trigger's on a whisper, it could go off in your knee if you startle me.'

'I wish you'd tell me what it's all about, Michel. We are on the same side – aren't we?'

'I said quietly, Audrey.'

She clamped her lips tightly together and watched him unclip the flap of the Hermès crocodile bag; her eyes had lost their bemused look, she was no longer mystified, or curious; she was bloody scared, and didn't care who knew it.

Gerrard peered inside the bag. 'Well, well, well!' He smiled into her dark, worried eyes. 'I'm not a field agent. I'm a – what was it you said you were, Audrey?' He held up a small but businesslike French automatic pistol. 'And what do you carry this around for?'

Gerrard inspected the small weapon. He turned it over in his hand and tested its balance, then aimed it through the windscreen.

'Nice little weapon this, Audrey,' he said shortly. 'You like French guns, don't you?'

'Don't be coarse, Michel – it doesn't suit you.'

She watched disinterestedly as he reached over the back of the seat and jammed the small automatic into the side pocket of the back door. When he straightened up he emptied the rest of the contents of the bag on to her lap and riffled through the assortment of clutter that fell out.

He selected a small leather-bound address book and a bunch of keys from the debris and swept everything else off her lap on to the floor.

'You bastard!' she hissed. 'I need all that.' She bent forward automatically to retrieve her things and ran her face straight into the oily-smelling Mamba. She jerked her head back as quickly as if it had been its namesake.

'I didn't say move, Audrey,' said Gerrard reprovingly.

'Don't be so juvenile.'

He waggled the bunch of keys in front of her. 'Which of these opens the front door of 16 Hillman Court?'

'You're being a bore, Michel.'

Gerrard touched the tip of her nose with the Mamba and fanned the keys out in his hand. 'Last chance, Audrey.'

She refused to turn her head. She sat rigid, looking directly ahead at nothing. Her bottom lip was clamped bloodlessly between her teeth in a sullen expression of stubbornness.

'Have I got to hurt you, Audrey?'

'Sod off!'

He tapped the side of her head lightly with the automatic. There wasn't sufficient force behind the blow to cause pain, but Audrey didn't see it that way – the gesture was enough – the shock of the touch of metal sent a tremor all the way down to the pit of her stomach. She didn't try to hide it. She turned a white startled face towards him.

Gerrard nudged her again. 'Which key, darling?'

'Don't you darling me, you bullying bastard!'

Gerrard smiled. 'You haven't been properly hurt yet, Audrey. I'm only just getting in the mood. The next tap'll probably need about fifteen stitches to stop the flow of blood, so, point to the key – and be quick about it! That one, is it? Good. Thank you.'

'Drop dead!'

'I'm glad you mentioned that! Let's go and say hallo to your boy-friend.'

They walked across the paved courtyard in silence and passed through a pair of large iron-framed glass doors held open for them by an elderly veteran in a navy-blue uniform, and strode unhesitatingly across the hall to the waiting lift.

Audrey pressed the button for the fourth floor and turned to face him.

'What made you turn against me?' She broke her self-imposed silence in a voice like a child who'd broken one of the rules, but didn't know

371

which one. 'Was it something I said, or something I did?'

Gerrard folded his arms and leaned back against the padded interior of the lift; he looked down at her with genuine regret.

'It was both, Audrey. When I asked for your help this morning it was exactly as I described – I needed it. You were the only person I trusted – there was no one else in London I could turn to.' Gerrard stopped smiling. 'Then you made a big mistake – you mentioned the Irishmen's farewell party at Mile End.'

Audrey looked puzzled. 'I don't see how . . .'

'You wouldn't,' rasped Gerrard. 'But I'll give you a clue! The only people who knew it was I who pulled the plug were General Sanderson, a man in Paris, Clive Reason and his bang-maker friend – and one other.'

'Who was the one other?'

'The violin player, the man who looks after the IRA's intelligence in- terests in Whitehall – your friend who lives just along this corridor.' The lift door opened of its own accord and Gerrard surveyed the two passageways that led off in opposite directions.

'But I don't see how you can turn that into a black mark against me,' complained Audrey.

'But I can,' said Gerrard. 'Quite easily. Only one of those men could have told you about my involvement because he was the one who set the meeting up. He arranged for me to be there, but by some fluke, which he'll probably tell us about before he dies, failed to turn up himself to collect his share of Semtex. He's the man who told you how it happened, Audrey – Mr Brocklebank.'

'My God, Michel Gerrard, you've got a bloody nerve!' Audrey looked, and sounded, indignant. 'On that flimsy little pretext, and without asking for an explanation, you proceed to violate my body and bash me across the face with a pistol? How d'you know Reason didn't tell me?'

'He didn't,' stated Gerrard. 'But it doesn't matter because your second bit of stupidity would have been enough on its own. Your know- ing about the explosion only put me on my guard.'

'I can hardly wait to hear what it is I'm supposed to have said.'

'I wouldn't have thought you'd find this boring, Audrey. Look at all the fascinating things you're finding out about your chosen profession.'

'Are you going to be unpleasant again?'

'You must stop bridling at the word "profession", Audrey. It's begin- ning to show a niggle of complex under that lovely exterior. Do you want me to go on?'

'If you must.'

'Well, the really silly thing you did was to spend all that time in the ladies' lavatory at the Ritz and take only five seconds over your phone calls. All that walking up and down Piccadilly, Audrey! I hope it didn't give you ideas?'

'I wish I knew what you were talking about!'

'Audrey, you didn't ask anybody about the number I gave you. You called Mr Brocklebank direct. You didn't need to unravel it, you had the number in your head.'

'You followed me, you bastard!'

'I was in the lounge bar, round the corner from you, when you were doing your stuff. That was the quickest phone call I've ever seen anybody make. And, Audrey, about Charlie Phelan? You didn't wait for me to give you his address, you galloped off with just a name and told me he doesn't live there any more. Last seen, you said, waving his little handkerchief from the deck of the Fishguard ferry! Don't make me laugh, Audrey!'

'You clever bastard! Phelan won't make you laugh – in fact I'm rather looking forward to the two of you meeting . . .' Audrey glanced down at her watch, 'which might be a lot sooner than you expect.'

Gerrard took her by the arm. 'Don't get too optimistic, Audrey. Come on, let's go, I'm tired of standing in this lift. Which way?'

She inclined her head to the right, down the black and white tiled corridor and indicated a large panelled door with a discreet number 16.

'What are you going to do?' she asked, scathingly. 'Charge in like a rampant bull, shooting at everything that moves?'

He smiled. 'Sounds a good idea, but I think this is a better approach.' He took her hand and placed the keys in it, then, drawing the automatic from his waistband, urged her gently forward. He stood close behind her and hooked one finger firmly into the neck of her dress. 'Keep the thought running through your mind, Audrey . . .' he murmured into her ear, 'that if your friend in there gets nervous and starts shooting he's going to have to come through you before he can get at me. And if I get nervous I'll do the same! If I were you I'd start calculating the odds before you think of doing anything that'll make either of us itchy – you might end up being the only one to get hurt!'

Audrey shivered involuntarily but managed to speak in a normal voice. 'I've gone off you completely, Michel Gerrard. I never thought I'd ever hate a man as much as I hate you!'

'Shhh!' he warned and pulled her close so that her body was touching his. 'Tell me about it next time you come on heat.' He smiled grimly and gave a little tug on her dress. 'Don't talk any more. Open the door.'

Inside was a short passage with two doors – one to the right, and one further down to the left. Gerrard, with his finger hooked securely in the back of Audrey's dress, brought her to a halt in front of a large ornate mirror suspended over a heavily gilded credenza. He looked over her shoulder and studied her expression in the mirror. She showed no fear. He was puzzled, and wary.

'Why aren't you afraid, Audrey?' he asked in a whisper.

Her confidence was rising by the second. Gerrard frowned and tugged on her dress and started the question again, but the constriction round her throat made her cough.

This immediately brought a voice from behind the door on the right.

'Is that you, Audrey?' The voice didn't wait for an acknowledgement. 'I'm in here. Come on in – and bring Monsieur Gerrard with you.'

Audrey raised her eyebrows to Gerrard's reflection in the mirror. He nodded.

Her face, still blank, told him nothing. He didn't like it, she was far too calm – and so was the voice that came from behind the door. Gerrard felt a familiar tingling at the base of his spine as he urged Audrey towards the door.

Without hesitating she opened it.

He didn't give her time to say, or do, anything. He moved in quickly, pulling her in front of him as he lurched to one side of the door. There he stopped, his back firmly against the wall with both arms encircling her waist. He pulled her into him, tight, so that she gasped with pain, while the snub nose of the Mamba, poking snugly from between his clasped hands pointed directly across the room.

There was only one other person in the room.

A large man, powerfully built, stood by a large Georgian sideboard. He was relaxed and showed no surprise and continued pouring from a decanter into a heavy cut-glass tumbler. He finished what he was doing in his own time, replaced both glass and decanter on a silver tray and offered his hands to Gerrard in an open, almost deprecating, gesture.

'There's no need for that, my friend,' he said calmly. 'I knew you were coming. If I'd wanted to play bandits with you I could have had the entire floor filled with first-rate marksmen.' He inclined his head condescend-ingly. 'Tuck that thing in your trouser belt if you want, and although I'm sure little Audrey's enjoying her cuddle, I'd find it much more congenial to chat over a decent glass than across her shoulders.'

374

Gerrard ignored the man's words. 'Keep your hands exactly as they are,' he ordered. 'And walk towards me. Don't say anything more. Move slowly and do just as I say. That's it. Stop there. Now turn around.'

The man did exactly as Gerrard asked. His expression of amused tolerance remained intact when Gerrard pushed Audrey to one side and ran his hands rapidly over his body and legs. When he'd finished, Gerrard stepped back against the wall and, with the pistol now held by his side, said, 'Thank you. I'll have that drink now.'

'What'll it be?'

'The same as yours.' Gerrard smiled amiably. 'And from the same decanter, provided it's whisky.'

The man smiled back mockingly. 'You've been watching too much television, Gerrard! It's Grouse, will that suit you?' He didn't wait for Gerrard's agreement. He kept the smile in place and addressed Audrey: 'And you, my love? Something for your shattered nerves? I don't think I've ever seen you looking so hot and bothered – perhaps you'd like to go and tidy up first . . .?'

'No, she wouldn't!' barked Gerrard. 'Stay where you are, Audrey!' He didn't take his eyes off the man by the sideboard. Audrey hadn't moved an inch. 'Give her a gin and tonic,' he ordered. 'Then take your own drink and go over there and sit down on the sofa. You too, Audrey – go and sit beside him. I'll help myself.' Gerrard moved sideways towards the drinks tray and poured himself a good measure of Grouse from the decanter.

'Cheers!' said the man.

Gerrard nodded, and sipped from his glass.

'You've surprised me. I expected to be meeting Colonel Harris.'

The man on the sofa didn't reply immediately. He stared at Gerrard for several seconds over the rim of his tumbler then turned his head sideways to study Audrey's profile. She looked at neither man, and her eyes, centred on the far wall, remained expressionless; but in her nervousness she crossed her legs, and knew instinctively that both men were staring at her.

Gerrard lifted his eyes from Audrey's knees and met those of Mr Brocklebank again. Commander Roberts gazed back at him steadily, a trace of humour in his eyes, waiting for the next question.

'Where's General Sanderson?' demanded Gerrard.

Roberts hunched his shoulders and held out his hands like a Jew at prayer. 'Gone,' he replied. 'Vanished like a puff of smoke. One minute he was there directing the battle, and the next minute . . .' He made his tongue hit the roof of his mouth.

'Dead?' asked Gerrard.

The gesture again: 'If I thought that, and had the slightest proof of it, I wouldn't be leaving the sinking ship quite as quickly as I intend.' Roberts took time out to swig at his whisky, then ran his tongue over his lips. 'I don't know where you got that idea from, but if you'd like to take it from an old cynic you can scrub any thoughts about Sanderson lying flat on his back somewhere with pennies resting in his eye sockets. His sort don't succumb like us ordinary mortals. Take it from me, Gerrard, when the dust has settled you'll find our estimable General having a quiet few drinks with your lot over in Paris while events go according to his plans over here.'

Gerrard frowned. 'You say that with some conviction – have you any evidence to back it up?'

'I don't see why I need to back anything up,' said Roberts. 'It's what I think – and I'm usually right. Sanderson laid his plans and buggered off – he doesn't want to be available for any last-minute changes. You're as much involved in the devious old sod's thinking as I am – we ought to shake hands and stick our fingers up at him. You mark my words, Gerrard, I know the way the bugger's mind works.'

Gerrard ignored the lead Roberts had laid for him and asked, 'What, then, about Colonel Harris?'

'What about him?'

Gerrard's lips tightened. 'A word of warning, Roberts. If I'm going to have to claw answers out of you, phrase by phrase, then I might as well put you away now and move on to Audrey there. I'll ask the question again. Don't try to think of something clever, just say the first thing that comes into your mind. What about Colonel Harris?'

Roberts took heed of the warning. 'He's dead,' he replied.

'That's all you need to have said in the first place. You can tell me about it later.' Gerrard looked sideways at Audrey and felt a bead of perspiration detach itself from his shoulder blade, tickle its way down his spine to collect in a damp patch at his waistband. She looked too comfortable – too calm and relaxed on the large sofa; slim legs elegantly crossed – unexcited, like Madame Récamier waiting for the new boyfriend. She sipped delicately at her gin and tonic and, sensing his scrutiny, turned her head to glance mockingly at the automatic in his hand. There was still no fear or worry in her eyes and no panic in her manner. It worried him. It shouldn't be like this.

And there was something not quite according to the script about

Roberts too.

He should be cringing for his life; he should be shaking with at least a trace of pale fright in his ruddy complexion. There was none of it. He was as relaxed and at ease as if he were in his office gazing out at the shiny towers of the new London. Something was very wrong.

It was time to find out what it was.

Gerrard put his glass on the sideboard. 'OK, Roberts,' he said. 'You know why I'm here. Before I do what I've been paid to do pehaps you'd like to tell me why it's been made so easy for me?'

Roberts stared at him. 'I didn't think you people were supposed to have curiosity, Gerrard.'

'Call it a Frenchman's curiosity – it's different from everybody else's.'

'Is that so, Audrey?' Roberts turned his head and smiled enigmatically at the woman sitting next to him. He laughed briefly then turned back to Gerrard. His tone was serious. 'I don't think "easy" is quite the term I'd use. It's taken a lot of intelligent guile to get all the scenery and props into place . . . not easy, Gerrard. Not easy at all – unless of course I've read the whole bloody thing upside down. And I don't think I've done that. Have you not realised that I invited you here? That I wanted you here for a reason?'

Gerrard felt the patch of sweat turn to ice around his waist. He raised his glass from the sideboard, sipped from it and replaced it on the tray. Without a word he raised the automatic and brought it into a firing position. It pointed unwaveringly at Roberts's right eye.

'Time's up, Commander Roberts,' said Gerrard quietly. 'There's something about you that's making me feel uncomfortable. I think we'd better have you out of the way. Say goodbye to the lady.'

'Geoffrey! For God's sake stop playing with him!' Audrey broke her silence with a frightened gasp. 'Tell him quickly or he'll kill you! Please! I know him – he's going to do it.'

'Tell him what, Audrey?' Gerrard continued looking down the barrel of the small automatic at Roberts. But some of the conviction was fading. Gerrard's finger loosened on the trigger. He still hadn't tapped Roberts's fear ducts. But he'd spotted something else hovering just behind his bland expression – something like a fairly high trump card – and it was about to be flourished. Gerrard was running out of patience, and curiosity. 'Or better still, Geoffrey,' he said evenly, 'you tell me. But take her advice and make it quick because she's right, you haven't got a lot of time. And I'm not going to count to ten!'

Roberts gave in reluctantly. 'You can put that thing down, Gerrard.

You won't be using it, not on me anyway. You'll find what you're looking for over there . . .' He pointed his glass at the other side of the room. 'The telephone, Gerrard. That'll confirm your problems. Just stroll across to it in your own time and ring the number of the house you slept in last night.'

The entire contents of Gerrard's stomach turned over. He lowered the automatic fractionally for a better search of Roberts's expression.

'And what's that supposed to mean?' It was all he could think of saying.

'Would you like me to repeat the whole thing in French?' Roberts indulged himself in a small smile of triumph, but it was out of character and he allowed it to sink quickly into his glass as he raised it to his lips.

'I don't know who you're trying to impress with your wit, Roberts, but if it's me, you're losing.' Gerrard felt short of breath. He knew the symptom – fear. 'Because I'm just as inclined to put one of these through your head before you come up with another witty remark and then play games with Audrey. Tell me again, what d'you mean by "the house I slept in last night"?'

'For Christ's sake, Geoffrey!' Audrey butted in again. 'I've had enough of this. I've told you before – don't play games with him, he's not one of the hobnailed Provo brigade! If you won't tell him I will.' Audrey stood up and walked towards the sideboard. She held her empty glass out for Gerrard's inspection. He nodded and she proceeded to gurgle a large measure of gin into it then threw in a handful of circular ice globules. She watched the glass frost with condensation as she swirled the contents around, then reluctantly looked into Gerrard's narrowed eyes.

'We've got a man baby-sitting the Lambdon girl,' she said hurriedly. 'He's not a very nice man. You know his name . . .' Gerrard's face was set, and she swallowed nervously. 'Charles Phelan. A thoroughly unpleasant Irish thug. I don't know where you got his name from, but I hope they told you all about him.'

'You tell me.'

'Charlie Phelan is Ireland's number one blood-bath. At the moment he's sitting with Melanie Lambdon on his lap waiting for permission to get on with it.'

Gerrard didn't trust himself to speak. He was almost mesmerised by Audrey's moving lips and, without realising it, he'd lowered the Mamba away from Roberts's face so that it hung once again by his side. Audrey was still talking.

'Geoffrey here is the only man Phelan will listen to. Kill him, or even hurt him, and you kill Melanie Lambdon. This is the game you've allowed yourself to be brought to the table to play.'

Audrey stopped talking. She glanced briefly at Roberts, then back at Gerrard and almost smiled. The almost smile was a mistake.

Gerrard took a step towards her. She shuddered and stepped back quickly, but he ignored her and placed his glass on the tray. He then took two paces across the room and stood in front of Roberts.

'All right, Roberts,' he said, with a calmness that was all show, 'I'm going to assume that this bitch here,' he jerked his chin at a startled Audrey, 'is telling the truth. Tell me what you expect in return for Melanie Lambdon – untouched, unharmed.'

Roberts accepted the replenished glass from Audrey. He tasted the whisky, nodded approvingly, and looked up, unhurriedly, at Gerrard.

'I don't want you to assume anything,' he said casually. 'I want you to do what I asked earlier; I want you to ring the number. When you've spoken to your young friend, and then to my Irishman, we'll talk about the price you'll have to pay for her return. But a word of warning, Gerrard! Don't try to be clever. If you do she'll die. And that's the only promise I'm giving you. Now go and make that call.'

Phelan allowed Melanie only the one word. When he took the phone away from her Gerrard had gone. Phelan's day was ruined.

Gerrard threw the receiver on to the table and walked back towards the centre of the room.

In the silence the high-pitched voice could be heard screaming tinnily down the untended phone.

'Go and quieten your animal down,' Gerrard spat at Roberts and went back to the sideboard and poured a solid half-glass of Grouse down his throat to kill the worms wriggling around inside his stomach.

Roberts put the phone down and came back to his place on the settee. 'You might be a fairly high card in the extermination game, Gerrard,' he said, 'but I wouldn't pay you tuppence for the amount of tact you carry around with you.'

'I'm not interested in what you think, Roberts.'

'Oh, yes you are – unless you want to hear another couple of screams from little Shirley Temple! You're not dealing with rational beings, Gerrard – you're dealing with Irishmen, and with Phelan you've hit rock-bottom. I suggest you start counting up to a hundred and ten before saying what's on your mind.'

Gerrard wasn't impressed. 'You can forget the bullshit, Roberts. Just tell me what the price is.'

'Not high,' said Roberts with a smile, 'provided you take into account that you're the fellow hanging on the stirrup and I'm the one who decides where we go and whether we trot or canter.'

'I asked you what you wanted for the girl, Roberts.'

Roberts shook his large head benignly and allowed the smile to drift away. 'I want you out of my way for twenty-four hours while I go about my business. I can't afford to have you sniffing around, turning over the traces and generally making a bloody nuisance of yourself. I want to make an orderly departure. I don't want you getting in my way. Agree to that and in two days, probably less, you can have your young playmate back, sound, and hopefully none the worse for wear.' He gave a little apologetic shrug of the shoulders. 'Well – almost none the worse for wear.'

Gerrard stared into Roberts's face, as if recording it for future reference, then tucked the pistol into his waistband and buttoned his jacket.

'Agreed,' he said tonelessly. 'Goodbye.' He turned towards the door.

'Sorry, Gerrard. It's not that easy!' Roberts almost smiled again. 'When I said I want you out of my way I didn't mean that literally – in fact I meant quite the opposite. I want to be able to see you right up to the minute I empty the sand from my shoes. I want you to come on a little trip with Audrey and me. We'll take your car in case somebody suddenly notices odd little bits of paper, and other things, missing from my waste-paper basket and starts looking for me.'

'Get to the point, Roberts,' said Gerrard, his voice tight with fury.

Roberts didn't take umbrage – he was on the winning side. He beamed into Gerrard's face. 'You're going to drive us all to the seaside – where, as a small bonus, you'll be reunited with Freddie's little girl. How does that suit you?'

'When do you want to go?'

'Now.'

'Let's get on with it.'

'Do I have your word on thirty-six hours' quiet co-operation?' Roberts half extended his hand, thought better of it, and dropped it to his side.

Gerrard didn't hesitate.

'You have my word,' he said brusquely. 'And don't forget that your life depends on the girl's welfare as well, so, if you can remember how to do it – and any of the words – start praying that your animal keeps his hands off her.'

CHAPTER 40

'Stand up!' squeaked Phelan in Melanie's ear.

When she didn't respond he dragged her out of the armchair, slapped her face twice to wake her ideas up and stood her on her feet. He left her swaying while he bent down and untied her legs. He threw her back in the chair and allowed her one scream when the blood rushed into her feet; then he hit her again – hard. She bit the second scream into a whimper.

When she'd partly recovered the use of her legs he dragged her across the room towards the front door. He propped her against the wall and put his face close to hers. The smell of whisky, tobacco and the foulness of his breath repelled her. But she now knew enough to keep her revulsion to herself.

'In a minute,' he hissed, 'we're going out through that front door and into the street. We're going to walk along to a post-office van parked by the kerb. When we get to it you're going to climb into the back – quietly; no fuss, understand?'

She turned her head and closed her eyes. She thought that would be sufficient acknowledgement.

It wasn't.

He slapped her face again. 'I said: understand?'

Out of the corner of her eye she could see Harry Smythe's legs jutting out from behind the partially closed door. She hadn't realised what incredibly long legs he had – it was almost as if they'd stretched in death. It gave her something to think about. She averted her eyes quickly and looked back into Phelan's face.

'Yes,' she whispered.

'Right. Put your shoes on and pick that coat up. Here, give it to me. Hold your hands out.' He draped the coat over her arms to hide her bonds. 'And pray like fuck somebody doesn't come up and ask you the time!' He didn't smile. The Luger was cocked and in the open brown-paper parcel – and Phelan's hand was in there with it.

He slammed the bright yellow door behind him and stepped out in the sunlight.

After a quick glance up and down the street he took Melanie's elbow and pointed her to the right. 'You see that red van?' he muttered.

She nodded.

'Good. Then walk towards it naturally and stop when you get to it. I'll be right behind you, and don't forget – do anything stupid and you'll hear a little pop; it'll be me shooting you in the back. You won't feel anything – not until you wake up on the pavement and find you've got nothing to make your legs move.' He made it sound like an invitation to coffee and the promise of a Danish pastry. Melanie shivered in spite of the warmth. Phelan took her arm again and steered her towards the post office van.

'Stop here!' Phelan spoke without moving his lips.

He angled himself against the side of the van and studied the parked cars along the kerbside. He saw nothing to upset him.

He opened the big rear doors and beckoned Melanie towards him. She stepped gingerly off the pavement and waited. He turned her by the arms so that she faced him with her back to the open van. He allowed himself another quick look over his shoulder, another glance round the side of the van's body – then he pushed her. He did it suddenly and without warning. She had no time to cushion the fall and hurtled helplessly backwards into the van. No time to scream; no chance to save herself, her head crashed against the hard metal ribs of the floor with a sickening thud and as her legs came up Phelan grabbed her ankles and slid her on her back until she lay full length on the floor of the van. Shocked, and dizzy with pain, she tried to raise herself, but another upward jerk on her legs sent her crashing back on to her head again.

It was enough. With a quiet gurgled moan she slipped back for the second time, almost gratefully, into a deep, black, bottomless pit.

When the yellow door opened Murray lowered the back of his seat and slipped completely out of sight. He stayed there, flat on his back, until Phelan and Melanie disappeared behind the post-office van.

He waited until the postal van passed him before springing the seat back into its upright position. He jettisoned an almost untouched cigarette through the window, started the Scirocco's engine, and with a grunt of relief at the prospect of a change of scenery manoeuvred the car out of its slot. He mounted the pavement with a jarring thump, reversed rapidly and brutally until he faced down Miller Street, then cooled down and moved cautiously in Phelan's wake.

They trickled in procession through the centre of London. Phelan was on his best behaviour.

Murray hung well back, keeping two or three cars between himself and Phelan as they crawled through Aldgate, twisted into Commercial Road and settled down at thirty miles an hour. Orange traffic lights, zebra crossings, and all the laws of the road, written and unwritten, were scrupulously observed by Phelan.

Murray whistled cheerfully through his teeth as they slipped into Limehouse, out again, then on to Poplar and straight past the Blackwall Tunnel. *Where the bloody hell's he going then?* Murray stopped whistling and tried another cigarette. He didn't have time to light it.

The van's left indicator flashed briefly and it slid off the overpass and dropped down into Canning Town. The Scirocco crept shyly behind it. Phelan did a sharp left and immediately flashed his right indicator to turn into the Donovan Place cul-de-sac.

Murray stayed on the Barking Road. He'd seen enough. He continued for a short distance and pulled into the first petrol station he came to.

He took a chance and tossed the keys to a slack-jawed attendant.

'Fill it up, son,' he told him, 'and check the oil and battery. If I'm not back when you've done that move it out of the way. There's a couple of quid in it for you. OK?'

He didn't wait for the boy's response. He moved quickly, just short of a jog, back to the turning where the van had left the main road. He looked up at the street sign: Donovan Place, a good address for an Irish patriot. He glanced casually to his right before stepping off the kerb, and saw Phelan's van parked half-way down the road. And no way out but this – it said so with a capital 'T' in red and white on a pole at the entrance to the cul-de-sac.

Murray walked past the end of the road; only one other vehicle – a light-blue, late-registered Transit backed up close to the back of the post-office van. He didn't look again down Donovan Place but carried on another hundred yards along the road then turned back.

The blue Transit now stood on its own, pointing in the right direction. There wasn't a soul about. Murray allowed himself another sideways glance as he crossed the road. But he didn't linger.

He walked slowly back to the petrol station. On the way he found himself an unvandalised telephone box outside the local working men's club.
It was nice and clean. He lit a cigarette and dropped the spent match on
the floor.

'Murray here,' he said when the phone answered. 'If I cut off suddenly
don't wet your knickers. I'm running after a face named Phelan. Yeh,
Phelan – pee, aitch . . . Comes out of the Falls, and listen; he's stopped
off for his Guinness and chips in Canning Town so I haven't got a lot of
time. No – I said listen, and don't ask bloody questions! Harry Smythe
went into a house in Miller Street, Highgate; number 14, bright yellow
front door – have you got that?'

'What about it?'

'He didn't come out.'

'What happened to him?'

'Fucked if I know! Go and have a look will you.'

Murray replaced the receiver. He wasn't laughing. His jaw-bone
stood out in a jagged line from his face and his teeth were clamped together in a hard, set expression. Murray had been quite fond of young
Harry Smythe.

He walked slowly back into the petrol station forecourt, paid his bill
and dropped two brass coins into the open hand of the black attendant.
He reached inside the car and turned the key to check the petrol gauge –
the dial flashed 'full'. He grinned at the lad and hoped it was petrol and
not water.

Twenty yards along the road he drew into a pub car-park, switched off
and waited.

The wait was three-quarters of a cigarette long. Murray was glad he'd
resisted the temptation to dash in for a quick pint. He'd have been just
about half-way down it as the blue Transit edged its way into the stream
of traffic heading east.

He ducked out of sight as it passed the pub and allowed two or three
cars to fill the gap before joining the slow procession. He overtook the
van once – as it crawled past the Boleyn at West Ham – and made sure it
was Phelan at the controls, then dropped back again a few cars behind.

Barking came and went and they moved across the Dagenham hinter-
land and cut into Eastern Avenue. When Phelan took the left swing at
Gallows Corner Murray casually overtook him – just in case the Irishman was getting edgy about a black Scirocco playing silly buggers behind
him, then dropped his speed to that of Phelan and stayed where he was,
cruising half a mile ahead with nothing to worry about except lunch.

384

The pale-coloured Transit stood out in the Scirocco's rear mirror like the Eddystone lighthouse and Murray was able to relax as they joined the A12 and cut into the nowhere regions of East Anglia. He let the van pass him occasionally, and even had time to buy himself a packet of crisps and a tin of warm shandy at a service station – it was a poor substitute for a pint and a wedge of home-made pork pie, but Murray wasn't complaining. So far, apart from Harry Smythe probably having been sifted into the urn, it hadn't been too bad a day . . . And it wasn't even raining.

CHAPTER 41

Gerrard drove in silence and without haste through the eastern out-skirts of London.

Roberts, at least, seemed relaxed and in no hurry. He appeared totally unaffected by the strained atmosphere inside the Citroën; the only thing that seemed to be disturbing his peace of mind was the smoke from Gerrard's Gitane that swirled around his head. He wound down the window a few inches to change the air and breathed deeply.

'Ever been to Suffolk?' he asked Gerrard when they hit the A12.

'No.'

'You haven't missed anything.'

'What happens in Suffolk?'

'Passage to fairyland – snow and pink vodka.'

'Geoffrey?' Audrey leaned forward from the back seat. 'Why don't you draw him a map, save him a bit of time when he decides to come and kill you?'

'Gerrard's not coming to Russia to kill anybody, Audrey.' It was a message for Gerrard wrapped in a warning. 'Am I right, Gerrard?'

'It's your argument, Roberts.'

Audrey ignored Gerrard. 'I'll ask you that question again if, when we get along the road, we find that Phelan's eaten his girl-friend.'

'Read your book, Audrey, there's a good girl!' Roberts didn't look round or move his head. 'Did Sanderson suspect me?' he asked Gerrard.

Gerrard made no reply.

'I don't suppose he could have done,' Roberts answered himself. 'Because you obviously hadn't a bloody clue, had you? You thought you were crawling into bed with Harris.'

'Roberts,' said Gerrard, 'I said I'd drive you to wherever you were keeping Melanie Lambdon. I didn't say I was going to sit here chatting with you about your dirty habits.'

Roberts didn't take umbrage – he actually smiled. 'I'd have thought a man in your occupation, Gerrard, would always be interested in another's dirty habits. Don't tell me that you're taking up the Bible and sticking your thumb in your ear because some young girl let you put your hand between her legs?'

Gerrard wound down his window and threw his cigarette out into the slipstream. He left the window down, the noise of the rushing wind drowning out any attempt at further conversation. After several miles of cleansing air his curiosity got the better of him. He wound the window up again and lit another cigarette.

'Tell me about your dirty habits, Roberts.'

Roberts looked sideways. 'I thought I hadn't misjudged you! OK. When did the Soviets turn me? Don't bother asking, it's the inevitable first question.'

'OK, I won't.'

But Roberts did want him to ask. He was dying to tell him. 'I wasn't turned,' he said without pause. 'I've always been on their team.'

Gerrard raised his eyebrows. 'I thought Communists were made – not born!'

'I'm talking about nationality. I was born in Kiev, Leonid Agaronoff – my old man was a cowherd – hadn't got a brain in his bloody head. I was bright, good at languages. They marked me down for an Englishman when I was fourteen. That's efficiency of the System! Never left the Soviet Union until I was twenty-two – I'm a patriot, not a bloody traitor!' Roberts managed a grunted laugh.

'How do you make that out?'

It was the right question.

'I changed places in 'Forty-nine with a twenty-year-old Intelligence Corps sergeant – National Service – on his way home for demob after ten months in Berlin. You probably don't remember the Hook of Holland – the bloody place was swarming with England's red-blooded youth drinking their way back to civvy street. Our boy was handpicked. A Welsh lad from Caerphilly – Geoffrey Roberts, fitted the bill all the way down to my size shoes. We had some lovely little things about at the time – willing young Swallows – the poor bloody deprived British squaddie in the Forties could hardly tell the difference between a Zulu and a Swede, let alone a Russian girl and a Dutch one! It wasn't too difficult – Geoffrey Roberts told her everything about himself. He's probably still buried there in Schiedam – crumbling bones underneath a new shopping arcade . . . !'

'You're romancing, Roberts.'

'Am I buggery! I went straight into the Met' and three years later was in Special Branch. You see, I'd learnt a bit of Russian in Berlin! They liked that!'

'What about Roberts's parents – his family?'

'Father killed in the war. No brothers or sisters; just a mother. She died of natural causes at about the time her son was demobbed.'

'Natural causes?'

'Forensic in those days wasn't what it is now! I went straight to sleep – I was a long-term project, but when Centre saw me moving up the scale in the Branch they began covering my tracks. I think they saw a future Commissioner of Police in the making. Everybody who'd had any contact with me – even the dear little Swallows – went into the ice tub. I was taken off the files and known only as a number at Dzerzhinsky Square, and even then by no more than three individuals at a time. Total anonymity!'

'So why the death wish?'

'What d'you mean?'

'The Irish.'

'Ah, the Irish!' Roberts shook his head and thought about the Irish for several minutes. Gerrard didn't push him, and Audrey was bored with the conversation; she stared out of the window at suburban Ipswich. Roberts came back to life.

'The Irish were one of the biggest mistakes made by the KGB since they allowed Philby to be uncovered – but that's another story. The whole structure of my security, built up over years of anonymity, was jeopardised the minute my name was reactivated and handed to the IRA. Christ knows what Moscow Centre thought they were doing – it was a weak link in the chain, they listened to somebody instead of chopping his bloody head off!' Roberts reflected for a moment then gave Gerrard a sad smile. 'It's the America factor again. The KGB's obsessed with following the Yanks down any rocky path they choose to take. They knew the Americans were probing the IRA structure – Christ knows for what purpose; only they know that. But it's the same bloody story – if the Yanks are interested then there must be something there for us. We've always had a good working relationship with the IRA political wing through our Dublin Embassy but never a direct military involvement. Some silly bastard decided that we'd start along the road to nowhere by offering them the best source of Intelligence any country had in another's security structure. That was the beginning of my end. Moscow wouldn't listen even when I told them that it would mean the end of Geoffrey Roberts, future Commissioner of the Metropolitan Police. I started packing my files the day it was broken to me.'

'Are you taking anything with you?'

Roberts tapped the briefcase between his feet. 'Not a lot! Only enough to neutralise Britain's intelligence network in just about every country in the world. They'll have to start again, there'll be nobody left – it'll take ten years for them to get back to where they are at the moment. I've also got a bit of American stuff as well, but they're a bit more tricky. Still . . .?' He shrugged his shoulders and left it at that.

Gerrard looked askance. 'That should earn you a decent pension. And a nightmare or two.'

The prospect of nightmares didn't appear to upset Roberts. 'Pension's guaranteed,' he said. 'I also hold the equivalent rank in the KGB to a British Army brigadier – that'll increase when I move behind my desk in Yakutskaya Street.'

'Maybe they'll pay you by the head!' Gerrard was bored with Roberts's prospects. He changed the subject. 'What alerted Sanderson to the leak?'

'Somebody nudged the CIA that British Intelligence circles had been infiltrated near the middle to top. They in turn tried to get the SIS excited but I think the word was too vague – interest faded and then the Anglo-American old-boy network came into play and it was "a word in your ear, Richard!" that started him off. But you can't underestimate that old bugger. Look at the way he played the Lambdon card. I hadn't got a bloody clue that Lambdon wasn't what he seemed to be. I assumed that everybody had a price and Lambdon had got the right one. But I was wrong. Funny though – I thought we all had a price. Do you have a price, Gerrard?'

Gerrard stared out of the windscreen but said nothing. Roberts was undeterred.

'Of course you have,' he said softly. 'She's lying flat on her back somewhere further along this road, with an evil Irishman standing over her with his cock in his hand waiting for the starter's gun to fire.'

Gerrard didn't stop staring, but the muscles in his face were stiff with the effort.

'And what about you?' continued Roberts, conversationally. 'The way he managed to con the people in Dublin that you were the only one with the right-size balls for the job was a classic. He told me he suspected the IRA had bought themselves a French trigger-man for something special but he couldn't place him, or what the job was to be; he said he'd got this whisper from a good reliable contact in Paris. Very reliable, he said – almost unimpeachable. Christ! I couldn't believe my ears. He put a large whisky in my hand and said, "Geoffrey, I want this bugger, whoever he is – I want him found and I want his every movement logged. But most of all, Geoffrey, I want to know what he's up to. I'm very worried about him, Geoffrey," he said, "so get your ear down and find out what it's all about." You'd have thought by the expression on his face that the end of the bloody world was round the corner!' Roberts snorted into his handkerchief. 'It gave you the green light as far as I was concerned. My word counted. If Sanderson wanted you that badly and showed signs of having first-degree burns around the anus over it, then that was good enough for me!'

A word of caution came from the back of the car. 'Don't you think you've told him enough now, Geoffrey?' Audrey leaned forward to join the two men. Gerrard looked over his shoulder and briefly caught her eye. It took her by surprise – she'd discarded the bitch and let in a reminiscent look of the moonlight kitten. She dropped it quickly. But not quickly enough.

Gerrard said, 'How did she come to be swimming in your stretch of water? Did she come with the blankets – or did you bring her over from the fatherland and worm her into the business?'

'Let him find his own answers, Geoffrey!' Audrey reached forward and touched Roberts's hand. He looked at hers for a moment, then patted it gently, almost affectionately.

'I agree,' said Roberts, and changed the subject. 'I gather you've never met the good Colonel Harris, Gerrard?'

Gerrard shook his head.

'Well, don't bother looking – you never will now. I gave him to Phelan – that's the guy wet-nursing little Melanie Lambdon. Funny how everything seemed to close in at the same time – poor old Peter!'

'Where is he now?'

'Christ knows! Phelan's probably buried him in his back garden; I don't know what these mad bastards get up to – I never ask for details. At the moment I'm just hoping we can prise him away from your girl.' Roberts didn't wait for comment from Gerrard; he stuck out a stubby forefinger and pointed up the road. 'D'you see that sign there? Turn right and go slow. Carry on down the road. Be careful, it's a twisty road and you might have problems with your steering being on the wrong side of the car.' He laughed cheerfully to show he was relaxed. The worst was over, they were almost up and away.

Gerrard drove slowly into the village. Roberts pointed down the narrow street. 'Take the left fork and you'll see a pair of gates about two hundred yards further down. Turn into the drive and follow it right up to the house – and Gerrard, don't get out of the car until I tell you to. There'll be a rifle aimed at you the minute this car is sighted from the house so just sit tight for a minute or two. Audrey'll keep you company – won't you, Audrey?'

The house was old and sat low against a wooded background of large elm trees. These were interspersed with a secondary jungle of self-sown seedlings and a mixture of cultivated forestry. A three-quarter-acre shrubbed lawn emphasised the stark whiteness of the building and from its walls the odd oak beam stood out in contrast to the plain front façade. In front of it the road split the lawn down the middle and ran into a semi-circular gravelled entrance.

Gerrard stopped the car on Roberts's instruction and switched the engine off. The silence was audible.

'I'll take that gun from you now,' said Roberts quietly, and held his hand out. 'Do it ever so slowly,' he warned in a lower voice, 'Phelan'll have a telescope sight on you right now, probably focused on one of your eyes, so don't make any sudden or threatening movements.' He waggled his chubby fingers. 'The gun, please.'

Gerrard stretched his body stiffly and straightened his legs out under the steering wheel. He took the Mamba from his belt slowly, held it delicately between his thumb and forefinger and passed it carefully into Roberts's safe-keeping. Roberts smiled his thanks and pocketed the snub-nosed weapon. He repeated his warning again about not moving and disappeared into the house leaving Gerrard and Audrey alone in the car.

'Michel . . .' A softly whispered voice came from the back of the car.

Gerrard ignored it. He was busily inspecting the windows of the house.

'Michel, listen!' insisted Audrey. Her voice was urgent and compelling.

'I'm listening,' grunted Gerrard. He'd spotted it – the far end first-floor window; wide open with the latch swinging freely and the curtains tucked untidily to one side; the interior of the room was dark, but that's where he'd be; tripod, rifle and gunner – all standing deep inside the room.

'What do you want?' He kept his eyes glued to the window.

'Phelan's going to kill you, Michel. He won't give you a chance. The minute Gerrard and I clear the house Phelan's been ordered to put you away. As far as Roberts and Phelan are concerned, you're already dead.'

'What about the girl?' Gerrard spoke between his teeth without moving his lips. He kept his face pointing dutifully towards the front, making sure he was in full view of the window with the open curtains. He moved his eyes fractionally to one side of the window and caught the suggestion of a movement – a white shirt picking up the glimmer of a stray light at the back of the room. But the knowledge meant nothing – except that Roberts didn't bluff. So what? And why should he? Gerrard felt a tiny muscle twitch in his right eye as if it were irritated by the hair-lines of a telescopic sight zeroed on to it. He asked the question again.

Audrey seemed to be having difficulty with the conversation she'd started. The silence from the back of the car was broken by the agitated flicking of a cigarette lighter. After a second it was followed by the softest of whispers – an apologetic, unhappy whisper.

'I'm sorry, Michel, it wasn't meant to be like this.'

'Oh? What was it meant to be like?'

'Like . . . Well – I think you should assume she's dead. I'm sorry, but we haven't got time to waltz around the subject.'

'Are you sure?'

'No, but I know Phelan. And Geoffrey wants both of you out of the way. Will you take advice?'

'From you? You must be joking.'

'Listen, you ungrateful bastard, I'm trying to help you! About Melanie Lambdon? If you get an opportunity try a gentle probe on Phelan – see if he's still got her in one piece. Not that I think it's going to make any difference, her name's already been ticked off. Phelan'll kill you as soon as blink. And, Michel, if you're going to try and make a bolt for it cut down your odds and wait until we've gone. Another thing, if Melanie is still in one piece, the chances are that Phelan's got her wired to a bomb – bombs are his speciality so for God's sake make sure you know where he's put her before you try to ram his teeth down his throat!'

'Why this sudden compassion, Audrey – and interest in my welfare? You're not expecting me to climb over the back of the seat and have a farewell quickie to show my gratitude, are you?'

'Don't kid yourself, you supercilious bastard! You've had all you're ever going to get from me. I was just trying to undo something that I regret.'

'You disappoint me. I forgive you, Audrey!' He glanced quickly at the first-floor window. White shirt had gone. The room was empty. 'How about a farewell kiss then?'

She was surprised, but it only took her a second to get over it. She leaned forward between the seats and, half standing, kissed the side of his mouth. As she built up enthusiasm, Gerrard's hand crept round the back of the seat and fumbled urgently in the pocket on the back door. Before she sat down Gerrard had retrieved the small French automatic he'd taken from her bag in St John's Wood. He stuck it between his thighs.

'Goodbye, Audrey,' he said. There was no warmth in his voice.

'You wouldn't understand, Michel, would you?'

'No,' said Gerrard. He carefully slipped the automatic under his shirt and jammed it into the front of his waistband.

'I could have loved you,' she said softly.

'Goodbye, Audrey,' he said again. 'But just a minute. Before you go –'

'What?'

'Two things . . .'

'Quick!'

'Who decided that Melanie and I go in the hole?'

'Roberts – all on his own. He told Phelan to kill you both. What's the other thing? Too late! They're coming! Watch Phelan – he's coming in from behind . . .'

'I've seen him. Tell me – when and how are you two leaving?'

There was no reply from Audrey, just an exaggerated exhalation which sent a stream of smoke scurrying over Gerrard's shoulder to eddy in a shapeless cloud through the open front window. It was pushed aside by the long barrel of a marksman's rifle that stopped with its muzzle resting lightly in the soft patch behind Gerrard's earlobe.

The now familiar falsetto followed it in. It came from an out-of-sight area; a patch of dead ground near the rear door of the car.

'Get out slowly, Frog. And stand still! Right – turn round and put your hands on the roof of the car.' He took his eyes off Gerrard's back for a fraction of a second. 'Search him,' he hissed at Audrey.

'No need,' said Roberts as he came up from the house. 'I've taken his gun from him. He's got nothing else.'

'Search him!' repeated Phelan.

Audrey shrugged her shoulders and ran her hands over Gerrard's body. Her heart wasn't in it. If she felt the small automatic it made no difference. 'That's all he's got on him,' she pronounced, and placed a silver Dupont, a packet of cigarettes, a leather wallet and a small credit-card holder on the bonnet of the Citroën.

'OK, Phelan,' said Roberts, 'put that stuff in your pocket and bring him inside. And keep your eye on him – he's a tricky bastard!'

'So am I!' rasped Phelan. 'I wish he'd try a couple of his tricks on me!'

'Just get him in here, and stop waving that bloody elephant gun around.' Roberts turned his back on the group and disappeared through the side door of the house.

The interior offered a welcoming coolness from the sweaty heaviness of the temperature outside. But the welcome stopped there. It was an unlived-in house and Gerrard's nose twitched at the overwhelming smell of mustiness. It had all the quality and homeliness of an underground car-park. Audrey didn't stare around like a woman seeing a house for the first time – she knew the place and Gerrard followed her through the main room into a large farmhouse kitchen. She walked round the table towards the window that looked out on to the garden and rested her back against an old stripped-pine dresser. There she folded her arms and surveyed the rest of the party. Gerrard exchanged a brief glance with her. He felt a glimpse of her concern for him, but there was no time to develop it.

It turned into a grimace of anger when the rifle barrel jabbed him sharply in the base of the spine and Phelan's squeaky voice hissed in his ear.

'Sit down, Frog. Don't move and don't talk.'

Gerrard ignored Audrey's warning glance. He turned grimly to face the Irishman. 'You wouldn't like to put that thing down and try touching me with nothing in your hands?' he snarled.

The rifle swayed out of reach but remained pointing at Gerrard's midriff. Phelan stared back and bared his teeth. It was almost as if he were enjoying himself – all that was lacking was blood, and with Phelan on stage that was never going to be very far away. He might even have been happy to take Gerrard on at his word. He narrowed his eyes, sniffed wetly, and looked Gerrard up and down as if measuring where the first kick was going. But there was no kick. Phelan gave no chances – it was death or nothing.

His voice remained high-pitched – matter of fact, but strangely cold

394

and unemotional. It sounded worse. 'I don't mind wasting time with you, Frog. If you don't mind burying your girl-friend in a jam jar.'

Gerrard stopped dead. He knew what Phelan meant. He stared into Phelan's flat black eyes and tried to work out the rest of it. Phelan kept him waiting.

After a good half-minute of silence Gerrard said to Roberts, 'What is he talking about?'

Roberts shrugged his shoulders. 'Ask him.'

Phelan didn't wait to be asked. 'She's sitting on three-quarters of a pound of quality C4 – Semtex – and she's got nearly an hour left on her clock.' He stared for several seconds at the watch on his wrist, shook it, and held it to his ear. 'That was before you wanted to show me what big balls you've got!' He didn't smile. He stared into Gerrard's eyes. 'Now it's less.'

Gerrard used all his will-power not to throw himself at the Irishman's throat. It wouldn't have done any good.

'You've just reduced her lifespan by ten minutes.' Phelan's lips parted in a death's-head grin. 'It'll take me ten minutes to get to her and one minute to strip the wire – I reckon that gives her about half an hour.'

Gerrard sat down slowly.

There was no triumph in Phelan's eyes. 'And I'm quite happy to come and sit down too. Perhaps we could listen to the bang together?'

Audrey had listened in silence. She'd had enough. She looked over Gerrard's head at Phelan.

'Where have you got the girl?' she asked. She avoided Gerrard's eye. 'I don't like the sound of your time limits, Phelan. I hope you're not trying to be clever by cutting it too fine. We don't want any bangs around here – at least not while we're still in residence. You can do what the bloody hell you like after we've gone, but the people around here are as allergic to explosions as anybody else!' She threw in the nearest thing she could muster to a friendly smile.

It didn't work with Phelan.

'Mind your own bloody business!' His voice rose to its normal pitch and bounced off the old oak timbers in the ceiling and wall. 'Shut your mouth and leave the fuckin' demolition work to me!' He was still calm and collected. He'd established the strength of his suit; he'd got everybody worried about the time of the day, and how fast the second hand was whizzing round the dial on his wrist – everybody, it seemed . . . he looked again at his watch . . . except Gerrard. He jabbed the rifle barrel between Gerrard's shoulder blades and put his mouth near his ear.

'Lost your voice, Frog?'

Gerrard remained mute and immobile. He'd looked at his watch – another five minutes had gone, and it had been squandered entirely on Phelan's squeaky invective. He refused to take the bait. He could accept anything Phelan wanted to throw as long as he threw it quickly and cleared off to stop the clock ticking. If Phelan told him to run up the wall he'd do it. But for Christ's sake, Phelan, stop talking and do something!

But Gerrard wasn't the only worried man in the room.

'That's enough now, Phelan.' Roberts's voice was firm and authoritative. 'Let's stop playing bloody games. I don't want any complication down here so you'd better pray to whoever has claim on your spiritual destiny that your watch is correct and that the Lambdon girl doesn't leave us prematurely.' He stopped frowning at the ugly Irishman and jerked his head at Gerrard. 'You know what has to be done, Phelan. Don't play with the bloody man – do it!'

Roberts turned away and opened the kitchen door. For a moment he stood framed against the encroaching wood; the broad sunlight saw the door open and rushed in, cutting shapes round the big man's substantial figure and brightening the old kitchen with a series of finger-like beams. Nobody else moved.

Phelan had gone very quiet.

Gerrard gritted his nerves against the urge to turn his head to find out what was going on behind him. Instead, he watched Audrey's face. It was like a mirror. He had no time to duck. Audrey's eyes widened in horror and his neck muscles tightened instinctively to take the blow.

Phelan transferred the rifle to his left hand. He stood on his toes and swung his leather sock against Gerrard's head. It was a perfectly timed stroke. Gerrard didn't feel it; there was no pain. The red and white star that split his vision exploded into a million fragments and he watched each one flicker and die until the whole galaxy dived into a black stodgy vortex and sucked him, feet first, into it.

Phelan watched the Frenchman's head crash on to the table without blinking. There was no pleasure in the cold flat eyes; no twitch of satisfaction, nothing, not even a self-congratulatory smile. He picked up Gerrard's head by its hair, held it for a moment then allowed it to drop back on the table. The thud resounded round the low, oak-beamed kitchen. Phelan looked up at his audience – there was no humour in his eyes.

'One Frog,' he rasped, 'about as dangerous as Fanny's left tit!'

There was no movement, or sound, or comment from Roberts. Audrey remained rooted where she stood with the expression that had forewarned Gerrard still etched on her face. She gave a gasp of horror, then shuddered and turned away.

'Was it true what he said he'd done to the girl?' she asked Roberts. She made a point of keeping her back to the Irishman.

Roberts made no reply. He pulled a face and raised an eyebrow in Phelan's direction.

Phelan answered for him. 'Of course it's bloody true! And it's no longer any of your bloody business. I told you to leave the worrying about demolition work to me. Before you two have had time to wring your socks out, this,' he rapped the side of Gerrard's head with the rifle barrel, 'and the woman'll be floating above you like a packet of corn-flakes! Worry about yourselves – not them.'

Audrey shuddered again when Phelan bared his teeth at her.

'Will you stick the needle in him, Missus Gilling? I don't mind bash-ing his head with my sock every five or ten minutes to keep him quiet, but it ain't going to do my arm a lot of good!' He nearly smiled, but changed his mind. 'I don't want the bastard waking up until tomorrow – you know how much?' He looked at his watch and held it to his ear again, then frowned and shook it again under Audrey's startled eyes. 'Another ten minutes – plenty of time!' It was Phelan's idea of a joke.

After he and Roberts had loaded Gerrard into the back of the Transit, Phelan looked across at Gerrard's Citroën and said, 'Are you going to have any use for that?'

Roberts shook his head, then frowned. 'Yes, I'll need it to get down to the beach. Why? Do you want it?'

'Christ, no. But I think the People'll be around like bloody flies when the Frog's been minced – we might as well take some of the buggers out at the same time. You've no objection?'

'None. But I don't want to go up with it.'

'You won't. Leave it to me. I'll give it a button job. A packet under the seat.' Phelan walked across to the car and peered into the interior. He stared at the dashboard for several minutes then nodded his satis-faction. He went back to Roberts. 'I'll connect a couple of pounds to the cassette player. You won't be playing music on your way out?'

Roberts laughed. 'I'll make bloody sure I don't!'

Phelan didn't laugh with him. 'When you've finished with the car, switch the player on and turn the ignition off. I'll stick a cassette half-way in. Don't touch it. When they push the cassette in – or take it out – Whoomp! And we're half a dozen Brits on the slate!'

'I thought you told Audrey there was only another ten minutes on the girl.'

Phelan pulled a face and looked at his watch again. 'I was hoping to see her pee herself! Don't worry, I've got enough time to fix this, and have about three minutes to spare.'

'You're mad, Phelan . . .'

'Yeh, so they say.'

CHAPTER 42

From his vantage point at the base of a low-slung bushy cypress Murray watched the two men dump Gerrard's unconscious form into the back of the Transit.

He stood up gingerly and, still covered by the tree, stretched his aching limbs. After a few moments he slipped cautiously back into the shadows of the wood and out of sight of the house. Once clear, he moved quickly away at an angle from the house and rejoined the path he'd discovered earlier. It led back to a collection of farm buildings, out of sight and largely overtaken by the wild undergrowth.

It had been Phelan's first stop. He hadn't looked over his shoulder. If he had he'd have seen Murray breathing down his ear.

When Phelan had turned right off the A12 Murray knew that he couldn't go much further east without falling into the sea. He had gambled on the first village they came to being the one that Phelan had come to to buy his stick of rock. It was a one-street village with a pub and a shop, and nothing visible beyond the street but fields.

Murray parked his car in the pub's forecourt and strolled through the village on foot. He continued until he passed the last row of cottages and came to the open countryside. It didn't put him off. He lit a cigarette for company and stared along the empty road. That's it, he decided – we've dropped a bloody bollock! Never mind! We'll go a quarter of a mile along this tarmac and if we don't see a blue Transit parked outside a broken-down shit-house we'll go back and get the car and try the next village . . . He flicked the unsmoked cigarette into the hedge and strode on.

A hundred yards and the road forked.

'And that's just what we need – ' he hissed under his breath, 'a bloody choice!' He hesitated briefly, flipped his mental coin, and veered to the left. He walked briskly on, a little less confident, a lot more hot and sweaty, and after a couple of hundred yards stopped briefly to look down a broad drive leading from an unpainted five-bar gate. A long white farmhouse sat comfortably at the end of the drive; but there was no light blue Transit van parked in front of it. All the windows of the house were closed and shuttered – it looked dead and unlived-in.

Murray grunted his disappointment and turned his back on it.

Another three minutes down the road and he nearly gave in to the urge to return to the fork and try his luck with the right-hand branch; but he stuck with it and set his sights along the wooded verge to a point where the road veered into a shallow curve.

He didn't reach the curve.

Twenty yards on he nearly tripped over a grass-covered concrete wedge spanning the open ditch on the side of the road. Stepping back and staring over the hedge he could see through the undergrowth the beginnings of a cracked and long-disused concrete road. Murray studied the marks on the old road; then he looked upwards at the over-hanging mixture of elm and bramble branches and inspected the recent white breakages among the thinner and more brittle of the branches.

As if to confirm what he'd already decided a motor started somewhere in the distance. He cocked his ear and listened. No mistake. A diesel – a Transit? – and somewhere down his road! A moment's hesitation; a quick look through the trees – there was nothing to see . . . But the sound was enough – he threw himself into the undergrowth on the other side of the rusty gate.

He was just in time.

The roar of an over-accelerated engine thundered up the disused concrete road and echoed round the silent wood. Delicately, Murray parted the prickly undergrowth and stared along the overgrown road as the burst of starting power levelled off and the quieter, normal sound of an engine in motion brought behind it the slow-moving Transit. Without moving his head he watched the vehicle approach. His eyes gleamed as it passed him, then hardened at the ugly, but welcome, sight of Charlie Phelan's skinny shoulders hunched over the steering wheel.

The van turned right at the disused entrance and roared off in the direction of the village. Murray listened as it was taken down the road in a high-pitched complaining second gear. He waited for Phelan to put it out of its misery, but instead, the engine slowed to a normal pitch and almost faded. Murray waited. After a ham-fisted grinding of gears the tortured engine screamed again but, instead of coming from the direction of the village, the sound now filtered through the woods immediately behind him.

The bloody great farmhouse down the road! Murray patted himself on the back. No corner shit-house for Phelan – nothing but the best for Sinn Fein's military wing! He stared down the neglected concrete road. But what the bloody hell had he been doing along there?

Leaving his cover he moved cautiously through the trees but stayed within sight of the old road. The road was shorter than he'd thought, but it still took him several sweaty minutes to reach its end. It was nothing spectacular – just a collection of old farm buildings. He stopped, and, remaining within the cover of the trees, inspected them for signs of life. They were dead. It looked as though nobody had been here for years – if you didn't count Charles Phelan and his Transit van! It could have been a dry well in the middle of the Kalahari; nothing moved, not even the dust on the road. Murray moved closer. Only one of the buildings had a door. It was an old barn – fairly solid, it looked water-tight and secure.

He eased the big .45 Browning, already half-cocked, from its sweaty pouch under his arm and wiped the perspiration from its damp butt on the inside of his blazer. He rubbed his moist hand down the side of his trouser leg and pulled the hammer of the automatic back as far as it would go. He tapped the bottom of the magazine unnecessarily with the flat of his hand and moved towards the first of the derelict buildings.

The slow inspection of each one raised nothing but his adrenalin count. And then he was left with just the solid brick barn – the one with the door.

He checked the back of the building first. It was solid all the way round. There was only one way in. He returned to the front and placed his eye to a crack in the large wooden door. He could see nothing except a pile of old straw bales. The rest of the interior was in darkness – there were no windows or open ventilators.

The door was held shut by a lump of worn four-by-two resting in two iron brackets. Murray didn't touch it immediately. He stood and stared at it. He studied both ends, then both brackets, and then the length of the bar, before raising it carefully and placing it on the ground. It didn't go bang. Murray didn't relax his concentration. Next, with his finger preventing it from swinging open, he checked the door in the same manner. When he removed his finger the right half of the door swung squeakily open. Murray watched it flap to a halt before peering round the door frame from the protection of the brick wall. The interior, now flooded with sunlight from the open door, was as bright as day. It gave him a clear view of the entire inside of the building. He was glad he'd saved it till last.

The back half of the barn contained nothing but stacked straw bales; some in good condition, others useless, and none of them less than two seasons old. He stared for several seconds at Melanie Lambdon who sat, half propped, in a corner made of straw bales stacked against the brick wall. He wasn't the least bit surprised to see her. She stared back. Only her eyes and the top part of her face were visible over the grubby cloth wrapped around her mouth and jaw.

Murray leaned round the door post and ran his eye over the inside wall and the inside of the door frame before stepping gingerly inside for a closer look at her. He studied her bonds for a moment then slid his finger down the side of the cloth bound round her face; it had been tied cruelly across her mouth, with as much slack as Phelan would have given an informer's neck-string. Murray's eyes hardened – it must have been excruciating. He loosened the cloth fractionally, ignoring the look of gratitude that welled up into her eyes. He kept his own eyes turned towards the barn door.

Melanie's hands were still tied with the nylon stockings, but were now behind her back. When he eased her gently forward he could see that her fingers had turned blue where she'd strained against the binding and cut the circulation. He loosened the knot and retied it. Tears of pain flooded her eyes when the blood rushed back into her hands, but she lowered her head and clenched her eyes tightly to stem the flood that threatened to erupt.

'Friend of Harry's,' he whispered. 'Just keep very still and you'll be all right.'

When she opened her eyes Murray had moved away. He'd seen something else. He'd spotted what he'd been looking for since he came into the barn – Phelan's box of tricks.

The explosive was still in its oily wrapper. The rest of the works – 2-A initiator plastic, HD detonators: good modern Libyan produce – were all neatly packed in place. Without touching, Murray traced the wires from the battery to their terminals in a small white-dialled single-handed timer. Everything was connected. The surplus wire was tied carelessly in a tangled bundle and the whole ugly, lethal package lay casually in the shoe-box parcel that Murray had last seen in Highgate, tucked under postman Phelan's right arm.

He smiled unintentionally to himself and bent down to study the dial; but the smile didn't last – it wasn't very funny; there never was anything funny about nearly a pound of Semtex primed for time. He compared the setting with his own wrist-watch, made a minor adjustment to the hands of his large Rolex and straightened up. He looked across the room into Melanie's tear-filled eyes, nodded encouragingly, then turned away and walked out of the barn, closing the door as carefully as he'd opened it.

He stood for a moment outside, allowing his eyes to adjust to the bright sunlight, then headed in the direction of the big farmhouse. After scrabbling about in the bushes he discovered amid the undergrowth what had once been a well-used footpath. He didn't hesitate. He plunged into the tunnel of bright green bracken and overhanging brambles and, at an awkward crouch, moved silently towards the rear of the old farmhouse.

When it loomed through the thick intertwined branches of the wood Murray turned off the track and headed deeper into the trees to approach the house from a different angle.

He saw the Transit first. It was parked haphazardly on the crescent-shaped forecourt and blocked his view of the front door of the house, but, by careful manoeuvring, he was able to position himself so that the van helped camouflage his observation point. Tucking himself behind the thickest cypress he settled down for his first sight of Phelan in residence – and the guest for whom the Lambdon girl was being used as bait.

There was no doubt in Murray's mind who would shortly come strolling down the garden path. That was the easy bit. The difficult bit was the question he'd been trying to ignore for some time now – a question that refused to take a back seat in his mind . . . How the bloody hell did Phelan and the Frenchman come to be on opposite ends of the sticky pole? Something wasn't quite right. Murray had a nasty feeling at the base of his spine. It was a feeling he knew; it always happened when something was about to go horribly wrong.

He watched the Citroën arrive with sinking feelings.

The woman was a mystery. So was the man. Phelan he knew. And Gerrard. *But what is she? Definitely not on Gerrard's side by the way she's searching his pockets! And the big bugger standing there like Cyril Smith on the last day of Lent – who the bloody hell is he?* Murray let the bits and pieces rattle around his mind hoping that somewhere a pattern would form; but all he got was a bucketful of different-shaped patterns, and none of them with the slightest hint of substance. Nothing seemed to hold together long enough to make a lasting impression – except that Phelan didn't like Frenchmen. And if Phelan didn't like Frenchmen, then this one had to have some good in him somewhere. It didn't make sense – what was going on?'

Murray arrived back at the buildings and waited in the undergrowth. Five minutes later he was joined by Phelan and his Transit.

Murray watched Phelan dump the unconscious Gerrard into the dust and waited until he'd dragged him into the barn. After a few more minutes he left his cover and moved cautiously to the side of the building. On his way past he glanced into the back of the Transit. It was empty, except for a few sacks and a cardboard box at the far end. Another of Phelan's murder kits? Murray edged towards the large wooden doors. One of them, caught half-way between nowhere by a faint summer breeze, banged monotonously against the wall and masked the gravel-disturbing sound made by his feet. He wondered what Phelan was doing inside.

Murray put his eye to the jamb of the other door and stopped worrying. Phelan was hard at work. Murray stood and watched him.

'Come on, you big bastard!' Phelan grunted with the exertion of pulling Gerrard's body across the dusty straw-covered floor. He made heavy going of it until, with a breathless and final bad-tempered heave, he managed to roll him on to his face at Melanie's feet.

Phelan was very sure of himself; everything was under control and very soon the whole bloody place was going to be turned into powder – and these two with it . . . Into powder . . .? Phelan started. He leapt towards his shoe-box and stuck his nose close to the dial; one minute left. He didn't flinch, he was as calm as a sweating cucumber. There was no reason why he shouldn't be – Phelan was in his element, he was handling death. It was something he knew all about.

From behind the massive doors Murray looked at his watch. He heaved a sigh of relief; he wasn't as calm as Phelan.

Phelan disconnected the wires from the battery, reset the single hand on the clock and joined it all up again. He tossed it casually back into its box, turned his back on it and walked across the barn. He stopped in front of Melanie.

'I'm going to take this rag off your face,' he told her. 'But if you make a whisper or say one word out of turn, I'll shove it back down your throat so fast it'll make your fuckin' eyes pop out!'

Melanie tried not to shudder, and in fear that he might change his mind lowered her eyelids submissively and allowed him to pull at the knot at the back of her head. She held back a scream when the cloth was removed, and bit her lips when, with a rush of blood, the life zipped back into her face.

She moved her mouth experimentally, then grimaced showing her teeth as she fought the pain. It had no effect on Phelan.

'No noise,' he repeated. 'Not even a whisper.'

She looked up through her eyelashes and saw that Phelan had moved across the barn and was staring intently into his cardboard box. He'd made a makeshift table of straw bales and seemed intent on his bomb. His back was turned to the big doors and the sun had moved, sending in thick, golden-blocked shafts of light which solidified in the disturbed dust of the barn. Her eyes moved towards the open door.

She saw a pair of legs walking across the floor towards the Irishman. She brought her head up sharply, and stifled a gasp. Too late. Phelan heard it.

He turned and glared at her – and saw Murray walking calmly towards him.

Phelan's reflexes were in the right place. He didn't have to think about it. He swung round with his back hard against the straw bales and his arm outstretched as far as it would go. His left hand fumbled desperately among the folds of his coat, lying in a bundle beside the shoe-box; but he was too late.

He stopped in mid-flight and, slowly, spread out his fingers until his hand looked like a giant spider sleeping on top of the jacket. His mouth went dry and his eyes hooded like a wary chicken's when they met those of Murray. He allowed himself a quick professional glance at the huge automatic pointing solidly at his chest, then looked back, blankly, into Murray's eyes.

Murray said, 'Quite right, Phelan. Don't even blink – let's just stand here for a moment and look at each other.'

Phelan remained like the stump of a petrified tree. Under his out-stretched fingers he could feel the hard metal of the Luger. But there was no temptation to try for it. He continued staring into Murray's eyes until Murray nodded his head and said softly, 'OK, that's enough. Put your hands on your head and walk to the middle of the room.'

Phelan did as he was told.

'Sit down there,' ordered Murray. 'Spread your hands out on the floor . . . That's it. Now, legs out straight. Good. Don't move from that posi-tion – and don't talk.'

'Who are you?'

Murray walked slowly round to the back of Phelan and stood looking down at his head. He remained like that for several seconds. Phelan was just about to turn his head to see what he was doing, when, without warning, and without change of expression, Murray leaned forward and smashed the barrel of the Browning across Phelan's splayed hand.

There was a sickening crunch as the two outside fingers mashed into a bloody pulp. For a brief second there was silence in the old barn. Then Phelan's scream came up from his toes and echoed like a wailing banshee into the rafters of the barn. It ended in a strangled sob.

Melanie turned her head away from the horror, and looked anxiously at Gerrard where he lay on his face in the straw. There was no movement. She closed her eyes, took a deep breath, and looked again across the barn at the two men.

She watched as Phelan raised his shattered hand to his face and inspected it with stricken eyes. His mouth remained open with the remnants of his scream still there, but it was now under control and no sound came out except the low moan of a man fighting for breath.

The blood gushed freely down his trousers. It was like a miniature waterfall. Frightening. Phelan tightened his grip round the wrist of the damaged hand and tried to blow the pain away. 'You bastard!' he groaned, still studying the broken and smashed fingers. 'You dirty bastard!'

Murray dragged a bale of straw to the centre of the barn and sat down. Now that Phelan couldn't see his face he allowed a little smile to cross his features. 'I said don't talk until I tell you.' He leaned forward and tapped Phelan's shoulder with the barrel of the automatic. Phelan shuddered. Murray had got him in the right mood. 'Nod your head.'

Phelan nodded.

'Right. My name is Murray. Captain. Army Intelligence. Don't expect yellow cards or any of that sort of nonsense – I don't go by those rules.'

'You're Irish . . .'

Murray's boot hit him at the base of the spine. 'I'm British – and I said don't talk. You met another British officer this morning in that lady's house in London. What happened to him?'

Phelan's mutilated hand shivered uncontrollably as he tried to place it back on the ground. It was the only movement from Phelan.

'I asked you a question,' said Murray.

'Fuck off!'

BOOM! The roar of Murray's Browning sounded like a clap of thunder in an empty aircraft hangar.

The explosion thumped against four pairs of unprotected eardrums and bounced backwards and forwards off the walls of the building until it found its way out through the door. The noise took Phelan's mind off his sore hand for a moment. He opened his eyes and looked at the hole where the end of his shoe used to be; a two-inch square had been torn out by Murray's bullet and all that was left of his big toe was a bloody jagged stub. Part of his foot had gone with it and a small spring of blood gushed up from the hole like an old-fashioned drinking fountain. There was no real pain as yet. But Phelan fainted.

Murray sniffed and gently rubbed his ear and waited for Phelan to wake up.

Phelan opened his eyes and stared at the roof of the barn. Then he re-membered. He raised his head from the floor to look at his foot and nearly passed out again. The sight of the dreadful gap made his bowels loosen.

'Holy Jesus!' he whispered – then louder, 'Holy Mother of God!' His voice broke and he allowed his head to fall back on the floor. He closed his eyes and continued his litany. Nothing else mattered.

He was allowed a few more seconds' supplication, then Murray's foot descended on his shoulder and he was shaken out of church and back into the old barn.

'Sit up and answer the question.'

'He's dead.'

'OK,' said Murray, quietly. 'Let's talk about the Frenchman.' He glanced quickly at Gerrard and then back to the Irishman's shiny black hair. 'Tell me about him.'

Phelan swallowed to clear the sickness from the back of his throat and spat it into the dust by his right hand. 'Is this some sort of catch question you're asking?'

'Get on with it,' snapped Murray, 'or I'll take out another toe.'

Phelan didn't hesitate. 'He's working for British Intelligence. They brought him over to do a job of work. He's the Frogs' top hit-man. They called him Siegfried.'

Murray's heart sank. 'What's the job?' he asked.

'He's done it.'

'What was it?'

'The British used him to get in amongst the Dublin people. They were joining up with the Yanks. His job was to sort them out in a block and coffin the whole bloody lot.'

'Anything else?'

407

Phelan stared, mesmerised, at the bubbling fountain where his toe used to be. He had decided he'd said enough when, out of the corner of his eye, he saw Murray's Browning pointing at his other foot. Murray didn't have to say a word. Phelan started talking again.

'There was something about a talking bubble in London – the Movement's man in British Intelligence. Siegfried was paid to murder him.'

Murray shook his head. 'Is it still going on?'

'Fucked if I know! You're Army Intelligence – *is it* still going on?'

Phelan knew he should have kept his mouth shut. The Browning bounced off the side of his head, then its muzzle ground into the corner of his eye socket. He screamed.

Murray's voice rasped in his ear. 'Answer the bloody question. No comments – just answers . . . And the next time you think of something clever to say it'll cost you an ankle. Now go back to the question. Is the game still on?'

Phelan got it out quickly. 'He finished the big job. He gathered all the top Organisation people – IRA, INLA, some American experts who'd come over to help with the display, and an Englishman named Malseed – and blew 'em all into tiny pieces.'

'Malseed?'

'A Westminster mouth – real name Adam Follington.'

Murray wasn't interested in Westminster mouths. He took his eyes off the back of Phelan's head for a moment and frowned at Gerrard's recumbent figure. After a second he shook his head.

'You sure about that?'

Phelan nodded his head.

'How'd he get in that close to the cherry? Who worked him into your people's good books? Who was his contact?'

Phelan lifted his head and squared his shoulders with a faint groan. He raised his shattered hand from the floor and moved it delicately backwards and forwards, then grimaced with pain when the blood started thumping back into its mangled nerves. He decided not to offer his foot the same treatment for the time being. He was almost relaxed when Murray's boot caught him in the back again.

'Answer the bloody question.'

'A bloke called Lambdon.'

Murray's day was complete. But he didn't allow it to show. 'Talk about Lambdon,' he said.

Phelan grimaced. 'The Brits must have planted him. No one knows for sure – he disappeared just before the bang. But why don't you ask him.' He jerked his head at Gerrard's body. 'He'll be able to tell you when he wakes up.'

'What have you done to him?'

'Nothing serious – just a jab . . . Headache mixture – he'll be up and about if she did the thing properly.'

'She?'

'Girl in the house.'

'Who's the big fat guy?'

'That's the one the Frog was brought in to murder. He's a top Brit Intelligence man.'

'What's he doing here in the middle of Suffolk?'

'Going home. He's taking the woman with him.'

'Where's home?'

'Russia. The Frog flushed him out somehow.'

'You mean he works for the Russians?'

'No, he's not turned, he's real. He's KGB. He's Russian. They worked him in – years ago.'

Murray stopped and stared at the back of Phelan's head. Things seemed to be getting out of control – his mind felt like the pedals of a racing bike on one of the downhill mountain stretches of the Tour de France – nothing would stay still long enough for him to think. He tried again in a lower gear.

'When's he leaving – and how?'

Phelan thought for a second, then replied, 'Tomorrow – early dawn. That's when it's scheduled for. But he can put it forward or back if anything goes wrong. There's something out there waiting for him.' He pointed his chin at the end wall of the barn. 'It's been arranged.'

Murray studied the far wall of the barn for the best part of thirty seconds, then frowned at the back of Phelan's head. 'What d'you mean, something out there? Something out where?'

'In the puddle.' Phelan pointed to where he imagined the North Sea was. 'There's a Russian ship out there. It's either a trawler, a small tanker, or a submarine. Roberts says they're always hanging around in these waters and it doesn't take a lot of shouting from him to give them the nod.'

'Got a radio up there at the house, has he?'

'Yeh.'

'Were you going with him?'

'No. I had to bring the girl down to control the Frog. When those two up there go I'm back to London – and then Belfast.'

Murray shook his head slowly, but Phelan couldn't see it. After a second of two he made up his mind. He touched the muzzle of the Browning to the back of Phelan's ear. Phelan didn't move.

'No, Phelan,' said Murray, softly, 'I don't think so. I don't think you're going back anywhere this time.'

'What d'you mean?'

Murray leaned back out of the way, prepared his ears for another explosion and tightened his finger on the trigger.

Gerrard heard the mumble of voices through the roaring in his head and tried to remember what had happened.

It took a minute, then it all came back like a flash of pain. The old farmhouse; Phelan . . . Audrey Gilling's look of wide-eyed horror before the blackness descended, and now the sick throb from the soggy part of the back of his head. He kept his eyes closed and made no movement as he forced himself back to consciousness.

Groggy – no spittle in his mouth and a tongue like a piece of raw *boudin*. He pushed the *boudin* as far back into his throat as it would go and moved it around. The dry bitter taste it collected jolted him alive with a shock. He'd been drugged! So, how long had he been out? He didn't try to work it out. And then he was wide awake. Melanie! Phelan – explosive – thirty minutes! For Christ's sake, what have they done with her?

The voices droned on.

They sounded hollow, but it didn't tell him anything. He breathed in slowly and smelt straw and dust. The pistol? He pushed his stomach out and felt it dig with a solid sharpness into his waist. So, one of them, at least, was going with him. But which one?

He decided it was time to see what was going on. Slowly – very slowly, he raised one eyelid.

All he could see was straw. Straw and dust – lots of it, and everything he wanted to see was behind him. That's where the voices were coming from – over his left shoulder.

He recognised the grating high-pitched vowels of the ugly Irishman. And the other voice? English. Not Roberts. But he is still around, which means there are at least three; but only two talking. Maybe Roberts is sitting on a straw bale watching a Frenchman come back to life?

Gerrard kept his arm stiff and, moving only his fingers, delicately probed the gap in his shirt until they found the butt of the small automatic. He was warm and damp with sweat but he managed to slide it out of its hiding place with two fingers. It was small, but solid and reassuring, and fitted snugly in his hand.

And still the voices droned on, first one, then the other. No sound of alarm, or excitement – just a collection of words that became clearer as the throbbing in his head diminished. Words like boats – trawlers, tankers, submarines – and radios and, he thought, Belfast. He closed his ears to the mumble and timed and rehearsed everything in his mind.

He was lying on his left side. The Irishman and his friend were behind him, hard to say exactly how far away, but, if the bang on his head hadn't upset his hearing, they were slightly to his left. Behind and left. So, a quick roll-over, cock the pistol as he rolled, left hand wrapped round the right, two shots into the nearest one and then on to the next and the same for him – and then two for Roberts. What about Audrey? Play it by ear. Six rounds. Pray to God Audrey loaded the thing! He ran the sequence through his mind. It sounded all right. He ran it through once more.

Then his eyes were open and he rolled straight into the broad shaft of sunlight that cut through the door like a searchlight.

He was blinded. Through the red mist he saw a shadowy, blurred form rise up into a man's shape. He had no time to blink the flames from his eyes. He fired twice – bang, bang! The form disappeared. He blinked tears into his eyes and saw another vague bundle rise from the floor and vanish with an up-and-down hopping motion into the open doors of the blazing furnace. He sent two shots after the figure. There was no welcoming scream.

And then a voice shrieked from behind him.

Female.

He threw himself on to his other shoulder and steadied his hand – and pointed the automatic, unerringly, at Melanie's chest.

Murray was just about to squeeze the trigger in Phelan's ear when he saw Gerrard's body move. It was only a blur in the corner of his eye, but it was enough.

He swung the large Browning away from Phelan and aimed it directly at Gerrard's head. But he didn't fire, and too late, saw the small pistol nicely gripped and steady, aimed straight-armed at his throat.

Gerrard's first bullet whistled across his chest tearing a ragged crescent from the edge of his tie; the second fizzed like an angry wasp past the back of his head. He didn't wait for the third. He threw himself backwards over a pile of straw bales and landed with a crunch on the hard stone floor.

Phelan moved even faster. After the first shot he took off and hurtled

through the door on one leg. His pains and aches and wounds were forgotten in the euphoria of the unexpected offer of freedom. He threw
himself bodily across the threshold and landed outside the barn in a
shower of dust and straw. Gerrard's two shots, whistling harmlessly over
his shoulder, gave him extra impetus. He clawed his way into the Transit's cab, turned the key, and thumped his uninjured foot hard on the
accelerator. The engine turned healthily. But there was no accompany-
ing roar of power.

Everything else forgotten he stared helplessly at the petrol gauge –
what the fuck? It was half full . . . He screamed at it; he jabbed his foot
again at the throttle and turned the key frantically once more. He'd
flooded the bloody thing! Again – and again . . . His heart stopped beat-
ing. The engine gave a discreet promising cough but floundered again
on its overdose. He kicked it. He swore at it and nearly wept with fear
and frustration . . . He'd got his chance – but he knew he was going nowhere without the Transit, not with half a foot and three fingers missing.
And any minute now someone was going to come out of that bloody barn
and start pumping bullets into his head. He gritted his teeth and continued anxiously twisting the key in the ignition.

'Michel, it's me!' screamed Melanie. 'For God's sake put the gun down!
Oh, God! – you've killed Murray and let Phelan get away! Michel!' she
screamed again at the top of her voice as Gerrard tried to focus on her.

He wiped his sleeve over his face and cleared away the forced tears,
and with them some of the burning sunlight from his eyes. He lowered
the automatic and shook his head, dispelling the last traces of drug from
his mind, and frowned at the woman crouched on the straw bale.

'Are you all right?' His voice was cracked and hoarse.

'Oh, God! Don't bother about me – I'm all right! You've shot Murray
– he's one of ours . . . He's a friend! Michel, quick! Phelan's getting
away! Stop him!'

Murray's voice bellowed from behind the straw bales. 'I'm OK!
Quick, girl, for Christ's sake tell him who I am! Tell him not to shoot! Be
quick – say something before that bastard gets away!'

The engine outside the door was still being tortured. The screeching
and grinding of the ignition continued unabated; and then the engine
coughed – twice, three times, and died again.

Murray shouted again, urgently, 'Don't shoot, Gerrard! I'm coming
out from behind these bales – everything's going to be explained!'

'Michel, he's a British officer!'

Gerrard turned to face the front of the barn. The small automatic came round with him and pointed unwaveringly in the direction of Murray's voice.

The Transit's engine burst into life.

'Bloody hell!' Murray leapt on to one of the overturned bales. He showed Gerrard both hands – open and extended, and shouted as he jumped down, 'I can't wait for you any bloody longer – I'm not letting that bastard get away!'

He swept up Phelan's shoe-box and dragged the timer out. He turned his back on Gerrard, stared intently at Phelan's home-made mechanism then stuck his thumbnail against the zero mark and turned the hand of the dial until it stopped against the nail. He gave a short prayer. There was about an eighth of an inch of space left between the single hand and the limit it could go – three minutes at the outside.

Murray shook the sweat from his forehead, waved his empty hand at Gerrard and threw himself out of the door and into the lingering cloud of blue-grey exhaust.

The noise of the racing engine filled the small area of the yard. Phelan's foot was banging the accelerator like the drummer of a third-rate pop group as he jerked and cajoled the van round to face the exit. He managed to keep it upright and finally got it looking in the right direction; then, shoving his good foot down as far as it would go, he screeched the van past the old barn, its open rear doors crashing and banging against the wall as he swayed like a drunken maniac on the narrow track.

Murray pressed himself flat against the brick wall. He held Phelan's triumphant eyes for the briefest flash of a second as he roared past, then calmly tossed the loaded shoe-box into the back of the van. With his back to the wall he watched the Transit bump and sway down the narrow concrete road until it disappeared among the trees. He gave it another few seconds then edged along to the corner of the barn and, protected by the solid brick wall, peered round the corner and stared along the track as he waited for the bang.

He was too intent on the sound of the vanishing Transit to hear Gerrard move silently alongside him. He'd almost forgotten about him. Gerrard reminded him. He jammed the small automatic into the soft part of his back.

'Put your hands against the wall,' he said into his ear, 'and tell me why you think I should believe you're a British Intelligence officer.'

Murray stuck his hands out. He said in a hushed voice, 'Wait a minute and just listen . . .' He kept his face pressed tightly against the wall.

'Listen – he's still in first gear – he can't change up with that damaged hand. He's pulled straight out into the road. Go on, Phelan, right up to the bloody house and call your friends out to show them your missing toe! Hey! – just a minute . . .' Murray's voice changed to surprise, then disappointment. 'Oh, bloody hell!'

He tried to take his face from the wall but Gerrard stroked the pistol under his eye forcing him to return to his original position. But it didn't prevent him from talking. 'Bloody hell!' he repeated. 'He's turned left. He's going the wrong bloody way – the house is in the other bloody direction. What the fucking hell's he playing at?'

Murray stopped talking and crinkled his eyes up in anticipation. Gerrard did nothing except stare at the side of Murray's head. For a few moments the only sound to be heard was the van's engine disappearing into the distance. It seemed to go on for ever, getting further and further away. Then the sound ceased abruptly.

A white flash shimmered across the sky. This was followed, almost instantaneously, by an enormous explosion which rent the calm afternoon air like a clap of night-time thunder.

The noise rumbled back and forth, finally echoing away into silence. A few seconds later, like an approaching storm, the sound of metal bouncing like a tin rainfall on the quiet little road filtered through the trees. Then the blast from the explosion whispered across the roof of the barn, carrying with it a handful of loose pantiles which crackled into fragments on the stone part of the yard. Murray laughed mirthlessly into the sudden silence.

'Goodbye Charlie Phelan!' He squared himself against the wall and looked at Gerrard out of the corner of his eye. 'That's saved one of us a job. I'll bet there isn't enough of that murdering bastard left on this planet to fill half a matchbox! And I'll bet there isn't a person anywhere in the world who's going to cry about it.'

The birds stopped squawking in the high branches and settled down again, and the trees shuddered back to their permanent positions after the buffeting they'd received from the lateral shock of the explosion. Quiet was restored around the group of farm buildings; it was as if nothing had happened.

'On the subject of tears,' said Gerrard, quietly into Murray's ear, 'and now that you've had your little moment and shown me how you kill Irishmen, perhaps you'd like to show me a piece of paper or something that will stop me putting a bullet in your spine.' Gerrard ground the automatic into the side of Murray's backbone until its narrow muzzle edged against a disc. 'And I hope you're going to say you don't carry that sort of paperwork around with you so that I can squeeze this trigger and send you after your friend Phelan.'

Murray grimaced over his shoulder and pressed his body closer against the wall. 'Cut out the bloody theatricals, Gerrard,' he grunted between clenched teeth. 'You know bloody well I've nothing on me. I'll give you a phone number if you like, or there's a card under the carpet of my car.'

'Where's your car?'

'In the pub car-park. Why don't you send the girl for it before you start flexing your muscles?' Murray grunted in pain again. 'But first take that bloody thing out of my back, it's grinding against a nerve.'

Gerrard stared, unsmiling, at the side of Murray's face. 'I'm sorry if I'm hurting you.' He leaned harder against Murray's spine, but Murray didn't make a sound this time – he was getting used to it. 'I might believe a bit of that, but we'll stay where we are for a minute while you clear up a few other little doubts. Work hard, Murray – I have a suspicious mind.'

'Fuck you and your suspicious mind, Gerrard! Explanations, whether you like it or not, are going to have to wait. You're going to have to take my word for the time being. Listen. I haven't got a lot of time. Up there in that farmhouse is a bloke who interests me. I want a little chat with him before he slips his ice skates on and buggers off back to the Steppes; name of Roberts, the big guy who brought you down here in a wrong-drive Citroën.'

'That makes two of us. He's what it's all about so don't bother with the background on him – he gave it to me himself on the way down.' Gerrard looked at the back of Murray's head and resisted the urge to smash it into the wall – maybe later, he thought. 'I'm probably going to make a mistake with you, Murray, but, assuming I accept for the time being that you are what you say you are, I want the answers to two questions . . .' He removed the pistol from Murray's trapped nerve and stepped back out of range of his feet and arms.

Murray grimaced and rubbed his back before turning to look Gerrard in the eye. Gerrard stared back, arms folded, the automatic still pointing from under his arm at Murray's midriff.

Murray knew what was coming. 'You're going to ask me about Lambdon,' he said.

Gerrard shook his head. 'I'm going to ask you about two Lambdons. Fred Lambdon is number one; Marjory Lambdon is number two. And as you just said, Murray, we haven't got a lot of time.'

415

Murray made sure there was no expression on his face. 'It was a mistake,' he conceded. 'I'm as sick about Fred Lambdon as anybody but I'm still not convinced he hadn't turned his hat round. And neither was Phelan. Phelan was right inside with 'em and even he wasn't sure whose game Lambdon was playing. There seems to be an awful lot of confusion between arses and elbows in this trade at the moment . . .'

'Speak for yourself, Murray!'

'I am! We're all decided on who the enemy is – it's our team that's causing the bloody problems. We're all in too deep – no trust and no co-ordination. You know the answer – what about Lambdon? Was he straight?'

'He was doing a job of work. He was set up by his own people and planted on the Irish. His control was the only one who knew about it.'

'Who's he?'

'You're not in a position to show curiosity, Murray! Why did you kill him?'

Murray's face showed what he was thinking. 'It was an accident, I told you. I was trying to get information. It's a bloody shame, I know, but the blame's not entirely mine if it was being played that close to the nose? I understand what his master was thinking; tongues are bloody unreliable things when you start sharing secrets in our country. But make my day, Gerrard – did I break up his game?'

There was no softening of Gerrard's expession. 'No. He'd virtually finished. He handed the ball to me when I arrived – if you'd left him alone for another week we could all have been having a drink together tonight. What about his wife?'

Murray shook his head in regret. 'If only he'd tipped me the wink somehow. I'd been on to him almost from the beginning, from about the time he first pulled the green strip over his shoulders, and in all that time he did nothing to persuade me he wasn't as thick as shit with the Irish. If he was stringing them he was doing it bloody well – it was a bloody good game he was playing.'

Gerrard refused to make it easy for Murray. 'Before you knocked his head off did you give him a clue as to who you were, and what it was all about?'

'No, of course I didn't. Lambdon probably thought I was PIRA testing him out. He played it tight all the way through. Bloody hell!' The regret in Murray's voice was genuine.

'You were going to tell me about his wife.' Gerrard didn't really want to hear Murray's excuses about Marjory Lambdon – the pattern was a

416

familiar one – but the bitterness seeped out.

Murray looked into Gerrard's eyes reluctantly. 'It was all about you,' he said. 'I had to follow it up after I caught your meeting with Lambdon on Horse Guards. He wouldn't tell me about you so I had to take it to her. It seemed the right thing to do at the time.'

'Why did you have to kill her?'

'I played all my cards on top of hers to try and get her to open up. I could tell she knew all about you, but she played it close, tried to look after you. When I realised I'd burnt myself it became inevitable. Look . . .' Murray stared earnestly into Gerrard's unsympathetic eyes. He was trying to convince himself, a sort of soul-cleansing effort, 'I'm on every Irish death list that's ever been compiled, and some they haven't drawn up yet, and the only thing they know is my name. I had to assume she'd blow the whistle on me; that she'd draw pictures and all that sort of thing for Freddie's new chums – I dared not take a chance with her. From my point of view she was the same colour as her old man.' Murray looked for a trace of understanding, but there was no softening of Gerrard's manner, nothing to help him out.

'And now that you know she's not?' asked Gerrard coldly. 'And that neither was he?'

Murray could only shrug his shoulders. 'You never made a mistake, Gerrard?'

Gerrard made no reply. He turned on his heel and walked back into the barn.

Melanie sat on one of the bales still rubbing life into her hands and legs. She looked a little the worse for wear – a trace of tiredness, a look of awareness, a little more maturity in her manner. She looked up and smiled at Gerrard's approach.

'Nice to see you up and about,' she said warily.

Gerrard's mind was on other things. He shook his head and put the other two-thirds of the Lambdon family into the far recesses of his mind and concentrated on what he'd got in front of him. He stopped and looked down at her. He wasn't smiling. It didn't deter her. She uncrossed her legs and said, 'Come here.' She reached up and put a hand round the back of his head and kissed both sides of his mouth and the tip of his nose. 'Is it all over now? Can we go home?'

'Er, before you start getting cosy, Gerrard . . .' Murray's voice from just inside the barn door left Melanie's sentence in mid-air. 'I'd like to get on with the job. I'll collect my gun if that's all right with you?' Murray deliberately ignored Melanie. He wasn't a man who normally suffered embarrassment, but he found it difficult to look this girl in the eye; there was a conscience somewhere inside David Murray that didn't allow him to stand easy in the presence of a woman whose parents he'd killed by mistake. She caught his eye over Gerrard's shoulder, but he looked away quickly.

'Thank you, Captain Murray,' she called out.

'Thank you for what?' he answered gruffly.

She smiled at him. It was a genuine smile, nothing sarcastic or re-proving about it – he could tell the difference; and it showed she knew nothing about Murray's world – which was a small consolation. He didn't smile back. 'Thanks for loosening that dreadful rag round my mouth earlier on. I wondered at the time, but I can see now why you didn't take it off altogether. And I didn't know you were a friend of Harry's? Phelan killed him, you know.'

Gerrard straightened up from Melanie and frowned over his shoulder at Murray.

'Kind gestures, Murray?' he queried, without smiling. 'And who's poor Harry?'

Melanie answered for him. 'He was one of Captain Murray's officers. He came to help me when Phelan arrived at the house. Phelan killed him . . .' She broke off and looked away.

Gerrard's eyes narrowed again and he looked accusingly at Murray.

Murray shrugged his shoulders; why change a good story?

He collected his Browning from behind the straw bale and flipped the magazine out into his hand. He replaced the single round that had crip-pled Phelan and slid the magazine back in place.

'If you want something with a bit more punch than that toy,' he said to Gerrard, 'there's a long-barrel Luger under that coat. Used to belong to Charles Phelan – I don't think he'll mind you borrowing it!'

Melanie sighed and bit her lip. 'I thought it was finished – I thought we were going home?'

Gerrard shook his head. 'There's one more thing to do. We won't be long. Make yourself comfortable on a couple of these bales, and if any-body you don't fancy appears through that door point this at them.' He handed her the small pistol, which she dropped immediately on to an adjacent straw bale.

'No thanks,' she said emphatically. 'I haven't forgotten the last time you said you'd got a small thing to do. I'm coming with you – I've earned it.' She rolled up her sleeves and showed them the red weals which had risen around her wrists. 'That's my argument for coming. What's yours for stopping me?'

Gerrard stared at her for several seconds. She stared back, unyielding. Then Gerrard smiled crookedly, and turned to Murray.

'Have you got any cigarettes?' he asked him. It sounded like surrender.

CHAPTER 43

A few hundred yards away in the farmhouse, Audrey Gilling stared absently at the gin and tonic she was nursing.

When the explosion shook the house the tumbler went flying across the room. The shattering sound of glass was lost in the reverberating thunder and rumbling after-effects and her scream died in her throat. She stood transfixed.

The shock wave that followed caused the old house to shudder and shake in its 300-year-old frame but the oak joists rode the punch and settled down again to stand still for another three hundred years.

Audrey found her voice after ten seconds of shock.

'Geoffrey!' she screamed. 'Geoffrey!'

Roberts almost fell down the stairs. 'What the bloody hell's all that noise?' he demanded.

'That bang . . .?' she started. But Roberts stopped her.

'For Christ's sake!' Roberts's shirt was dripping with sweat but his face was dry and he showed no sign of concern or fluster; a thick coloured towel hung round his neck as if he'd been caught in the middle of shaving and he dabbed his neck and chin with its corner as he leaned against the door post. 'Phelan's been telling you about his bloody bangs ever since we got down here! What were you expecting – bursting feathers?'

'I wasn't expecting *that* – not yet! I thought . . .'

'Forget it. You just heard the mad Irishman's farewell fart – he's put the wrong wires up his arse and blown himself out of circulation. I'm not disappointed. Go and pour me a large whisky.'

Audrey's hysteria sniffled into a hiccup as the shock began to wear off. 'What about the others?' she asked, hoarsely. 'What about Gerrard and the girl?'

Roberts made a rasping sound in his throat. 'I don't think we're going to have to worry too much about them. Bits of Frenchman'll still be fluttering down over Southwold Marshes this time tomorrow! Don't shed any tears for Gerrard – he's got what he's been paid for. He's probably overdue anyway. Forget 'em!' It was an order.

'Geoffrey, that damned explosion's going to bring half the bloody county around here wondering what the hell's going on. There's going to be police and the fire people, and before we know where we are you and I'll be grinning idiotically at the television cameras.' Her voice rose again as a cold finger of panic touched her spine. 'What are we going to do?'

Roberts dabbed his face again with the towel and swallowed a large mouthful of whisky. 'I've already done it,' he said.

'Done what?'

'Changed our departure schedule. I've been chatting with one Rudi Chenkov who's sitting about fifteen miles from here in the cabin of a Soviet trawler. He's sending someone to pick us up.'

'Isn't that risky?'

Roberts shrugged. 'No more than anything else. But they're not silly – they'll be wearing an FRG ensign to show how well-mannered they are. Rudi's arranged tea and scones for us at half-past four. Rendezvous about six miles from here. They've arranged two alternatives. If one doesn't stick there's a back-up craft hanging about just off the Suffolk coast. But I think that's Russian over-caution – nothing's going to go wrong; nothing can go wrong – you won't even get your feet wet.'

'Where is this rendezvous, Geoffrey?'

'Not far.' Roberts refused to commit himself further. 'Finish your drink and I'll see you at the front door in ten minutes.' He put his empty glass down with a bang, nodded encouragingly at Audrey and started ponderously up the stairs to say goodbye to his wireless set.

Gerrard crushed his cigarette out in the dust and looked up at Murray. 'And all you managed to get from Phelan was that there's a boat waiting for them off the coast somewhere, and they're boarding at dawn? Nothing else?'

Murray flicked the cigarette stub into the undergrowth with his finger and thumb. 'He said Roberts spent a lot of time talking into the waves out there. Not just today, but on a regular basis. This is probably his contact point. Phelan said Roberts could change the schedule any time he wanted – and I use Phelan's words: if anything goes wrong.'

Gerrard, who had been moodily studying the distance Murray had achieved with his cigarette end, looked up sharply.

'If anything goes wrong? Wrong in what way? Would a huge explosion on his doorstep constitute something going wrong – wrong enough for him to want to change his schedule?'

The two men looked at each other in dismay.

'Quick!' barked Gerrard. 'Show me that track to the house you mentioned. Come on – move!' He pointed to Melanie. 'You stay close to me – and don't do anything idiotic! Run, Murray!'

They weaved hurriedly in Indian file along the narrow twisting path.

They hadn't gone more than a hundred yards down the track when Murray, a few yards in the lead, stopped dead and pressed himself against a large tree trunk. Without looking round he stuck out his hand and waved Gerrard off the track. He peered through the wood, listened for a second, then turned his head and put his finger to his lips.

'Listen!' he rasped, and inclined his head in the direction of the house.

'What is it?' whispered Gerrard.

'I heard a car door slam. There it goes again. It's moving away now.'

Gerrard thumped Murray on the shoulder. 'That's my Citroën,' he hissed. 'Quick, they're on their way!' He pushed Murray in front of him. 'They've got to turn it round – we might be able to stop them before they get to the drive.'

Gerrard set off in a crouched run after the younger, and faster-moving, man. He was still a few yards behind when Murray threw himself against a tree and, using its trunk to steady his arm, aimed the heavy Browning through the undergrowth. The roar of the .45 thundered once. It set the rooks off again.

Over the noise of a hundred squawking birds Gerrard shouted again. 'Did you see who was in it?'

Murray brushed green moss dust from the arm of his blazer and continued staring through the trees in the direction he'd fired.

'The woman was driving,' he said. There was no trace of excitement in his voice. 'Roberts was in the passenger seat. She turned right towards the village and shoved her foot down.'

'Did you hit it?'

'You'll need a new rear window – unless it's unbreakable glass.' He replaced the used round in the magazine, half cocked the Browning and shoved it back under his arm. 'I'm going for a little run,' he told Gerrard, 'as far as the pub in the village. My car's parked there. If you and Melanie make your way towards the village I'll come back with the car and pick you up.' He didn't wait for a reply. He turned briskly towards the drive-way and started trotting.

'Hey, Murray!' shouted Gerrard.

Murray stopped, turned sharply and scowled. 'What is it?'

'Leave your cigarettes, will you?'

Murray was back in less than five minutes.

Gerrard and Melanie clambered into the two-door car and it roared back through the village and out the other side towards the A12.

'Right or left?' asked Murray, grimly, as they approached the main road. 'Left'll take us back to London – right to Lowestoft. But whichever way we go the sea's not far away. All we have to do is point ourselves to the Imam's voice and you'll find nothing but bloody water!' A trace of ex-asperation crept into Murray's voice as he studied the two directions.

Gerrard touched him on the shoulder and pointed to the left-hand side of the road.

Shielded behind a screen of thin broom and gorse stood a gaily coloured ice-cream van. Three people stood at the side of it licking the tops off large cornets. Murray got the message.

'Be quick!' he snapped.

Gerrard squeezed back into the car and pointed to the right.

'A grey Citroën with a woman at the wheel squealed to a halt, then hurtled off in that direction.'

'Roberts didn't stop for an ice-cream then?' Murray sent the Scirocco screaming across the A12 leaving behind a startled audience to contemplate a cloud of blue smoke and an overpowering stench of burnt rubber. 'Where now?' he asked as he worked the engine up to 4,000 revs.

Gerrard pulled a face and looked over the back of his seat. 'Do you know this area, Melanie?'

'Nope. Not at all,' she replied. 'But according to this map I found on the back seat this stretch of road runs parallel to, and not very far from, the sea. It continues like that for about six miles. After that the road begins to veer sharply inland. It gets further and further away from the coast.'

Gerrard patted the nearest bare knee affectionately. He left his hand there. 'So?'

'Your old girl-friend won't want to stay on this road for more than about another four miles. The rough stuff, or isolated beach, is all that stretch on our right.'

'Thank you. Give me the map.' Gerrard turned back to Murray. 'Put your foot down, Murray.'

'We're already doing ninety-five! You were about to say something about the minor road – ' Murray broke off with a startled exclamation: 'What the bloody hell!'

Gerrard looked up sharply from the map.

A galaxy of cold blue flashing lights appeared in the middle distance. Gerrard swore in French and slammed the map book closed.

A police Land-Rover stood parked across half the road, and beside it, at a protective angle against the rear of a large white ambulance, stood a patrol car, its headlights blazing ineffectually against the sunlight.

'Accident!' said Murray, unnecessarily.

'Perhaps it's a Citroën, grey, left-hand drive . . .' suggested Gerrard, without conviction.

Murray snorted impatiently, 'It's a bloody lorry!'

A group of uniformed men stood round the rear end of an articulated lorry, its tail end poking at an angle from the depths of a large tidal ditch. It cut the road in half and reduced it to single-line traffic. Three cars waited patiently under a policeman's outstretched finger while a local single-decker bus crawled slowly past the obstruction from the opposite direction.

'Can you get past it?' asked Gerrard.

Murray smiled enigmatically. 'Might not be necessary.' He brought the car to a halt, switched off the engine and got out. He hesitated for a moment then leaned back inside and said to Gerrard, 'If you pull up the corner of that carpet by your left foot you'll find a plastic folder stuck to the underside. Toss it over here.' He closed the door and strolled across to the nearest policeman.

Gerrard and Melanie watched as Murray held out the plastic folder to a sceptical-looking policeman. The scepticism didn't last long. The policeman studied the inside of the small folder, nodded sagely, and the two men walked away from the line of cars. They stood talking and looking back along the road from where Murray had just come. Murray was doing most of the talking and all the pointing.

After a moment Murray and the policeman walked towards the first car in the queue. The policeman went down on one knee and spoke to the driver. It was a very short conversation. They moved on to the second. This one took longer, but when he straightened up the policeman looked much happier. He nodded earnestly to Murray and pointed back along the road. They had another brief exchange and Murray trotted briskly back to the Scirocco.

'Chap in that second car along there,' he said as he climbed behind the wheel, 'was behind a fast Citroën for about five miles. It had a frosted rear window, like a windscreen that had been clobbered with a brick, and it turned off just the other side of that rise back there.' Murray turned the ignition and the steering wheel at the same time. The effect was spectacular.

The car leapt sideways, squealed across the road, mounted the grass verge opposite and thumped back with another squealing, skidding whirl to point in the opposite direction. With a brief wave of thanks to a startled policeman Murray sent the Scirocco screaming off with another stench of burning rubber.

'How far back?' asked Gerrard. He hung on grimly to the bracket above the door until Murray had finished changing gears. 'And where does the turn-off go to?'

Murray was slowing down even as Gerrard spoke. 'This is it,' he said and swung the car into a narrow, hedge-lined road. 'The copper said it ran down to a wooded picnic area. That's where the road ends – you can't go beyond that. It's the edge of England – nothing but cliff and water. But don't look so pleased – there's an old cart track that cuts across an open field and leads to the remains of a ruined abbey.' Murray slowed the car almost to walking pace and glanced sideways at Gerrard. 'The abbey sits on top of the cliffs but most of it's fallen into the drink over the past few hundred years. The interesting bit is a footpath that leads down to the beach itself – not used a lot nowadays, according to my copper, because it's considered unsafe. And not only that – he said the beach below is nothing you'd want to write home about – just rock, sharp flints and dirty water. He reckoned it's only useful for beaching a rowing boat if you wanted to do a bit of fishing without getting your feet wet!'

'OK,' grunted Gerrard. 'Stop this thing and I'll get out and walk.' He turned to Melanie and put his hand on her knee, holding it there for a second and then sliding it under the hem of her skirt. He stopped on the silken softness of her thigh, then squeezed until she hissed in pain.

'If you move from the back of this car,' he growled, 'regardless of what's going on outside, I'll be so angry you'll wish you were back in the care of Phelan! Do you understand that, Melanie Lambdon?'

She nodded. She understood.

Gerrard slipped out of the car and, moving on the balls of his feet, doubled towards the next bend in the road. Only fifty yards beyond the narrow curve the road ended amidst a cluster of tall pines and a partially cleared area surrounded by bright yellow-blossomed, but scrubby and unkempt, gorse. It was the picnic area Murray's policeman had described. In the shade under the pines was the grey Citroën. It stood alone and untended. Of Roberts and Audrey there was no sign.

Gerrard brought Phelan's Luger from his waistband. He snapped off the bulbous silencer and checked the magazine. It was full. He held the weapon up and showed it to Murray before moving towards the clearing. As he moved he heard the Scirocco's door squeak open behind him. He knew it was Murray. He didn't look round. He concentrated on the area surrounding the car.

'You're wasting your time there, Gerrard.' Murray's voice came from just behind him. He'd moved up quickly and made no attempt to lower his voice – if anything, he spoke louder than normal. 'I've just spotted a black dot moving amongst those old ruins over there, and if you look quickly now you'll see a figure in a blue track suit. Have you got it?'

Gerrard looked across the field and nodded, and grunted an obscenity.

'The lady who was driving that car,' continued Murray, pointing his Browning at the Citroën, 'wore a blue track-suit top. And if you look quickly now you'll see a dark splodge just about to move into cover behind that big piece of wall.' He scratched the side of his head with the muzzle of the Browning. 'But what's he doing over there, when the foot-path to the beach is down here?'

Gerrard wasn't listening. He looked quickly over the Citroën and checked underneath. 'What did you say about footpaths?' he asked.

'There's a rickety old finger-post stuck to a tree over there that says: "To the beach". It points downwards, not across there at those ruins.' Murray put the Browning away and lit a cigarette.

'Can you hear anything?' Gerrard was listening intently, his head tilted in the direction of the sea.

'Like what?'

'Listen, it's a helicopter! It's not a boat that's taking them off – it's a chopper! There's something big out there – big enough to store a chopper in its hold! That's where they're being picked up; that's their land-mark . . .' He pointed towards the ruined abbey and gestured Murray back to the Scirocco. 'Quick! Try to get the car across the field. I'll open the gate.'

The nippy Scirocco darted forward like a startled pony and skidded almost sideways through the open gate. Murray barely slowed down for Gerrard, who threw the door open and jumped inside as the car swerved away across the field. Murray put his foot down, bumping in and out of the ruts of the cart track. He twisted and turned the wheel, grimacing each time the car's sump crunched against the lumpy boulders in the ruts, and suffered with the car the unkind treatment he was giving it. But he didn't slow down, or halt his suicidal dash across the field.

'Look!' Murray shouted above the noise. He took one hand off the wildly gyrating wheel and stuck it out of the window. 'Look at that bloody thing up there!'

Gerrard bent down in his seat and stared out of Murray's window. He narrowed his eyes behind Murray's pointing finger.

'I see it!' he said calmly. And then Melanie screamed from behind, her voice jerking with the erratic movements of the car.

'It's a great big black thing,' she shrieked, 'low down and just beginning to pull up over the cliff. It's coming up now, Michel – any minute now! Right in front of you – now! Good God! Look at it . . .!'

'Can't you make this car go any faster, Murray?' Gerrard was bouncing up and down in his seat like a man hanging on to a yo-yo. 'They'll be in that helicopter and away long before we get anywhere near them! Come on, man! Make the damn thing move!'

' . . . bloody foot won't go down any further! Not until one of these soddin' rocks makes a hole in the bottom . . . !'

'Shut up and look where you're going! Christ! Look out! You're going to hit the hedge!'

'Wrong!' bellowed Murray. 'I'm going through the bloody hedge – I can't bugger around looking for a gap! Hang on! You too, Melanie!'

Murray's luck found him the thickest and sturdiest portion of the hedge, which, against all the odds, still had a trace of mud in the shallow ditch beneath it. Murray realised his mistake and tried to change his mind at the last second. Too late! The car ground on; it swivelled and slipped as the hedge wrapped itself around its bonnet and turned them sideways with a grinding, screaming howl of tortured metal. Then the engine stalled.

'Fuck it!' Murray didn't apologise. He threw himself out of his door and rolled over in the dusty grass bellowing at Gerrard as he scrambled up, 'It's a couple of hundred yards to the first wall of the ruin. See you there!'

The deafening racket of the black helicopter, almost directly above them, drowned Gerrard's reply as he struggled to get across the front seats and out of Murray's door. He paused only to yell at Melanie.

'Get out and stay by the car. Keep down and if you hear shooting lie flat with your face in the grass.'

He ran alongside the hedge, crouched low with the Luger cocked and ready in his hand, and followed Murray's leap over a wooden stile and into the grounds of the abbey.

The helicopter zoomed upwards. It bore no markings. It was painted overall matt black and looked like an ugly giant crow as it lifted over the cliff edge for its second run across the abbey. The pilot must have spotted the two men. He thundered straight towards them. He knew how to fly a helicopter and attacked at full speed, only feet from the ground and almost scraping the stone wall. It sounded like a runaway express bellowing through a narrow tunnel. It drowned out all other sound and all feeling.

Murray and Gerrard hit the ground together and buried their faces in the sweet-smelling grass as the downward draught of the rotors hit them with a thump – and then, as quickly, it was gone.

Gerrard shouted across the space to Murray: 'Quick – before he turns, get under that low wall and watch out for Roberts. Move, now! I'll be right behind you!'

As he spoke three quick shots came from somewhere in the abbey ruins, but they sounded flat and harmless against the grinding of the helicopter's engine as it turned hard over for another approach.

'Roberts has found us – the bastard!' Murray called out, and threw himself to the ground again. 'He's somewhere behind that large buttress, under that broken arch. Can you see him? That last shot of his was too bloody close for my liking. One more sight of him and I'll blow his bloody head off! D'you want to talk to him again – or is he game?'

'Kill him!' answered Gerrard. It was a simple statement. Then his voice rose. 'Hey, watch it, Murray! This chopper isn't playing games . . . *Get down!*'

Gerrard scrambled level with Murray, leaving his fall to the last minute, and once again felt the down-draught scrape across his back. This time the thundering noise and the drag of air didn't go away – the helicopter hung above them blotting out the sun with its shadow and deafening them as it came even lower. Gerrard turned his face painfully upwards and screwed his eyes tight. He was just in time to see a small cylindrical object hurtle out of the opening in the fuselage.

'*Merde!* Down, Murray – *Down!*' He bellowed the last word at the top of his voice. 'Keep your face down – it's a bomb!'

The words were hardly out of his mouth when the shadow vanished and an enormous crack threatened to pull his hands from his ears. It was followed by a loud whoosh, and then a gentle anti-climactic hissing from a few feet away. It sounded like a punctured tyre. Like a punctured tyre ...? Gerrard opened his eyes, and closed them again – quickly. Everything about him was black. Jet black. He was blinded, he couldn't see a thing – the sun had gone out, blotted by a black cloud, and he was enveloped in thick, oily, impenetrable smoke.

'Murray!' he yelled. 'Can you hear me?'

Murray's voice came back through the darkness. 'Yes! – but don't raise your head, that bastard's still banging away over there, on the right ... He's moved his position, by the sound of that gun. Are you still there?'

'Yes, I'm going over the wall.'

'Look, he's trying to keep our heads down while the chopper comes in from the other side. And he's bloody well succeeding as far as I'm concerned! You all right over there?'

'So far! Listen – I'm going forward. I'm heading for the sound of that helicopter – the pilot's keeping the smoke in this direction with his blades, and clearing an open area for himself. Come through, but stay behind me.'

Gerrard ran forward at a crouch. He heard two shots, close, and recognised the Mamba's signature; then a thud as a third bullet ploughed the grass by his foot and a whistle as another hissed by his head. It was close enough to make him duck and fall over the remains of the first low stone wall. He ignored his grazed shins and felt his way along the pile of old masonry until he found the corner.

He could hear the helicopter hovering in the middle of the abbey, nudging the smoke delicately away from the centre before settling to take on its passengers. It pushed too hard, and for a second, through a gap in the smoke cloud, Gerrard saw the black machine almost touch down.

Murray must have seen it too. 'Watch out, Gerrard!' he shouted. 'I'm coming through.'

Murray appeared out of the thinning screen right behind his voice; he had a blue-spotted handkerchief tied round his mouth and had to raise the flap to speak. Gerrard dragged him down beside him and shouted in his ear.

'Watch out for that helicopter – he's sure to have something bigger than pea-shooters on board. When I give you the word, move in from the right. I'll meet you in the clear. Shoot on sight – but for God's sake make sure it's not me you shoot!'

With a brief nod, Murray slipped silently into the dark-grey mush. As soon as he'd gone, Gerrard stood up and moved forward. He kept running until he reached the last of the inner walls. He looked upwards; there the smoke was thin and sparse and the upper reaches of the massive wall stood out spectacularly through the whispery tentacles of what was now only thick brown mist. Through it, Gerrard could see the sun, a huge orange orb, discoloured by the swirling cloud but perfectly round and forcing its rays into the centre of the ruins. The noise of the helicopter's engine reached screeching point, and over its uneven beat Gerrard heard a hoarse bellow from Murray.

'Gerrard! It's on the deck! I can see it! The woman's on board and they're hauling Roberts in now . . .' Murray's voice died away, then came back again, louder and more urgent as the helicopter's blades began to race and its engine noise thudded into the walls of the abbey. 'Hold your fire – I'm going to tackle the bastard!'

Gerrard shook his head in disbelief and ran forward out of the smoke and into the clear, as, with a final crescendic roar, the helicopter's engines lifted the machine off the ground. He brought the Luger up in both hands and sent two shots screaming into the perspex-covered cockpit. It was like shooting at an elephant with a starter gun.

The helicopter ignored the shots and rose like a straining heron. And then, as if pulled up by a gigantic unseen hand, it burst through the smoke and rocketed above the ruins.

Gerrard dropped his arm and looked up in horror. Murray was hanging on to the landing strut by one arm.

His legs dangled loosely, and as Gerrard watched open-mouthed, they began to describe furious circling motions, as if he were riding a bicycle that only he knew about. Gerrard could see his startled face looking down, gauging the distance to the ground as if he were trying to make up his mind to jump now and only break both legs or hang on for a cleaner death later.

But the choice went quickly as the fast-rising helicopter slipped back into the dispersing, but still dense, smoke. The spinning blades dug into it and swirled it around like a small cyclone and, from the centre of the vortex, Gerrard heard the heavy, solid report of Murray's Browning.

BANG, BANG, BANG, BANG, BANG!

The shots thudded out one after the other until its magazine was empty.

The helicopter's engine note remained healthy and unimpaired.

'That was about the most stupid thing I've ever seen!' Gerrard looked

430

up at the black cloud and noticed that the ground was now clear of smoke. He could see Melanie standing on the wooden stile, waving with both hands and pointing upwards. He looked up and saw nothing but smoke.

She stopped waving and ran towards him, tripping over the foot of the stile and dragging herself up again in her hurry to get to him. He could see her mouth open, shouting urgently, and she was pointing to the sky; but nothing carried over the still-throbbing noise of the helicopter.

And then he could hear her.

'. . . it's Murray!' she screamed. 'Did you see him up there? He's hanging from the bottom of that thing!'

He took her in his arms and calmed her down. 'There's nothing we can do,' he said softly. 'If he can hang on until they put down he might be able to drop into the sea.'

She pressed her face into his chest. 'And what was all that white spray pouring out of the bottom of the thing after those bangs? What was he doing, Michel – shooting at it?'

Gerrard stiffened and pushed her away. He held her at arm's length and gripped her tightly, resisting the urge to shake her like a doll.

'White spray? What white spray, Melanie?'

He didn't wait for her reply. He pushed her aside roughly and brought both hands up to his forehead to shield his eyes from the sun. He stared critically at the helicopter, now diving for speed towards the open sea.

'It looked like water coming from underneath, just beyond where Murray was hanging,' whispered Melanie, but Gerrard was still staring hard at the helicopter and cut her short.

'Just a minute,' he said gruffly. Then, a second or two later, 'You're right! Murray's holed their fuel tank.' He stared down at Melanie, then back to the helicopter. 'The idiot!' There was a trace of admiration in his voice. 'They never change, these Englishmen! Mad, completely mad.'

As he watched, the helicopter slipped to the right and its nose went down.

'Hold on – listen!' he said gruffly. 'It's turning . . . It's coming back!' He tightened his arm round her shoulder.

'What's happened?'

'Murray did it! He's drained it. Listen, it's choking – they're down to the dregs. They won't make it! Come on – come on!' he urged, as if the pilot could hear and benefit from his encouragement. 'Come on, it's only a mile, that's all! You can make it . . . It's *less* than a mile!'

The helicopter's blades continued to turn, but they weren't being driven and the machine dropped lower and lower. It looked as though the pilot had realised he was not going to make land and decided that a controlled splash in the sea was better than a dead-bird plummet on to the beach.

As they watched, Gerrard and Melanie saw a minuscule question mark detach itself from the underside of the descending helicopter; this was followed almost immediately by the faintest suggestion of a splash in the water.

'And down went Murray!' said Gerrard softly, almost to himself. 'And about a mile away. I hope he can swim.'

The helicopter laboured wearily a few seconds longer then flopped into the water like a tired and travel-worn gannet. Gerrard narrowed his eyes against the glare of the sun and wondered how many other pairs of eyes were doing the same thing. But the drama wasn't finished yet.

Within seconds a brief splash of colour appeared alongside the stricken helicopter and blossomed into a large orange doughnut.

'Melanie.' There was undisguised urgency in Gerrard's voice. 'Take Murray's car, and as quickly as you can go and get the Citroën and bring it back here.' He swung her round by her elbows. 'And don't ask questions. Be quick!'

She gave him a quick, worried look and ran. The Scirocco started first go. She slammed it into gear and forced the wheels away from the hedge; the tyres spun with a high-pitched whine but the treads failed to find a grip in the soft moist grass. They skidded noisily in the same shallow and damp ruts that Murray had made earlier. She swore crudely, and stamped her foot on the clutch like a spoilt child. It didn't help. She took a deep breath and tried again, much slower, but again heard only the turning wheels and smelled the overpowering reek of burnt rubber. Still no movement. In a panic she slammed the gear into reverse and revved the engine, but much too quickly. It slid sideways – and deeper into the hedge.

'Michel!' she screamed.

'Leave it,' he bellowed, 'and run!' Then he lost interest in her.

He squatted on his heels and rested both hands on his knees. He could just make out three dots in the orange dinghy; the pilot, Roberts and Audrey . . . And what's more – he gritted his teeth in surprise – the boat was being rowed out to sea – not towards the shore!

After a few more minutes' floundering the downed helicopter lurched on to its nose and disappeared under the water. But the orange dot continued to make progress towards the skyline. Gerrard tried to measure

432

the distance but stopped at about six hundred metres. It was a long way in anybody's currency. He brought both hands up again to shield his eyes and, as he stared, there crawled into his vision something he'd been fearing for the last ten minutes – a large ocean-going trawler was coming to join the party.

It was a fast boat and it was using all the speed it had. Gerrard groaned aloud. He felt a cold wave of impatience surge into his stomach and gave in to the temptation to glance over his shoulder and across the field.

The Citroën was moving as if on broken glass. It crawled like a hearse through the open gate.

'For God's sake, girl!'

He stared across the field for several more seconds before the trawler drew his eyes back to the North Sea. His stomach dropped.

The boat had made better progress than the Citroën. Gerrard could see quite clearly the crested wave breaking high up on its bows as it powered on at full speed towards the dinghy. The distance between the two was narrowing by the second. He lit one of Murray's cigarettes and stood up and waited as the Citroën bumped spongily off the cart track and shuddered across the grass towards him. He directed it into a shallow depression behind a rise some ten yards from the edge of the cliff, where it snuggled out of view of any curious gunsights.

He ignored Melanie. He stubbed the quarter-smoked cigarette into the grass and with controlled haste crawled into the back of the car. He pulled the centre armrest down from its recess and depressed a concealed catch at the back of it. There was an audible, well-oiled click and the entire seatback sprang forward to rest on a long metal hinge. Gerrard glanced over his shoulder.

'Open the boot and take out the jack from the right hand bracket and put it over there by the edge of the cliff. When I tell you, get in the car and stay there out of the way.'

She did as she was told without question.

He came out backwards from the car with the long slim barrel of a PM sniper rifle, its highly polished butt cradled in his arm.

'Hold these,' he instructed. 'Don't drop anything.' He leaned back inside again and this time came out with a squat, leather-bound oblong case and a large, reinforced, shaped leather container with straps. Melanie cradled the dull metal rifle barrel as if it were a puff adder. The questions were burning inside her.

'Michel?'

'Shut up!'

433

She followed him the ten yards to the cliff edge then handed him the barrel.

He took no notice of her as he joined the sections of rifle together. When he'd finished he laid it carefully on its side in the grass and picked up the light moulded steel jack. He gave a sharp twist of its ratchet, and two short sturdy legs clunked down. He spread them at an angle, each with a small but thickly spiked foot splaying outwards into a solid heel to make a firm bipod. He positioned this in the grass and stood on it, shifting his weight until the spikes penetrated the hard soil as far as their restraining shoes. He looked up briefly to gauge the closing distance between the fishing vessel and the bobbing orange dinghy. He wasn't happy with what he saw. The trawler's bow wave had diminished to a bare crest. It was slowing down. It was now close, and well in touch with its quarry. Without looking round, he snapped, 'Get back to the car now.' Melanie didn't argue.

Gerrard crouched over the bipod. He slid the rifle barrel into its socket and locked it home. He looked up again at the fishing vessel – a quick professional glance at a barely moving target. Whoever won, it was going to be close. He opened the leatherbound box and carefully removed the delicate S & B PM2 power telescope from its snug blue-lined bed. It fitted easily and solidly in its mountings just above the breech. He tightened it into place with his fingers and lowered himself beside the rifle.

From inside the leather container he removed a cardboard box containing 7.62 boat-tailed cartridges. He held the box for a second while he glanced again across the water. The trawler was almost standing still. Sliding the lid off the box he studied the shiny cartridges. Each was segregated in its own tiny compartment. Three of the compartments were empty; another three had a cotton-thin red line drawn across their base – red for long-range death ... He removed one from its slot; a custom-loaded 190-grain boat-tailed finger of instant death – with a mercury-filled hollow cavity nose in case instant wasn't quick enough.

He chose one and wiped it with his handkerchief until it glistened with a dry lethal reflection. He held it by its rim, placed it carefully into the open breech of the rifle and locked it in with a slow smooth bolt action. He cleaned and polished the other two red-marked cartridges and rested them close at hand on top of the leather case.

Stretching himself flat on his stomach beside the rifle he brought the familiar butt comfortably into the small of his shoulder. His eye fitted perfectly on to the powered telescopic sight and, as he turned the focusing ring, the blurred orange mass that had filled the lens clicked almost noisily into shapes. He checked the reticle and range scale – 848 metres exact. Extreme. Almost too far. He'd loaded the cartridge for 800 metres – at the outside – who wants to kill at 800 metres? He looked again and blinked at the distance, then let his brain take over . . . Offset it by a fraction. How much of a fraction . . . ? He stared down the scope again and, as he began to zero on the dinghy, saw the grey prow of the trawler intrude into the edge of the magnified area covered by the sight.

Three shots . . . two good and one hurried before that thing takes my target. One for warmers, one for Roberts, and a rush job for Audrey.

Lucky Audrey!

He switched the telescope to maximum zoom.

He was suspended in solitary state. He was nowhere and completely alone. The only other living beings in the world sat in the crossed hairs of his gunsight. Every ounce of his concentration poured into the tube, and as the vision crispened the two hair-lines centred on Audrey's blue-clad leg. Gerrard's left wrist moved a fraction of a millimetre and the centre wires slid upwards to cross the broad shoulders of Geoffrey Roberts. Gerrard's wrist moved again with a feather touch and the cross-wires lowered to Roberts's midriff, two inches below his elbow.

Gerrard's finger tightened on the trigger.

His ears ignored the sound of the shot. There was no other indication that a high velocity bullet was on its way to cut Roberts in half. The solid platform had held the rifle as rigid as a battleship's main armament and the bullet flew true at 800 metres a second. Gerrard let out the breath he'd been holding.

'You're dead, Roberts,' he breathed.

He slid another round into the breech and put his eye back to the lens. But Roberts wasn't dead.

Roberts was still sitting in the dinghy, a smile locked on his face as he looked down into the flimsy rubber wall beside one of his fat knees. Gerrard could see quite clearly the look of surprised horror on his face as he turned and looked directly into Gerrard's eye.

Roberts didn't know quite what to make of it. It took a second or two for it to register, and no matter how hard he stared at the cliffs they told him nothing – at 800 metres he'd have been lucky to see a twenty-five pounder thumping away at him. But Roberts didn't need to see what it was – he knew when someone was shooting at him.

He looked down again at the clean hole in the side of the dinghy and tried to squeeze himself lower into the rubber boat instinctively seeking the protection of its flimsy walls. He'd measured the distance. If he could keep away from the next bullet for just a few seconds longer he'd be protected by the massive bulk of the now almost dead-still trawler inching agonisingly slowly, towards them.

It was too slow for Roberts. He took the only other option open to him.

Gerrard saw the splash as he heaved himself over the side of the dinghy. Gerrard turned the knob fractionally and searched for Roberts's head, but it was well hidden behind the slowly deflating orange wall. Roberts was nobody's fool!

Sorry, Audrey! Your turn now. Gerrard breathed Audrey's death sentence to himself as his finger moved to the trigger.

He was fractionally too late. Before his finger took the strain another splash in the telescopic sight told him that Audrey had received Roberts's warning. *So you can't be all bad, Roberts . . . !* Gerrard narrowed his eye for a glimpse of the pair of them in the water, but he knew he wasn't going to get one. *You could have left Audrey in the dinghy without telling her, Roberts; you could have let her take the next shot, by which time you'd have been safe behind the trawler's iron wall . . .*

He watched the grey hull of the trawler edge up to the dinghy, and waited for his orange target to disappear behind the protection of its bulk. He stared.

The eye looking through the magnified tube blinked. It was a blink of disbelief; incredulity; amazement – Gerrard went through all the emotions. He took his eye away from the lens, wiped it gently with the sleeve of his shirt and looked again at the comedy show. Then he allowed the smile to break through.

The trawler had come up on the wrong side – and there was no time for corrections. The remnants of the orange dinghy stood out against the black, rusty patched background of the boat's hull like coloured bottles on a fairground shooting booth. Gerrard continued staring. He couldn't believe it. But it was there all right – in orange on black; and there was no question about it – Roberts, who'd been lucky all his life had run out of luck, just when he needed it most.

The trawler was virtually at a standstill. Two rope ladders dangled down the short distance from the deck to water-level and a shirtless, muscular sailor hung casually by his left hand from one of them. He held the other ladder in his free hand, steadying it against the gentle dipping motion of the boat and waited, with all the patience of a deep sea fisherman, for his first customer to haul himself out of the water. Gerrard could see the good-looking young bronzed face, contrasting with the blondness of his hair and beard, calling encouragement to what Gerrard presumed was Roberts, nearest to the foot of the ladder.

Roberts seemed reluctant to leave the cold, but safe, embrace of the North Sea. Gerrard watched with slightly more than fascination. Roberts must have been trying to explain the shooting, and the necessity to put the boat between them and the unseen marksman, but it seemed he was being told not to waste time and to get on with it . . . Whatever the message coming down from the bridge was, the boat remained statically in position, like a basking whale, and Roberts knew he was going to have to run the gauntlet. Very soon the skipper of the trawler was going to start getting itchy feet and decide that he'd been long enough in unwelcome waters; any minute now he was going to have to consider quieter, less public places to compose his excuses for the loss of a KGB brigadier, and a Company helicopter – any minute . . . !

Gerrard continued staring at the tableau. *Maybe Roberts will send Audrey first to draw the fire? In which case . . .* Gerrard smiled again to himself. *It'll be your lucky day, Audrey!*

But something was happening. Roberts had made up his mind. A rope with a looped end came flying over the trawler's bulwarks and disappeared into the dark water. Gerrard centred the cross wires of the sight half-way up the unoccupied, loosely moving rope ladder – and waited. The ladder stiffened. He watched the sailor on the other ladder brace himself to steady it as the large bulk of the former Special Branch man rose out of the water assisted by the rope looped round his waist.

Roberts stood shakily on the first rung of the ladder and, as he steadied himself, looked lingeringly over his shoulder.

Gerrard's eye narrowed with interest. Under more charitable circumstances he'd have imagined the searching look to be one of sad farewell – perhaps a trace of unconcealable regret?

Gerrard's imagination was way out. There was nothing less charitable than the thoughts coursing through Roberts's mind, and the searching look was far from regret. It was one of fear; Roberts knew what was pointing at him and he had a good idea what was waiting for him half-way up the side of the trawler – the way Roberts threw his dice it was just a straightforward question of how good was the finger that was pointing at him.

He took another two hesitant steps up the wriggling ladder and moved his shoulder blades into the centre of the hair-line cross on the telescope. He paused conveniently to take his last breath, and in a brief

437

moment of optimism stretched across the narrow divide to hand his briefcase to the waiting Russian sailor.

The 190-grain bullet hit him half an inch to the left of his lower spine. It shattered his spleen and carried most of his stomach out with it to splash against the black wall of the trawler's side. To Roberts it felt like a hefty punch in the back. But he was dead before he'd fully worked out what it really was.

He dangled on the end of the rope, swaying in time with the trawler's movements as it rose and fell in the light choppy swell. Above him, a row of heads watched from the ship's side, unaware of the reason for their important guest's strange behaviour. But not for long. At a bellow from the sailor on the ladder they all ducked out of sight, leaving him to make his own arrangements. He didn't linger. He let go of the rope and dropped into the sea for safety.

The men on deck, hanging on to the other end of Roberts's line, began to pull him in. They were shielded by the thick steel bulwark and hauled on the rope from memory. Gerrard watched without emotion as Roberts's body rose up the ship's side, jerking in fits and starts, like an overweight puppet whose strings had finally given way, until what was left of him was hauled out of sight behind the steel wall.

And still no effort was made to place the solid mass of the boat between the people still in the water and the marksman who'd shown them how good he was at shooting people at extreme range.

The trawler remained in position while Gerrard replaced the spent cartridge. He had all the time in the world. When he put his eye back to the scope he saw that a head and shoulders had risen over the bulwarks and was peering nonchalantly over the side. A braver specimen! There was at least one in every navy. Gerrard smiled his admiration. It was probably the captain who wanted to get his boat out of this madhouse. He was gesticulating at the water, and his mouth was going like a man who knew a swearword or two. It worked. A few minutes later the blond sailor reappeared, timorously, to scale the ladder he had hurriedly evacuated. There was no sign of Roberts's briefcase in his hand – Roberts's plans for the disintegration of Britain's intelligence network floated away unnoticed.

Following the sailor out of the water, on the other ladder, came a dripping figure in a pale-blue tracksuit. Audrey wasted no time. Gerrard blinked coldly as he watched her climb blindly in Roberts's footsteps.

She started off with a vigorous zig-zag motion, too fast for an amateur. It was probably under shouted advice from behind the steel bulwark.

Gerrard fine-focused again on the back of Audrey's head. Her hair was plastered flat by the water – like a white skullcap – and she kept it turned protectively towards the rough featureless wall of steel as if the very action of pressing against it would at the same time protect her back.

Goodbye, Audrey!

Gerrard stroked the smooth trigger lazily, without pressure. He smiled. And as if on cue, Audrey's feet slipped and she was left swinging helplessly, hanging on to the ladder by smooth little hands while her feet scrambled madly in an attempt to retrieve her footing. The cross-hairs remained inexorably at the base of her spine and Gerrard blinked away the familiar vision, a picture as clear as if he was lying next to her: the smooth litheness of her exquisite body and the gentle womanly curve of her hips – he recognised the spot where the mercury-loaded bullet would enter, and he knew where it would emerge; he saw her soft lips and looked into her warm brown eyes and heard her laugh in the wantonness of her lovemaking. But the vision lasted only a second. He moved the cross-hairs fractionally up and squeezed the trigger.

Gerrard suddenly felt very tired.

He lay back on the warm grass and rubbed the strain from his eyes. After a few minutes he felt the tension drain out of him and opened his eyes. Melanie was kneeling beside him.

'I'm sorry for shouting at you,' he said.

She put her hand on his mouth and slowly shook her head. 'I don't think you are, but it doesn't matter now, does it?'

Gerrard closed his eyes again.

'Are you interested in David Murray?' she asked.

'Not particularly,' he grunted.

'While you were at war, a small motor boat circled round the spot where the helicopter sank. They must have seen him floundering around in the vicinity. They picked him up and the last I saw of him was just below us here. He waved before they took him away.'

'Good.'

Gerrard opened his eyes again and pulled himself up. He raised her chin so that he could look into her eyes. He could read nothing there. 'Shall I take you home?' he said gently.

She stared at him for a few seconds then lowered her head and kissed him. It seemed like forgiveness. 'Please,' she whispered. 'I hate this place.' She placed her hands on his shoulders and stood up. He lay on his back and stared up at her. 'Don't move,' she said. 'I'll go and get the car and bring it round here. You can tell me how to load that stuff,' she glanced contemptuously at the rifle, the butt resting on the ground, its barrel pointing harmlessly at the puffy clouds above, 'then I'll take *you* home.' She shaped her mouth into a kiss and turned away. Gerrard lit a cigarette and watched as she walked across the grass and disappeared behind the rise, then lay back and stared at the sky.

Melanie slid into the unfamiliar left-hand seat and after a moment switched on the ignition. The red light on the radio blinked at her. She turned up the sound. Michael Jackson screeched out of the radio trying to overcome the noise of his backing group. She pulled a face and turned it down.

Gerrard raised his head. 'Switch it off!'

She looked at the machine. Sticking half-way out of it was a cassette. She opened the door and by standing on her tiptoes could just see over the rise. 'I suppose Wagner's more in your line of country,' she shouted.

'Shut up and bring the car round.'

'I need music. What's on the cassette?'

Gerrard shot up on to his elbows and stared at her as she peered over the grass ridge. 'Melanie, I don't have any cassettes.' He was on his knees. 'Don't tou – '

'So, what's this then?'

She reached down into the car and removed the cassette.